HARD HIT

Poole gave a brief brief. He didn't reveal all. Didn't tell the true aim of the kill.

The point was to show Saddam a bit of lo-tech wreckage, some good old fashioned retro-war in which American soldiers, boots on the ground, could walk up to one of his paper tiger Republican Guard units and bloody some noses with modern warfare's equivalent of a knuckle sandwich. Shoot him with rifle fire. Kill him with a grenade. Up close and personal.

A helluva cool concept. Even so, that was not the point.

A tiny strike. Just the tip of an ice pick. An ice pick thrust into the cowardly heart of Saddam Hussein. A prick of fear into the chest of the madman and his two sons, who were in charge of the Republican Guard units. Oh, so fine. Still . . .

Good as that was: Make some noise, raise some dust. Upset the Sadman. Make radio reports fly. Monitor cell traffic. Watch for convoys.

Then bust a cap in Saddam's ass. Shorten the war by weeks and months. Maybe end the war before it began. Now *that* was a mission.

DELTA FORCE

PRELUDE TO WAR

JOHN HARRIMAN

JOVE BOOKS, NEW YORK

THE BERKLEY PUBLISHING GROUP
Published by the Penguin Group
Penguin Group (USA) Inc.
375 Hudson Street, New York, New York 10014, USA
Penguin Group (Canada), 10 Alcorn Avenue, Toronto, Ontario M4V 3B2, Canada
(a division of Pearson Penguin Canada Inc.)
Penguin Books Ltd., 80 Strand, London WC2R 0RL, England
Penguin Group Ireland, 25 St. Stephen's Green, Dublin 2, Ireland (a division of Penguin Books Ltd.)
Penguin Group (Australia), 250 Camberwell Road, Camberwell, Victoria 3124, Australia
(a division of Pearson Australia Group Pty. Ltd.)
Penguin Books India Pvt. Ltd., 11 Community Centre, Panchsheel Park, New Delhi—110 017, India
Penguin Group (NZ), Cnr. Airborne and Rosedale Roads, Albany, Auckland 1310, New Zealand
(a division of Pearson New Zealand Ltd.)
Penguin Books (South Africa) (Pty.) Ltd., 24 Sturdee Avenue, Rosebank, Johannesburg 2196,
South Africa

Penguin Books Ltd., Registered Offices: 80 Strand, London WC2R 0RL, England

This is a work of fiction. Names, characters, places, and incidents either are the product of the author's imagination or are used fictitiously, and any resemblance to actual persons, living or dead, business establishments, events, or locales is entirely coincidental.

DELTA FORCE: PRELUDE TO WAR

A Jove Book / published by arrangement with the author

PRINTING HISTORY
Jove mass-market edition / July 2005

Copyright © 2005 by The Berkley Publishing Group.
Cover design by Rich Hasselberger.
Cover illustration by Stan Watts.
Book design by Stacy Irwin.

ISBN: 0-515-13964-5

JOVE®
Jove Books are published by The Berkley Publishing Group,
a division of Penguin Group (USA) Inc.,
375 Hudson Street, New York, New York 10014.
JOVE is a registered trademark of Penguin Group (USA) Inc.
The "J" design is a trademark belonging to Penguin Group (USA) Inc.

PRINTED IN THE UNITED STATES OF AMERICA

10 9 8 7 6 5 4 3 2 1

As retired army colonel Roscoe G. Spangler stood in his office watching the world piss its pants about going to war in Iraq, the war in Iraq came to him.

One moment Spangler stood in pajamas tap-dancing with his fingers and toes in front of a keyboard at a belt-high counter, blogging, linking, reading, blinking, snickering.

The next moment his office temp of going on two years spoke up.

"Little early for the mail chick," Mary Grace Hale said. *No big deal* in the tone of it. *Still . . .*

It should have raised the alarm hairs on Spangler's neck. Because Mary Grace never made small talk, and besides, her boss didn't do small talk either. Not a rule or anything. Just that he didn't know how.

He never chatted, didn't gossip, was a rotten mentioner, couldn't pull off telling a joke, even one right out of *Reader's Digest,* and usually had stink-breath, so people kept him at max puff-distance anyhow. Shooting the breeze was beyond him. He had no war stories to trade because all his war stories ended in shame, his.

Unless.

Well, there was the one topic.

Terror. On terror, bullshit-wise, Spangler was a one-note maestro. Oh yeah, on the T-word, Spangler could have out-Pavarottied Pavarotti, belting it at 10K amps warp-blast volume. *Want to know the names of the thirteen terrorists in Lower Disgravia?* Fine. *Hear the one about the guy who refused his assigned suicide ride because it arrived with dented fenders?* Way fine.

But weather, food, clothes, movies, television? *Duh-OH!*

Nobody wanted to tiny talk with him anyhow. Because to talk to him you had to . . . well, *look* at him.

Spangler was hideous. Face scarred and burned from the 9-11 Pentagon attack. Slivers of glass and shards of debris still imbedded. Six surgeries into the attempted fixes of the unfixable he told them to go to hell on the seventh. *Cosmetic, my ass; look what you had to work with from the start.* So he told them to leave the detritus hidden deep in his pockmarks and rutted, ropey face. He knew what he was, and what he was was ugly with all the names to go with his looks: *Weird Science. Toad. Freak Show. No fixing that in six hundred surgeries.*

Spangler the unsung hero in the aftermath of 9-11. Unsung because nobody wanted to give him public credit. Because a sung hero looks like *that*? Well, who even wants to talk about it?

So. Mary Grace wasn't making small talk as she leaned toward the security system. Her focus was on a bank of nine security screens arranged in threes like the quiz show *Hollywood Squares*. She tripped nine rocker switches, one at a time.

Top right. The screen view of the camera hidden below the mailbox. A plain vanilla car, a Ford Taurus, white with no options, rolled into frame. The camera lens the left eye of a flower garden elf cast in the image of Winston Churchill. Spangler kept telling Mary Grace he meant to change that over to the right eye to suit his own politics. She never smiled. Not even the first of a hundred times he said it.

Top center. From the weather vane atop the house. She used a joystick to zoom in on the rear plate.

Top left. A long view from a birdbath on the front lawn. Three men. Two in the front, one in the back.

Middle right. The front door peephole lens. A still life of suburbia, Beaver Cleaver style. *Golly Wally, d'ja ever think we'd have nine cameras peeking outta our house?*

The rest of the screens empty of life so far.

Spangler didn't notice. He was off in worlds of his own. In the first world he typed a blog comment. In this world his fingers made the sound of a dozen cockroach legs rattling over the keyboard at upward of ninety words a minute. Fingers racing to keep up with his racing thoughts, advice to governments foreign and domestic on how to take down Saddam Hussein using methods both legal and extralegal. Fingers clattering away, bashing the whiners, meaning liberals, meaning the mainstream media, stopping only to jam his slipping black-framed, black-lensed specs back up to roost in the red dents of his pocked and greasy nose. Good stuff. Even brilliant stuff. Even better than when he was writing stuff in the basement of the Pentagon. Even if, just as in his army days, nobody nowhere was ever going to read it because all the bloggers were too busy reading their own stuff.

In the second world his feet brushed an urgent softshoe on the carpet. In that world he had to pee. But not until he finished turning hot thoughts into hard words. Not until . . .

"Uh-oh." Mary Grace saw both of the sedan's front doors come open at once.

Uh-oh? Spangler froze, his hands poised over his keyboard like a B movie ghoul. He poked at his slip-sliding glasses, laying down a greasy fingerprint on one lens. *Uh-oh?*

"We've got company, Colonel. Bad company."

"Contact."

Just the one word in his radio ear-bug, and Poole, Edgar, each a Captain, Delta Force, felt the gears start to grind.

Contact. Bo Barret had spotted the bad guys. Barret's voice the buzz of a pinhole in a stereo speaker. Tight pitch, tiny flutter. Barret jazzed. The Iraqis he was supposed to see in the place where they were supposed to be. A Raq division headquarters ripe for a hit. Tank division. Republican Guard. Make that *elite* Republican Guard, perky Katie. *Elite, baby.* Elite. *Shit.*

Poole could see Bo grinning. Bo don't smile, *really* smile. Bo just bared his teeth when he was happy. Bared his teeth when he wasn't. Like the baboons, wolves, and lions making animal threats. Except with Barret? No threat, man. With Bo it was an animal promise. You had to know the man to tell the smile from the scowl, tell the good nature from the bad-ass, the *aw-shucks* from the *aw-shit,* the pat on the back from the kick in the ass, the stab in the eye, the two-tap to the brain.

You hadda love a man what goes to war with a smile on his face, no matter what the nature of the beams.

Made Poole smile just to see it in his own mind's eye. His own big smile topping off his six-four frame, NBA small-forward build of the Cheetah. All that potential speed and grace even while sitting still.

Poole asked for pictures. "Got vid?" he said into the radio mike a kiss away from his lips.

"Roger, stand by for film at eleven."

That fast, Poole saw the target flicker before his eyes. Literally. As Barret turned on the video sender in his own night vision goggles. A scout didn't have to say a word to report what he saw. Just flip the switch on his helmet-cam and look at what he wanted others to see. Each man on the Delta Force attack team saw it, too.

Well, no wonder the Bo-ster was jazzed.

On his tiny heads-up screen Poole saw twice as many military staff cars as there should have been and two black Mercedes stretch-limo SUVs besides.

He saw the scurrying of Raqi ants around the headquarters, staff weenies and aides de camp running their asses around. General gotta have his favorite Indian tea, don't he? Didn't forget the Swiss chocolates, did you? Where's that French cognac? German brewskis iced down? Rooskie vodka frozen? Havana stogies humidorized? Gotta Hollywood donut for the rrhoids? Something with Michael Moore's face on it? Every Raqi ant wearing an I-love-Saddam 'stache. Poole thinking about growing one himself. Make him look older, maybe a little less like the regal Masai warrior prince he liked to think he was, although he damned well was an unhyphenated American and had not a clue to his Afro origins.

The pix, Edgar. Get your mind on the pix. Senior officers chewing junior-officer ass. Junior officers munching NCO butt. NCOs yelling at any enlisted not already stiff as day-old corpses. Shit flowing downhill. The Raqi army same as any other.

Cooks freighting ice chests full of cold drinks and thermal containers of hot finger foods for the VIPs. Senior officers stealing bites. Thinking life was good in the old HQ camp-out. Enjoy the bliss, Raq-man. None of them could know. War wasn't a week away like Saddam's own CNN network was telling him. Tonight, baby. Bloody a nose. Kick some ass. Take some name. What was the word? Terrorism? *Terrorize this, mammer-jammer. How's it taste, Sadman?*

Life *was* good, all right. Just not for the Raqs.

Bad company?

Mary Grace's words brought Spangler back to a third world, the real one. He whirled to face the bank of screens. The whiplash motion didn't even ruffle his slicked-back, silver-streaked black hair worn like a Speedo swim cap. He reflected the room off his prescription sunglasses, the lenses dark and thick as the bottoms of merlot bottles and just as big. He had gotten bigger specs in the last two years, a small kindness to Mary Grace, so she did not have to look at all of his face at once, did not have to bear the brunt of those eyes. Not that she'd care. She didn't shrink from him. More than that, she was so damned . . . *neutral.* As if his face were a blank slate instead of a moonscape. Didn't she care that he was ugly? How could she not? How could a woman look at a pile of maggots and not react? Or his face, which was worse than a pile of maggots, for chrissakes? How? What the hell was wrong with the woman? Just one more reason to love her.

She grimaced at him, impatient. *The screens, Colonel?*

Middle center. That one showed a movement in the side yard. It drew a flicker of pink eyes behind the black-green lenses. To the . . .

Middle left. A thick figure in a jumpsuit crept toward the patio doors in the back. Spangler could not see Jumpsuit Guy's full face in the shadow of the bill of a ball cap, but he could see enough black skin to identify his race. The outline of Kevlar body armor beneath the suit told of his career field. The man wore his fanny pack to the front, the zipper open at the top.

"He might be armed," Mary Grace said, giving words to Spangler's thoughts.

"Oh, he's armed all right."

She lowered her head and raised an eyebrow at Spangler. "Friend or foe?" She slid her own glasses off her nose.

Spangler smiled at the edge in her voice, his wet lips pulling scars white around his mouth. Mary Grace took off her glasses and five years of age with them. Those eyes. Hazel, intent, warm as a golden retriever's. He smiled a second time that she did not recoil from his first smile. So pretty.

"Grace have you ever thought about contact lenses?"

"Colonel, dammit, friend or—"

"Grace I only got the one friend," he said. "A CIA guy. How sad is that?" A CIA guy, who like his agency, was only a friend for as long as he needed you for something.

"Colonel—"

"The somebitch in my backyard? No friend, I'll grant you. Only a tattered lackey hiding under a pig's tail, to quote a hero of mine. But an enemy?" He shook his head. "Nah. Not a worthy one, anyhow. Ignore him. Let's deal with the pig in the white Ford."

Poole's bright and greedy grin froze on his face. Ready to kick ass. But. There was something else here. *Limos?* Nontactical SUVs? All that brass? Not what the intel said. Not just a division HQ of the so-called *elite* Guard. Bigger. Way bigger. How's come no—

His ear-bug crackled. A new voice, a warp in the voice from far, far away. The voice of UV white teeth and hair styled to the tune of fifty bucks. "Prosper Zero-Six, this is Saxon Three-Three, over."

—staff officer was butting in from on high?

Poole sighed. The number Three-Three in the call sign

told him it was some second-level staffer, an ops type. Some zit on a staff weenie's ass half a world away saw what he saw. Satellites. Damn things. The vid let a scout keep his lip zipped, but the sat sent the same vid around the world to the twenty-one-inch, flat-screen console of a different kind of enemy, some limp-dicked, wine-sipping, nail-biting, second-guessing, pencil-wringing, nose-breathing, designer-cologned desk jockey who lived in the suburbs and worked in bunkers below ground. A guy who didn't think he could fulfill his oath to protect and defend unless he split his ass-kissing lips to butt in on a mission in progress with some lame-ass—

The warp sounded like a stuck organ key, high and reedy, playing under the words. "Prosper Oh-Six, this is Sax Three-Three, over."

"This is Prosper Six," Poole said. By the ache in his face, he was wearing as much of a snarl as Barret's smile.

"This is Three-Three, roger. It's just that a number of us here just wanted to confirm that you could see that your target is larger than the one briefed by the J2."

I'm just saying is all. Son. Of. A. Bitch.

"Roger, copy." *Now. Outta my ear, willya.*

Saxon Three-Three might be a three-star general, a duty officer to a four-star, himself a horse-holder to one of the horse-holders to the SecDef. But here on the ground in Iraq, it was Poole's war, Poole's mission, Poole's men, their lives his alone to spend or not, if they'd just let him see to business. These men were more than stats on a sheet. They meant something to him. He needed to focus so he could be something of worth to them.

"This is Three-Three, roger. Just trying to help."

Yeah. Not so much to help the boots on the ground as much as protect the seat of government, in particular that part of the seat of government in the Pentagon on which a pink, fat ass now sat, the ass at the other open end of the very digestive tract now making noise over the radio in the middle of a combat op. Talking the talk, doing the two-step, the Pentagon's very own dance of the seven dwarves, the CYA shuffle. Cover Your Ass. Put it on the audio record. In case of a combat review board. Or even a court-martial. Testimony already in place: *Hey, I tried to tell the captain—whatsis name? Poole? Poole, I says, too many cars. Must be a corps or an army and not just a division.* Letting it be known off the record: *If you screw this up, Poolie, you're on your own.*

Fine. Now. Outta my face, asshole.

"Prosper Zero-Six, you copy?"

"Roger, copy," Poole said. "Prosper Zero-Six out." *Now. Ya mind?*

Funny. Guy didn't put the mission on hold. Didn't tell him to stand by. Case of shrunken scrotum. The staffer's scrotum shot his balls into his belly cavity, stopping the sparrow's heart, and bringing on lockjaw. Bunker commando's version of shell shock.

Poole waited. No comeback, not a word, a grunt, a whisper, a sigh. Nothing. *Shee-it.* A staff weenie and a slow thinker besides.

"Video off." Poole put out staff-guy's eyes and waited for the last word to warble in his ear. It did not. A slow talker, too from—

"Ah, Prosper Zero-Six this is, ah, Three—ah . . ." an open mike, but dead air. The guy wanted to say something, needed to speak, but had no words of weight. Just trying to figure out how to say: *Do you know who you're talking to here?* Trying to find a way to get that point across without putting an actual threat on record: *If you screw this up now, I'll lead the hanging party—make that two parties because we're going to hang you twice. Once by the neck, once by the balls.*

Spangler pointed to the top center close-up view. A full screen of the Ford's license plate: *U.S. Government For Official Business Only.*

"I saw it, Colonel. An al Qaeda ruse?"

"A ruse, Grace?" Spangler stared at her, his eyes glittering behind the wine bottle lenses. *Al Qaeda, Grace?*

"Ruse. A trick."

"I know *ruse,* Grace. But al Qaeda? Wasting a ruse on me? To the whole freaking world I'm a nobody and retired besides." *Al Qaeda? A ruse? On me? Some kinda fatwah? On me? Why would you say that, Grace? You take that back. Say it ain't so.*

"Who would have thought al Qaeda would hijack four airliners two years ago and use them as bombs?"

Spangler's face hardened into a lava field of scars. In fact he had, but . . . well that was another story. The guys outside?

"Not an enemy, Grace." Not in the al Qaeda sense anyhow.

"Friend, then?"

"Hardly. But not al Qaeda, either." There. He said the words aloud. They sounded tinny to his ear and hammered a gong in his heart. *Al Qaeda, Grace?*

Had being close to her every day dulled his internal alarm system? Had that heart-shaped face and porcelain skin charmed him out of his good sense? Those eyes of amber pitch. Had they—?

Mary Grace pointed at the top left screen as the door of the Taurus opened and a military policeman in uniform stepped out.

"Colonel, you've got about twenty seconds before your unfriendly friend or friendly enemy rings the bell." She turned to him. "Course of action?"

His heart wasn't in it. Still . . . "For you, let's go with sex-kitten maid."

She grasped at the neck of her prim black dress with

the fingers of both hands. With a quick pull she opened the dress to her belly button, revealing a curtain of red satin held by strands of red lace.

She saw him looking. He saw her disgust at his seeing. A cold twitch played at the corner her thin, flat-line mouth as she popped one snap back into the wrong fastener, making a pucker at the front of her dress. "And you?" One raised eyebrow warning him off, *Not in your wildest dream, buster.*

"Mmmm? Beg pardon, Grace?"

"Your role?"

"Right?" he said. "Dirty old man." Indeed.

She pointed to a TV screen. The sneer on her pouty lips told him. *Move your ass.*

Middle right. The MP stiff-stilted his way up the walk. *Gee, Wally, ya think that's Audie Murphy coming to the front door? Our front door?*

"Blue team," Poole said. "Rally on me. Weapons hot, mikes cold."

Telling them to assemble. All weapons ready to fire, a round in the chamber, safeties off, so no metallic clicks would give them away when they moved into the attack. Radios off. No chatter out.

And, by the way, telling the staff officer all the same things, putting it on record. *Outta my face.*

His order caused an eruption of dark shadows on the desert floor, lit up by a nearly full moon. The shadows floated toward him. *Move it.*

Poole had to act fast. Three-Three would find his tongue. He'd have his own horse-holder put in a call to a horse-holder of a horse-holder. Until he found a decision-maker to put the Delta Op on hold until some first-echelon horse-holder could drop a note on the SecDef, maybe drag him out of a meeting to call off the hit.

Poole saw six shadows flit from bush to bush, closing on him. Not fast enough. Give a staff guy a minute and . . .

"Move it," he said, although nobody was straggling.

He had to get his mind off the bunker rats. He had a fight to fight. The one outside his head, the one on the ground a couple hundred meters away. He had to strike. Before Three-Three's balls warmed over and redescended.

Poole ran down his five-paragraph field order in his head as he waited for Blue Team to assemble.

Paragraph One, the Situation. In terms of the acronym WETT. *Weather, Enemy, Troops, Terrain.* The *Weather* colder than a Raqi well-digger's ass. The *Enemy* a division headquarters-plus. The *Troops* an even dozen Delta operators all told in his command, divvied into two teams. He had eight with himself in Blue Team. Lieutenant Alberto Solis with the others in Green. The *Terrain* an oasis in an ash can the size and shape of Iraq, a rare lush spot in this region of Iraq with a water seep oozing into an ancient river channel and flowing for less than thirty meters before calling it a good try and sinking out of sight.

Paragraph Two, Mission. H-hour, D-day, attack the second Republican Guard Army Division headquarters and kill its commander and staff and as many other enemy as possible.

"Whaddya smiling about, Cap?" Barret. That bad-ass-smile-thing of his own going on.

Poole lowered his head and cocked it a notch: *What the hell are you doing down here? You damned well better have left a pair of eyes up yonder.*

Barret could not see Poole's eyes behind the NVGs, but he could read the tilt of his captain's head. He gave a tweak of that one-size-suits-all grimace.

Poole could read the nuance like a billboard even before Barret said, "Michelotti?"

"Sergeant?"

"Bo wanna know. Got your eyes on?"

"Yes, sergeant."

"Ears open?"

"Affirm, sergeant."

Barret grimaced again. Poole hit the high-beams on his own smile.

"What?" Barret said.

Poole wanted to say: *Hell, Bo, I'm smiling because you da man. I'm smiling because on paper the mission is to "inflict maximum casualties." Screw inflict. Kill the sons-abitches. Kill their commander. Kill their staff. Kill their wives and children and all their dogs and cats, too.*

You inflict somebody's ass when you want to get their attention. You kill his ass to get his buddy's attention, maybe keep him from joining up to get the terrorist team signing bonus. But Poole couldn't go into all that.

So he said, "It's good to be back in action, boys."

A group grunt told him the boys agreed.

"Master Sergeant Ballard?"

"Sir."

"Head count?"

"Team Blue is all present and accounted for, sir. Eight souls. Security out. We're all-ears." Ballard cleared his throat. "Or else."

"Roger." Poole knelt in the sand and drew it up like a sandlot quarterback. His men knelt with him, their heads close. Back on the sandlot with his buddies. "One last time. Let's go over the OPLAN." His band of brothers. "Situation . . ."

The doorbell rings once, its effect that of a starter pistol.

Spangler watches her on bottom center as . . .

Grace breaks like a sprinter from the blocks. She leaves him standing and races up the stairs, twisting her skirt on her hips, pulling her pantyhose into bunches at the knees, picking thick strands out of the hairdo piled on her neck.

Spangler swallows his testosterone.

The doorbell rings twice.

Spangler calls out, "Make him wait." What the hell, she knows that.

"I kno-o-oow-*UH*."

Spangler clumps up the stairs in his heel-less flip-flopping slippers, his arthritic knees giving him the Frankenstein walk. Slow, but as fast as he can go after standing in one place for two hours. Besides, his heart isn't in it anymore. Not after what she said. *Al Qaeda, Grace?* He's doomed and he knows it.

He sheds his pajama top, a moose-and-squirrel pattern, and tosses it to the floor of the entry, a foyer that shields the view to the rest of the ground floor. He leans against a credenza to catch his breath, rattling drink glasses against a crystal decanter.

"Are you all right?" Mary Grace asks as she opens a closet, pulls out a knotted plastic bag, and tosses it to Spangler.

"Fine." He drops his bottoms, sheds his T-shirt, and stands in boxers, a Union Jack pattern, as he tears open the bag. There's no shame at his squat body, no sexual intent apparent in this well-rehearsed act. Its only effect is to remind Spangler of two things: one, he has yet to pee; and, two, he's had no time to do it. He puts on wrinkled, stained, plain-white but yellowed boxers over the Union Jacks. He smells the stained T-shirt pits as the doorbell rings twice. He grimaces. *Doomed.*

"This is too clean, Grace, too clean."

"It's a prop, Colonel. Stop your whining." Grace pulls an apron out of the closet, ties it on crooked, and wrestles a rolled rug. She's plenty disheveled now, her blouse opening tunnels of view to the red lace, her hair a mess.

She looks up halfway, sees the bulge, looks up to his face, and catches him staring at her.

"Help me out here, Colonel."

Which brings him back from a dark fantasy he knows she'd never satisfy, not for money, not even as a deathbed request.

Poole gave a brief brief. He didn't reveal all. Didn't tell the true aim of the kill. Hell, they could figure it out. If CentCom just wanted to hit a military unit, they could toss a smart bomb from the edge of space. Shoot Tomahawk missiles from the ocean. But making noise and killing from long range wasn't the point.

The point was to show Saddam a bit of lo-tech wreckage, some good old fashioned retro-war in which American soldiers, boots on the ground, could walk up to one of his paper tiger Republican Guard units and bloody some noses with modern warfare's equivalent of a knuckle sandwich. Shoot him with rifle fire. Kill him with a grenade. Wipe out a general and his staff with a shoulder-fired rocket. Up close and personal.

A helluva cool concept. Even so, that was not the point.

A tiny strike. Not a display of might and sound and craters and rubble that the tip of an explosive iceberg might create. No, just the tip of an ice pick. An ice pick thrust into the cowardly heart of Saddam Hussein. A prick of fear into the chest of the madman and his two sons. Uday, my son the psychotic and Qusay, my other son the psychotic, in charge of the Republican Guard units. Oh, so fine. Still . . .

Good as that was, that was not the point, either. You know, strictly speaking.

The point-point was: Make some noise. Raise some

dust. Upset the Sadman. Make radio reports fly. Monitor cell call traffic. Watch for convoys.

Then bust a cap in his ass. Shorten the war by weeks and months. Maybe end the war before it began.

Now, *that*. Was a mission.

Too bad the troops couldn't know. Not because they couldn't handle the truth. But because it didn't pay to give them nice-to-know intel. Knowing the real mission might give them a kick in the ass, a secret smile, a love-a-ly sense of i-ron-y. But.

If they failed in the mission, a Raqi interrogator would turn nice-to-know into Al Jazeera-will-know.

Of course, Delta men had already vowed they would not surrender. In that vow Poole trusted them. But nobody could trust the fortunes of war to act so kindly as to let a man have enough time to fight to the death or even kill himself. He might wake up with a net tossed over him. Or he might be blown unconscious in the detonation of a mine or grenade. It had happened. And if an unconscious man were somehow to fall into the hands of the Iraqis, everybody assumed no rules of war among the Hussein barbarians now occupying the Cradle of Civilization. People would tell what they knew. A given. So they could not know. Poole alone of the men on the ground inside Iraq knew the ultimate mission. He had already briefed the men on a side mission for each of them. His double indemnity clause. Somebody else might be taken alive, even if only by accident. But no way could the Raqis take Poole. Not alive. If only one bullet remained on the team's arsenal, no matter who had it, it belonged to Poole. *S'long, boys, give it to me gentle-like.*

He reviewed the execution paragraph of his field order. Again, in brief. He and Blue, eight men, would strike the camp from the south. Team Green was to stay out of the action. Green was to cover Poole and his team on an arc to their east, then north toward Baghdad. Once they were

clear, Green would follow. Then the two teams would travel in overlaps. Again, toward Baghdad.

A simple plan. Run toward Baghdad instead of away. Let the Iraqis search farther and farther outward, toward their borders. As the Delta team inched closer to home.

That was that for Poole's Delta team. End of mission, end of war.

The open, embedded-reporter war was to begin on its schedule, with regular troops plowing furrows of destruction through the fields of Saddam's armies. Other Delta forces would pull off their various missions of sabotage and assassination. This Delta team would not be extracted, could not be. Not until American ground troops had bypassed them.

"Above all," Poole said. "No shooting, looting, rape, or plunder after tonight, so make the most of it." His men each reacted in his own way. A smile here, a wink there, a nod, a twitch, a snort, a sniff. Poole loved these guys. Able to see humor in the utter dark before the very dawn of battle. "After the strike, our job is to sit tight, outta sight, outta mind, outta the line of fire." A grunt, a sigh, a shake, a sniff, a snort, a twitch of one lip.

To strike and run away was one thing. These guys didn't like the idea of going cold turkey on the fighting. But. No troops could be spared to pull their asses out of the fire if they should get into it.

Poole kept his silence, kept it a long time. Until each man gave his attention to their leader. Until each man stopped fidgeting.

He gave them the admin-log of his order, the beans and bullets. *Try not to starve. Oh and, by the way, when you dig in, better go deep enough to strike water. Because no way are you going to be able to carry enough for three to six weeks.* "Oh, and don't be going Donner Party on each other, either," he said. "Because you will get hungry.

"Command and signal." Poole gave the men a time

hack, reviewed the radio frequencies and procedures. No need to discuss personal locator beacons, because each Delta operator had one implanted under his skin. It would reply to a signal from a satellite, on cue. Each man might get killed. But somebody upstairs would damn well know where his body fell. If somebody was captured and taken in for interrogation, somebody would know where to direct a rescue effort. Rescue effort. Right. The party line. Guys knew. The PERLOBE was a homing beacon for a two-thousand-pounder. Never know. A little friendly fire, a soldier's worst enemy, a politician's best friend.

"Last thing on signal," Poole said. The shuffling started up again. The men did not want to hear this. He cleared his throat. They grew still. "The DIC," he said, talking about his own double indemnity clause. "It's not a matter of love, godammit. Not loyalty. I know things. I know things that you do not know about this mission. If I go down. If I have to be left behind. If I'm unconscious. Even if my godammit head is blown off. You have to do it." Not a groan, not a breath, not even a pair of eyes answered him. "And what is the double indemnity?" Nobody answered. "Blue?"

Blue Dolan did not hesitate. "You get the double tap. Two shots to the punkin, even if your punkin's not on your body anymore." He would not hesitate when the time came, if he was around to do it. Because he was Delta to the core, the essence of the killer without the psychosis. Good man, Blue.

"Affirm," Poole said. "Any questions?"

He did not expect any. He did not get any.

Guys had made their private blood pacts already. SOP in Delta. In the same standard operating procedure that men in other wars had promised each other that they would take back messages to loved ones, written or oral. This was not quite the same, because this was Delta. This was a war on terror. No quarter asked, none given. The pact: *You want to do the murder or the suicide? Or we gonna go out a double-homicide?* You had to choose one before a fight. You could not go into a battle with loose ends on this issue.

"Hot mikes," he said as he turned on his own radio. "On my go." Three beats of every jackhammer heart as he checked his watch. "Move out to attack positions. *Go-go-go-go-go.*"

The doorbell rings a third time.

They unroll a stained rug laden with fuzz, cat hair, a cigarette butt, gum, and sundry trash.

Grace stamps down the rug's curled edges and kicks the debris around. "I've got the rest. You go spruce down. *Go-go-go-go-go.*"

The Delta men didn't need Poole's *go-go-go.* He knew that. He said it for the staff weenie on the other side of the world. Let the guy know they were back on the air. Let him know that the team was rolling in hot. Put a wild hair up his ass. Make him think they were talking about him while they were off the air.

Nothing but a thin static trickled into his ear-bug. Guy wasn't gonna pull the plug? They were still on?

Oh, yeah. Still hot, baby. About to poke an ice pick up Saddam Hussein's single brown eye. Hit him right in his low-slung heart of hearts.

Grace raps the side of a flour sifter, dry-painting a shower of dust into the corners of the foyer. She sneezes, but it is not hers, but Spangler's heart that stops. She glares at him. She kicks the Colonel's PJs against the wall. It lights a fire under him at last.

He hobbles into the kitchen, his knees now oiled a bit with the activity. There he takes down the only items inside a corner cupboard: a jar of peanut butter, a tin of smoked oysters, a fifth of Stoly he's pre-mixed with olive juice, his own dirty, breathtakingly warm martini, and a plastic bag.

The doorbell rings a fourth, fifth, sixth time. Spangler smiles. A seventh, eighth, ninth, and tenth time. Spangler cackles. He dances an antsy jig as he smears peanut butter over his teeth. He rinses with Stoly and swallows. Not bad. He pulls at the bottle again, then cracks the tin of oysters. He mashes some in his hands and rubs the mush under the T-shirt into his pits. He puts the rest of the oysters into the plastic bag. He's lost one oyster on the counter. He leans over and laps it up. He licks up the oil slick. He washes it down with a third shot of vodka—with a not too diligent effort, he could learn to like the combo of oysters marinated in salty Stoly. He crams the bag of oysters into his shorts on the way to the living room.

He swings aside a painting on hinges to reveal a one-way glass looking into the foyer. There stands Mary Grace. In the mirror side she slaps on lipstick and smears her mascara. She winks, pours herself a whiskey from the decanter and transfers a fat, red half-kiss onto the rim of a glass.

One detail makes him swoon. The sight of the skin stretched tight over the line of her nose, a white glare of a highlight on porcelain. If she were a Sleeping Beauty, and he an Ugly Prince, he'd choose his kiss carefully. He'd skip her lips, kiss the white line of skin on her nose. He'd inhale her breath until his lungs burst. His knees buckle at the thought.

He sighs the sigh of a man who knows he'll never mean a thing to her, not even in his wet dreams, where even there he cannot make the fantasy work. "What would it take?"

"Take? Take what?" Her voice comes through a speaker hidden in the frame of the mirror.

"Never mind."

Poole kept to the near side of the ridge. He watched the boys split into two teams of three each and halt. Waiting. As Barret scoped out the Raqi camp twice more. First with his NVGs. Then with an infrared scope in case the Iraqis used IR searchlights at night. The Raqis had night vision devices, too. Mostly the crude and bulky Russian versions from yesteryear, the knockoffs of early American Starlight technology. Russkies, man. Never throw anything away. Sell you their garbage before throwing shit away. Sell you used condoms—if they used condoms. Raqis also had the French NVDs, good for peeping Toms in gay Pair-ee but not worth a crap in the Raqi dust and heat.

The *elites* had German NVDs. Good shit. Optics superior to even the high-tech NVGs of the Delta team. The Raqs could do more than spot a target in the ambient light of the moon and stars. What's more, they were radio-linked to fire direction centers. An Iraqi soldier at an outpost could spot his target in his night vision binoculars, mark the location with a GPS system, self-contained, and transmit a wireless signal to an artillery battery. A Raqi with a sixth-grade education, by pushing a series of three buttons in turn, could unleash a barrage of 122-mm artillery on Poole and the boys in less than a minute.

Except.

The Raqis didn't give the kraut NVDs to just anybody. General officers and trusted staff officers. Very trusted.

Made sense. Who in his Iraqi-general-right-mind was going to trust a hand-held fire direction center to the likes of a Raqi Jethro Bodine with a Kurdish grandmother and Shi'a sympathies?

Barret gave a thumbs up and crept over the ridge. No IR. Barret had the drill down. Stay outta sight. Creep like an Indian. Stop often.

Indian. Bo trying to be one like his hero, Robert Night Runner, the Marine Corps gunnery sergeant who had gone into Afghanistan on Poole's team after 9-11. Night Runner. Deep breath. Close your eyes. *Wish I may, wish I might, wisht I had a Runner tah-Night.*

Poole exhaled. Opened his eyes. No Blackfeet warrior. *Night Runner, man.* Making the plays, making the people around him play better. *Da Larry Bird of Battle. Da Jason Kidd of Kombat. Da Wayne Gretzky of . . . something-something.* Guy's mind always three moves ahead. Seeing the enemy in the empty spaces before they got there. *Slipping up on the Ta-Ta-Taliban and—*

Forget Night Runner. Not even on this side of the planet. He had eleven excellent fighters and himself. Delta, man. Best in the world. Live with it. He could do dat.

Watching Barret crest the ridge behind a stand of shrubs, moving into a herd of basalt boulders big and black as Angus cattle, becoming one with their shadows. A second team of three kept watch from the shrubbery. As the two men with Barret, Artemis and Winston, slid into the black, sleeping herd. Barret jammed a thumb at the sky. He and his team took up the watch as Poole and the second team crept into the basalt.

Barret and his two men were really outta sight now. For a full ten minutes. Working their way down a fold in the earth, a protected slope, until they were in position to rub out the listening post.

Michelotti, one of Poole's favorites, nudged his elbow.

"Suicide squad reporting for duty, sir," the kid said as he put a forefinger to his temple and dropped the hammer of his thumb. Poole gave him a smile and handed over a black box the size of a package of cigarettes. Michelotti already had three in his hands.

Poole didn't let go of his. "For the luvva God," he said, "don't—"

"Right, right." Michelotti shook his head. *What you think? I'm stupid?* "Think, Cap'n. I'm the mechanic of this outfit. I'm not the guy gonna set one of these off by accident."

"It's not you; it's the box I don't trust."

Michelotti snorted. "You're forgetting, Cap'n. I modified every one a these damned things. I fixed them all with my own two hands."

"Right. Yeah. Sure. You broke the seal and diddled with the electronics and a quarter pound of CX-11. Enough to blow down the walls of Jericho. What, me worry when I got Alfred E. Einstein on my side?"

"Thanks for the vote of confidence, Cap."

"Book it. Settem up. You got ten minutes."

Poole used the time to study the landscape.

The division was set up near an oasis, with a spring flowing from the basalt ridge. A great bivouac site. Regular resort. Shade by day and plenty of fresh water. Caves carved into the side of the ridge, not big caves, not big enough to hide more than a couple tanks. But plenty big enough to hide a couple fat-ass generals and a gourmet mess for flag officers. The Raqis didn't allow vehicles, even general officers' vehicles, to drive up to a cave entrance. That would be a neon sign: *BOMB HERE* in the eyes of spy satellites.

Only one walking post lay between Poole and his target, a pair of guards trudging, rifles slung, in the dry stream bed on the dark side of the headquarters. Close to the network of tents and tracks. Convenient for the duty officer, in that he barely had to step away from the razor wire around the command post to check on his men. But flawed tactically, because the men were so close to the CP that any rifle fire that passed through their bodies would penetrate the tents and awnings that shielded the site from sun and sand.

The listening post was in a good tactical spot, two hundred yards up the ridge. Two soldiers, one on duty, one asleep.

The Raqs had not put a fighting position in place to support the listening post from below. There was only the walking post next to the tents. Then, on the far side two BMP armored troop carriers. Like all mechanized troops, these men hated to dig. *A foxhole in this sand? Get real, Sgt. Abdul.* Poole knew the drill for them. In every army, the guys had to face general officers day and night and there was more saluting than shooting, more spit-shining than spitting, more loving than fighting, more drilling than killing. If they had to fight, they would choose to fight first from inside their vehicles, shooting out of the firing ports. If forced to dismount, they would try to fight from behind their vehicles. If forced to fight in the direction of the hillside, they would have nothing, no prepared positions, no foxholes. *This war, man. Great discomfort to my style, know what I mean?*

In the distance, the division's tank elements had spread out on a line parallel to the ridge. The nearest regular unit was a tank regiment, augmented with an infantry battalion, as near as Poole could tell. It was deployed in an arc about a mile's distance from the division headquarters, with the command post as its focal point. Near enough for security, far enough for the noise and diesel fumes of tanks not to disturb a general's sleep. The tanks were not a particular problem. If any of them reacted to Poole's attack, it would take them a full ten minutes to arrive here, long after the Delta operators had left.

The infantry. A Company of regulars encircled the headquarters. Barret had reported them as a threat, and

Poole could see Bo was right. Good troops well led. They had dug in on the best tactical ground near the headquarters. They used camo over their positions. They filled sandbags to rig overhead cover at least two feet thick and raked to look like a desert mogul. They had ports so they could either fire toward the desert or turn and fight toward the ridge. On either flank of the headquarters camp, a platoon had chosen good ground, partway up the hill so as to be able to defend in all directions. Each platoon had listening posts up the slope. One had even sent three men to a lookout on top of the ridge a klick away. Each listening post had a fighting position behind it where men could give fire support once the scouts were called back in. Good work by crack troops.

Except.

Except for the area directly behind the command post. There the headquarters troops would man a post. And man it they did, in the way that all hindquarters troops did. Half-assed. Giving Poole the chink in their chunk.

Poole checked his watch. The second had swept up toward his H-hour. He trained his night vision goggles on the spot where Barret was to pop up. He did. Even on low zoom, Poole could see his bared teeth. *Note to self: tell Bo to camouflage his teeth next time out.* So his deadly smile would not give him away. Guy would love it, skulking around with teeth painted the colors of the desert, the total warrior. Hell, the tattoos on both his forearms were already done in desert tones. Why *not* his teeth?

Poole checked his watch again. He held out his right hand toward Barret, his thumb and all four fingers extended as he watched the second hand. Starting with his pinkie, he counted down, folding his fingers one by one, then his thumb into a fist. He pumped it twice.

Barret clacked his sparkling teeth three times. Three men oozed toward the listening post, flowing like shadows cast by some slow-soaring night bird. Three angels of death swooping toward the pair of Raqi sentries.

The doorbell buzzes, rattles, and bongs. The guy on the other side of that button is pissed.

Spangler puts a hand to his chest. "Be still."

"Speak up, Colonel. I can barely hear you."

"The crystal," he says. "Don't forget the crystal."

"Hold your water." Grace opens the credenza, puts away the clean glassware, and brings out a dusty, dingy set of glasses and a can of PAM spray, garlic flavor. She points it at the mirror.

She hesitates. "Showtime?"

"Not quite."

"Awwww, not the cat."

"The cat's good."

"The cat stinks."

"The cat's the reason the neighbors never ring twice."

She sprays a mist of garlic oil onto the mirror, leaving a clear spot in the center for him to see. Then she drops out of sight for a second. She holds up a square Tupperware lid and tosses it into the closet. She sprays the garlic oil into her mouth and grimaces as she lights up a smoke. She drags hard, pulling the coal a quarter-inch into her lungs. Mary Grace sighs the foyer full of smoke. She's a smoker, all right. Spangler knows that. He's known it for a long time. He'd forgive her if only she would feign sleep for just ten—

The bell goes nuts. Mary Grace flips the can of garlic PAM into the closet and slams the closet door. Hard.

He can't help himself. The sluttier she gets, the more he loves her.

Poole watched Barret and his team at their work, hands dancing with boisterous, silent signals—finger shouting.

Barret put Trendall, his best shooter into place as one more rock in a pile of boulders. Trendall, packing a new add to the Delta arsenal. Instead of the Mod-4, Trendall shot a .17-caliber varmint gun, off the shelf. Then fitted with a synthetic stock, full desert camo, 8-power scope, and silencer. Poole had seen him pull off a head-shot on a grasshopper in training for this mission. *A head-shot on a grasshopper!* On a moonless night, with a night vision scope so sharp the grasshopper looked like a mutant alien invader on a drive-in movie screen. Poole saw it with his own eye, through a second scope. Watched as the grasshopper's head fell off, the grasshopper still clinging to a stink weed, an instinct that something was wrong, bunching up to hop off and take flight. Bug's instinct about something wrong? *Right on.* Bug's head gone. Fricking bug dead and didn't even know it.

Trendall was Barret's insurance policy, in case he was spotted on his sneak. If an enemy soldier pointed, picked up a radio, or looked as if he might sing out, Trendall was to go grasshopper on the guy. Put an eye out.

Barret and Winston did not go directly at the Iraqi guard post. Not daring to sell short even a hindquarter soldier. Instead they swept along like two lazy gusts in a slow, black breeze, stopping often. Until they drew level with the Raqs. Then went at them from the side. The Raqs alert in two directions, up the hill where a deadly enemy lurked; and down the hill where a deadly friendly lurked. An officer of the guard might slip up and catch them goofing off, hand out kitchen duty for a month. Or a beating. Court martial. On a night like this? With so many VIPs around? Trial by pistol. Summary execution. SADS. Sudden Adult Death Syndrome? It could happen.

Barret and Winston moved at the guard post one at a time. As one man lay with his rifle and night scope on the guard post, the other overlapped him by ten meters in turn, each growing more cautious as he drew nearer. At any moment two silenced rifles kept a single head in a crossfire.

Poole watched like a kid. A regular nature special. Two killer lions closing in on a fawn. Each foot tested the ground before putting weight down. Each back bent lower as the distance shortened. At twenty meters, Barret shucked his pack. Winston slipped up beside him. To use the pack as a rifle rest for his M-4, four-power scoped, night-capable, silenced 5.56 mm. Bo gonna go the rest of the way by his lonesome.

Bo, Derek Jeter in the batter's box. Pulling on his skin-tight leather gloves. Bo, black as night except for that damned shit-eating grin. Tests to see his bayonet is fixed to the flash suppressor of his rifle, an issue M16A1. Fixed. Runs a leather finger across the lenses of his NVGs to clear the dust. Pulls at those damned gloves again. Poole waiting for him to tap mud off his cleats with the butt of his rifle, dig in, elbow cocked. Wait for the Roger Clemens heater.

Then he was off, working downhill to stay out of Winston's line of fire. Balancing on the knuckles of one gloved hand. Boots, working slowly, surely, silently finding quiet footing. Shoulder blades jutting against the back of his jacket. A lion, man, a fricking lion hugging the ground. Getting to lunging range. Only thing missing from the nature picture the twitching tail.

At ten meters Barret stops to check all around. Collects himself. Gives and gets a thumbs-up from Winston, Trendall, and Poole in turn.

Poole checks his watch. Less than five minutes from H-hour. On course, on time.

Barret creeps the last ten mikes in slo-mo. Nut-crunch time. Too far for a bayonet attack—too much ground to cover if the sentry spots him.

Poole catches himself breathing for Barret. Through

his nose, and slowly. He hears the tattoo of both their heartbeats in his own ears.

At five meters, Poole lets himself relax a little. Both for Barret and himself. This is close enough for a rush.

At three meters, he sighs in relief. Sign the death warrant. This one is all but over. Two giant steps and a bayonet thrust. Fork the bastard out of his hole like a snail. Iraqi escargot.

The man with his head up was already dead, except for the mere formality of a rifle slug through the skull. He belonged to Trendall. Or Winston, the backup shooter, in case of a glitch.

Bo had the Raq in the hole, outta sight for the last ten minutes. Probably napping.

Two meters and . . . . *Shee-it!*

Poole is outta breath, outta words, when it happens. No way to affect the fight or even sound an alarm. Too fast for him to do anything but flinch.

As Bo leans in to strike. As he raises his bayonet, giving the shooter his signal.

The Raqi turned to Barret. *What the hell do you want?*

As a voice calls out. Not from the sentry position. But from below. In Arabic. Poole making out the words: "What's going on up there? What are you doing out of your position, soldier?" Talking to Bo. *That's what Bo wanna know.*

Trendall shoots.

Winston shoots.

Barret dives into the Raqi position.

Then, nothing.

Poole waits.

A few seconds later.

Still.

Nothing.

Except a roaring of white noise in Poole's ears. *Where*

the hell'd that static come from? His heartbeat? He forces himself to begin breathing, to concentrate on listening.

"Bo?" Forget radio protocol.

Two seconds. It all came apart in two damned seconds. Poole damned himself good. He shouldn'ta been watching the sneak. He shoulda been eyeballing below. Shoulda seen the guy come up the slope to check on the guards. Maybe the guy *was* sneaking, to see if he could catch the sentries asleep, or goofing off. Instead he catches Delta Force in the act of the attack. Shit. It ain't the way it's supposed to be. *My bad, Bo.*

"Barret? Speak up, man."

A grunt in his ear-bug. Then, "Ten-by here, Cap. Just got trapped between two dead guys is all."

Poole could see the image in replay. The head-shot sentry had fallen like a body-slammed wrestler. Backward, over Barret. Okay good. But what's the rest of the story. "Trendall?"

"My guy is head-shot." A note of disgust. "He flinched, and I missed the eye. I think maybe the cheekbone."

Whining about the cheekbone being the killing shot instead of the eyeball. The ego on these guys.

Made him laugh in that empty, silent, scared-shitless place at the top of his gut. It's what he loved about them— they could make him laugh right in the middle of a matter of life and death.

Death. Poole replayed the sound of the bullet's impact at three thousand feet per second in his mind's ear. The bullet too long, too sleek. The sharp nose of the slug hooking like the curl of a candy cane as it struck bone. The bullet tumbling inside the skull. The over-pressure making a pop louder than the silenced report. The slug delivering every last ounce of energy to the soft mass inside the head before exiting. The Geneva Conventions forbade mushrooming slugs and splitting jackets like the sporting rounds, but hey? *What're ya gonna do?* Slug bends on impact. Not like there's a rule-a-war against it.

Poole remembered two more sounds as well. The louder report of Winston's .223 slug, not as well silenced. He replayed the cry of pain in his ears. The third man, the one from down-slope.

"Winston?"

"I hit him hard. Upper body."

Poole heard the note of dismay in it. Waited for Winston to fess up.

"Possibly not fatal," Winston said. "Sorry."

Forget sorry. "Bo?"

"Bo'll gitter done."

Poole watched. A liquid form. A black puddle of ink pouring out of the guard post. Flowing down the slope. No pistol, no rifle. Just the bayonet, black matte, now unfixed from the rifle and re-fixed, in his right hand. Getting down with the wet-work.

Get him, Bo. Do him. Gitter done before he hollers out. Situation like a fourth and one in O-T, clock running out. Poole started to stand up to see better. Caught himself. Sat down on his heels. No damn football game. More like a disaster in the making. That Raqi gets away and—*Well, shit, he can't is all. Stop him, Bo. Whatever it takes. The man. Has got. To die. Stop him or—*

Poole saw a second figure on his belly, trying to slink away. Damn him. The final gun no more'n a couple ticks away.

Guy hurting bad. Crawling slow. Till he hears sounds behind him. Sounds-a-death. Guy takes off slithering, but only for a short distance. The man hurt way bad. But quiet. Lung-shot, maybe, maybe throat-shot. He'd-a called out by now, loud.

Poole hears a cough in Bo's mike. *Throat-shot.* The guy was throat-shot.

Poole went into the Raqi's head. Man knew he could never escape. Thinking he might hide out. Trying for a patch of dark brush. A bush too far. Grabbing for it. Coming up short. A dark form flowed over him, engulfed him—

"Tango Uniform. Bo clear here."

—Killed him. Tango Uniform. Tits Up.

Bo not even out of breath.

"Nice job, Bo." Poole dared to breathe.

Bo'll gitter done. Poole could hear the smile in the words. Could-a heard it better without the static, though. Thinking maybe Three-Three was messing with him. Naw, guy wouldn't do that. Would he?

Grace drags another hit of smoke into her lungs and yanks open the front door. She blows the smoke at the military policeman on the stoop. He backs off a step, comes back, then recoils. Spangler sees the poster boy is holding his breath against hers of smoke and garlic.

"We already bought," says Mary Grace. "Girl Scouts beat you to it."

The MP speaks through one hand clasped to his nose. "Colonel Spangler, Ma'am?"

"I look like a Colonel Spangler to you?"

"No." He's a touch giddy for lack of breath. "No, I mean: Is the colonel in?"

She turns and bellows. "Colonel? Some guy—" She whips her head back to the MP so fast her hair flies out of its knot. "What kind? Navy? General? What?"

"Sergeant, Ma'am. Army."

Mary Grace hollers. "Some sergeant-man-army."

Spangler's knees buckle as her hair comes free. The sight of it hits him harder than the open door to her slip and bra. But he keeps his head. He sees that they are not the only ones wired for sound. A tiny wireless is rooted in the MP's ear. *Assume he's miked.*

Spangler shuts the hinged painting and ruffles his helmet of hair into a wild tangle of spikes. In the reflection of the glass he sees a shape through the curtains behind him, a shape on the patio is trying to peer inside. Spangler is across the room in three giant steps. He peels off his glasses and yanks aside the curtains, coming face to face with the intruder. Jumpsuit Guy out back falls on his ass, gets up, runs away from what he has just seen.

Grace shrieks at a newer, higher pitch.

"Colonel Spangler-r-rrrr? You hear me-*UH*?"

The MP now stands well away from the door, trying to keep his nose into a rivulet of fresh air, his eardrums perfed. Spangler, hiding behind dark glasses again, staggers into the foyer and kicks the square Tupperware box of cat stogies. He's far from drunk and not even acting loopy. He just wants to stir the stench.

"Yeah, Grace?"

"Army-guy here wants to see you." She gives him a look of disgust about the cat box. "I gotta go."

Spangler chooses to believe that the flinch in her lips is not for him but at the smell of cat scat. Has to be that, at least in his head. Which feels a bit dizzy right now. Is it the Stoly? Or just the sight of her, her hair free and wild, her skin blinding white in the light of day.

She stands hipshot, waiting. She's gotta go, but not until. Spangler hands over a wad of greasy twenty-dollar bills. The MP takes a deep breath, then leans in to see his man, then backs off at the newer, more rancid smells.

Spangler doesn't care about the MP. He takes a huge risk. "You're beautiful, Grace." He nods toward her. "With your hair down like that." He means it.

Grace sneers at him. Not like before. A full sneer now, no hint to it, no real-fake-sex-kitten maid, not even a fake-sex-kitten maid. Spangler can see the revulsion. She drains her drink, burps just shy of vomiting, sets her lip-decal and its glass down, and skitters away down the walk, pulling at a wedgie under her skirt, her hair bent and un-ruly, swishing behind her, flying wild, right out of the wild-hair before-ads. *Helluvan act, Grace.* Except for the ad hominem sneer, exactly on script. Spangler means it when he leers at her, no fake to it, takes a deep breath, and turns to the MP. *Ah, well, go to work now; gotta git it done as the real soldiers say.*

"What can I do for you, Sergeant?"

Poole treated himself to a sigh of relief. He closed his eyes, took a deep breath, let it out. The number one lesson of a combat leader. The lesson he had to keep learning over and over. The battle always gets off-plan. No matter how good the plan. No matter how small the battle. Always. Guy who pulls a new plan out of his ass? Guy who cobbles a new plan on the fly? Guy that's always a step ahead? That guy. He wins. Every time.

Gotta stop hoping things'll work out. Never hope in combat. Just gitter done, as Bo liked to say.

He ordered the rest of blue team down off the ridge, moving toward the camp for the attack. One by one, the blue men rogered him. Okay, put a check in the plus column for blue.

"Green?"

Solis rogered: "Green is ten-by at Position X-ray." X-ray being across the main access road to the Raqi head-quarters. In a wadi, the dry streambed that ran perhaps once or twice a decade. Okay. Time for time-check. Running behind. Where did the time go when you were kicking ass?

He picked his way down the slope toward Barret, trying to make up ticks. Even with his attention at his feet, he sensed a change in the night air. He stopped to check out the camp. Activity. Frantic activity. Men shouting. People running back and forth. *Shit. Busted?*

His ear-bug crackled.

"Shit." Barret.

Poole heard it in the word. *Busted.*

"Give it to me," Poole said.

"One of the dead guys," Barret said. "He had a radio."

"A radio?" Poole believed it, but . . . "I didn't hear him snitch us out."

"He didn't."

"He didn't?" Poole didn't feel like playing Twenty Questions.

"Bo did."

The hell's he talking about? "C'mon, Bo. Give it up." He watched through his NVGs.

Barret held up a handheld radio, wet. "He couldn't talk in it—shot through the throat. So he locked down the transmit button. They heard me talking. In English. Bo snitched us out."

"Roger." *Shit is right.*

Fricking little things. Everybody in America worried about WMDs, poison gas, anthrax, dirty bombs. But one smart Raqi, now dead, could undo the first combat mission in the war against Iraq by leaving his damned phone off the hook.

He ran a soldier's prayer through his head: *Lordy-Lordy, save us from our own damn selves.*

"Look like they gonna send the duty officer up here, maybe a relief squad." Winston.

"Perfect," Poole said.

"We got 'em right where we want 'em, boss." Bo.

It brought a flash flood of a smile to Poole's lips. "Move on down toward the HQ. Keep off the trails. Get close enough for hand grenades. Turn this little rat screw our way."

•

Barret snickered over his open mike. "Want Bo to stand up and holler that Saddam's old lady's got skid marks in her skivvies?"

Poole saw smiles on the other men. Barret laughed out loud. "Bo amuses Bo."

"At ease. From now on, no more speaking the English."

Poole thought of Michelotti, who didn't speak any of the Iraqi dialects. "Mitch, I want you on my hip the rest of the way."

"Oger-ray, ir-say," Michelotti said.

Poole didn't even try to stifle the laughter. *Delta men.* Eight guys playing sneaky-Pete in the middle of Bum-fuck, Iraq, to attack an entire Raqi division. Laughing all the way.

Giddy laughter, yes, nervous black humor, for sure, to cloak each man's dread that he might die here. But what god was it that smiled upon him this way? Letting him command such a group of men at such a time as this?

The MP sees Spangler's scarred, pitted face. Before he can get over that shock, Spangler parts his wet, fat, leering lips to reveal crooked teeth framed in peanut butter, chunky style. The MP grimaces. Spangler goes for the jugular. He lowers his glasses to fire both barrels at once, two pink irises beaming at the MP over the tops of the black lenses.

The MP looks away. He says, "I want you to come with me." It's a lie. He wants to run away.

"Sir. You want me to come with you, *SIR.*"

"Yes. Sir. Come with me. Sir."

"You gotta ask nice, Danny."

"Please. Sir." A weary look. The kid's seen the movie, heard the line before, probably used it himself.

Spangler doesn't care. He can't let this be too easy. "You have no jurisdiction. I'm retired."

Spangler hides his eyes behind his shades. The MP collects himself. He flashes credentials, complete with a star.

"I'm deputized as a U.S. Marshal." They both let a long pause hang in the air. "Sir."

Spangler looks shaken. He's not shaken, but puzzled. *A military guy deputized as a marshal? Chrissakes. They can do that? Ah, what the hell, whether they can or can't, got to let the guy bust balls.* He manufactures a tic to pick at his cheek.

The kid sees the tic. "So. Sir. Are you coming?" Boldly. "Peacefully? Sir?"

"You got a warrant?"

"Do you want me to have a warrant?"

A good line. Spangler wants to reward Danny with a smile. But he can't seem at ease. His argument is not with the green cop. It's with the prick in the backseat of that Ford out there, the Big Bad Pig.

"Want to come in while I call my lawyer?"

The MP flinches. He has left the volume too high in his earpiece, and Spangler can hear a tiny bark. The MP speaks the cues from his ear to his mouth.

"You can use my cell phone."

The kid strains to hear. Spangler bites back a grin.

Spangler holds out his hand.

"Sir?"

"Your cell phone? You said I could use it?"

The tiny voice barks.

The kid says, "It's in the car."

Spangler stares at him.

"Sir," the poster boy says. He's flat-out whining now.

Spangler gives all the body language of protest. He stammers. He looks left, right, up-right, down-left. He scratches his head with oily fingers. He shrugs and takes a step back into the house. He leans away. Letting the guy think he might run.

The MP leans in at him. He's a cop. The chase he understands. He'll follow, if he has to. It's an instinct, as automatic as a terrier's. You run; he chases. Even if he has to hold his breath for ten minutes.

Spangler remembers his tic. He gives it a few more tics, then mumbles a surrender. "I have to get some pants. I need pants, don't I?"

The tiny voice slaps at the MP's left eardrum. The kid leans his head to the right and squints one eye. As if he could get away from the rant with that.

"Sir," the kid says. "I must insist." Please? Please-please-*pretty-puh-leeeeze*.

Spangler sighs. Moment of pity for the kid. He doesn't deserve this. He's just another lackey. The true object of Spangler's disaffection is out there in the Ford, just down the walk.

I'm on my knees here. The very words right there on the kid's face.

Spangler looks beaten down at last. He steps out in his underwear, stained with lemon Kool-Aid. The MP is bewildered yet again. He follows Spangler to the Ford Taurus. He hangs back, walking clear of Spangler's wake, on the grass, out of the rancid draft.

Poole had the Blue Team tucked away between the dead sentry post and the HQ. Tick-tight. So when the Raqis reacted, they'd be looking up the hill. If the Raqs used IR to scan the slope, there'd be no Delta hits. The tents and vehicles would shield them from line of IR sight. Hiding in the IR shadows.

Now came the tough part. Now came the wait.

Tanks rocking and rolling. Funny. At night, no white lights. Scaring the shit out of men on the ground. Guys shouting and waving and cussing at the black hulks moving along at ten miles an hour behind rooster tails of dust and exhaust. Like running the bulls or some shit, only in the dark.

Just the kind of rat-screw Poole had hoped for. Let them run over a general's ass. Worse yet, get some dust all over his finger foods.

More rat-screw. The rear-echelon commandos coming up to the wire to gawk. Couple stepping over the wire. Creeping up the base of the slope. Trying to see into the night, cupping hands over their eyes, as if that would help. Yapping it up like the hindquarters troops they were. "See any sign of them?" "I can't see my hand in front of my face." "That Jafar, he's always pulling pranks." "This time some officer will pull his trousers down and give him fifty lashes." "This time it's not so funny." "Not with all god's generals here." Laughs. Curses. Whispers. "I wouldn't go up there, if I were you." "I'm going." "I dare you." "I could."

Was that Barret smacking his lips? *Come on up, shit-for-brains. Come to Bo.*

Fricking REMFs. Rear-echelon-mothers not even armed. Bare feet. T-shirts. Ready for the rack. A few packing chow, chunks of meat and rough hunks of bread. Chatter puffs. The Raqis doing what all soldiers do when they don't know what to do. Shoot off their mouths. Thinking out loud that the outpost had gotten lost. That the duty officer had gone up to check on them and got lost himself. That he was too red-faced to answer the radio calls to him.

The guy red-faced, all right. Red-necked, too.

One Raq getting warm: "A parachute landing. Maybe. It could be." Other Raqs shooting him down. "Nobody would be so stupid as to parachute onto a tank division." "Not just any division—we're the Republican Guard." "No, the *elite* Republican Guard." That brought laughter.

Poole shook his head. Funny. Even the enemy listened

to CNN. Even the Raqis laughed at the nets. The Raqi thinking it ironic that they should get so much respect from the enemy press.

Call it unanimous. Both sides calling it the enemy press and thinking it ridiculous besides.

Then came the real break. A clatter of gear. A rough voice. "Get out of the way, you sheep's asses. Real soldiers need room to pass. Make a path; make a hole."

Line troops. Grunts quick-marching to the base of the slope. Fanning into line without a pause. Darting up the slope in small groups. Moving in waves. Good troops, well trained, well led.

REMFs left to look on in awe. Only a few wisecracks. Guys shrinking away. Thinking if there was trouble up that slope, they would be in the line of fire. More Raqis getting the idea. Party over. Back to the rack.

Except for the usual 10 percent, the idiots. One moron ducks down behind a bush. One douche bag pulls the flap of a tent around his ass and peeks over. The mother of all nimrods squats in place. Lights up. Passes the butt to a pair of his nimrod buddies. Too kewl. Too stupid. Too Darwin.

Poole listened. To tanks stopping just beyond the CP. To the hum of the IR searchlights. To the whine of electrical motors and the grease-muffled chattering of gears as tank turrets swept from side to side.

Time. He reached to his right to find—nothing. Michelotti was not there, goddam him. "Mitch!" Into his open mike, into the static warble.

"Ere-hay, ir-say." From his left, on his hip. Right there. Right where he was told to be.

"Sorry. Light them up."

"Oger—"

"Put a sock in the pig Latin shit before I—"

Michelotti cut him off with the suicide squad. An assault full of sound and fury signifying an infantry e-attack.

All bark in a little black electronic gadget pack. Ambush in a box.

All the special ops forces had them for a while now. The first versions came in suitcases, later briefcases. This one, one per man, in a jacket pocket. Light as a stick of butter. Computer board, half a dozen fiber optic light projectors, three ear busting miniature Bose speakers, and a plastic explosive charge, CX-11, a space-age explosive with ten times the bite of the same weight of C4. The charge its only teeth, the rest noise.

When Michelotti set it off by a remote control the size of a Game Boy, the suicide squad opened fire. It shot beams of laser light at nearby rocks and bushes. The light blasts were engineered to look like muzzle flashes from half a dozen spots, with an occasional half dozen more positions opening fire. Some single fire, some full-auto. Michelotti used a dozen sound effects: small-bore mortars, RPGs, helicopter rotors, and the sound of an F-16 strike against the ground troops, including kicking in afterburners to climb out. Overkill, to be sure, but that wasn't the point anyhow. Make noise enough to spark a response.

Which it did. The Raqi infantry went ballistic. Forget about dead sentries. *The bad guys are shooting at us, man.* The Raqs opened fire before their officer told them to.

Ten times the noise. To cover the Delta team's true attack. As soon as the Raqis opened up, the Delta men with silencers started taking out targets. Four men began to kill Iraqis around the CP, including firing into the tents. Barret and three others aimed their fire up the hill, taking out the platoon leader first, then the light machine guns. Before long the CP troops opened up, spraying down the slope— and their own men. Finally the tanks opened fire, first with machine guns. Then the big guns.

Poole made it a point to take out the three morons sharing the cigarette. *See, man, those things can kill you, huh?*

Brief moment of regret. Shoulda let them live. Expand the idiot gene pool.

An HE round went off in the middle of the laser light show. Tank gun. The suicide squad went silent. A blast of the CX-11, set off by Michelotti. A bump in the rattle of small-arms fire from the Raqs.

Poole looked to Michelotti. He was hunched over his control panel, shucking and jiving, his teeth practically a laser light show of their own. *Note to self: Barret and this kid both camo their pearly-whites.*

In time the Iraqi fire petered out like the last of the popcorn kernels popping inside the microwave bag. The Raqs thinking it was over.

Michelotti snickered. He jammed a finger into his button cluster and brought a second suicide squad to life. An attack helicopter thrown in for good measure.

Setting off a new panic. *Choppers, man! Shootem down!*

The sky lit up with tracer fire from every corner of the Iraqi camp. The hill blossomed with high explosives. Michelotti shook with laughter, his teeth glittering from the muzzle flashes of nearby Iraqi rifles.

Fine and funny. But Poole had other things to tend to. He put down his own rifle and armed two hand grenades. By the time he was ready to toss, so were the other Delta men.

"Go deep!" He grunted into his mike, even as he cut loose with his high lob. He saw three grenades bounce onto the top of the CP canvas. His own went over. In quick succession each man threw a second grenade into a different spot.

Then they all hit the ground and covered their heads. The explosions came in two waves. The first set of grenades set off a rolling blast in and around and on top of the command post. The second wave, five seconds later, reached out farther. The first blast got everybody's attention, including the infantry on he hill. The second blast, which included two white phosphorus grenades, hotter and brighter than the sun, would blind anybody looking toward the screaming and destruction at the command post.

Before he could give the command to move out, Poole heard a grunt of pain. He turned to see Michelotti clutching his chest.

"Mitch, are you hit?" Poole sorry that he had snapped at the kid for using pig Latin, the best joke of the war so far.

Michelotti smiled. "No, but they got my second squad." He poked at his control panel and pointed up the hill. One of the tank rounds had knocked out the black box.

"You little bastard." Poole's smile belied the words. "Send in the reserves."

"Oger-ray . . . I mean, Roger, Sir." Michelotti tapped out a three-key code, and the hill came alive with the sights and sounds of two more infantry squads on line.

The Iraqi camp went nuts. Time to boogie.

The Delta Force team slid into the gully that ran at an angle to the headquarters to get away from all the wild fire from every point of the compass.

The sights of tracers and cracks of slugs flying overhead filled Poole with awe. Like AAA tracers over the night sky of Baghdad during Desert Storm. All of it set off by a couple chips in boxes costing maybe two hundred bucks apiece. All that—

He stopped in place, and Michelotti ran into his back.

"One more thing."

"Honest, Sir," Michelotti blurted, his teeth flashing through his grin. "I didn't mean to use pig Latin that last time."

"Not that. I forgot to throw out my calling cards."

"Shit!" Michelotti began patting down his jacket pockets. "Me, too."

Michelotti found what he was looking for. He held it up. A pack of playing cards.

Poole held out a hand. "Give me yours, I'll do them along with mine."

"No way, Sir. I'll fix it for the both of us."

Poole nodded. The kid had a right to play a part. "Do it here."

"No, Sir." Michelotti tossed a nod toward the lip of the gully. "We have to leave them where they can find the proof that we've been here. Up top."

Poole gave the idea a once-over. "Negative on that shit," he said. "We don't have time to go back."

Somebody else cleared his throat on the radio net. Barret. He was right to be antsy.

Poole's hesitation gave Michelotti the go. He ran up the slope, shucking the two packs of playing cards into one hand.

"No, don't—" Poole bit off the rest: *Get down, you little shit, get back down here.* He didn't want to say it in English.

At the top of the ravine, Michelotti drew back his arm. As it came forward, his head burst into a mist of red.

"No!"

Yes. Michelotti snapped back into the gully, riding the gravel under his back as if he were a sand sled. The decks of playing cards blossomed into a mushroom cloud against the sky and fluttered back to the ground, some outside the gully, some down the slope, some spinning to rest on Michelotti's body.

Michelotti's dead body. Poole saw it as soon as he reached the man. His favorite son. Funniest kid on the team. Had to be dead. What, with half his head gone. He looked up at the top of the slope past the glitter of scattered cards reflecting the light of explosions, the flicker of light on teeth exposed in the kid's death mask. Mitch. Dead.

A stray round. Nobody had shot again at the spot above the gully. Mitch. Killed by one wild shot, possibly some Raq who never even looked up. Just held his AK on auto and stuck it out of his BMP. A wild-ass shot up the slope. *Damned war. Damned Saddam.*

He leaned over the kid. In his pocket he found the control panel for the suicide squads. And one spare black box, which he also took. He set the ten-second arming delay. He stuck it under Mitch's body. A booby trap. Not the kind of thing an officer'd want to brag about. Not the kind of thing the SecDef'd write in the condolence letter to Mom.

Michelotti. Dead. Shit.

Poole saw that one card that had fallen on Michelotti's body was the ace of spades. Saddam Hussein. Proof that Americans had been here. The other cards a list of the most wanted. The joker being Osama bin Laden's face with the international sign—circle and slash—across it.

And now proof of death. Michelotti's corpse.

Poole pulled his pistol. In truth, there was no need to. Michelotti was dead as Abraham Lincoln. But he had agreed to this pact. He could not expect any of the other men to do this for him if he was not willing to do it himself. Fire for effect. Two silenced shots, the double tap to the kid's head, already pulverized. And, as a last act of kindness, two extra grenades propped under the body, set to go off if somebody tried to molest Michelotti's corpse. Or, barring that, in two hours, according to the timed setting on the suicide box, blowing the kid's body to vapors. Michelotti had already left his DNA sample in a vault back in the states. It'd go to the lab for positive ID for burial purposes. Put the collective Michelotti family mind at ease. Shut up the press corps vultures. No MIAs among the Delta Force. No POWs. And no body to parade down Broadway in either Baghdad by the Husseins or New York by the press.

Booby-trapping bodies, for shit's sake. Not policy. But a Delta pact. Leave me lie? Or blow me in place? Mitch's call. Tell that to his mom: *It's what he wanted, Ma'am.*

Poole dredged up a prayer from his distant past. *Now I lay me down to sleep. I pray the Lord Michelotti's soul to keep.* If he had it right. If it fit. It was the only fragment of the only prayer he knew. It'd have to do.

Barret cleared his throat again.

Poole picked up the kid's M-4 and took out the bolt. Bury it later. He stuck the M-4's barrel into the ground above the place where Michelotti's head would be, if he had a head. It was all he could think to do.

Then he was off, jogging to join up with the others, glad for the NVGs pulled down over his face. It just wouldn't do for the men to see their bad-ass leader with tears in his eyes.

A weary Spangler flops into the backseat next to a four-star general, Caranto, by his name tag. Of the three kinds of staff weenies in the world, those who memo you to death, those who bitch you to death, and those who bore you to death, he was the fourth, a wearying combo of all three.

"Catch you with your pants down, Ros—?" Caranto flinched. "Jeez, what's that dead-fish smell? Is that you? Or is it that woman?"

Spangler sniffs the air. *What smell?* It's all he can do to keep a straight face.

Caranto slides as far away as the seat allows, backs up to the door, rolls down the window. Spangler extends an oily hand, and Caranto takes it without thinking. He jerks away, rips a hanky from his pants and wipes his hand.

"General? What brings you here?"

Caranto starts to put away his hanky, then thinks better of it and drops it on the floor of the car.

"Friendly welfare check, Roscoe. Just seeing how you're making out. Doing a lot of fishing, are we? From the smell of it, dumpster diving."

"No, I—"

"Playing in the latrine, then?"

"Your sergeant mentioned a warrant?"

"Actually, you mentioned the warrant." Caranto pinches his nose. "Shit, man, don't you ever take a bath?"

"Saturdays."

"God bless Omar Bradley, you, you . . ." *Speechless. Guy goes speechless.*

"Checking on my welfare. That's so thoughtful, General—"

"Welfare. I don't give a shit about your welfare. I want to see your welfare ass doing twenty to life in Leavenworth."

"For screwing my maid? That's a crime?"

"Not that. I—She lets you *screw* her? You?"

"Sometimes." *In my dreams, although I do have to use restraints on her, even in my fantasies.*

"Hell, yes, it's a crime. A crime against nature. What the hell's wrong with her? She blind? Smell-deprived? Mental?" He puts a hand to his face, pulls it away at the smell. "She ought to have a handicapped parking space in your driveway, if she's screwing you."

"She does stay pretty drunk, now you mention it. *Gaaah!*" Spangler scratches frantically at his balls.

"What the hell are you digging at?"

"I think Grace give me the crabs."

Caranto hides his nose in the crook of his arm.

"For the love of—Get. *Out!*"

Spangler gives him a look of shock. *Me? Out?*

"Yes, you. *Out!*"

Spangler is deep in thought. "Out?"

"Now!"

Spangler blinks, coming awake at last, from the look

of it. He steps out. He leans down to look into the Ford.

"That's it? No warrant?"

"No. I was supposed to ask you to come back on active duty. Offer you your stars—"

Spangler fakes a laughs, then sobers up. He's no longer faking his emotions or his state of mind. He lets out the truth of them both. "Fuck you very much, Tony."

He regrets the lapse at once. In the first place, his words don't have the effect he wants. Caranto smiles. With a croc, you might not know whether it was about to smile or eat you up. But with Caranto, you always knew—knew it was reptilian chow time.

"And I was worried you'd take up the offer. I'll relay your response to the lady in the red coat. Word for word." He pats his chest. "Better yet, I'll play it back for her."

Spangler flinches. *The lady in red? Word for word? Shit!* Knowing he was miked? He let slip his control? *Double-shit!*

Caranto gives him a gotcha smile. "One last thing, Spangler."

Spangler doesn't care about a last thing. He's still upset over his lapse. What was it Churchill said? *If you have to be blunt, better you do it in manner and attitude, not actual words that can be reported?* Or recorded.

"I know what you did on 9-11, Spangler. I know you left General Bowers to die in the fire. I will be back, toad. I'll be back with a warrant as soon as I have the goods—*a-ack!*"

Caranto sees he has put his hand in a warm puddle of slimy oysters and oil on the car seat. Caranto shrieks as a hot-smelling, wet stain oozes across the fabric.

"You pissed my car? You pissed your pants in my car?"

Spangler, a wide peanut butter–eating grin on his face, isn't as happy as he looks. *The lady in red?* He'd said those things for the ears of Lady Redcoat?

Still. The Ford peels out, three men hanging their heads out windows. Any soldier in the line would pay a hundred bucks to see what he was seeing, five hundred to do what he just did. Except . . . .

Lady Redcoat was going to hear him disgrace himself in his own words? *Shit-fire.*

Poole found his voice at last. Had to. Had to right himself for the sake of the living. Get back on plan. React. Adjust. Get the hell out of this goat rope. Slip in to a hidey-hole. Outta sight, outta mind.

"Delta Green," Poole said into his boom mike, "we're on the egress to the rally point. When we pass through, you got our six."

"Wilco," Solis. "Nice war."

"Roger." *Like hell.* Like losing a son—okay, a brother, because he had no idea what having a son was like. He didn't say a word about Mitch. Later. When—

He saw Barret slow down near the mouth of the gully. Check out the wide sand funnel. Cautious.

He caught up to Barret and the rest. By force of habit he counted heads. Came up one short. Shook his head. *Mitch. Not short.*

Barret was right to stop. A long, low black shadow fish-tailed away from the CP. Toward them. He dialed up the zoom in his NVGs. A vehicle like none other. It didn't belong in a combat zone. Something right out of Hollywood, the town. A stretch SUV. Mercedes. Shiny, not even done up in matte black.

"Taker out?" Solis.

Poole did the math: SUV = VIP. Stretch SUV = Big VIP. Armored SUV = Big-ass Brass.

Kill a big fish? Or just get away clean.

Firefight easing back at the camp. Fifteen seconds, tops.

Get your ass in a crack?
SUV hauling ass.
Solis coughed.
SUV fishtailing.
Let him go?
Ten more seconds, and he is gone.
Take him out?
No time.
Barret cleared his throat.
A no-brainer. "Boomers out."
As soon as he cut loose with his own grenade, aimed for the roadway, Poole wished he could have it back. Not the grenade, but the command. He'd just blurted the words. Didn't say how many, didn't say who should throw. From the look of it, all eleven Delta men from both teams had gone through the same quick thought process. All had come up with the same solution. Each man with a boomer at the ready. All had cut loose as one.

Each saw the result. A dozen hand grenades out. Ready to blow at once. Another goddamned fiasco in the making.

They hit the ground. They stuck thumbs into their ears. They wrapped fingers around their electronic eyes. To save their hearing, to keep their night vision goggles from washing out. Cut down on the blast of sand on glass.

Three-two-one.

A sputter of explosions, a regular cluster bomb. A drum-thump in the chest, a string of stinging blasts in the side.

Poole waited an extra second for a late boomer, then, was up like the rest of the team. How did the Delta guy cross the road? In a fog. Of dust drifting at them white and thick. A rain of sand and gravel pitter-pattering off their heads and bodies.

They reached the road, churned up dust, and found . . . *nothing?*

The chill breeze blew away the last wisps of the dust cloud. Poole and his men stood gawking at ant-lion craters in the dust.

Nothing else. Nothing.

For one idiotic second Poole felt as if he were in a Roadrunner cartoon. They'd blown the SUV into the air. He cringed. Thinking it'd down and smash him flat. He fought back the idiot impulse to look up into the sky.

They'd missed?

If so, the generals in that car were now on the radio—?

"Here." Barret. Near the berm.

Poole came to his tactical senses. "Off the road."

Barret led the way, walking between an arc of tire tracks. The stretch SUV had veered away from the road, blown or steered off course. The tracks curled over the bank of the wadi.

Barret and his two men formed a line and went tactical before sticking their heads over the edge.

Poole caught up. "Green?"

"Blue." Solis. "We've got the SUV covered. Who the hell is in this ride? The Dixie Chicks?"

"If only," a voice said. "We could blow it in place."

"Cut the chatter," Solis said.

"Good work," Poole said.

"No work to it. Thing like to run over us."

"Any sign of life?"

"Nada."

"Can you get in?"

"Sí, send up the designated jacker."

He meant Michelotti. The kid had a civilian rap sheet for all kinds of auto crimes. The words hit Poole like a knuckle-rap to the chest. "That's a neg. He's, uh, a casualty."

Silence. Then, "Roger." A long, stuttering beat before, "We can get in while you cover your tracks across the road."

Nice way to put what he really meant: *Get your head outta your ass, Captain. Brush out the tracks.*

"Roger—"

Before he could give the order, Barret was on it. Sweeping away their prints on the road and at both edges. Barret at work kicking dirt into the craters. Two men stood security, three others used uprooted desert bushes to wipe away the traces. It took less than a minute. The team huddled in the wadi, eight men on watch. Poole, Solis, and Miller focused on the SUV, the car on its side.

Everybody froze as a convoy of three vehicles, more SUVs, tore down the road, rumbled over the craters, and escaped the CP. Poole breathed easy. The traffic would wipe out the last traces of the ambush. They'd have time before anybody missed the SUV. Down the road, back toward the CP, tanks rumbled. The big guns fired into the hill now and then. Hell, the Iraqis might not have even noticed the boomers going off all at once.

Behind him, Poole heard a snap. Electric door locks.

"How did you do that?"

Solis smiled. "Miller. He just hit the driver's door lock button."

Poole shook his head. *How?*

"The boomers blew out the front glass."

"It's not bulletproof?"

"Probably is. Still in one piece. Just flat blew it out."

"Any—"

"No sign of life inside. Miller just climbed in and hit the lock."

"Coming out," Miller said into Poole's ear-bug. "Don't you be shooting me, dammit."

As the driver's door of the SUV opened to the sky, Poole moved around to the front grille and looked inside. The plate glass between driver and his passengers had glazed all the way across, and he couldn't see a thing except the driver's shoulder, which Miller stood on.

Miller climbed out and walked over the side of the vehicle to the rear door. He grasped the door handle with one hand, and pointed his silenced Glock with the other. One of the other Delta men, Ballard, stood down from watch. He climbed up onto the vehicle and held out a boomer.

"If you resist," Miller said in Arabic, "we will fill your car with hand grenades. Do not resist. Or you will die." Nothing.

Miller pulled the rear door open an inch and said it again. No response. He flopped open the hatch. Said it again. Again, nothing.

Ballard stowed the boomer on his web gear. Poole knew. No sign of life.

Miller bent over. First he stuck his pistol in, then his LED light, then his head. "Four bodies in back," he said. "Cover me."

Poole had a mind to order him out. Eight quick and quiet pistol shots, two per head. Sooner or later patrols would sweep the area. He wanted to be long gone. Get some digital proof of the deaths and then bug out.

"I need some pix," he said into his mike.

"Holy Mother of Christ." Miller.

"Put a lid on it." Solis.

"Jesus, Cap'n you gotta see this." Miller.

"No, I don't," Poole said. "Checkem out for intel, maps, ID. Snap some shots. Grant them eternal. We gotta—"

"Jesus, no, you gotta see with your own two personal eyes."

"I don't have to see; just give me a report. I'll believe it."

"No, Cap'n, ain't nobody gonna believe this. Hell, I'm seeing it, and I don't believe it."

Jesus is right. Poole climbed up the rear of the vehicle and traipsed over the fender to look inside.

To see Miller, holding the heads of two men. *Two heads? He found a pair of heads?*

No, he could see by Miller's light—the heads were on bodies. Just cradled under each arm, the faces aimed at the sky.

Poole blinked. He wiped off the lenses of his NVGs. The mirage did not clear up.

Jowls and cheeks bunched up beneath Miller's arms. Still . . .

"Kiss my ass," Poole said into his open radio mike.

A burst of radio squelch. "Can you hear me now?" An echo in his ear.

Somebody Poole didn't want to hear from. Three-Three, the staff officer in the sky who'd been silent for so long. Guy had to butt in, had to know what was going on.

"Prosper Zero-Six, this is Three-Three, I've been trying to contact you for the last one-zero minutes, but we've been jammed. Your mission has been put on hold. I say again, hold off your attack. Acknowledge, over."

"Too late."

"Prosper Six, say again, you're cutting out."

"I said that ship has already sunk. We already carried out our attack."

"Prosper Oh-Six, say again." Agitated.

Kiss my ass.

"Prosper Oh-Six, say again." Pissed.

"Kiss my ass."

It looked like any other Pentagon conference room, except it was a five-minute high-speed train ride away from the Pentagon. Accessible only by a rail system known to a select few with top secret clearances and the need to know. The room was part of a no-frills office and survival complex two hundred feet below Arlington National Cemetery. The DEOC, Defense Emergency Operations

Center, called the Bat Cave by the few who knew of its existence. Accessible only by a series of train tunnels and a mini-Metro system from the White House, the Capitol, CIA Headquarters in Langley. Conspicuously, no access from the State Department. Accessible to only a select few in the executive branch and even fewer in the legislature, this was a place to go when all the options available through State had gone fruitless. Built during the dawning of the nuclear age after World War II, the Bat Cave's technology and communications kept pace with each new computer chip. No administration had ever run the country from here. A few, the Carters and the Clintons, for instance hadn't even been briefed on its existence. Some people, even people in high places, did not deserve to know. Others simply could not be trusted.

Always guarded. Always swept and dusted and maintained by top secret staff. Always supplied with fresh stocks of water and a year's supply of survival rations and perhaps the world's best library of movies going back to film and music back to 78 rpm platters, it seemed as if no administration would ever use the Bat Cave after the collapse of the Evil Empire. In effect, the place did not exist. Which made it ideal for meetings that did not exist of groups that did not exist on topics never open to debate, the press, the public, or even the very idea of existence.

In this nonexistent room sat several nonexistent suits. Some wore military suits, a marine three-star, an admiral of four-star billet, and an army major general. Two civilian exec-types sat, nonexistent, on the side of the table opposite the admiral and the marine, and a comely nonexistent woman in a red coat headed the table. The men looked to her to open the nonexistent session with no published agenda, no minutes, no record, no memos, no notes, while she gazed at each of them in turn, passively, as if they truly did not exist, waiting. A phone buzzed. Nobody dared answer. Until she nodded at the army two-star, a gofer standing at attention against the wall. Two-star took the call.

As four-star air force general Caranto entered, took off his coat, sniffed it, and hung it up. He sniffed his hands and wrinkled his nose.

"So glad you could make it," the woman in the red coat said, no note of glad in it.

"Sorry I'm late," Caranto said. "I had to change my uniform." He held up the palms of his hands, sniffed them, grimaced.

Nobody in the room cared. Two-star handed Lady Redcoat the phone, she *Mm-hmmed* once, then went silent, then stopped breathing. Then she went the color of her blazer.

Lady Redcoat did not react until she hung up the phone, and then only in a fervent whisper, not really a word at all, except she shot the first consonant so hard between her front teeth and lower lip and cut it so sharp on the end.

"Ma'am?" The suits acting deaf.

She said it again, loud and clear for the suits. "Fuck."

They waited for Lady Redcoat to tell them the news, nobody daring to ask what.

She walked out, leaving them with only the one word.

Outside Spangler's House, the Winston Churchill elf's eyes blink open.

Inside, Mary Grace touches a pair of keyboard function keys. Her eyes go wide at what only she sees. She looks behind her, at the back of Spangler at work.

Without a word, Grace gets up and hurries out of the room and up the stairs like a warm draft.

In the foyer, Mary Grace opens the door. She nods a greeting and steps aside.

In his office, Spangler's head comes up. Did he just

hear the front door shut? He spins his chair around to see all nine security monitors on.

On two monitors, upper center and upper left, there is Grace scurrying away from the house.

He hears footsteps inside.

Spangler jumps up and runs to slam the door, but Lady Redcoat steps into his face, comely but harshly. He couldn't have startled any worse at Freddy Krueger. He staggers backward into his stand-up counter.

"I . . . Grace?"

"She won't be back. I wonder if I might have a word with you?"

Spangler, barely out of recovery from one scare, finds himself suffering a new one.

Grace. Et tu, Grace? He'd known it in his heart when she came up with that al Qaeda remark. He'd never mentioned any part of his role in going after al Qaeda. He'd not even hinted at al Qaeda having an interest in coming after him. "You know Grace?"

"Indeed. Whereas you, in fact, do not."

"Not Grace?" Then, off her lack of reaction. "She works for you? You know what I do?" They are not questions, really. Clearly, she knows everything Grace knows. *Damn that Grace.*

He looks past her to the stairwell. Empty. He checks the monitors. Empty. At least Lady Redcoat didn't bring a posse. He flops into the chair that belonged to Grace, whatever her name was.

He looks past the Lady in the Redcoat. "You didn't bring backup?"

"A vote of confidence in you. That you'll reconsider my offer to return to duty." She waves a manila file folder his way. "A word, please?"

"About my language to Caranto. I imagine he let you listen to the tape—no, I'm certain he did. That'd be just

like him. Well, that's not the point. The point is, I apologize—"

"Don't apologize, Roscoe. Only the weak have the better manners, to quote your hero, roughly. I like you better
when you're a bully."

"Still I shouldn't have used that lang—"

"Fuck your language. I sent Caranto here on a simple
errand, and he blew it." She shook her head. "But that's
O-B-E. Make that O-B-N-E."

Spangler gave it a thought, then shrugged. He knew the
one acronym. "Overcome By Events," he says, "but I
don't get that last."

"Overcome By a National Emergency." She balls a fist,
not so much at him but as if to concentrate her thoughts.
"I don't have time to debate. The country doesn't have
time. We have to act now and never debate it. Ever."

Spangler opens his mouth. She shuts it with a look.

"No, Roscoe, no more small talk. I tell my story. You
listen. I hand you some papers. You sign." She holds the
file folder level, its edge pointing toward his throat like a
horizontal blade of a guillotine. "I go to work. You go to
work."

Spangler's eyes go wide beneath his glasses. He in-
clines his head toward her, body language for: *I go to
work for you?*

"For me."

Spangler leans back in the chair, all ears now. He'd
made his vow already. He'd never go back to the basement of the Pentagon. Not after the role he had played in
the post–9-11 war against al Qaeda. He'd been to the
mountain top. He'd never serve in that basement again.
He thought he'd peaked, that his life was all downhill after the work in Afghanistan. But . . . ? *Work for her?* He'd
never even envisioned a new mountaintop, a higher, more
heady job. *Working for her?* He could do that. He—

He remembers himself and bolts to his feet, staggers at

the pain in his knees, and braces himself against the counter. He points an open hand at the chair.

"I'll stand." She tosses a nod at the counter. "I always work standing. You do, too. Like Rummy."

He'd seen Rumsfeld work on his feet. The day he retired, he met the SecDef in a private audience, as if Rummy, as she called him, were the pope, which he was. Pope of the Puzzle Palace. Ever since that day, Spangler had worked standing up. If the old fart could do it—

"I'll bet that hurts," she says without caring.

"Only in the knees." Why would Grace tell her about his arthritis, too?

"I mean if you fall asleep and hit your chin on the counter on the way down."

She smiles at her little joke. Spangler gives her a twitch of a smile only. A thought splashes in his head like a bursting water balloon.

"What else did Grace tell you?"

Lady Redcoat smiles, the first genuine smile she has ever shown to Spangler. He knows she likes him—at least in a bemused way. He'd known that from day one, 9-11. On that day, he'd briefed her on Swift Sword, the plan for preemptive strikes against terrorists around the world. Swift Sword.

"Her name is Andrea," she says.

"Grace? Is Andrea." *Right.* Spangler does not believe that name, either. He has been stupid before. *Mary Grace Andrea Hale, my ass.* Whatever her name, she did not matter. Not anymore. He is already in love with somebody else. A woman with power. A lady in a red coat.

"Andrea works for you."

It wasn't a question, and she didn't even grace the remark with an answer beyond the raising of an eyebrow. *What else?*

"What else did she tell you?" *For chrissakes.*

"What do you think, Roscoe?

"The smoked oysters?"

A wide, thin smile, and fake.

Spangler gives her an *aw-shucks* smile and lifts his hands a little before letting them flap against his thighs. *All in a day's work.*

"She didn't tell me that you planned to leave a puddle of urine in General Anal's car like something out of a goddamned *Seinfeld* episode."

"Well, that was . . . spontaneous, a dark angel impulse. Childish," he said.

"That, too. But if only I had known, Roscoe." She wagged her head wistfully. Her slit of a smile cracked like a jagged line on an ice pond. "I would have sent him over earlier."

She'd set Caranto up, too? God, he loved her. "You had a national emergency you wanted to talk about?" He had to keep some kind of edge to himself, flimsy as it was, and not let her believe that he would tell her anything she asked anytime she wanted it. He had to keep at least one shred of his pride intact.

Didn't he?

She narrowed her eyes at him. "This is so—"

"Classified?"

She flicked an impatient hand his way. *Don't interrupt with stupid questions.*

He saw something there. Lady Redcoat in distress. Nothing to do with him, but disturbed with a part of her ordered world somehow turned upside down. By what he could not guess. He'd seen her on 9-11, at the moment when the first of the Twin Towers collapsed to rubble. She'd betrayed distress then, too. This was different. This was a personal distress.

An instinct kicked in, a sensation dormant in Spangler since he'd hung up the uniform, that predator's sense. He sensed not blood, but vulnerability. Whatever she was about to tell him was not so much a national problem. It was a personal problem. She was stepping out of channels. She was about to step into a shadow world of the not-quite-legal, not-very-ethical, quite immoral. Of course. His world. She was assessing the risk of venturing into it herself.

Spangler all at once felt the earth shift like a pool table. All the balls rolling toward his corner. He put on a dumb look to hide his insight. *Come into my parlor.*

She glanced at him. Seeing his stupid, blank expression, she decided he might not be a risk to her. She tried a tentative foray into the spider's realm.

"I'll begin with the punch line," she said. She hesitated at one last doubt. He could see her weighing her way to salvation, a nano-glance toward the stairs. She could still go away without touching the tar baby, avoid getting mixed up with him.

Spangler laid another layer of stupid onto the moon crater of his face: *I'm so-o-o confused.*

He could see her waver. Then something else. He'd already won the battle. She was dying to tell him. Whatever it was, she was near bursting with her dirty little secret. She had to share it with somebody who could appreciate its magnitude. Any second now.

She burst. "Delta Force is in Iraq."

That's it? "So what?" No need to fake a reaction to this. This was not news. Be a national disgrace if they weren't in there, ready to recon, sabotage, direct fire, secure the bridges, hit the SAM sites and SCUDs, and all the rest. *That all you got?*

"The Preemptive Terrorist Team you put together after 9-11."

He shrugged. *And?*

"They captured Uday and Qusay."

"Saddam's sons?!" They said the words in chorus. His part the question, hers the emphatic answer.

Uday and Qusay.

Whaddya gonna do now, Captain?

You're not just Delta, man. You're the Preemptive Terrorist Team. No prisoners. Standing PTT order.

But this! This was Uday and Qusay.

My ass, man. They extra baggage. Can't unloadem, can't killem, can't leavem behind, can't ignorem. Uday and Qusay, man. Whyja have to go and tell the staff weenie you even haddem?

He couldn't keep his head on straight. He had a mission. The team'd pulled it off. Too well, except for losing Michelotti. Now this.

Uday and Qusay. In his custody. In his care. Right outta *Alice in Wonderland.*

Sure, he'd visualized success in this mission. Even fantasized. Hell, who didn't take a visualization one teensy step into the realm of the unreal? *But this?* This was as undreamable as the notion that teams of terrorists could hijack four commercial jetliners and fly them into some of the most visible, most important landmarks in America. He—

He had to get the crap out of his head. Get a plan going.

He should've dropped a pair of grenades into the disabled SUV. That *would've* closed the book. *He could've—*

Arrrgh! Get off the shouldas, wouldas, and *couldas?* He had to deal with the *what-it-bes,* not the *what-if-it-ain'ts.*

He had to take inventory, to get back on track.

He took in the sights and sounds of the night. *What it be?*

Quiet, except for the storm of static in his ear. No gunfire. He did hear an explosion, what was it? An hour ago, or just twenty seconds ago? Some Iraqi had kicked a dud round, maybe picked up one of the black boxes that Michelotti had left behind. Or even Michelotti's booby-trapped body. Put that one in Michelotti's column.

The mountain was still lit up by no less then two dozen white-light searchlights. They were looking for their attackers and not finding them. They were pissed that they had no bodies of the invaders.

But, hey, forget the Iraqis. Deal with the situation at hand.

Uday and Qusay. He had to take them. Of that he was sure, even in the absence of orders that Three-Three tried to give him but couldn't because of a new round of the radio jammers.

Orders. Now that he'd made his report, there'd be no undoing things. When he did get orders, they'd come from on high, that was for sure. And they'd conflict. Constrict. Contradict. And afflict, yes, afflict—that was a certain outcome.

Hell, the on-high commands of his own country would afflict the Delta team as much as Saddam's orders. Hiding out closer to Baghdad didn't look like such a bright idea anymore.

Saddam's sons. In his custody. In person. *Alive.*

Uday and Qusay. Can you spell *disaster?*

He became aware that Lieutenant Solis was standing by his shoulder, that Solis had cleared his throat for the third time.

"Yeah?"

"Recommend we un-ass the area, Cap."

"Roger."

Solis just stood there. *Roger, my ass, whaddya wanna do? Where do ya wanna go? Like, now that we have these two birds? Got orders? I mean besides the* roger-thingie, *a plan would be nice.*

"Go east a ways. Find a place to hole up."

"Take the prisoners?" *What say let's leave them here?*

"Uday and Qusay." The two Iraqis looked up at the sound of their names. Weird. Weirder even than just saying their names out loud.

A smirk under Solis's NVGs. *Who else? What say we kill them and say we didn't?*

"Affirm."

"Take them? Or leave them?"

"Take 'em. Alive." Not exactly an excess of conviction. Leaving it open to question for Solis.

"What if they died from injuries in the car crash?" *It could happen.*

"Uday and Qusay died in the crash."

"Sure. They crashed; they burned. Total accident. Fucking shame."

And there Poole stood, emperor of his tiny desert empire of the shifting sands. One word, a thumbs-up or thumbs-down. Uday and Qusay would live or die at less than a word, a mere gesture.

Shit-fire.

He could get away with it. That was not the problem. His men would go along, a wall of silence, a brotherhood tight as titanium, hell, depleted uranium. He knew these Delta fighters. On their deathbeds eighty years—or ten minutes—from now they wouldn't brag about killing the scourge of the Kurds in the second Iraq war.

"Cap?"

"Right."

"Kill 'em then?" A broad smile.

"Wait." What was wrong with him? Poole had never felt so off his game. Kill these two just because they might inconvenience him? Kill them because he could and get away with it? Or spare them because of a sudden attack of morals? A loss of nerve? Hell, Tyler's training test of two years ago revealed that he could kill in cold blood if he had to, but this? Tyler never trained him for this.

Man, the hassle he was gonna get back in the world. Either way. But if the two just up and died trying to escape? They'd put him up. For sure. Article 32 investigation. The works.

"Cap, where the hell are you with this?"

"Negative." Thumbs-up.

"Don't kill 'em?"

"Do not. Kill them."

Solis stood there. *Just asking* in his body language. *Why not?*

"National security." It sounded lame, even to his own ears.

"Roger, sir. National security it is." Solis turned to his troops.

"Wait."

Solis looked back, hopefully.

"We can always kill them later," Poole said, and wished he could eat his words at once.

Solis's mouth twitched in disdain.

Poole telegraphing a weakness. Just couldn't keep his fat mouth shut.

"We'll never let them be taken alive by the Iraqis."

"Right, Sir." Solis went to work prepping the prisoners for the march. Flex cuffs and duct tape. "National security and all."

Leaving Poole to his head games. What the hell was wrong? Scruples? Practicality? Gutlessness?

He should have been able to say it, the one word, without a hitch in his voice. *Affirm.* Kill them. *Negative.* Spare them. No indecision. No eating his vomit. Leaving no room for Solis to give him shit.

An hour ago, he'd have said the word, one of them, and gone on with the mission. But now? What was eating at him?

The loss of Michelotti? Was he just shaken and needing some time to recover?

Or was it something deeper? Something more permanent? Some flaw in his character that was always there but had never had the occasion to rise to the surface till now?

Till those two came along.
Uday and Qusay. Damn them.

Spangler gave her a squint of: *Can't be.*

"It's true," she said. "Two days before Bigfoot's dead-line for Saddam and his two sons to go into exile, and our guys capture the little bastards."

Spangler pooched his lips.

"Holy cow, Roscoe, I thought you'd be head over heels at the possibilities."

Spangler was, in fact, fully engaged in trying not to pass out. The possibilities, indeed. They ran amok inside his skull, his thoughts like rats in a scrum, thirty rats at once.

"They say that war is mainly a catalogue of blunders, but this—"

"Not *they.*"

"What?"

"*They* didn't say that. Churchill did. You're quoting Churchill again."

"Right." She was a genius of the mind-screw, letting him know she knew as much about his hero as he did. Just to mess with him. It worked. "This," he said, a quaver in his voice. "It's terrific."

"But what?"

"But your little windfall comes with a shitload of prob-lems." Trying to give it back to her.

"You don't know the problems."

"What's this got to do with me?"

"I want you to get those two out of Iraq alive."

His laugh was a spray of spit. "Me? What the hell can I do? You've got all of Delta, all of CENTCOM, all of the Pentagon at your disposal, and you come to *me*?"

He spread his arms. *Look at me.* Exhibit A. *Just look at me, for chrissakes.* He looked down at his sunken chest, his paunch, his spindly legs. He lifted his eroded face to the light. *This is your Bruce Wayne, your Clark Kent, your Peter Parker?*

"Delta. CENTCOM. The Pentagon. Those people don't belong to me." She left it unsaid but hanging there in the air between them: *But you do; you belong to me.*

"I'm your Plan B?"

"You're my Plan B, my Plan C, my Plan Z."

Spangler leaned back, soaking up her bizarre need, her adulation—whatever it was. She *needed* him? *Why, for chrissakes?*

"Delta, CENTCOM, the DoD," she said. "They have rules. But you, Roscoe. You are the king of no rules."

He gave her a catbird smile. He had her by the balls.

Her face went hard and angular, pinching off all her natural beauty. "You're gloating?" She looked toward the stairs. The way up and out of here.

"No." He lied fast. "I'm just . . ." He shook the rats out of his head. "It's just that I'm not what you think. I'm just an over-the-hill guy."

She squinted, taking a long, long look. "Here you are, walking up to the garden and running away just because the dog growls." She let a smile play at her lips.

He recognized another quote and smiled. "I'll give it a shot."

"You have to want to do it, Roscoe. You don't want to? Just say no." She stared, unblinking. "It's all you have to do."

He saw her let a smile leak through the slit in her lips. They both knew she'd won.

"Not a question of want to. I have no resources," he said, protesting too much but not too seriously. "I'm a no-body, hell, less than. I'm a nobody with nothing."

"You have to do this, Roscoe. Get those two out of Iraq. The men in Delta trust you, and I need a wheeler-dealer."

Nah. She needed the evil twins. Leverage with Saddam. Leverage for her in the halls of power. Spangler? A fall guy. He'd seen it all. Hell, fall guy was his career MOS. He'd made an art of it.

"You can do this."

"I'll try."

"You'll do it."

"I'll do it."

"You've got carte blanche." A greedy, gas-pain of a smile crossed her full lips. "Uday and Qusay," she said, looking up into her head, practically swooning. A sneer wormed its way across her face. She became a caricature of herself, a wicked stepmother right out of one of the Disney features. Everything but the dry-washing of greedy hands and the coat made from the skins of a hundred and one spotted pups.

Spangler felt it. Just the idea. Saddam's cretinous sons in custody. He caught her mood, caught himself dry-washing his own hands at the thought, caught himself wishing he had a puppy coat, too.

Karim-Assad Ibrahim al-Hasan al-Tikriti. Only nineteen years old and already the most important man in Iraq. Those very words from the mouth of Saddam Hussein. Two, sometimes three times a day, for about an hour each time, most important. Perhaps *the* most important man in the world.

Saddam always said it with a big laugh, as if this was some new, huge insight. Usually with a heavy clap on the shoulder from Uncle Saddam and hard enough to hurt. Never by accident. And always followed by the observation: "We keep trying to fatten you up. How can we put some muscle on those bony shoulders? Don't we feed you enough good food? And how are you feeling?"

Karim-Assad always answered the same way, in the

same manner, never varying a word, a gesture, a tone, a shift of his eyes. His very life depended on his ability to convey he felt just as fit as he did at the last meal.

"Oh, I am feeling most exceptional, Uncle. Thank you for asking," he would say. "Why I just ate a wonderful meal not an hour ago, prepared in your own kitchen, thank you, Uncle. Most nutritional, yes. I feel very plump even now." Then he would bow from the waist, almost touching his nose to his knees, for he had been bowing for years now, and was perhaps the best bow-er in all the country, in spite of his potbelly. Then he would come stiff and straight, and say with great solemnity, "I am most honored and most proud to be of service to you, Uncle. Most proud, most yes." With all the sincerity and gravity that he could fake. Knowing all the while that part of him truly was the most important man in Iraq. His pot-gut and his roiling, overfed, simmering-with-spices stomach.

He would take his position in a nearby corner of whatever palace Saddam chose to eat this meal and stand by, an armed guard of Saddam's personal bodyguard at each shoulder.

Saddam and his guests, always men, usually including Karim-Assad's cousins Uday and Qusay, would eat. The same food that he had taste-tested in the presidential kitchen an hour earlier. Every course—no matter that he did not like curry-flavored dishes, and Saddam ate curry at almost every meal.

Karim-Assad had to taste at least three tablespoons of everything. Every sauce. Every meat. Every pastry and dessert, which was not all so bad. Every beverage. Water, liquor, wine, brandy, coffee, tea, soft drink, iced tea, lemonade—everything that Saddam might sample from the table, three tablespoons.

Then he would stand by for an hour. Literally, on his

feet. In the presence of those two guards. With the kitchen staff. Everybody watching that food, left on warmers or in coolers, depending on how the food should be kept.

After Karim-Assad tested the food, the cooking staff could add nothing more to it. If a scoop of butter was to go into a sauce at its finish and just before serving, Karim-Assad had to taste of that butter the hour before. Three tablespoons, no matter how much Karim-Assad begged.

Just before the set meal time, the entire kitchen staff would bring out the meal, under covers, so nobody could slip a drug into it at the last moment. Each course would be served from a side table. The meal, once prepared and taste-tested by Karim-Assad, never left the sight of half a dozen of Saddam's personal bodyguards.

The bodyguards were to ensure the integrity of the meal. And to keep watch on Karim-Assad. Should he become ill, even dizzy, the meal planning would end. Saddam's medical staff, always at hand for meals, would pump the contents from Karim-Assad's stomach. Not so much to save his life as to analyze them, to find the poison that had made him ill. In such a case everybody on the cooking staff might have to die. Not from food poisoning but from hanging. Or from the torture that proceeded the hanging, all part of the investigation, all part of life lived close to Uncle.

Karim-Assad himself would not die, unless somebody at the table became sick. Then he'd take what all Uncle's staff called the three steps to death. The torture, then the interrogation, the hanging, with the threat of step one being repeated often. Although Karim-Assad knew better than that. Uncle would never hang him. That was too quick and clean for a member of the family suspected of betrayal. He might be laid out in the garden of one of Uncle's palaces. In the sun. Held in place by a sharpened fencepost driven through his gut and into the ground. Left to die, Uncle's guards ordered to water him hourly. With urine.

He had many a sour laugh about the logic in killing a food taster. What was he? A suicide taster? What idiot would poison himself just to get at his uncle? Questions he could never ask aloud. Just asking them would bring suspicion on him. *Why are you obsessing over taking poison?* A short leap from there to: *How long have these thoughts of poisoning the great Saddam been on your mind?*

Should the issue ever come up, Karim-Assad had his answer, of course. Ironic and why not? *Obsessing over poison? Me, a food taster? The first to die if ever a dish does get laced with cyanide or strychnine or dioxins? Why would I worry about poisons at all?*

His life's work to stuff his mouth and fill his belly with rich food. His death to have that plump belly pierced and to use his mouth to beg at last for a drink, even to ask evil men to piss into it. Such was the life of a distant nephew of Saddam, and such would be his death.

Once, he thought it had come. On the night of roasted game birds imported live from France, when Uday had doubled over, slapping the table with one hand, holding his throat with the other. His eyes bulged, and he looked as if he might disgorge his tongue.

It was quite a scene. Half the cooking staff fell to their knees, howling their last prayers and testament to Allah. The principal chef fainted. The assistant chef wet his pants. The pair of bodyguards at each of Karim-Assad's shoulders pulled pistols. Each put his muzzle to Karim-Assad's temple. Quite ridiculous, really. Had they fired, they likely would have killed each other as well. More ridiculous because how would they ever know if he was sick if they blew apart his head? Most ridiculous, in fact. The bodyguard were all too eager to kill him. It was nothing personal for them. It was just that by killing him, they might save themselves. Karim-Assad had heard of it before. A condemned man under torture might implicate any other people around him, guards, for instance, whom he did not like. Everybody knew that Karim-Assad did not like these two. Or any of Saddam's personal bodyguards.

In any event, nobody died but the principal chef that night. And not because of anything to do with poison.

Ten seconds into his convulsions, Uday sat up straight. He laughed excessively loud at his little joke, as trivial jokesters were prone to do. Uncle Saddam thought it not so funny. For he had stuck the handle of a spoon down his throat and had vomited on his plate before the joke was revealed.

After an awkward ten seconds more, while Uday was getting the evil eye from Saddam, Uncle burst into a laugh. He had seen the hysterics of the cooking staff. Calling attention to their hysterics made his own pale by comparison, or so he seemed to think.

The principal chef died of heart failure, the only casualty of the prank.

Karim-Assad had seen a lot, had learned a lot from that experience. He had seen the cowardice of Saddam. He had seen the cruelty of Uday, and the stupidity— willing to risk his father's wrath by pulling such a stunt. And he had seen the quiet, steady stare of Qusay. Qusay had not panicked, had barely even stopped eating. He saw in an instant that his brother was faking. Karim-Assad watched his eyes. Qusay also saw his father's fearful reaction. He watched in disgust. He said not a word. But his look spoke volumes. Karim-Assad saw him vow in that dark silence to someday kill Uday, to dispose of him when it was necessary to rule Iraq after his father. His expression said that he would not put up with such folly, so great a lapse in protocol and in front of the kitchen and security staffs. He showed that he would be a far sterner leader than even Uncle himself.

Perhaps he had shown that side of himself before. But this was the first time Karim-Assad had seen it. From then on, he made a study of the men in power. Those who came to the table every night. Those who came as guests. Little people on the staff. And the important ones sitting down to eat.

Someday, he would get a chance to show that he was more than a gut. Karim-Assad would eat wonderful food every day, every meal. In great quality and variety. In five years, he had developed a refined palette for the best whiskeys, champagnes, brandies, cigars, wines, and liqueurs. He could detect spices by name and amount in French cooking—only stifled by the excess of curry that Saddam called for so often. He observed the cooks at work—he was not allowed to make idle talk with them—that was too great a risk of collusion in an attempt on Uncle's life.

That night of Uday's prank, he learned many other things, too. About himself, for instance. He felt the smile on his face when Uday choked. And barely had time to stifle it before the guards turned their attention—and their pistols—toward him. He knew there was no poison, of course, because he would have been the first to know. He could hope, though. He did hope, too. He hoped that the greedy eater Uday had choked on a sharp bone, that he would inhale a piece of the bird and die of suffocation. Uday dying blue. Such a vision. It would almost be worth the belly piercing if somebody had actually poisoned him. He did not know that he could have such feelings in him. Revealed by a bold knowing look and no more. The closest feelings to bravery he had ever felt.

From that night on he paid closer attention to the nuances of food. More important, the nuances of people. He could identify a good deal of a man's motives and personality in less than a minute in their presence.

So he knew of the serious trouble this night, long before anybody spoke a word of it.

Something terrible had happened. In a trice, Karim-Assad deduced that, in the absence of Uday and Qusay, whose places at the banquet were set but not occupied, that a terrible something had happened to the two infamous sons of Saddam.

He could barely keep the smile off his face.

Lady Redcoat, true to her word, gave Spangler carte blanche to get Uday and Qusay out of Iraq. No challenge to his wish list, not even the one he cringed to say aloud.

"I need a military jet," he said. "With pilot."

"Done," she said, and that was that.

So Spangler was streaking west across the blue-black ahead of the morning in an F-16 fighter equipped with wing tanks for extra fuel. To Malmstrom Air Force Base, Great Falls, Montana. Good thing that she didn't ask him what he hoped to achieve out west. *You don't ask, I don't lie.* Fact was, he had no clue.

How to get former Marine Gunnery Sergeant Robert Night Runner back into action with Delta Force? He couldn't come up with a reason why Runner would say yes.

Lady Redcoat—she told him her name was "Madelaine-don't-ever-call-me-Maddy"—gave him the details, few as they were, of the Delta Force find inside Iraq.

"You're sure they're not body doubles?" he said.

"It's an A-1 report. Impeccable source, no-fail contact."

He winced at the certainty she was selling.

"Okay, not 100 percent. I know nothing is ever 100 percent. We give it 95 percent certainty. It's not a lock until we get DNA."

Spangler doubted 95 percent. Even if it was a Delta report.

But she kept selling. She grew animated, walking around the rooms, her hands flying out now and then at random, snatching ideas out of the air like gnats, ideas that lent credit to her hopes. "Think, Spangler, think. Who sends doubles to a meeting of the Republican Guard's division commanders? At night? Saddam wouldn't send fakes who might attract a smart bomb at a sit-down with all his top officers. Not with war a couple days away."

Selling herself as much as him. She had to be right. *Delta has Saddam's two sons. Had to be them. Had to be.*

"Uday and Qusay? Alive?" Lady Redcoat shook her head. "What pure dumb luck."

"Or un-luck, as the case may be."

She showed him a game smile. "That's what I like about you, General. I saw it in your eyes, as I was telling my story. Thinking half a dozen moves ahead."

"Two days ahead. The president's drop-dead day for Saddam to go into exile. But now you have his spawn in custody. That's a bit problematic, as they say."

"It's a pain in he ass is what it is. We can't reveal we have them until a day or two after the ground attack."

"On the other hand, Saddam can't reveal they're taken."

"Too big a loss of face on the Arab street."

"And yet . . ."

"And yet, if Saddam—or anybody else in the world on that side of the street—sets them free, they'll be instant heroes in the Arab world. A victory for Saddam."

"A defeat for us."

Her smile petered out. She handed her folder to him at last.

"We'll be goats no matter how big we win the war. For sending in attack forces before Bigfoot's forty-eight-hour ultimatum is expired."

Spangler caught it. She was lying. "Why?" he said as mildly as he could. "There's no rule against gathering recon and putting sabotage forces in place." He shrugged it off. "Is there?"

She cleared her throat. "These guys went in thinking they were going to hit a headquarters and make Saddam stick his head up for a second. So we could bash him like one of those gopher games. Except with a stealth bomber."

"And?" He was beginning to see her problem.

"Bigfoot pulled the plug on offensive operations. No air. No attacks. Just get into position until his ultimatum ran out."

Spangler felt the crush of her drift. "But Delta didn't get the word. Carried out the attack. By accident, as it were."

A twitch of one eyebrow. *Obviously.*

"And snatched the sons of hell besides."

She sighed.

"Helluva dilemma."

She had nothing to add to that.

"You called me *General* there a second ago."

"That agreement you're about to sign makes you brevet major general."

Spangler opened the folder and saw the title on the top sheet: *Recall to Active Duty.*

"Pocket orders? This is no agreement. This is involuntary."

She shrugged, a smug smile playing at her thin lips. "As a member of the Individual Ready Reserve, you're being recalled to active duty." She shrugged. *So what?* "On the best of terms. To do what you do best. To do your deeds in the dark."

She had a point. He signed without reading. He closed the folder and handed it over.

"A move up," he said. "A second star?"

"No stars, except for pay purposes. You live in civvies on this one."

Too bad. He'd have liked to see himself in uniform as a two-star, see if the stars elevated him beyond toad stature. "Why not hire me? A contractor? Consultant? Civilian?"

She shook her head. He knew why not and that she wasn't about to say it.

So he said it. "You want to keep me subject to the Uniform Code? Why would you want to keep me liable for court-martial?" Not wanting to hear the answer.

"The Uniform Code?" A wry smile crossed her thin lips. "Why would you bring that up?"

"9-11. The Pentagon fire? Bowers?"

"Bowers?" She shook her head. "No. It's not a crime to run from a fire. And you did save the OPLAN that gave us the team that gave us bin Laden—or at least our shot at him."

Spangler dared to breathe. If that's all they had on him—

Her wry smile turned into a thin grin. "Even that thing in the hospital ICU . . . ."

She let it hang. Spangler blushed. Deeply. *That? She knew about that? How much* did she know about . . . *that?*

"What did you think, Roscoe? That we wouldn't keep an eye on him?" Lady Redcoat gave him a coy smirk. "He was the Pentagon's top antiterrorist officer. We had a security camera on him."

Oh. That much.

"Of course." Said the spider in the red coat.

Spangler found himself back in the hospital ICU room.

A burned, seeping body lay on the bed, his boss, Lieutenant General Randall Bowers IV, a casualty of the 9-11 strike on the Pentagon. His name and rank not released. He'd not been honored in the SecDef's memorial service. No mention that al Qaeda had been so lucky as to get America's top military antiterrorist officer in the first strike. Yet so unlucky as to get Spangler in his place.

Spangler saw himself sift through the cords that connected the barely living scab to life-support machines. He saw a woman doctor burst into the room, the latest of his many self-made enemies.

"What the hell are you doing?" Not a question but an accusation.

For Spangler held a pair of cords in both hands at his chest, trying to decide which to pull from the wall outlet.

Lady Redcoat held both hands in front of her chest, miming him and mocking him at once. "Praying the rosary, Roscoe? Praying the rosary?"

As the life-support monitors went nuts and the seeping body died in a puddle of himself.

"I laughed myself silly." She laughed again, silly again at the memory. He faked a laugh of his own. He saw through her laugh. She wasn't laughing at that scene as much as her position. On top. Letting him know she knew. She had the pictures. She had the attack dog in Caranto. She'd use them both, if she had to. She had his balls in her hand. Without leaving a fingerprint. And he, Spangler, with that stunt with the oysters and ruining the car seat, had handed Caranto all the motive he needed to go for the kill, if, *if, IF* she ever let the four-star off his leash.

She pinched off her smile and grew serious, inch by inch, even as she inched closer to his face.

"I confess. I do have a dark side. But next to you, I'm the morning star and the setting sun." She shook her head. "No, next to your light-less soul, I'm the brilliant fireball of a bursting nova." She stepped into his face, using up all his oxygen. "I need your darkness to complete me, Roscoe. With you, I can be the black hole in the galaxy from which not even the light can escape. Take my light, Roscoe. Make me a dark star, make me black like you."

Spangler glazed over at the dark sensuality in her words. He was hers.

"What do you want me to do?" he whispered.

She was nose-to-nose, her expression that of the were-wolf.

"Get them out of Iraq."

"Delta?"

"Delta." She shook her head, coming out of the trance. "What the hell do I care about Delta. Don't be an idiot."

"Uday and Qusay? You want me to get them out? How? With what?"

"Whatever you want. I'll give you money. I'll give you access. I'll give you resources. You can be a one-man army. Or you can recruit a legion of demons. Whatever you want, Roscoe, whatever you want."

He could not say what he wanted; he had not the power of speech to put words to the fantasy now running through his head.

She pulled away from his face for a second to dry-spit to the side.

"I'll feed the media the occasional taste of shit to keep them hungry. You'll do the grunt work behind the head-lines."

Spangler leaned away. She got back to nose-to-nose contact. No woman had ever gotten this close to his face voluntarily, not his mother, as he recalled. *Hell, not even the occasional whore.*

"Whatever I want?" He growled in his throat to get back his voice. "Whatever I want."

"Anything," she said. "Bring me Quday and Usay. Do anything. Or anybody. No rules. You and me, Roscoe, you and me."

"You can't pull them out with the Delta men?"

She glared at him in disgust, pulled away, gave him back his air.

"Of course not," Spangler said. He leaned toward her, pulled by her magnetism. She cut him loose with a twitch of her head: *Not another inch nearer.* "You would have already done that."

"They're trapped behind the lines. Deep behind the lines. And now the whole Iraqi army is more into finding that Delta team than they are into defending against our attack."

"Why no extraction?"

"None foreseen. Delta was supposed to stay in place, out of sight, out of mind, until the conventional attack rolled on by. Now we have to wait until tomorrow night at the earliest to send in an emergency chopper." She shook her head. "But with Bigfoot's order about letting the ultimatum run out, we can't even do that now."

"You've considered ordering Delta to kill them outright." Now his mind was hitting fourth gear, getting up to speed.

"Dammit, Roscoe." She went wild-eyed. "Even if we wanted to, we're being jammed. Goddamned Russians. But even if we did, what good would it do?"

"Right. The dead bodies don't mean much if we can't show them on Al Jazeera. Even with pictures of the bodies it's a rumor until you produce the corpses. You need the bodies to get any vid value from them. If you can't get them out alive, you have to pull them out dead at least."

She shook her head. "I don't know, Roscoe."

"What?"

"This isn't the mind I saw praying the rosary with the life support cords in that hospital room. I'm a little dismayed here."

He shrank into his chair. *Why?*

"You're so slow on the uptake. Have you been doing dope?"

"I'm a little out of practice. Give me a break here." Spangler scratched his head, digging for something both wise and evil. "As a last resort," he said, leaving the words hang. "You can just kill them, even if you lose the PR value."

She shook her head. *What the hell are you talking about?*

"You've thought about sending a two-thousand-pounder down the chute to evaporate the brothers. The Delta boys, you know, collateral damage?"

She dry-spat into his face now.

"You call that dark thinking? Don't make me regret I brought you onto my team, Roscoe. Of course we thought about a smart bomb. Even that shit-for-brains Caranto could come up with that. Hell, that was Caranto's first lame idea."

Caranto? Comparing him with Caranto? Spangler was offended. "Of course, of course." He tried backfilling. "The president has too many scruples for sacrificing American boys—"

"Scruples, hell. The president doesn't even know. He can't know yet."

"The president can't know?"

She reached out and lowered his own glasses for him. She stared into his naked red eyes without even blinking. Disarming his trick before he ever had a chance to use it on her. Showing him he dare not try.

"Officially? It's too sensitive for Bigfoot to know." She shrugged.

Spangler nodded. Deniability he understood.

"Somebody else is going to have to fall on her sword for this," she said. One corner of her mouth twitched in the imitation of a smile. "Or *his,* as the case may be."

He shuddered. Very like a *his*. Now that he'd signed over his soul. She pulled out of his personal space once and for all.

He slid past her to Mary Grace Andrea Hale's workstation, opened a drawer, and plucked one of her cigarettes from the open pack she left behind. He lit it as Lady Disdain began her transformation back from a she-werewolf into a comely professional woman in a red blazer.

She gave him a look of surprise. "And I thought I knew all about you, Roscoe. Since when do you smoke?"

"About three seconds ago."

Spangler's belly rose into his throat as the fighter began its descent into Malmstrom.

Two Delta men worked on securing the captives. Poole was over their celebrity status by now. Uday and Qusay. Big deal. Nothing to him but a double-barreled pain in the ass. Like his ear-bug bugging the hell out of him with static. A click. A warble. One broken word punched a hole in the noise.

"Traffic." Solis.

Yakking at him from the edge of the wadi where the team had posted its security detail to overlook the road and watch their six.

Poole waited, pissed at the scratchy white noise in his headset. Three-Three called it jamming. Saddam jamming? A satellite? *Nah.* How could he? He didn't have the tekkies to dick with the Big Bird. *Did he?*

More noise, like somebody blowing bile. Poole heard word fragments eking through the static. "Say again," he said. Nothing but racket.

He saw he was standing with the overturned SUV between him and Solis. When he had cleared the vehicle and was sure he had line-of-sight to Solis, he spoke up.

"Say again."

"We got us a convoy," Solis said, an edge in his voice. Pissed at having to repeat himself. "Better get ready to fight."

"Roger." Kay. So the radios hooked up if you got line-a-sight, radio-to-radio, with only a few meters between transmitters. The white noise was still there, the static, and the sound of a clarinet playing at half-speed in the background, but they could talk.

Still no Three-Three. The satellite jammed like a plugged toilet. Had to be. What else could keep a staff weenie so quiet for so long? He tried a call.

"Three-Three, this is Prosper Zero-Six, over."

Nothing but the sound of a penguin feeding her chicks.

He peeled back the sleeve of his jacket to check his high-dollar wristwatch with digital compass, GPS screen, text messaging, and weather data. Nothing. Nothing, that is, but partial LED symbols and numerals flashing hiero-glyphics. The damned thing wouldn't even tell time. Everything, the compass, GPS, the weather and the time was coming from the SAT. Everything gone bat-shit.

Jamming, definitely jamming the Big Bird.

He looked to the watch on his other wrist, a twenty-dollar Casio. It worked fine, although he did not like the news it gave him—a little more than an hour till dawn.

He caught a glimpse of Uday and Qusay. A couple raggedy asses, they had perked up. Sound of the convoy. Uday and Qusay flashing their chewers. Not sly grinners, but hopeful. Thinking they might be rescued.

They were still smiling when Foucault and Artemis laid a foot-long piece of duct tape over their mouths, both at the same time, taping those stupid smiles in place.

Poole winked at them. He made a pistol with his fore-finger and thumb and shot each of them in the head with it. A wasted insult. They could not see him in the dark.

Their flaps weren't taped over. They could hear.

"If these two try to call out, cut their throats," he said in their language. "If they try to escape, cut off their legs. If it looks like the Iraqis might overrun us, shoot them both."

"Affirm." His men both answered at once, also in Arabic.

"In the head."

"Affirm."

"Twice each."

"With pleasure."

"With extreme pleasure."

The Husseins cowered. He turned to deal with the issue of the Raqi convoy. Wondering.

What the hell was eating him? Ruthless, yes. He decided long ago, even before Tyler's training test for ruthlessness in the Nevada desert, that he could be cold as he needed to be in combat, killing terrorists without compassion. That was his job. Leave the second-guessing to the embeds with the troops, the wet-beds back home, staff officers, and politicians.

But cruel? Where did that come from? Nowhere in the mission statement that he had written for himself did he find cruel, sadistic, or barbaric. That was for the Husseins, all of them. He didn't know he had it in himself till now.

Breakfast was early, well before sunrise. Which meant Karim-Assad was called to taste food bare hours since last night's meal. Ugh!

He still felt stuffed, even ill before eating his first bite of poached sweet honey-lemon-drenched orange wedges dusted with cinnamon. They were always on Saddam's menu. A treat, really. But he could not deal with them. At least not feeling this way. So, in secret, and silently so as not to raise an alarm, he vomited into a mop closet far from his room in the basement of the palace.

When the meal was served, Karim-Assad stood by,

bracketed by his Mukhabarat guards. He again saw the stress in Uncle's eyes. All the staff looked to Saddam for cues on how to act, what to say, what to feel. He spoke excessively loud and boisterous to Karim-Assad as they each went through their false lines.

"Don't we feed you enough?" Uncle asked. "And how do you feel this morning?" The rote was loud but empty of even a shade of emotion.

Karim-Assad recited his script with ease, not missing a word, not reacting to Saddam's dark, darting eyes.

Why wouldn't Uncle show stress? The great Satan America had threatened war. Saddam had laughed at the idea at this very table a month ago. And at a different table every other meal since, as the mobile kitchen staff moved around from palace to palace.

Uncle was off his game in the pre-meal chatter. He was dull and distracted, thus his high staff fumbled as well. They talked of the weather, of all things. *The weather!* Might as well discourse about the sun. It seldom changed, either, except on its daily cycle across the sky. They repeated fragments of conversation from previous meals, fawning over Saddam by quoting his words back to him, repeating words and phrases without context. One line of chatter did not follow upon the next. Parrots reciting words just this side of inanity.

Then Saddam went silent. He did not eat or even ask that somebody serve him. He drank only water, French sparkling water at first.

When Uncle put the French water on the floor beside the table, the high staff went silent. So did the kitchen staff, if it were possible to go even more silent than they already were, not letting even a blink of the eye or a whistle through the nose, or even a loud heartbeat call attention to them.

Uncle called for Italian sparkling water.

He put on a forced smile. "I hate the French fizz. Ever since they started putting petrol in it."

The high staffers roared with laughter. Karim-Assad reined in his own smile—at them. He saw it in their faces. A staff filled with fear. Dread actually. Dread that the next word out of Uncle's mouth might condemn one or more of them to death. His little joke about the French. That broke the dam of emotions.

But only for a little while.

The high staff tried to keep up the patter, speaking louder and faster, as if their babble might make sense if they spoke it apace.

Uncle withdrew into himself. He grasped his sparkling water too hard, Karim-Assad saw. He went too deeply into the study of the bubbles clinging to the side of the lead crystal glass. His eyebrows bunched over his eyes, swollen with worry. Gradually everybody at the table spoke lower. And slower. Until finally the room was silent except for the sputter of candles. Not a tinkle of gold silver on bone china. Not a breath, not a cough. Not a single appetite.

Everybody seemed to fear what Karim-Assad knew would come next. Uncle would begin to talk about his feelings, the reasons for his stress. Such talk always pointed to some form of betrayal of trust. Or incompetence. Such talk always lead down the hallways of the palace, any palace. They all had the stairwells past the underground sleeping quarters to the far wing of the labyrinth of tunnels. They all had halls that led to the guest bedrooms set aside for those found guilty of any kind of betrayal, from overdone lamb chops to the accidental mention of the name of a previous traitor. Nobody wanted to go to the ubiquitous basement bedrooms. If they did go, some were never seen again, never even talked about, for if you mentioned them, you might join them. Those rare few who did come back were never quite the same as before, always frail and flighty, like abused kittens.

Saddam took a deep breath.

Everybody else held their breath.

"The staff is dismissed," Uncle said.

Karim-Assad was glad to be going. Somebody in that room was about to hear his name called. Somebody was going down the stairs. Through the hall. To the guest bedroom. In the basement. Somebody—

"Karim-Assad Ibrahim al-Hasan al-Tikriti."

A full body shudder shook Karim-Assad. He stopped at once, faster than his guards, who were so slow of wit that they did not even know his full name when they heard it. As he whirled in place to face Uncle, he pasted his easy smile into place. He did not feel at ease. Not one bit at ease. But he could act it until the torture began, he supposed.

"Uncle? How may I serve you?"

Then he saw it, a look on Saddam's face, a look he had never seen before. His smile froze. And so did his heart.

One glance. One blink-long look at Montana told Spangler to flee. Go into the terminal. Book a new flight. *Fly away, Roscoe, fly away.*

Here he did not belong.

From the moment he stepped off the plane at Great Falls and felt the chill of the tarmac through the soles of his shoes, he saw the proof in all things Montana. *You. Do not. Belong.* The Arctic air double-clutched his lungs like the first drag of a first-time smoker. *Go. Back. You still have time.*

Today's high of minus-twenty? At noon? With a lousy fifteen-mile-an-hour breeze sending the chill down to minus forty-five in fog that gave way to light snow? Who *did* belong here? You couldn't even piss in safety.

He'd stopped his rental SUV to drain his lizard of too much coffee farther back along US-89. He couldn't go through with it, though, couldn't even draw down his zipper. One glove off, he had to cover his scarred right ear from the harsh wind fangs on tender tissue. Then his hand went numb. When he tried breathing through his nose, the damp hairs froze stiff. He tried to pinch back some warmth with a cluster of frozen sausages that were his fingers, and he felt the needles of ice puncture him inside his nostrils. A bloody nose from snow needles.

And what? Expose his hairless gopher? What was he? Nuts? Thinking this even as he stood fumbling with his zipper, raising his windward shoulder to shield an earlobe, he caught a picture of himself near death, his penis frozen to the rear bumper of the Dodge Durango where he'd accidentally touched it like one of the ubermorons in the *Dumber* movies.

Hell with that. He'd rather piss his pants. Die of shame. He had more experience in that anyhow. He'd died a daily death of shame for weeks at his court-martial for cowardice back when. Hell, every day for years on end at the Pentagon was a day of death. Junior officers and the enlisted took one look at him and shied away, bumping into walls and each other to get shed of him.

He didn't belong in Montana. God, what if he went off the road? *Hell, what road?* He couldn't see a road, only an occasional pattern of black patches breaking through wind-blown drifts. That'd be it. He'd die. He'd never walk out. Walk where? They'd find him dead, stuck to the rental Durango seat, frozen on a Golden Pond of his own making.

If the Natives found him, they wouldn't even turn him over for burial. They'd just throw him to the wolves or coyotes or grizzlies or polar bears or whatever the hell roamed this *Here-be-furry-dragons* wasteland. A white guy whiter than the winter with pink eyes and a military

ID in his wallet. A general. Hell, a brevet major general. Just like George Armstrong Custer. Scalped for good measure.

He didn't belong here, at the fringe of the Blackfeet Indian Reservation. No military officer belonged here, where red, white, and blue meant nothing to do with the flag. Here, the memory of bluecoats meeting red men was a stain on history, a history of conquest, the most ruthless blue-on-red attacks coming General-Tecumseh-Sherman-like in winter on camps locked in white fog and snow. The massacre on the Washita, for one.

Spangler felt a flash of shame about that one. He wished he could make things right—he would if he could. If only he did not die on the side of this road. He would walk up to the first red man he saw and offer his hand, apologize. He would express his regret that the braves out on a hunt that day when Custer hit their village—

A *village!* He saw a village!

At least the sketch of one. A mere blink in the storm gave him a glance of straight lines and angles that did not belong on the prairie. Low, squat houses. Fade to white-out. Another blink. Trashed cars. And there a fleeting, slinking glimpse of an animal, spotted and brown. Then another blink of Heart Butte. *Saved!*

What was that? A hyena? They had hyenas in Montana?

His Dodge plowed through a snowdrift, sending a puff of white into the wind.

He shook his head. Heart Butte. *Sad looking place.* Where did people go on days like this? Where was the workplace? Could you just pound on doors until you found your man? Night Runner. How in the hell was he going to find Night Runner?

He felt the need to flee again. Back into the storm. At the risk of his life, if need be. So he might be anywhere but here.

There it was again, the hyena—no, merely a spotted brown dog with low-slung hips and sagging teats that looked like a hyena. And another dog. No, a whole pack of dogs, perhaps eight in all.

What did feral dogs eat anyhow?

The question was rhetorical. He didn't want to know.

"My family," Saddam said. "My son."

Karim-Assad took his deepest bow. To give himself time to think. There was a warmth in that voice, perhaps for the first time ever. He knew it by its scarcity. And that look, too. A look of feeling. For him, Karim-Assad.

He touched his nose to a knee. On the way up, Karim-Assad took in the eyes of those at the table. All the eyes on him. All in great relief that he was the object of Uncle's attention now. A few curious glances. Mostly hopeful. Hopeful that Saddam would send him to the bedroom. Nothing personal. Just that it might spare them.

"And how have you been, my son?"

Karim-Assad saw that Saddam was looking him in the eyes. Never had he done such a thing before, not like this. In the past, if he did meet Karim-Assad's eyes he was only looking at Karim-Assad's belly through them. Did the taster's eyes betray any sign of pain, any onset of spasms? Only a belly. That's all he had ever been to Uncle Saddam, a distantly related belly.

But now. *This!*

This was it. His moment. Karim-Assad knew it because he saw in Saddam's face. All these years he had spent in studying nuance at tables like these, among men like these, the most vicious, jealous, practiced at their craft in all the world. Never saying what they mean, always with secondary motives to their words and acts.

He could still play the belly, the dumb and greedy eating machine. Take no chances. *What's to eat? What may I taste for you, Uncle? Would you like to hear what's on the menu for our next meal? May I suggest less curry in your cooking?*

No.

This was it. His time.

"Uncle, I am fine. Perhaps too well fed. But fine in every other way. How may I be of service to you?"

A broad, warm smile.

Karim-Assad saw it coming.

"Sit."

There! There it was. One word to put him on a level with every feral mind at this rich table. No false praise in it. No word games of any kind.

The men of the high staff were aghast. A lowly food taster? At the same table with them? All their fears about Saddam's mood seemed to give way to what was, to them, a more base emotion. Jealousy. With one word, he was a threat to their grand status. A lowly serving boy sitting at table. With *them*? Were they not worth more than he? A moment ago they feared for their lives. Now they feared only for their rank in the never-ending jostle to be nearer to Saddam's hand. High status. Karim-Assad allowed himself a small smile at a thought: *The easier to suckle Uncle's broad ass.*

What they did not know was that Karim-Assad read books. Western books in translation as well as Eastern books. Not the Iraqi trash that Iraqi writers spewed to praise the exploits of Saddam as the modern Nebuchadnezzer, either. But many truly great men wrote coherent, inspiring works. Karim-Assad had found his way into the libraries of some of the palaces. None of these jostlers for favor at the table would know that he read books, for they did not visit libraries. Neither did Uncle, or his cousins, Uday and Qusay. But that was beside the point. He learned things. Of all the things he learned, he retained only a few, a handful of pointers on how to succeed in one petty life on earth.

Of these, the most important was to recognize the moment, the single instance or event that can change your life. Even more important than to seize the moment was to know it for itself. Then to act upon it at the very moment it showed itself; act without hesitation. Ever to be ready to act was even more important than acting.

The word was *sit*. It was the offering of his moment. Karim-Assad saw it for what it was. Just as clearly as the others did not.

Should he take the chance? Seize the moment? Remain a food taster? Or grasp for a golden rung on the ladder?

He strode toward the table. The eyes of the high staff looked to the last chairs, below the salt, they called them. There were five empty chairs down at that end of the table. He could have any one, including that at the opposite end to his uncle.

Two pairs of eyes, ranking generals in the south of Iraq, suggested he take the side chairs. One pair, the chief of Mukhabarat, demanded he bypass the end chair. The commander of Saddam's personal guard simply told him to die now, at his own hand, or die at the hand of one of his men later.

He did not take the recommendations of any of their eyes. He looked only to his uncle and read in them a moment of confusion. Uncle's eyes gave him permission to take the far chair, if he liked. When Karim-Assad did not, the sad eyes forgot their stress for a moment, to say: *If it pleases you to take one of the other far chairs*.

Karim-Assad read it in the eyes. *So be it*.

When Karim-Assad walked past the near end of the table and marched toward Uncle, the brow lifted. His eyes smiled. The crow's feet at the corners revealed it as a true smile. Uncle glanced at Uday's chair, to his left. They gave even that permission: *All right then, sit there if you like*.

Karim-Assad heart soared in his chest.

Yet he walked past the chair.

The dark, heavy brows lifted in surprise. *What now?*

Now, indeed. The instant most dangerous in Karim-Assad's life, perhaps the very hour of his death.

He walked between Saddam's back and the two personal bodyguards posted behind him, not six feet away, at the wall. They took a step forward. Karim-Assad put his left hand on Saddam's shoulder. Gently.

The guards took two more steps. They could die for this. Their commander was at the table, and saw it, too. Somebody at Saddam's back. It would not take a dagger to kill him. Not even a letter opener. A steak knife plunged into his ear, a butter knife into his eye, a broken shard of lead crystal from Germany slashing his throat.

Karim-Assad gave the thick, sloping shoulder a loving squeeze.

Saddam, fully aware of the guards moving toward his nephew, raised his right hand, the same offhand gesture he used when saluting a crowd of cheering Iraqis. The guards hesitated. They looked to their boss at the table. The general lowered his head a mere centimeter. The guards stepped back, the hatred in their eyes palpable. If they lived through this night, if they did not have to accept an invitation to the guest bedroom, they would wait for a chance. To get even with Karim-Assad.

He glanced at them. He did not smile as he went past Saddam's right shoulder and released the left from his grip. No need to antagonize or to gloat. Yet, what he did was worse. He looked quite through them. They did not exist for him. Not now. Not ever again. They were dead to him. They would hold no sway over him from now on. For he was about to sit in the favored son's chair, at Uncle's right hand.

He stood behind the tall, formal chair, crafted in Italy, upholstered with fabric from China. One in nearly every palace. Each chair worth ten thousand dollars American. A hundred thrones for Qusay.

He looked into Saddam's face, his eyes asking: *May I sit, uncle?*

"That chair belongs to Qusay."

Karim-Assad unleashed his warmest smile, full of love and deepest empathy. He knew it by its feel, well-practiced before the mirror.

"Our loving Qusay had no need of his chair last night, and I regret to say . . ." He pulled out the chair and sat, the gasps of the high staff audible even from the far end of the table, first at his boldness, then at his words, "It appears that Qusay will not have need of it this morning, either."

"Big-ass convoy."

The report through the static in his ear stopped Poole's heart.

"Four BMPs, two more SUVs. Probably more bigwigs booking it under escort. Coupla tanks, coupla trucks."

"Roger. Heads down." Take a memo. No ability to report it to higher.

Poole moved in closer to the Demonic Duo, studying the faces in his NVGs, checking them out. Flex cuffs, the nylon handcuffs. Hands in front, zip-tied to each man's belt, buckled in back. The Delta men duct-taped the men's hands into gloves of camo tape.

Two more small convoys passed by, a platoon of tanks grinding by at full speed, and a company of infantry in trucks. All the activity gave him the jitters. Especially the combat convoys. They traveled with white lights blazing. Too risky for the team to stand up and roll. Too great a chance of getting caught in the sweep of headlights.

They had to wait for a break.

Poole stepped up to each of the brothers. Uday was taller than he'd thought, and thinner. Crooked. In the physical sense, too, his body leaning to one side. Poole knew that he was leg-shot in an assassination attempt. The car crash might have made it tender. He winced every time he tried to put weight on it. *Tough.* Poole poked him in the chest with a forefinger. Just to see if the guy was real. Guy with a rep as an animal. Kidnapping and raping a bride on her wedding day. Uday grunted. More a whine. Uday, afraid. The serial rapist. Rumored to have more perversions than J. Edgar Hoover and Jeffrey Dahmer combined. Whining. Uday, whose video games involved authentic swords and real blood and genuine guts in the old man's prisons. Raqis afraid of him. Nobody could predict who'd die next. Anybody in the room. Everybody at risk. Uday. In Delta hands. Afraid. But hell, who wouldn't be afraid on the wrong end of a Delta ambush?

Poole wished he hadn't called it in. He poked the man again. Again a whimper.

"Uday," he said. It was not a question.

Uday tried to talk through his tape.

"Shh-h-h!" Qusay shushed him through his nose.

The tall brother glared at Qusay. He grunted through the tape. *Screw you,* in the tone of it. He turned to Poole and grunted at him, too. *I'm not Uday, asshole.*

"Too bad," Poole said, a twinge of cruelty infecting his words. "If you're not Uday, you're not worth anything to me. If you were Uday, I'd keep you alive. Since you're not, I'm going to have one of my men open your belly and pull out your guts, fill the cavity with sand, sew you back up."

Uday whimpered. Probably seen it done.

"Tape an electrical charge to your genitals. Leave the wire contact open. Let it stay open until you have to piss. When you piss you burn off your privates. See how long you can hold it."

Uday's eyes filled with tears. He tried talking through the tape. Poole lifted his NVGs on their hinge and shined a flashlight between them, as if to see Uday, but really to let Uday see him, his face. *See there? No pity.* He put a strip of tape over Uday's eyes.

He turned to Qusay. Qusay, the tougher nut, according to intel. He pulled wrinkles into the tape with an even broader grin. He knew better, or thought he did. Americans. They might talk about it, but they didn't pull the kind of stunts he and Uday and Saddam had pulled ten times before lunch. It was all there in the eyes. Americans had no stomach for torture, for personal violence, for evisceration, for outright murder, for war crimes.

Poole wished he could get the smile out of those eyes. Maybe cut off a body part, one of Qusay's, and stuff it into Uday's mouth. Tape it there. Let Qusay watch Uday choke on it, his parts. Let the bastard anticipate the moment he would cut something off Uday, something disgusting and maybe even diseased—

"Got more traffic." One of the scouts out, speaking into Poole's ear-bug. A more edgy report than the last. Everybody was getting more agitated by the delays, by the notion of having to deal with prisoners, by the never-ending cacophony of roaring, howling noise. By the promise of a dawn that'd leave their asses hanging out.

And Poole. Talking mutilation. *Shee-it.* Where the hell was his head?

Shoulda been on plan.

The plan had them a mile or more from here by now. The plan did not imagine this twist.

Poole felt a kick of tactical urgency. Forget crimes against the Geneva Conventions, forget crimes against nature. He had the here and now to deal with. And he used to think Tyler was nuts. Now he understood Tyler too well. Hell, he *was* Tyler now.

The tactical situation. Get your mind on the tactical. Got it?

Okay, got it.

Okay, what was the report?

Okay, traffic.

What's it mean?

More traffic by day. Search parties. New parties. From Baghdad, looking for this pair of devil spawn.

Deal with it.

Poole threw the tape onto Qusay's chest and spoke to one of his men. In English. "Keep them apart." He switched to the Raqi language. "Do not let them jeopardize the lives of our men in any way."

It sounded better than the death threats, far better than the sadism of before.

Poole studied Qusay, Saddam's clone. Shorter than he thought, with much more hair, blown about by the concussion of the grenade and the crash. Not an imposing guy, unless you knew his rep as a killer. Poole reached out to adjust the hair, so he could get a better look. Qusay did not flinch at the touch, was not afraid. His face tightened under the tape. Out of hatred. He did not want an American to touch him. Poole smirked. Wait until day, when he saw that a black man had handled him. Wait until—

"Truck." Solis spoke over the roar in Poole's ear-bug. "Slow-moving. Flatbed semi. A lowboy hauling a tank."

New sounds, worse sounds than the traffic on the road. The popping, buzzing roar of helicopters.

Poole had to smile at the idea that crept into his head.

"Can you take the truck?"

"Take the truck?"

"Can you? Take the truck?"

"It's a flatbed, Cap."

"Dammit, can you take it or not?"

"It's a truck. Of course I can take the truck. What the hell do we want with a fricking truck?"

Solis pissed? All this crap and now a balking officer? What next?

"Take the truck," Poole said. Loud enough to be heard over the jamming, loud enough to make his point with Solis and the rest of the Delta team on the net that he didn't want any more of their bullshit.

"Take the goddamned truck."

A dark satin look broke across Saddam's brow. All at once, he went from filial to lethal.

A cue for the chief of Mukhabarat. He sprung to his feet. "I demand to know how you know that our noble Qusay will not join us here at the table. What spy—?"

Saddam raised a languid salute and got his silence. His eyes, hooded and aglitter pinioned Karim-Assad. "I ask the same things as the chief of secret police, nephew."

A sudden shift in his status. Not *son*, but *nephew*.

Karim-Assad belched. The lurch of his gut came just shy of dry vomit. *Just the curry. Not nerves. Just the curry.*

No reason to panic. He had seen gush and bluster at table before. Rather than act so weak, he reached for a bottle of fizz water, French. He twisted off the cap and poured a glass full. *Take your time.* He held the bottle for one last clinging drop to drip into the crystal goblet. Showing them all how his hand did not quake. Why would it? He had drunk liquids and eaten foods that might well be laced with poisons and acids. For years he had risked death. He took a long, slow drink now. He might not know what the future held for him. He did know this one true thing: He was no longer a belly, but a brain. This was a big risk, yes. But just a risk. He had made his peace with Allah long ago.

He set his glass down without a splash and barely a ripple.

He looked into Uncle's eyes. "Your face tells me that you slept hardly at all last night. You are worried about them both, Father. Especially Qusay. You did not mind that I would sit in Uday's chair, but it made you uneasy that I would sit here. The very words of your most esteemed police chief just now confirm it. I was right to worry about your dear sons. My dear cousins."

Saddam's eyes filled with tears. His lower lip trembled.

Karim-Assad looked around the table. He saw that the most vicious men in Iraq could not stand the sight of Saddam about to weep. He knew why. "May I dismiss the kitchen staff, Uncle?"

Saddam's chins fell to his chest and bunched up.

Karim-Assad stood up. "Out," he said. He liked the voice he heard, strong and sure. He liked the response to it as well. The kitchen staff were off like a herd of clowns at a circus. They ran into the doorway and each other. To see Saddam in tears? Who could live in peace after that? If they could be out of sight of teary eyes, they might live another day—or in the cycle that they lived, perhaps as long as another meal.

In a most reverent voice, Karim-Assad said, "I think those at the table should give my uncle a moment as well. This is a hard time for him. This is a time for family."

The high staff left in almost as much a hurry as the kitchen staff. Except for Saddam's chief of police, the secret police, and the personal guards. Karim-Assad looked at them, one eyebrow raised.

"We are family, too," said the chief of police.

"Closer than you," said the chief of guards, a threat in his voice.

Saddam put his hands over his face. "Go." The word mashed in his palms. "All of you."

A smile eased onto the faces the two officers. *You, too, son of swine.* Karim-Assad stood up. Saddam's wet right hand closed on Karim-Assad's left. He did not let go.

Karim-Assad looked to the others. He sighed. *I am needed here. What can I do?*

Truly. What *could* they do, but leave the room?

Karim-Assad looked to the two guards behind Saddam. They were confused. He gave them an out by tossing a nod to the doorway. They started. Halted. A sense of fear caught up with their need to flee.

"Go," Karim-Assad said to them. "You may keep us in sight from the hall. Stay out of earshot."

To them a good plan. They bolted to watch from afar. The shock of being bossed by a pup who was minutes ago a lowly food taster had not yet sunk in.

Karim-Assad did not care. He was alone with his uncle. Indeed. At this moment, the second most important man in Iraq.

Only one thing kept Spangler from U-turning and driving back into the blizzard. The dark and ragged figure that loomed from a cloud of snow in front of the Dodge. *Right damned in front!*

He jerked the wheel left and stood two-footed on the brake. The Durango spun left and slid. It kept to its line, straight down the street but spinning still. Right at the man. *Get out of the—*

A slam of metal against body and bone. Spangler could not stop, could not go. The brakes didn't stop him. The gas didn't drive him. He tried both to no effect. Finally the Dodge came to a rest on its own. Pointing back the way he'd come. The way out of town.

Then the SUV began to slide again, this time toward the edge of the street. He tried the brakes again. Nothing. Again. He tried the gas. Nothing. Until the tires of the Dodge came to rest in a rut of snow at the side of the road.

He looked for a fallen, broken man, that quick dark thing, short as a dream, that had flashed in his face before the white swallowed him up. Nothing. It was a distant dream now. It was a dream. Right?

Sure.

A dream.

Spangler saw the way out. Just hit the gas and drive back the way he came. In seconds the storm would hide him. He began to make his excuses to the rental agent about the dents in the Dodge. A deer. A deer had jumped onto the road. He—

He saw the dark figure again. Stumbling toward him out of the white wind. It was no hit and run after all. His heart leapt with joy. He should get away now. He could. And now with a clear conscience.

The storm closed around the Durango.

Spangler didn't care. He was getting the hell out of Dodge.

He poured the coals to it. In the blind. Eyes out for a break in the blizzard.

It came as a dark shadow in the white. Out his door glass. The figure. An Indian. Holding on to his mirror. Running alongside.

Spangler gunned it.

The figure ran faster.

Spangler floored it. The engine roared, the tires sang.

But the Indian kept up, humping it, bobbing, gasping, running as fast as the car.

Spangler shrieked in agony. A dream. He was dreaming this.

The Indian, hair long and greasy, specked with snow and lashing his wolfish face, finally let go. He stood outside the door laughing.

The Dodge still roared, the tires sang yet.

But the Durango had not moved.

Spangler had sat in one spot the whole time, spinning his wheels on ice. While the man mocked him.

Stuck. The Indian's face had gone slack. The joke over, he had a look of murder in his eye.

Spangler gave up trying to get out of the snowbank. He started thinking again about apologizing for Custer at the Washita.

The dark figure walked up to the front of the truck and banged on the hood. That sound of metal against bone. A fist banging on the hood. A shout that he could not make out. The hand raised, fingers spread to ask man's ever-asked, ever-unanswered question: *What the fuck, over?*

Spangler didn't know what. He was glad enough that he had not hit the man—at least not enough to injure him. So there was no need to run, after all, really. Right? The figure walked around to the passenger door and jerked on the door handle. Locked. Spangler had the foresight to do that anyhow.

The figure began to pound on the window glass.

"Hey, knock it off." He didn't say it all that loud.

The Indian did. "Open this door before I bash—"

Spangler unlocked it. He could deal with the man, maybe, at least he should try. Because if the glass were gone from that window, he'd never be able to drive back to Great Falls in this cold.

The Indian got into the vehicle and sat. He smelled of liquor, fresh, sharp whiskey on his breath and sweet, stale alcohol oxidizing through his pores and clothing. The dusting of white snow on his face began to melt in the flow of the heater. A monster out of the mist, gasping for breath. Sure. Why not? All that fake running. It *was* funny.

"Pretty funny, running in place like that." *What the hell? Try to disarm the guy.*

It didn't take.

"You trying to kill me?" Again the one hand in the air holding up the sky with a fist. Spangler saw that there was only the one hand. Disarm indeed. The other hand had been taken off at the forearm. An open denim sleeve flapped like a pennant. For a second, he thought that he had taken off the man's hand. But no, that could not be. The guy was just a derelict. Probably passed out on a train track to sleep it off and found out a train had cut it off. Probably—

"You bastard." This from a derelict. Talking to a two-star.

"I'm sorry."

"For what?"

Custer. He almost said it. "I didn't mean to hit you. I didn't see you—"

"You didn't goddam hit me," the Indian said. "I hit you as you went by. With my fist." He held up his good hand clenched. "Called you a few names, too, you son of a bitch."

A mean derelict. But one who spoke with good diction for a drunk.

"I'm sorry." Spangler could not look at the man. That broken sleeve. That stump. That smell of stale alcohol. That he was stuck. That he would die here. That some-body would find his burnt corpse inside the stripped-out Dodge, tireless, left upon cinder blocks. Maybe in the spring. In the soot on the dash they'd find a note scratched, his last testament a nod to the *Fugitive,* Richard Kimball's mantra: *It was the one-armed man done this to me.*

"I need a drink."

"I'm sorry."

"Stop being sorry, goddammit. Why should you be sorry that I need a drink?"

"Sorry—I mean, sure, I need a drink, too. Is there a place we can get one?" Okay, okay, maybe he was going to get out of this after all. He dared to look at his man at last. He saw that he was young, but tired, his anger more alive than the man himself. A man, for the moment, in-credulous.

"I don't want to drink with you."

"I'll buy."

The Indian laughed, the short bark of a startled dog. "Damned right you will."

"Sorry—I mean, sure. If it's okay with you."

"You can buy me a drink."

"Really?"

"Not that way, not like we're buddies or something. Just give me some money. You damned near killed me. You should buy me a drink. A lot of drinks."

"Of course. I'm sorry—"

"You say that one more time, and I'm gonna break your goddamned face." He studied Spangler's scars, taking inventory of his face, and gave another bark.

"What?" Although he knew perfectly.

"Not that much to break, is there?"

Less than perfect diplomacy, which was to tell plain truths without giving offense. Still, the Indian just about pulled it off with the open, big, clean smile. This was a good-looking guy once.

Spangler was glad he'd not given him the red-eye over the tops of his sunglasses. The man was no longer comfortable with his smile. He was nearer the brink of his rage. Go from an open look to a closed fist.

Spangler fished for his money wad and clutched it between his legs to peel off a twenty without the guy seeing the whole roll of cash.

A smile of a different kind creased the bristled, pained face. Spangler was astonished at how good the teeth were. He was more astonished that he, the original phantom face of the opera, pitied some other soul for what he lacked in curb appeal.

The Indian snatched the bill from him. As soon as he had it in hand, his mood swung low. "Now you'd better get your ass out of town." As if he couldn't abide a man who gave in to his extortion so easily. "Some people around here aren't as gentle as me." At a simmer now. "Man like you? White and ugly? Well, I guess that's redundant, isn't it?"

Redundant? Forget the nasty edge to the attack. A derelict uses *redundant?*

"White guy could get hurt around here." The derelict shook his head. "Worse than you've already been hurt."

Was that a return note of pity there? Were they brothers in pity now? Spangler grew bold.

"How'm I gonna leave? I'm stuck." *Redundant? He says* redundant?

"No, you're not."

"What?"

"Stuck."

Spangler touched the gas pedal. The Dodge's front tires chattered and the rears spun in place. He lifted his eyes up his hairline. *See? Stuck.*

"I'll get you out in two minutes."

"I—don't know what to say."

"Say you'll pay me fifty bucks to get you out in two minutes."

Gladly. "Fifty bucks it is." Spangler smiled. He felt a rush of his old self returning. And why not? He was a career army officer, hell, a two-star general. Hell, he'd run in the first military teams in the war against al Qaeda. For chrissakes, his men killed Osama bin Laden—or maybe just his clone, but still—

What did this guy have on him? Nothing, that's what. The guy was a drunk, and all he wanted was a handout. Give him what he wants. Make him go away. The minute he was unstuck, he was out of here. This drunk no more than the shadow of a cloud passing through his memory. Nasty is as nasty does, to borrow from the philosophy of Forrest Gump.

"Two minutes," Spangler said. An inspiration struck him. "If you don't have this thing parked in the center of the road for me in two minutes, you have to give me back the twenty, besides."

The man barked at the challenge. He slapped the twenty down on the dashboard. Chrissakes, the guy was glad that he'd showed some backbone.

"Let's see it, General."

"What?" Spangler swallowed his tongue, then coughed it back up. "What did you say?"

"General Grant. Let's see your fifty." The man wiped his empty sleeve across his eager mouth, the denim greasy as a dish rag. "Or maybe you don't have the balls."

Spangler felt his smile stretch and whiten the scars radiating from his lips. "Make it a Franklin." He slapped down two fifty-dollar bills on the dash.

"A hundred bucks? To get you back on the road?"

"No, fifty bucks to get me back on the road—in two minutes. And another fifty if you can answer one question for me besides." He flapped a hand carelessly. A little reckless generosity with other people's money wasn't going to kill him. "I change my mind. The twenty is yours no matter what."

The drunken Indian seemed not so drunk anymore. He puffed up and slapped himself across the chest with his greasy flapping sleeve. "Easiest hundred bucks I ever made."

"How do you know? I haven't asked you the question."

"You can't ask the question I can't answer." The man piled out of the Dodge, slammed the door, and high-stepped through the snowbank around to Spangler's door. He pulled open the door and ushered Spangler out like a rough parking valet.

As Spangler stood stamping in the snow, his legs throbbing with his natural aches and unnatural cold of the day, the Indian slid behind the wheel. He gave the grin of a dog baring its teeth as he rode the seat back a full six inches.

"Cake."

Cake? "How can you be so sure this'll be easy?"

The Indian refreshed his canine grin and turned the steering wheel with a forefinger. Spangler saw the problem at once. He had been trying to drive out of the snowbank with the wheel still cramped to the left. The Indian put the Dodge into reverse and, barely touching the gas pedal, eased off the four ice patches that Spangler had created by spinning the tires in four-wheel drive. As he backed up, Spangler had to step aside so the open door could clear him.

"I'm starting my stopwatch," he called into the storm, the wind snatching his words away.

Funny, he didn't feel so cold now that he was not alone. Yes, he was with a crazy Indian, crazy and drunk besides, behind the wheel of his Dodge. But he was not alone with the blizzard anymore. True, he had bought the man, as he had bought hookers in the past and long-gone Grace, whatever her name was, his erstwhile office temp. But, bought and paid for, he had a friend for a time.

The Blackfeet man eased the Dodge forward, rolling past the frozen patches, past Spangler. The cold, dry snow squealed at the crush of the tires.

"You got to be gentle with the gas," the Indian said as he went by. "Let the tire claws catch a grip."

Spangler gave a lame smile. He clutched his North Face parka to him. All that layering he'd bought in Great Falls, and still he felt a chill, a new chill. He should have gone for the windshear layer. The salesgirl in the yellow Polo shirt tried to talk him into it. He argued he'd never need it because he didn't plan to do anything but walk from his car to a guy's house and back. What the hell was he thinking?

"Better start that watch," the man said.

Spangler didn't need to. He saw that he had already lost the fifty bucks. He would gladly lose the other fifty. If only the man would answer his question. If only he'd step out and turn the Dodge back to him.

He caught up to the Dodge, idling in the center of the street, connecting the words to his question. As he came near, the Indian closed the driver's door. Spangler's heart snapped. No, that was just the sound of the door locks. The window cracked open an inch. Then his heart did snap as it picked up a salsa beat, catchy but irregular. *No!*

"Looks like I win," said the voice from inside the Dodge. All Spangler could see was a twinkle of an eye, and the glitter of fine white teeth, even rows of candy-covered Chiclets gum.

Spangler felt a spike of hope. "How can you say you've won when you haven't answered my question?" The chill in his lungs went straight to his heart. He knew his answer before the door window slid shut, before the Dodge idled forward again, down the middle of the road or track or whatever it was that passed for a street in Heart Butte, Montana. He had known before he could ask. The grin his answer. Not the grin of a sly dog on that bastard's face. It was the grin of the wolf in the last instant before taking its prey.

Wolves? Dogs? Spangler looked around himself. *Hyenas?*

For one brief, insane moment, Spangler felt an urge to race after the Durango. Like one of those idiots in the movies was always doing. It was no smarter to call after the Dodge. But he did. "Come back," he said into the wind. He laughed, giddy at the pure nonsense of it.

The moment of irony did not long last. He swung to a dark side of himself. True, he was not a brave man, but leave him adrift in the city, and he could fend for himself. Here, though—

He turned in a circle, looking for dogs and hyenas. He thought he saw a blur of something between buildings but it might have been just a snowflake on a lash.

He felt so cold. No sound but the howl of wind and the pattering of ice crystals against the hood of the parka. No feel but a chill over all his body. The wind biting at his exposed skin. Another kind of chill swept inside the coat with all its Gore-Tex and high-tech insulation. It came from the core of him. He'd lost the ability to taste anything but his own bile. All he could see around him white and shades of gray. Shifting images of snow, clouds and curtains of snow. No true color but the one last glimpse of red, the Dodge's taillights winking out in the storm. The very picture of death. His own. Torn apart by hyenas. Or feral dogs. Hell, velociraptors for all he knew. *Wouldn't make much of a difference which, now would it?*

Cold. Alone. At the mercy of this frozen hell on earth.

He was going to die, sadly, lacking even a foul-weather friend.

It was all he could do to keep from crying. The only thing that stopped him was the idea that his eyes might freeze shut, the notion that he might not see the dogs coming for him.

Not many men alive could say they had been left alone with Saddam as Karim-Assad had. So great was the danger of assassination in Iraq, real or perceived, that seldom were fewer than three people in a room with Saddam. At that, never three people who did not compete with each other for their status, their future, their very lives. Certainly never men who might plot as one against him, in even the remotest scenario.

Karim-Assad knew all of this as he sat down to the table. To wait, only to wait. Before long, the shoulders stopped trembling, the multiple chins stopped quaking.

Saddam took out a hanky and wiped the tears from the creases in his neck. He dried his face and sniffed. He let out a long sigh.

"This is ridiculous," Saddam said, a broad, wet grin on his face. "Nobody should have to see the great Saddam blubbering like a child." He cast an evil eye at the guards in the hall. They decided to count the mosaic tiles at their feet.

"No," Karim-Assad said. "You are right to grieve for them, Father. What do you know of their safety?" *Is it possible they are dead? Could I be so blessed?*

But Saddam wasn't ready to discuss his sons; he wasn't through with himself yet. "For shame. Tears from the great Saddam."

"The great compassionate, caring Saddam. What father does not love his sons? What father would not shed tears for them? But they are not dead." *I fear it in my heart of hearts.*

"Do you think so, my son?"

Karim-Assad smiled. *Ah, a son again.*

Saddam needed a son. Others he ruled by fear. But a son. A man could rule a son with love. Or greed. Or, in the case of Uday, fear and the threat of withholding sex and drugs. But a real son like Qusay, a son that could succeed him in rule, love. Only with a son could a man like Saddam show intimacy. Now he feared that both were gone. Uday was no great matter. In fact, it might be a relief to Saddam as well as the rest of the citizens of Iraq if he were dead. But Qusay. He was the Hussein to come. If he did not return home—

"Until I know about Qusay, I need somebody to talk to."

Karim-Assad forced his own hands not to recoil from the clammy hands of Saddam. *Until I know about Qusay!* He kept his head from recoiling at the threat in Qusay coming back alive.

"I need Qusay."

"Of course you do, uncle."

"For now, I will confide in you, my son. Call me Father."

"Tell me why you are so distraught. What you know of their fate? Father."

Saddam smiled. "Of course." With that, Karim-Assad knew he had the man's trust. Saddam told him the story in full. A combined ground and air attack. That was the report from the division headquarters. A devastating bombing, backed up by a division of airborne soldiers. A surprise attack, treachery of the Son-of-Satan Bush, made worse by the treachery of the infantry company detailed to secure the headquarters. They had collaborated with the enemy. They had given up valuable intelligence to the Americans. They had turned their rifles on the camp and tried to kill all the senior staff. Luckily, most of the traitorous infantry company was killed. The rest taken prisoner.

"The reports are that many Americans were killed," Saddam said. "We will parade their bodies in the streets of Baghdad as proof of the invincibility of our armies."

"An excellent idea," Karim-Assad said. "That will teach them the cost of invading a sacred sovereign state."

A moment of silence. Saddam traded his grief for shock at Karim-Assad's words. As if his new son had spoken his very thoughts.

Karim-Assad wondered how many lies were told to save the lives of the generals at that meeting. He wondered, too, what this had to do with where the Hussein sons now were. What their fates were? But he must not seem too eager.

"What do the reports say about the numbers of the invaders killed, Father?"

"Dozens, perhaps hundreds."

"Excellent. It will be a long parade."

Saddam gave a gas-pain smile. He did not care about a

parade of bodies. "Uday and Qusay were in that camp," Saddam said.

Karim-Assad covered the leap in his pulse by patting Saddam's forearm in a quick rhythm to match the sudden spike in his own heart rate.

"They fought bravely," Karim-Assad said. "No doubt."

Saddam blinked, even he doubting that scenario.

"They escaped then, surely." *Say it is not true, that I am wrong, that you know of their demise. Their dead bodies are aboard helicopters this very moment, a day of mourning, a public funeral to go along with the parade of American corpses. A parade of two corpses in particular. Better yet, say they were captured. By the Americans. No, the Israelis . . . no, the Kurds! Say they have fallen into the hands of the delightfully wicked Kurd, Adnil Mustafa-something-something-Kirkuk, whose name is a kilometer long and the synonym for terror in the Iraqi mind. Tell me that Adnil has them. Tell me—*

"They are gone from the camp. We have heard no word from them. Not even a response from the GPS receiver in their car. The French satellites . . . nothing. Not a word."

Saddam's eyes welled with tears again. Karim-Assad fought back his own impatience at that. Did not want to seem cold. Did not want to betray his own high emotions.

"Then there is hope, Father. They might have escaped. They might be hiding out. Perhaps they turned off their GPS receiver."

"Nobody can turn it off."

"Then they are hidden inside the cave. Or perhaps a deep ravine. There are a thousand places, Father. A million. They will come back." *If God could be so cruel.*

"Do you think it so?" The sagging face braced itself. The sagging eyes pulled the swollen, blued lower lids tight. "That they will come back?"

"With all my heart."

"Roger," Solis said. "Take out a frigging flatbed truck."

Poole heard the pitch of Solis's voice. Still balking. Solis saying: What Delta man couldn't take out a truck and driver? And, oh, by the way, *Why the hell would we want to?*

Poole got a grip on his anger. Took the edge out of his own voice. No time to go Hillary on the team now. Keep a cool head. Make it go down like iced tea.

"Don't take out the truck."

"Roger." A bit cocky, thinking he got his way.

"Snag the truck. Without a fight," he said. "Capture the truck." *I know you can do this.* "Keep the driver and crew alive." *It means a lot to the mission.* "No shooting, no boomers." *It's almost impossible for ordinary soldiers, but you guys are Delta troopers, man—* "Can you do it?" *Or not?*

Solis slow to answer. Unmoved by the tact. "Just to clarify, Cap. It's a truck. A semi-tractor, a flatbed trailer with a tank on the ass-end."

A mile away, a white light stabbed into the darkness, sky to ground.

"Screw the truck." No more room for debate.

"Roger." Cocky again.

"Hold what you got."

A second light funneled out of the night. Searchlights. Two choppers. Then a third. Word out. Raqis saying to hell with blackout drive. The Raqs not looking for little Satans anymore. Now looking for daddy's boys.

Poole gave the daddy-boys a glance. They'd perked up. The tape on their mouths crinkled. Grinning again.

Poole cupped a hand over his mike. "No rescue for you," he said. "If we can't sneak you out of Iraq, we'll just take your heads as proof we captured you. Maybe sell you to the Kurds."

The wrinkles in the tape flattened out.

He left Uday and Qusay in the care of Foucault and Artemis.

He marched through the line of Solis and the security detail.

Thinking. That cruelty shit. Why did he go there with those two?

Aw, well. Screw it.

He waded into the ankle-deep dust, fine as talc, and stepped up onto the running board of the Raqi tractor that labored in slow fits and starts. The driver, occupied with all the boomer-caused potholes, didn't even see him.

Until Poole yanked open the door of the truck and jammed a pistol into the side of his face.

"Stop this truck or I'll kill you right here."

Loud enough for the driver and his buddy on the passenger seat.

Loud enough for his men.

Well more than loud enough for Solis, damn him.

The driver stood on his brakes. Poole grabbed onto the steering wheel to save himself from getting bucked off.

Poole switched to English. "Foucault in front with me. Stow the brothers in the tank or under it. Everybody else outta sight. Hide your asses from the choppers. If I see so much as a goddam boot sticking out, man, I'm going to put a bullet in it, so help me, Jesus."

Nobody mistook him this time. No subtext here. No subtlety. No nuance. No tact.

Poole talking pissed. Simple as that.

The Delta men did what every unit does when they don't want to get in the line of fire of a pissed-off officer. They flew into action, all assholes and elbows, to do what he said.

Saddam gave a full body shudder, as if struck by a sudden chill. He radiated his chill to Karim-Assad like some black sun quite able to absorb the heat of every body in its sphere. As fast as that, Saddam's grief died—to Karim-Assad it seemed his tears dried as if they'd dropped on the hot tarmac in Baghdad instead of the cheeks of a tired, aging man swollen by the lack of sleep and exercise, and by the surfeit of alcohol, cigars, and rich food. In aspect, quite harmless.

Saddam's slumped shoulders went square, and his back snapped to attention. He looked at Karim-Assad through dark, glittering slits, his face that of an angry, eager, practiced killer. Quite able to do sudden harm.

Karim-Assad was cautious. "I do worry about one aspect of the report from the front."

One eyelid opened as if pulled up by a string in its center, revealing one black pupil through an angry triangle.

"I worry about the security," Karim-Assad said.

"My very concern." Saddam threw up his hands, fingers splayed. "Where was our security?" He crashed both hands on the table as fists that rattled the crystal and goldware. The guards in the hall shrank, their backs against the wall. "Faulty security around the headquarters. Where were the local area defense missiles? The regional antiaircraft radar? Security patrols?" He held up his right fist. "None of these detected an airborne attack?" His forefinger shot out from the fist. "Swarms of the infantry dropping from the sky?" A second finger shot out. "Light infantry against a tank division?" A third finger joined the first. He closed his fingers again into the fist.

Karim-Assad waited for him to slam the table again. But Saddam did not. Instead, he went into a brief, deep meditation, one finger tapping the tabletop, an exotic green-grained wood from Africa.

Karim-Assad had seen this look before. He knew what it meant. This was the Saddam who could rule a country. Not by fierce emotion and bombast, although he did at times resort to that when the cameras were rolling. Rather, by clever thinking and decisive action, quick and deadly.

"Lies." Saddam looked at Karim-Assad and nodded slowly. "Of course. The first reports are always lies." He sighed. "Very sad. Men always feel the need to lie. They lie because they are afraid to die, and now, because they lie, they die." He shook his head as something caught his eye.

Saddam's eyes followed the point of a finger toward the entrance to the dining room thirty feet away. There stood an officer. Karim-Assad did not know the man's name or position on the staff. He did know he was a second-tier officer who sometimes carried a note to one of the peacocks who always found a way to get to Saddam's banquet table. Karim-Assad sometimes amused himself by theorizing that the peacocks took turns sending notes to themselves at the table, notes they had written themselves. So they could look important as they excused themselves to attend to some matter of state.

The peacocks. The peacocks were afraid of Saddam and especially his sons, who could wield the power of life and death even at a meal. The peacocks. The peacocks were afraid to stay away from the table, too. For fear that to be absent might mean to slip down the hole to anonymity. At times of greatest danger, though, the peacocks sent this messenger.

"He brings bad news," Saddam said. "They always send him when they have bad news." He shook his head. "So sad. They have deluded themselves into thinking that if I do not kill this messenger, I will not kill them." He laughed. "As if I did not have other options. I could spare him and kill them. Or kill him and them as well."

The last had the effect on Karim-Assad's spine of soldiers marching over broken glass, screeching, squealing, crackling, broken glass and bones. Karim-Assad sighed to cover his own shudder. Saddam had as much as said it. *Somebody must die.*

The officer stood at attention, waiting to be summoned, as if he could wait for the rest of his life, no matter how long his life.

Saddam pointedly ignored him.

"A friendly wager, my son." Saddam uncovered a plate of elaborately decorated chocolates. "He who comes closest to predicting the content of this report wins these French chocolates."

Karim-Assad smiled. A little more than an hour ago, he had eaten three of those very candies, at random. "I will take your wager, Father."

"Several of the general officers at the meeting were killed," Saddam predicted. "He bears this news on behalf of the high staff, even now very busy directing the battle against the invading Americans. I am not to feel sad for the dead, because it appears that they are to blame for the lapse in security and the loss of my sons." His eyes filled up, but the wicked smile never left his face. He gestured to Karim-Assad, hooking the four fingers of one hand at him. "And your prediction?"

Karim-Assad spoke with no hint of irony. "Such good fortune that only the incompetent officers and soldiers died in the attack of the Americans and none of the competent ones. Such bad fortune that no bodies of American invaders were found. Or very few."

"Aha! You suspect commandos, not regular forces." Saddam said this over one raised finger. "As do I."

Karim-Assad answered over a raised finger of his own. "I caution you, Father. Events will prove you right, but only eventually. This report will not admit to such a catastrophe wrought by only a handful of men. The division is out in force looking for entire brigades of invaders."

Saddam nodded, slowly at first, then vigorously. "I believe it. You are right. How do you understand so much?"

Karim-Assad cocked his head. *Isn't it obvious?* He spoke, an effort to keep the flattery out of his flattering words. "I have observed you for years now. Every day, two or three times a day, I watch and listen at your table. Unless I were an idiot, how could I not learn from you?"

Saddam's eyes narrowed. "You are anything but an idiot." He spoke the words almost to himself.

Again, Karim-Assad felt that chill that he'd seen in others.

"Tell me, my son. Were my sons betrayed to the Americans, do you think?"

Karim-Assad learned something new in that very moment. To be the object of that chilling gaze was tenfold the effect of watching another man's blood curdle. *Only honesty now. No flattery. No lies, no shades of truth, no jokes.*

"I doubt it," he said. "Uday and Qusay took every precaution against betrayal. Your system is not subject to failure. The invaders, I imagine, set out to attack the headquarters only. The loss—the temporary loss—of my brothers was only an unlucky coincidence."

"Bad luck, indeed." Saddam chewed his bottom lip and used the side of a forefinger to stroke his mustache. "But why strike a well-armed headquarters at all? Why not a bridge? A dam? A power plant? Why not send bombs? Or one of those damned flying missiles?" He waved his arms at the domed, thirty-foot ceiling. "Why not here? Or any other of my abodes? Why not try to kill me?"

"I am no military expert."

"Still, why not try to strike me? I *am* Iraq. I am the Islamic struggle against the West. Why not me?"

"Father? How could they? They could never find you. They would strike at empty air—"

The fists slammed the table again. "Exactly. You are more right than you know. Here now, let us get the report." He beckoned the waiting officer. "Let us see who wins the chocolates."

Spangler stood swaying before the wind. But not for long. He wouldn't get the chance to freeze to death if he stood like a china closet in the street so a car could run him down the way he had run down that drunken Indian. Well, almost. He could feel his feet wicking up the cold from the ground. Six hundred dollars and change he had spent on winter clothing. Of all things, he had skimped on boots and socks. Street shoes. He had walked into an arctic Montana winter in street shoes. He might not freeze in an hour. But if he didn't move soon, his feet would turn into a couple of cods right from the freezer. He'd lose his legs at the knees.

He stilt-walked to the side of the street. If it was a street. *There!* The first sign of life. A liquor store with the lights on behind barred windows. The front door was papered over with hand-lettered signs. *No checks! Not even checks from your mother!! Cash only. Cashier has less then $50.00 on hand, the rest is in a cash drop. No credit! No checks, No credit, No BS!!!*

"Okay, okay," Spangler said. He pushed on the door. Locked.

A fresh sign fluttered on the outside of the glass: *Counter service closed due to storm. Drive-up/Walk-up Window Service ONLY!!*

All right, all right. No need to shout about it. Can't a guy step in to make a phone call? Wait for AAA? Maybe a cab? Spangler stamped his feet. They did have taxis around here, didn't they? Call the cops and then a taxi. A one-armed guy stole his car.

Jeez, Mack? A one-armed guy stole your ride?

Yeah. What? One-armed guy gets a pass on theft?

So, you leave it unlocked?

Sorta.

Sorta? Keys?
In the ignition.
Guy break in?
Not exactly.
Jack it? Pull you out at the point of a gun?
Not exactly.
Well? What exactly?
I let him drive and he drove off.
You let him drive?
Yeah. And he just kept going.
How is that a stolen car?
Ummm, let's just say that unwisdom prevailed.
Dumb shit.

Spangler shook his head. To get that scenario out of his head. He walked to the side of the building and looked down a narrow gap between shacks. Nothing but lumps under snow. A slatted pallet of snowboards, a crushed box draped in white, tires stacked as tall as a man and fringed in fluffed arcs, an old refrigerator lying on its back, the white of the porcelain not as white as the weather.

Movement!

Spangler pressed himself to the side of the liquor store.

The door to the refrigerator opened like the lid of a coffin. An eruption of snow. A man sat up and shook the dry crystals off. He looked around. Surprised. Coming out of a dream where he slept inside a Kitchen Aid in a blizzard only to awaken and find himself in both. As his reality dawned on him, the man took a deep, relieved breath, smoothed the knife edge off a snowdrift that had crept up to the lip of his bedroom, and patted smooth a shred of canvas as if it were nothing less than a rumpled goose-down comforter. He saw Spangler, and a snarl curled over his mouth, showing off broken, yellow snags for teeth.

Spangler couldn't hear through his parka and the wind

battering his head, but he could read lips well enough. *Get away from here, you bastard. This here is mine. Get your own goddamned bed.*

Spangler stepped back to let the man know. *Your bed, buddy. All yours.* The man lay back down, closing the lid to a slit. Spangler saw a pair of angry eyes staring at him, eyes wary of a sneak attack from the white man who would evict him from his winter camp.

Spangler felt a hole in his heart, a strange feeling he decided to call empathy. A feeling he did not know, did not want to know. He could see the guy's point, though. With the wild hyenas and raptors running around Heart Butte? Maybe sleeping in a fridge was a good idea.

He went to the other side of the store to get away from the vision of an abject side of humanity that he'd never expected to see. He was a general, for chrissakes. Generals didn't—

Humanity.

Thank goodness. A clutch of men leaned into the shelter of the building, shifting their weight from foot to front, doing a slow tap dance in the snow. They passed a brown-bag bottle among them. Three men, no, four. And behind them a window. Like any ordinary burger joint drive-up window. Except this one dispensed liquor, wine, and beer.

He walked toward the men. He realized he was pulling the strings on his parka. Not against the cold, but to hide his face. So anybody who looked at him could only see his nose and sunglasses and parka. *No need to cause a riot here, just ask a couple questions, find the local constable, call a taxi, and lacking that get a room for the night, calling the AAA cavalry—*

All four men stared at him, no longer tap dancing.

Okay, so he was a vision to them, too. Spangler rehearsed his opening line in his head. He decided he should be firm, assertive, anything but let them smell fear. Isn't that what the *Reader's Digest* would tell you as the first of twenty-one tips on how not to be a victim of violent crime?

"I'm looking for a guy," he said. About the right mix of bold and clear.

"Nice coat," said the tallest of the four, a lean and hungry look etched in his face. "What's that there? No face?" He leaned closer to Spangler, towering over him to read the logo on his parka. His eyes were black dots swimming in yellow the shade of Post-it notes.

"No face?"

Even in the swirl of wind, Spangler could smell the rancid breath. It made his stomach lurch. He smoothed out the wrinkle in the coat's logo.

"North Face," Spangler said.

"No face."

Okay, now what, Reader's Digest? The twenty-one tips didn't have a trick for this gig. *You bastards in Pleasantville don't have a clue—*

"Cat got your fucking tongue, No-Man?"

"Frosty the fucking No-Man, bro."

Spangler didn't catch who was talking to him exactly. He said the only thing that came to mind, as firm and assertive as he could and screw the *RD* script:

"North Face," he said. "The jacket is a North Face brand. It says North Face."

"Who gives a shit?" one said.

"Not the parka." The other spewed the words at him, his breath laced with cigarette smoke, whiskey, and some powerful, unknowable herb dug from a hot, rich mulch pile, wild onions, and dog shit. As close to vomit as breath could be short of chunks. On the word *parka,* he peppered Spangler with spit that froze in the air between them and hit him like stinking sleet.

"I'm talking about you, white man. You got no face."

"Robert Night Runner," Spangler blurted. "I'm a friend of Night Runner's. We were in the service together."

The four men pressed in on him, and all at once. Spangler's world became a jumbled sea of sensation. Dark skin, deep brown like the light grain in walnut, not red at all as Fenimore Cooper wrote. No whites in these eyes, either, only black obsidian and that 3M yellow.

"I like your gotdamn coat," said one, maybe the tall one. Spangler wasn't sure, they were so many and so close. "Gimme that fuckin' coat, white man."

"Buy me a drink."

"Buy us all a drink."

"Loan me some money. I need twenty bucks to get my car out of hock."

Spangler fought off a dizzy spell. He tried to think of descriptions. *Yes, descriptions.* He would need to be able to tell the constable the descriptions of his assailants. Because, yes—goddamned *Reader's Digest* or no—he was going to be assailed.

The staff officer gave a terse report. He did not quake or quail. He was not afraid. Karim-Assad liked him for that. Rarely did he see such courage among the higher staff who came to fawn and bow and scrape and flatter. Although, he had to admit, it did come so easy, to flatter. He had done it this very night.

Saddam listened, staring down the table as if he were hearing a radio instead of a man. When he was done, Saddam said, "Bring a phone." He dismissed the staff officer with a wave of his left hand.

While the staff officer brought up a phone, unreeling a cord behind him, Saddam spoke in a low voice, "One dead American, his body blown up by charges laid under the corpse. Killing half a dozen of our own." He laughed. "It gives new meaning to the term *suicide bomber,* doesn't it?"

Karim-Assad joined him in his sardonic laugh. *There!*

There it was, the flattery again. So easy when you were so close.

"A draw," Saddam said. "The wager is a draw." He used the edge of his hand to divide the candies, giving well more than half to himself.

Eager not to notice, Karim-Assad put one of the chocolates into his mouth. Then he spat it out into his hand at once.

Saddam looked almost human again, and alarmed.

"Oh no, Father, no poison." Karim-Assad put the candy back into his mouth and talked around it. "There is nothing—wrong with the chocolate. It is delicious. I was a glutton—lacking in manners to eat one—before you." *And again, the flattery.* "If you will forgive—me—my only defense is to say—that it has been my job for years to taste—the food on your—behalf."

Saddam laughed. He pushed his share of the candy away. "No matter. I have no taste for it."

No taste. But he kept the candies in his pile. Far away from Karim-Assad. He did not want what he had won. Yet he did not want anyone else to have it, either.

An item for the notebook of Karim-Assad's mind. A tidbit about the perfect tyrant. Never did he give in, even on a tiny point. A rule of the winner at every game, big and small.

"So much to learn from you, Father." This Karim-Assad said with no trace of flattery.

"Gimme some money, No-Face."

"He's a No-Man, bro, a No-Face-Frosty-the-No-Man."

The four found this hysterical.

In the middle of a pure-ass blizzard roaring down from the most remote region of Canada, Spangler could not catch a clean breath of air. Nothing but the used, bad breath of four thugs. He tried to gather his wits. It was the shortest one who demanded money. A short Indian in denim. On second look, they all wore denim, blue jeans and jean jackets, just like the one-armed man. He was going to have to work harder to get the descriptions down.

"Am I being mugged?" he said.

"Mugged? White man wants to know if he's being mugged."

"Not mugged, North Face."

No-face. Spangler almost corrected him.

"We don't mug people in Montana, white man. Not on the rez."

"Okay, well, that's a good thing," Spangler said. "You had me worried there for a—"

"On the rez, we rob people." Another occasion for hysterical laughter, laughter in the voices, laughter in the faces. No laughter in the eyes, though. The 3M eyes deadly serious.

"Rob 'em and feed 'em to the dogs."

Dogs, then, not hyenas or raptors. Okay, so that's cleared up. No comfort in knowing it, but . . . Think, Roscoe, think. The tall guy. He was sure the tall guy said they were going to rob him. *A tall guy with acne scars, a crooked nose, and pigtails. No, not pigtails. Braids. Call them pigtails, you just piss off the cops, too. Probably Indians like these.* Be just his luck.

"You gonna give me some money or not? Or maybe you leave this place with no face."

"Yeah, no face, No-Face." They found this, too, a good joke and laughed the air full of stink again.

"You're robbing me?" Spangler said. "A friend of Night Runner's? You'd rob—"

"Who said anything about robbing you? You say anything about robbing the white man, Crooked Finger?"

Crooked Finger. A name. Now he had a name to give the constable or cops or whatever. If they left him alive.

"Somebody ought to call a cop," the short, fat, round one said.

Spangler giggled at his own thought. The man had turned his own idea into words. "Well, there's no need for *that*. I'm sure we can sort this out—"

"I'm a tribal cop," said the one called Crooked Finger. He leaned into Spangler's face and breath-gassed him big-time. "Call me, whydoncha?"

Saddam picked up the phone. He barked a command into it, and Karim-Assad could hear tension in the voice on the other end. The voice knew who he was speaking to.

Saddam put a hand over the mouthpiece. "It is a marvel of the Soviet technology—stolen from the Americans and the Japanese, of course. The wonder of modern science that I can be in radio command of any unit in my vast army." He shook his head and spoke Karim-Assad's very thought: "Until the American bombs start falling."

He picked up the phone line in his left hand and snapped his wrist, sending a coil shooting across the banquet room. "Likewise, it is a marvel that something as simple as this telephone line taking my voice across the room as easily as that is all I need to defeat the electronic ears of the American Satan." He leaned across the table and whispered to Karim-Assad, "They listen to me, you know. From satellites." He pointed up. As if the American's ears could hear him in this very hall.

Karim-Assad found himself mirroring his uncle's behavior. He whispered back, "I thought so."

"But this line? It's fiber optics from our Russian friends. Do you know this fiber optics?"

"No, Father."

"It does not leak words like copper wires. And to be even safer from those who would try to intercept my words, it travels underground. It splits into other lines in the tunnels beneath the city. Each time I speak an operator diverts my words down a separate line." He used his arms and hands to demonstrate, shooting lines of communication out from his body to every corner of the banquet hall.

"It cannot be jammed." He shook his head at Karim-Assad. "I'm sorry, do you know this term? *Jammed?*"

Karim-Assad shook his head.

"It means to interrupt radio communications. I have asked the French to do this for me, even before the American ultimatum expires. I wish to make it difficult for them to talk to each other."

"Jam the Americans? You can do this?"

Saddam smiled. "I can do this. Even to the satellites." He pointed to his phone. "And with this, my voice comes from as many as a dozen towers, as much as forty kilometers distant from each other." He laughed. "The American spies must think I can be in a dozen places at once. Or that I travel as fast as a thought from one transmitter to another."

Karim-Assad lowered his head and looked up from beneath his brows at his uncle. *You don't expect me to believe that?*

"Of course I speak in jest. Now if you will excuse me, I must call a meeting of those responsible for the disaster tonight." He gave Karim-Assad the back of his hand, the same dismissive flip that had sent the others scurrying, from kitchen help to messenger to general officer.

And Karim-Assad knew full well he had much work to do to cement his new spot as a son of Saddam.

Poole seated himself beside the trembling driver and made room for Foucault by putting the assistant out with the rest of the team. His top NCO carried bundles of papers and maps he'd tried to cram into an attaché case from the SUV.

Poole still pissed, turned off his radio. He sighed at the

sudden silence in his head. He glanced over his shoulder at the load on the flatbed. All his men were hidden. He told the driver to drive and turned to Foucault. He felt the flush of shame for ragging on his men, for showing up Solis in front of the troops. It showed.

"All due respect to the L-T," Foucault said. "Screw 'im. Next time, he'll take the truck. First time you tell him."

Poole laughed. "What you got?" He indicated Foucault's intel booty.

"Lots," Foucault said.

"Such as—?"

The Iraqi driver drowned him out trying to cram his truck into gear.

"I've heard quieter gravel crushers," Foucault said.

Poole noticed the Iraqi's eyes, full of tears. He stared at the road, although the truck had not moved an inch. The man bounced in his seat, working his feet, trying to cram the shifting lever into gear.

"Guy's like a kid in the driveway playing in the old man's truck," Poole said. "Fake-driving."

"Scared to death," Foucault said.

Poole could see it. It was a kind of a buck fever, the man zoned out, going through motions literally out of sync, getting nowhere. He had seen soldiers in combat empty an entire magazine of an M-16 without firing a shot. For them, the battle had started with the safety on. When the gun didn't fire, they ejected one round from the magazine, pulled the trigger, found no result, ejected another round, until the gun was empty. Then kept ejecting rounds. Until somebody slapped them upside the head.

Hitting the driver didn't seem the right thing to do just now. He put a hand on top of his and pulled back to stop him from grinding away on the transmission.

"Relax," he told the driver in his own tongue. "You know how to drive this truck, isn't that right?"

The driver sobbed.

"Take your time. You're a good driver. One thing at a time."

The driver took a deep, ragged breath.

"Now we are getting somewhere," Poole said. "You can do this. Low gear. First put it into low gear." Poole released his grip on the driver's shifting hand.

"I don't think—" Foucault.

The sound was high-pitched and loud, drowning out Foucault. Like turning the ignition key while the engine is already running.

Poole yanked the driver's hand back to the neutral position, his nerves on edge. He needed to be moving. A stalled truck in the roadway was an invitation to trouble for a search party or combat patrol.

The driver sobbed. "Don't kill me."

"Got a nervous wreck on our hands," Poole said in English. "You know how to drive one of these things?"

"Hell, Captain, you know I can drive practically anything on wheels, half the boats in the navy, and most every damned helicopter made, if I have to. But you don't think it's a good idea for me to get behind the wheel, do you?" Surely. Delta men were cross-trained to drive, fly, and sail most any craft, James Bond–style, but— "What if we get stopped at a roadblock?" Foucault looked at Poole's black cheek. Right.

"Right." He patted the driver's shoulder. "Relax," he said in the man's language. Then, in English to Foucault, "Help me out here."

Foucault had the same easy manner in the Iraqi's language as he did in his own, laid-back, gentle, encouraging. The quality that made him a superb interrogator.

"Of course you know," he said to the driver. "The first thing is not to put it into gear." He gave Poole a nudge: *No offense, Captain.*

"But he said—"

"Forget what he said. Put the clutch pedal down first.

He's a good officer but not a good truck driver." Another nudge to Poole's elbow.

The driver wiped a dusty sleeve across his face, smearing mud. He looked from Poole to Foucault, waiting for the officer to take out a pistol and execute the NCO right on the spot.

Foucault nudged Poole again.

"What? Oh." In the driver's language: "He's right. I'm not a good driver."

"But *you*—you are a good driver," Foucault said to the Iraqi. "Now, why don't you drive it? Drive the way you always drive. Pretend that we're not here."

Both Poole and the Iraqi driver laughed at once. Ridiculous. It took the tension out of the air.

After jabbing at the transmission a few times, the truck slipped into gear with a snap and a jerk. The diesel engine roared, the turbocharger screaming like a jet engine on takeoff. As the driver let out the truck's clutch, the truck leaped forward, jerked to a stop, bounded forward again, bounced, labored, rattled, and bucked. A smell of burning wool filled the cab.

"Drive the way you always drive," Poole said through the wide grin on his face.

"I am driving the way I always drive," the Iraqi said.

Poole patted him on the shoulder. "You're doing a fine job, too."

The driver mashed the accelerator to the floor.

"I can't wait until he shifts gears," Foucault said in English.

The tach needle went to red-line-plus rpm.

"If he ever does."

After the driver settled into a cruise, Foucault said, "I've been in plane crashes that weren't this bad."

"Now, what do you have?" Poole said, picking up the conversation where it was before they had to retrain the driver.

"Maps, plans, orders. Of course I only had time to skim it. But I think we have picked off the game plan for the Republican Guard. Defensive positions, counterattack plans, demolition targets—bridges, dams, mosques, shrines—shit with strategic value and shit with propaganda impact."

Poole whistled. "Whoa. Good shit."

"Every time they claim we bombed a shrine we can release a document that shows they blew it themselves."

"Perfect."

Foucault shook his head.

"What?"

"There's a bit of bad news, too."

"Copping the battle plans for the Republican Guard is bad news?"

"No, that's good."

"What, then?"

"In the car. The dead guys."

"What about them?"

"The driver, the guy in the front, the two guys in the back—I mean, besides Mutt and Jeff back there—the four dead guys?"

"What about 'em? A driver and three Mukhabarat agents? So what?"

"The guys in back? They weren't secret police. One was a Frenchie, the other's a Rooskie."

Shit. Poole heard himself try to explain it to a court-martial: *They were dead. I swear, they were already dead.*

What about the double tap in each man's head?

Okay, now. That. I admit it, that looks a little bad. See, they weren't all the way dead, so we had to shoot each of them twice in the head to be sure they could not get up and compromise the mission.

But all he said was the hiss-crack from his own lips and teeth, "Shit."

Of long habit of being flicked off like a bit of nose glue, Karim-Assad felt the effect of that backward flip of Saddam's hand. He sprang to his feet, sending his chair skittering backward across the hardwood floor of the dining room. He bowed once, not as deep as he used to. He crabbed toward the door. Like any other menial, he did not turn his back on Saddam.

Indeed, even the high staff scuttled out of Saddam's presence in this very way. Karim-Assad often joked—to himself—that a man close to the seat of power never showed his back for a different reason. Namely, that he did not want a dagger sheathed in it.

Karim-Assad now felt strange. As a servant, he was always relieved to be sent away. Now he was one of them, a competitor for the attentions of Saddam. In a trice he found it risky to be away from the man's presence. One brief moment in the dark sunshine of Saddam? That's all there was? Now he was slinking back to his cubbyhole? To return to a life as a food taster? Living out of a cheap textile bag? On the move again tonight in the back of a truck without windows? So nobody could report to anyone where Saddam would take his next meal?

"My son!"

Karim-Assad came to attention and turned full-face to . . . what? Uncle? Father? Dictator?

Saddam bellowed for his staff officers. They stepped out of the hallway, a pack of lapdogs waiting for his beck.

Saddam pointed at Karim-Assad.

Karim-Assad felt his blood curdle. More than ever he felt like one of them. Worried that he had aroused the sudden, arbitrary anger of Saddam. Afraid that he was the next man in Iraq to die at the dictator's hand. His mind raced. How had he offended? *The flattery? The lack of flattery? His excess of knowledge? The chocolates? For heaven's sake, not the chocolates clutched to mush and melting away in his hand? Surely.*

Spangler's heart went dead for two beats. His mind let loose of details for the police report. One of the muggers was badged? He was dead.

"Gotdamn Night Runner," said the one called Little Brother. "You're a friend of his then?"

Okay. So. The guy didn't like Night Runner. "No, not a friend so much. I'm just saying."

"Saying what?"

"I knew him. In the service. I was just passing through here and—"

All four broke into guffaws. Spangler had no idea what joke he'd made.

Crooked Finger said, "Nobody passes through Heart Butte, bro." He snapped a frozen drip off the tip of his nose with the back of one sleeve. "It's not on the way to anyplace."

Guy had a point.

"Nobody white." Said the third Indian, his first words. "Nobody white gets through. This is like the Greasy Grass to a white man."

Greasy grass? Spangler didn't get it. *Was that like a case of diarrhea?*

"Little Bighorn."

"Custer, bro."

Custer. Spangler felt his eyes well up with tears. Had to be the cold. Surely he would not cry. Custer? Maybe he could apologize for Custer's sins. Still. He did not dare.

The fourth Indian caught his eye. This one did all his talking in sign, slitted eyes, the sign of anger; lifted lip, the sign of scorn; clenched fist, the sign of rage barely held in check. Spangler needed a breath, a heartbeat, anything to keep from swooning. If he went down now—

"So you were in the marines?" Crooked Finger.

"No, army—" And Spangler felt his heart seize again.

That finger came up in his face. "Night Runner was a marine." The tall man's finger. It was, indeed, crooked, bent at the second joint and withered at the tip.

The guy saw him looking. "Snake bite," he said. "T'sow I got my name, bro."

"Right. Crooked Finger."

"Night Runner was a marine." Back on topic.

"Of course. I know that."

"Then why did you say army, Bro?"

"I just . . . blurted."

"He blurted," said Little Brother. "I thought I smelt something." It amused them. "You shit your pants, too?" It killed them.

"No, I was going to say—"

They stopped laughing, letting him have his say. But Spangler couldn't find the words to begin to try to explain. A joint op against al Qaeda? The army details a marine into a Delta Force hunter-killer unit. To track down Osama bin Laden? *Where to begin?*

If only he could get a fresh breath of air, some room in his lungs for oxygen. That might help him think better. He felt he might pass out from secondhand liquor breath. He—he realized they were waiting for him still. He had to say something. He should start with the classified material. That should impress them. And anyhow, he didn't care—

"White man who served with Night Runner? Seems like he ought to know the right gotdamn service. Don't you think, white man?"

"I can explain—"

"Blackfeet people, some of us, we don't like to go into

the army. Maybe marines but not army. Some of us don't forget what the army done to our people in the olden days."

And to Spangler, every bloody scenario that he had dreamed of on the drive to Heart Butte was about to come true. Here he was, on the plains of Montana, surrounded. A flash of déjà vu. Of another brevet major general. So this was how Custer felt back on June 25, 1876, the day he died. *Well, screw him.*

"Screw who, bro?"

He'd said it aloud? "Custer."

Hysteria again.

Spangler was near panic. Custer. The Sioux and Cheyenne did not scalp Custer. Spangler was about to lose his hair—he just *knew* it. These men did not want to talk. They were dying to hurt him. Hurt him and take his money. Scalp him. Feed him to the dogs.

The money he did not care about. It wasn't his anyhow. Lady Redcoat's cash to use and lose as he saw fit, and he'd already budgeted a quarter-mill for bribes and salaries and goodies like fake passports. It was the hurting part that bothered him. He had a low threshold for pain anyhow. Because of his scars and diseases, which always throbbed to the near side of agony, it didn't take long for him to reach and pass over that threshold. He hated it now that his life was nailed to the cross of thought. While most soldiers, especially the good ones, the ones in Delta, were nailed to the cross of action. If ever there was a time for him to switch crosses, it was now. Still . . .

These men wanted to hurt him. If he threw a punch, he might land one blow. One lousy blow. He didn't expect it to have much effect, at least on them, except to piss them off. Then they would hurt him all the more. *Dammit! He was not a hitter. No, he was just a sheep in fleece clothing. Forget hitting.*

So he did the best thing he could. It worked before. It might get them to back off, might give him a breath. He'd run. He might not get far. But it was the best thing that he could come up with in his oxygen-deprived state.

Slowly, so as not to alarm them, he raised his hands. "I just want to get my wallet."

"Yeah, get your wallet."

"Show you my ID card."

"Hell with that. Show us the money, bro."

"Yeah, show me the money."

"Hey, I saw that movie." Little Brother laughed.

"We're not really robbing you," Crooked Finger said.

"You're not?"

"No, bro."

"Hell, no."

"It's a loan, bro. You loaning us some cash is all."

"How much?"

"Twenty bucks."

"Twenty?" *No problem.*

"Screw that. Fifty."

"Hunnerd."

"Okay." *A hundred bucks?* He was going to get out of this for a lousy hundred bucks?

"Apiece." Finally, the fourth Indian had a word to say, his still-clenched fists the exclamation points.

"Okay." *A lousy four hundred bucks?*

"O-kay," three at once.

"A hunnerd bucks."

"Apiece," the man of only one word said.

New problem. Spangler had the cash. In that wad. But, if he pulled that cylinder of green right now, they'd take it all. Not that he cared *so-o-o* damned much. He could afford it. But once they became felons to the tune of five grand or so, they might decide they had to kill him to keep him quiet. Back to the scalp-and-dogs scenario. A moose and squirrel battle raged in his chest, his panic the moose, his courage the squirrel and . . . of all things. Squirrel won.

Or maybe it was the one thing to do.

Spangler's hands barely paused at the zipper of his parka. He kept them going up. To his head. With his left, he pulled back his parka hood, exposing his warped and wrinkled face. With his right, he pulled off his black specs, exposing the four men, licking their lips all, to the red-eyed glare of his diseased eyes.

"This young man," Saddam bellowed to the staff. He jabbed a finger at Karim-Assad.

Karim-Assad felt his body wracked by chills.

"You all bear blame for losing my sons. Until they return to me alive, this is my son. If any of you should treat him as less, I will be as offended as he."

The words sucked all the air from the room. The members of the high staff moved their lips but could not talk, nor breathe, nor even gasp. Their eyes went wide, then narrowed. Surprise, then hatred.

Karim-Assad was as much in dismay as any of them. He could not even find glee in the words. Less than an hour ago, he was a lackey. At a word, these men were *his* lackeys? If they offended him, he could make them pay. *Such power and so sudden it was, too.*

How fleeting, though? Karim-Assad was no fool. He had seen men fall from grace. Saddam had said of Uday and Qusay, *Until they return to me alive.* Twice now he had said it.

Saddam's words gave himself free play to shift meaning. To suit his purpose and no one else's. Nobody could ever pin him down.

Until they return to me alive . . .

Karim-Assad was as afraid as any of the high staff. Uday and Qusay. When they returned, if they returned, Karim-Assad was out.

He looked into the faces of the staff officers. They had heard the loophole as well. He saw the hatred in their faces give way to sly looks bearing threats. *Treat us with respect, you little bastard. Or else have us killed. Because if his spawn should return to Saddam alive, you will be nothing more than a wart on a camel's ass. We will slice you off from Saddam with a sharp knife and burn you to ash.*

Karim-Assad gave a long blink of dismay. Inside his head he could see his way as clearly as the pattern of stars pointed the ways to north and south on a desert night. Saddam had his goal, to redeem his sons at all cost. The high staff had theirs, to protect their own interests, and once that was settled, to dispense with Karim-Assad. Yesterday a food taster, today a threat. Now he had his own goal as well, from the same set of words: *Until they return to me alive . . .*

Uday and Qusay. They must not come back, except as dead men.

Foucault and Poole rode in silence. Even after Foucault pointed out that the tank on the flatbed was a Soviet T-76, Poole couldn't get it up. The T-76 was a juicy detail, if only Poole could report it. The Raqs were thought to have only ancient T-55s and the T-72s dating back to Desert Storm. The more modern T-76 was another violation of the weapons embargo, damn Russians. But it didn't exist if Poole couldn't tell anybody about it.

It didn't matter so much, either, if the Russians could come back with: *Yeah, but nanna-nanna-boo-boo, you killed our peace emissary to Saddam, two shots to the head.*

Hell, nobody would care. All anybody cared about were the weapons of mass destruction. If he found nuke rounds in the T-76, then maybe the press would get a hard-on—not to print the fact but to discredit it. Until they'd satisfied themselves that he and his Delta team planted the tank. At the direct direction of the president of the United States. No winning with those butt-weasels.

Still, Poole had to try. He called Three-Three a few times as the truck bucked along the dirt road. All he got for the effort were squeaks and bubbles in the ear. So he gave up. To deal with more pressing problems.

Dawn, for one. Much less than an hour away now. Riding the truck from the ambush site would gain them some ground but what then? What could they do by day? He wasn't going to sell himself as a Raqi.

Foucault spoke like a native. He might pass.

Poole's language skills were good enough. Not his race. Even if he bathed his black skin dusty white, he wasn't going to hide his nose flare and his lips. If they ran into a roadblock after sunup, he was just going to have to hide on the floor.

Ah, well, screw that. He was *not*. Gonna get his ass killed playing like some damned high-school kid sneaking into a drive-in movie.

"Where were you going when we stopped you?" Poole said to the driver.

"A tank repair factory."

"Where?"

"At the outskirts of Baghdad."

"Well then, go there." Poole trained his eyes on the dusty road ahead. He ignored the incredulous stare of the driver on his left, incredulous that he would be going into the heart of the city. Just as he ignored the incredulous stare of Foucault on his right, both of them thinking: *We're taking the road more traveled? The road to Baghdad?*

Maybe, maybe not. He had some time. He'd think of

something by then. Maybe the flatbed'd sprout wings by sunup. Fly up a monkey's butt and hide there.

They also had the time delay on the demo charges Foucault and Blue Dolan had set back on the stretch SUV. After piling the driver and the Secret Service bodyguard from the front seat into the back, taking the count back up to four bodies. Although the undercarriage of the SUV was armored, one of the Delta men had found a spot just big enough, an arm's reach into the chassis, next to the gas tank. White phosphorus grenades went into the passenger compartment, their spoons tied down with rubber bands. The grenade on the gas tank would start the fire. When the rubber bands broke, and the Willy-Pete went off, the interior of the vehicle would go white-hot for five minutes, then burn like a kiln, reducing metal to puddles and everything else to ashes.

That might give them even more time. The Raqis would see the fire from the air and respond. They would never get the flames out without hazmat trucks, and it might take a day or two for the fire to cool enough for them to extract the four lumps of ashes.

If they found any forensic evidence of all, it would be of the two holes in four skulls. It would take much longer to determine these were not the Hussein boys. Poole guessed they might have as much as three days while confusion reigned inside the Raq at the very top levels.

Maybe things weren't going so bad, after all, mission-wise. He was supposed to prod Saddam into a careless act of movement or communication so that high-flying stealth bombers could strike him and perhaps bring a quick end to a war without ever fighting a war. A year from now, given the small odds that he would even survive this fiasco, as he stood his court-martial, he could claim that he accomplished his mission in spades. Whatever else they did to him, he did that in the service of his country. *I regret that I have but one life, yada-yada.*

Be a good thing to say when they let him speak his last
words before torching him with old sparky.

I done my duty, butt-weasels.

Spangler's red eyes drilled Crooked Finger first. The guy
fell back.

Just a step or two. That's all it gave him, but good
enough.

He fired a glance at each of the others. Each of them
fell back, too. Indian number four, Mister One-Word,
went down in the snow. He cursed about his bum knee.

The three others went at him.

"Now you're going to get it."

"Frosty the No-Man gonna get it now, bro."

"Kill your ass."

Moose took charge of his chest, and Spangler . . .

Spangler darted into the gap left when One-Word
went down.

He'd go for the front door of the liquor store. Far
enough on gimpy knees. The four would have to peel him
from the door handle. Beat him in public. Scalp him in
plain view, but—

Spangler smashed his nose into a tree trunk.

Dazed, he crumpled.

A tree trunk? In the middle of a drive-up lane?

He lost his specs in the snow. On his hands and knees,
he began to feel for them. The cold did not matter now.
He would never be able to drive through the blinding
white back to Great Falls without them. Not that it mattered. This was his dying place, bright and cold as a bad
dream. He sat back on his heels and put his hands to his
face. Funny. The cold felt good. He drew fresh air into
his lungs. He hadn't noticed how fresh the air was here in
Montana. Good to breathe, refreshing as a drink. *You
know, when you're not at death's teepee door.*

He waited for the blows to begin. A line from a film came to him. *A good day to die.*

He thought of the man in the fridge. He wished he were there now, safe from white weather and Blackfeet. *Screw it. Not a good day, Little Big Man. Not a good day at all.*

As the sky grew lighter, Poole's mood grew darker.

The farther the tractor and its flatbed went, the thicker the traffic. Trucks and utility vehicles passed them coming and going. Convoys of trucks thrashed the road in both directions, whipping the road into a fairy dust, a white liquid. Soldiers hung out the sides of the trucks like bird dogs on the way to the hunt. The Raqs just trying to put their faces into fresh air, trying to keep from choking on the clouds of talc in the air. Even in this truck with the closed cab the dust enveloped them like a snowstorm.

Funny. The Raqs in an uproar. Could happen in anybody's army. Hell, Poole had seen it plenty of times in his. The Sadman hadda be calling for heads. Heads'd roll, too.

At the half-hour mark before sunup, a chopper circled them, keeping them in the glow of its spotlight.

The Raqi driver cursed. He tried blocking the light with one hand. The truck lurched under his unsteady foot. "I can't see."

"You're angry," Poole said.

"I'm most sorry."

Poole shrugged. "What would you do if we weren't here?"

"What do you mean?"

"If somebody blinded you like this, what would you do to get them to stop shining the light in your face?"

"Curse them. Wave at them with an indecent gesture."

"Do it."

"What?"

"Wave at him. Curse at him."

The driver gawped.

"Do it," Poole said. "If you try to send any signal beside an obscene gesture, any kind of warning at all, I will kill you."

The driver stared.

"And if you don't start waving, I will kill you anyhow."

The driver did his best to wave off the helicopter, cursing aloud, which was pointless. He did gesture with the finger to match the signal for road rage the world over. Poole would have been nervous, except that the truck had grown as wild as a rodeo bull. Any second now, he expected to go through the windshield, out and over the hood. He held on, counted to eight. The helicopter flew off before he got bucked off.

The driver brought the truck under control.

"Eighty-point ride," Poole said.

Foucault got it. "I've been thrown from gentler."

"Sarge, you ever wonder?"

"Bout what, Cap?"

"About how our army's the same as this guy's army?"

"Don't let on," Foucault said. "We'll be out of a job."

"No wars. Just rally in the desert and throw one big keg party between armies, man."

Poole shook his head. Trucks and tanks plowing the ruts in the road. Helicopters shining lights on their own traffic. Every Raqi jumping through the hoop of his own ass. Total goat-rope. Instead of downing a few brews and telling lies, guys trying to kill each other.

He checked his two-dollar compass. Caught a glimpse of himself in the compass mirror. Forget his skin color. In this world, everybody was the same, gray as auto primer paint. Maybe he could use a bandanna to hide his lips and nose. Keep going by day.

He looked down at his M-4. Naw. The Raqis get one look at that and keg party's over. Just throw down and start shooting.

Barely fifteen minutes before the SUV was to blow and the sun was to come up, an oncoming tank column forced the driver to the side of the road.

The semi pulled to a stop, and idled for a full ten minutes as the tanks passed. Reinforce an entire Raqi division with yet another tank battalion? Man, what were the Raqs thinking?

Maybe they were trying to kill him with dust blowing off the rooster tails of the passing tanks. He looked back on the flatbed. The T-76 was white as a marble sculpture. He pitied the Delta guys back there. Felt a moment of shame for busting Solis's balls by showing him up. Ah, well, the L-T had to learn. Some L-Ts, the ones with hard heads, had to learn the hard way.

"Drive on," he said in Arabic as the last of the Raqs went by.

Poole began thinking ahead. To roadblocks. The Raqis knew roadblocks. Sooner or later, they'd hit one. Scared the bejeezus out of him. Delta'd be better off to abandon truck. Avoid roadblocks. Avoid a fight. Avoid—

The truck lurched as the driver let up on the gas. Poole saw it the instant Foucault said it—in close-up through the windshield—just before he hit the glass with his face. "Goddam!"

"I am most sorry," the driver said.

"Got a roadblock." Foucault said it in the tone of a funeral prayer.

Poole couldn't stop himself from laughing. The Raq driver gawking at a crazy black Satan-type. Blood trickling down his face. Busted windshield. Roadblock. The Three Stooges themselves couldn't have made up a more ridiculous scenario. Not funny, but ridiculous. He'd have liked funny better.

If only.

"Get up, General."

General? Spangler found strength. Somebody knew his rank? Still blind, he lurched to his knees. Didn't he recognize that voice? Who knew he was a general? Who even knew he was here?

"Night Runner." One of the Indians. Little Brother.

"Night Runner?" *Here?*

"You bastard." Crooked Finger. Spangler knew his voice, too.

He opened his eyes right at the level of a greasy, empty sleeve.

"Night Runner?" Spangler looked up into the face of the man who had stolen his Dodge and the hundred twenty bucks.

"I didn't steal your Durango."

Spangler shook his head. Had he made the accusation aloud? "No, I didn't think you actually stole it."

"Yes you did."

"Yes I did." Spangler fitted his prescription sunglasses to his face as best he could, bent as the frames were. Chunks of slush slid down the lenses and froze into place. He found he could not just let go of the metal stems, as they froze to his fingertips. He pulled free of the glasses, thinking he might have left skin, and stuck his hands in his pockets. At least he thought they were in his pockets, because he could not feel either them or the pockets.

"What happened to your arm?"

"I lost it in Vietnam."

That left Spangler silent. *Vietnam?* That didn't make sense. Night Runner was too young for the Vietnam War. And besides, Spangler had known him after Vietnam, just two years ago in fact. "How—?"

"I'm not allowed to say," Night Runner said.

"Ah-h-h." After going into Afghanistan with Delta, Night Runner had returned to his Force Recon marine unit. A black mission into Vietnam, a—

"Bastard." Crooked Finger again.

Spangler was surprised to see that Crooked Finger was not talking to him, but to Night Runner. The four Indians stood shoulder to shoulder. They looked sober now, and more angry at Night Runner than even at Spangler moments ago.

"Man said he knew you in the army." Crooked Finger.

"Didn't even know you was in the marines." Little Brother.

"He was in the army," Night Runner said. "I was in the marines. We worked together."

"A joint operation." Spangler tried to clarify. Night Runner's face knotted up. A look of *Shut your hole.*

"You two was running drugs? Like in the CIA, bro? I heard about them bastards doing that."

"Drugs? Where the hell—?"

Night Runner stared Spangler silent.

In all his years at the Pentagon, if Spangler learned one thing, it was that look. *Zip it.* He bit into a lip sandwich. He had no part in this now. He kept his gaze lowered. He did not even dare to wipe at the slush sliding down his face.

The tall one raised his crooked finger at Night Runner. "Maybe you was together too long. Maybe you as white as he is."

Little Brother was amused. "Not that white, bro. No-Face-toad-Frosty-the-no-man there whiter than sunup tomorrow."

Toad? How'd the guy know people called him that from K through 12?

Crooked Finger de-amused Little Brother with a sharp elbow to the side of his head. For a second there, the assailants looked as if they might assail each other.

"What's going on here?" said Night Runner.

"We ain't robbin him or nothin." Crooked Finger looked to the three others, who, in turn shrugged, nodded, and wagged until they came to a silent consensus. *No rob-bin here, bro.*

"No," said Little Brother, "we ain't robbin him."

Night Runner looked to Spangler.

Something had come over the former marine. He had called up a bit of that military bearing of his. His eyes now de-glazed. He looked as if he would kick ass on all four of these thugs, if Spangler gave him the word. *Well, try, anyhow.*

Spangler cocked his head, thinking it over. No, he did not want to waste this man—what was left of him—on four ne'er-do-wells.

"We were negotiating a loan," Spangler said. Better to play it in low key, see if they could get out of this without a clash.

"That's it," Crooked Finger said. "A loan."

Night Runner flashed those teeth again, teeth whiter than the day. A genuine smile. An approving smile. *Good call, General.*

The smile infused Spangler with warmth he had not felt since coming to Montana. A glow radiated from his core, from a fire set by Night Runner. He felt something he had not felt for two years. The real leaders and true heroes could do that to an ordinary man. They could ignite fires even in him, give him the will to charge into hell. If they had to fight today, Spangler felt he could do it. *Night Runner. There, by the grace of God, goes God.* One word from Night Runner, and he'd just start throwing punches, no matter that the strongest thing he'd ever punched was a keyboard. One word and—

Night Runner raised an eyebrow at Spangler: *Earth to Toad, earth to Toad.*

"Sorry."

"You were saying?"

"Oh, a loan. We were talking about a loan."

A look of: *Okay, I'll bite.* "And how high did the bidding go?"

"A hundred bucks," Spangler said.

"Apiece," said the fourth Indian for the third time.

"That's what he was saying about the time you came up," Spangler said. "He's a bit wearisome on that point."

"You didn't agree to it?"

Spangler wagged his head, but Crooked Finger wasn't having it. "Yes, he did. A hundred bucks apiece. That's what he said." The other three began to nod. "Four to one."

"So it was a vote, was it?"

"Not exactly," Spangler said. "I didn't get a vote."

"Liar," Crooked Finger said.

"A hundred bucks, bro."

"Apiece."

Spangler shrugged. "See what I mean?"

"Wearisome."

"It's still four to one, Runner," Crooked Finger said. "Even with his vote."

"Four to one, bro."

Four to one? Spangler winced. Technically, it was four to two. Why did bullies always assume he was worthless in a fight? *Er,* rather, how did they know he was a man of wit rather than hit?

"Four to one sounds fair to me," Night Runner said. The four stiffened, ready for combat.

"I mean a hundred bucks," Night Runner said. "Apiece." The four sagged in relief. Three of them began dancing on the spot, not a native dance, but that eager soft-shoe again, as if the cold had numbed the soles of their feet. Or was it just the sudden reminder of the need of drink?

Spangler fished for his wad of cash.

He felt a nudge against his elbow. He looked down and took the keys to the Dodge from Night Runner's hand without protest.

"Go start the Durango. Warm yourself up. Wait for me."

Spangler pulled at his roll of cash, so thick it stuck in his pocket.

Night Runner held his stump to Spangler's elbow, keeping his arm from pulling out the wad. "Don't need it." He held up the two fifties that Spangler had forked over earlier. He fanned them with his thumb and fingers, folded them together deftly with one hand, stuck them between his teeth, and tore them in half. "A hundred bucks," he said. He tossed them toward the four men. The blizzard caught the paper and blew them away like any other of the dozens of pieces of litter, the nickel fliers, plastic food market bags, the aluminum beer cans drifted into heaps against walls and fences with the snow.

Little Brother dove and tackled two of the pieces. The third Indian ran toward the building stamping in snow as if killing fire ants, trying to pin one piece of the loot to the ground. Crooked Finger saw his odds halved and slouched after the others, leaving the slit-eyed one alone.

"Apiece," Night Runner said to this last man standing, the one Spangler saw as the least sane. "One piece for each of you."

Everything in Spangler's alternate universe came to a halt. The trio stopped chasing the wind, stopped crawling through the plush pile of the white carpet, stopped stamping oversized footprints in the snow. Spangler stopped breathing. Even the blizzard held its breath. The only movement was the fourth Indian, clenching and unclenching both fists by his sides.

"Unless Sneaks Low wants a piece of me," Night Runner said.

Nothing happened. No snow, no wind for a full ten seconds. Sneaks Low stopped clenching his fists, ready for battle.

"That's your answer then," Night Runner said.

Crooked Finger broke the impasse. "We got them all." He held up the four pieces of two bills. "Come on, Sneaks. I'm buying the house."

Spangler laughed. His third or fourth Indian name in as many minutes.

It was a cue for the blizzard to start up in double-fury to make up for its lapse in energy.

Sneaks Low turned his body but not his head and glared at Night Runner as he walked away.

Spangler shuddered. "Man scares me," he said, more to himself than Night Runner.

Night Runner kept his own gaze locked onto the slitted, hateful eyes and spoke in a low tone. "The man who scares me in a fight is the one you have to talk to twice."

"What?"

"I told you to go to the Durango."

Spangler spun on the spot and jogged as fast as his jolting knees and barely defrosted feet would take him. Only once did he look back. His four would-be assailants stood with four brown bags outside the drive-up/walk-up window of the liquor store. They drank and slouched and soft-shoed, the weather no big deal, the face-off a nonevent already forgotten.

A last glimpse of them dancing in the snow through his fogged and icy glasses was all he got before they vanished in a gust of white wind.

Night Runner had vanished, too. A sudden fear gave Spangler new life in his body, new flexibility in his knees. He was actually running. Hell, he hadn't run since that helicopter fire so long ago. He—

Ran out of the fog and into the Dodge parked in front of the liquor store, knocking both knees numb.

Over the hood of the semi-tractor Poole saw a dusty soldier advancing in the glow of headlights, rifle slung, waving a hand in front of his face.

"Don't stop," Poole told the driver. "Idle forward." He needed time to think. "Slowly." A lot of time. "Slower." *While you're at it, would you mind not grinding the gears into a pile of filings?*

The driver shrugged, his shoulders shaking. *Doing the best I can here, boss.*

The truck eased forward, bucking and jerking, as Poole's mind raced to invent, to improvise, to survive. *An armed soldier. Not good. Rifle slung. Good.* Behind him, other armed soldiers milling in the liquid dust pools as deep as their boot-tops. Good. Soldiers being soldiers, taking a break while others worked, pointing at the truck driver and laughing at his driving. *Vehicles parked to the edge of the road, not to block it. Very good.* A troop truck. Its front end raised. Beneath it, a utility car. *A car crash. A simple car crash. Superb.* Soft red lights arranged in groups well off the road. Men smoking and joking, rapping and napping. *No alarm here. No roadblock. Excellent. Deep breath. Exhale.*

"A traffic accident," Foucault said. "Thank Christ."

"No more English," Poole said. "And lose the Christianity."

"Sorry, Cap." In Arabic.

Okay. So. Situation. A troop truck had run up over the back of a command car. More Iraqi leadership damaged. If he got out of this alive, he'd have stories to tell forever. Wearem out at the VFW.

The guy coming on an infantry type, an NCO. Waiting for medics. Not a real cop who might check papers as a matter of routine. Raq a country of permission slips. Delta in the hall without a pass.

Mission. Get on by without a fight.

"We have to move on," Poole said in the driver's language. "Tell him. Tell him this is a combat emergency. By order of the division commander." He hid his M-4 between his knees but kept a hand on it.

The driver did a take. "One tank with a seized engine is an emergency?"

Poole glared into the man's eyes. *Now the guy was getting a backbone?* "A matter of life and death," he said. "Yours."

The Raqi NCO called up to the cab. A squad leader.

"Tell him," Poole said in a low voice.

The driver sold the emergency tank story hard, practically begging. Poole was afraid the Iraqi was going to start crying.

The NCO wasn't moved. He shook his head, raising a dust cloud from his round helmet. "Even so. You can't go on."

Poole heard a note of indecision in the voice of the young NCO. He nudged the driver in the knee.

"We have to go on," Poole whispered.

"We have to go on," the driver said. "I told you, by the general's orders."

"You can't. It's a traffic jam. Another convoy is behind the crash. And another is coming up the road."

The Raqi driver, near tears, shouted, "I tell you, my general—"

"I have a general, too." The young NCO waved at the crash site. "He's dead. Crushed under that truck. Three other men dead. Four others dying. Too many hurt to count. Don't tell me about your general."

"Don't piss him off," Foucault said.

"What?" The NCO and the driver as one.

"Ask him if there is a way around," Poole said in a low voice. *"Be nice about it."*

The driver did as he was told.

"Through the desert?" the young NCO asked.

"Of course the desert."

The driver threw up his hands. "Of course the desert."

"I don't know," the soldier said, at last over the issue of whose general was more important. "I could take a look."

"*Take a look.*"

"Take a look."

The NCO balked.

"*Please.*"

"Please."

The NCO shrugged his shoulders and turned about, walking off the road across the desert floor. Now and then he stamped his feet on the crust of sand and gravel. As if that might tell him something about the load-bearing weight of the desert floor.

"Follow him," Poole said. The driver looked at him. "Drive after him, as if he were guiding us."

The tractor bounced forward, rocking and jerking as it left the river of dust.

At first the NCO stopped in place and tried to wave the truck driver to halt.

"Keep going," Poole said.

As the truck came at him in fits and starts, the NCO gave in at last. An oncoming tractor? Nearly out of control? Wary, he turned his back and found his way across the flat ground, checking over his shoulder to make sure the semi wasn't going to run him down. Poole relaxed a little. To anybody watching, it would seem as if an NCO had taken charge. A guy takes action to solve a sticky problem. Nobody was likely to mess with a guy actually doing something right. Before long they met up with a ground guide and a vehicle coming from the opposite direction. The Iraqis in the convoy had gotten the same idea, perhaps on their own, perhaps following the NCO's lead.

In no time, they were back on the track. The truck pulled to the side to await the passage of another tank convoy.

"How far to Kuwait?" Poole asked after the driver had

finally jammed his truck into low-low gear and sat at the idle.

"Perhaps three hundred kilometers," the driver said.

Poole looked to Foucault. They exchanged winks in the dim light.

The dirt track gave way to a rough gravel road only slightly less dusty than the track they had been on. Gradually this widened into two lanes full of potholes from the heavy military traffic.

The sky was brightening. Poole checked his watch. Anytime now—

An explosion on the horizon behind them. A daylight flash of lightning.

No pilot flying within twenty miles could have missed it. And sure enough all the lights in the sky converged on one point, like moths to a bug zapper.

His chest sagged. He drew a deep, dusty breath.

Spangler's impact on the Dodge felt soft. He did hit it hard enough to hurt. And he did lose his feet and hit the ground. But the snow was deep, and as he looked over his spectacles he saw the Dodge door, dented in two places by his knees. A sheet-metal cushion. He gave a wild laugh. What was it, an hour ago? Or a month ago? When he thought he'd run into a man? How to explain that to the Hertz people? *No, the Dodge didn't run into a thing. I ran into the Dodge. How? Welp. See, there was this one-armed man? And four muggers?*

A burst of adrenaline shot him to his feet. *Those thugs.*

Then a growl. *Wolves*? He rolled over, got to his knees, tried to fix his glasses to the dents in his nose.

No wolf. A dog. No. Not just one dog, but half a dozen. In a half circle around him.

Ready to pounce.

The brown one, black-spotted, hanging teats. Up close

her eyes crusted with dried—or frozen—pus. A couple stupid-looking mutts with flop ears and mangy fur. Stupid-looking except for the teeth.

Teeth bared in a pack smile. The buzz of a pack growl, low and harmonic like a bee swarm.

Spangler thought he might dive under the Durango. He might even yank open the door of the SUV and get in with only one of the creatures hanging onto him, maybe trying to pull him back out into the storm like a rag doll.

Then again—

He grasped two fistfuls of snow and stood up shouting and cursing. He threw the half-clamped snowballs, kicked out in his street shoes, went after the dogs, hyenas, raptors, and all the gremlins in the snow. In the street. In his mind.

They pack-yelped as one and skittered into white safety.

"Somebitches." He laughed, giddy at the irony in that.

He pulled open the driver door and piled in, talking to himself aloud and proudly. "After what I been through? Couple damned dogs? Somebitches."

He wiped at the crust of ice on his glasses. The door locks snapped shut.

Spangler yelped and tried to see through lenses of ice.

"Just me."

"Night Runner. You scared the hell out of me."

"You did okay with the dogs. They've been known to tear up a poor soul that passes out drunk. A few kid attacks every year."

"Spooky," Spangler said. "But nothing like those . . . four."

"Better get going," Night Runner said. "Sneaks Low will do more than scare you if he finishes off his bottle of Mad Dog and finds you still in town. He won't even growl first like those dogs."

Spangler needed no more. He fumbled with his keys,

dropped them, picked them up. Sorted them. Stuck one into a hinged joint in the steering column. Cursed. Gave up. Thrust the keys at Night Runner.

"I can't even see to put in the key. You drive." He sat there staring, tiny sheets of ice floating down his black lenses.

Night Runner took the keys. "It will cost you."

"Name your price." Drops began to fall from the lenses like tears.

Night Runner laughed. "Forgive the debt, the one hundred dollars I took from you and gave to them."

"Best money I ever spent."

As the sun arc-welded a line across the horizon, Poole could feel it. The claustrophobia. Riding in the confines of the truck cab by day? Bad call. Fight from here? No way.

Besides. The driver was back to grinding gears. Every shift set his teeth on edge. Wasn't the bad driving, though. Hadda play the odds. Next roadblock? The pros'd be running it. Raqi cops. Checking papers and IDs. No bluff was going to cut it.

He felt Foucault squirm as the sun came at them long and low. Like a spotlight. Time to cut bait.

"Pull over," Poole told the driver.

This was a flat stretch of desert, the road deserted. For the time being. Act now or forever.

The truck rolled to a stop at the edge of the desert.

Poole yanked the driver out of the cab and hauled him to the front of the truck.

The man's lower lip began to tremble. "Don't kill me."

"Quit whining."

Poole pushed him backward, lifting his butt up onto the bumper of the truck. The driver did cry now. He huffed his last prayers.

Poole felt an instant of shame. The cruelty thing. At

least this time it was not cruelty for its own sake. He had to do this. His mission. His men.

"You want to die?"

The man folded his hands. "I have children."

"Sit here."

The driver nodded.

"Don't move."

The driver wagged his head, and the muddy tracks of his tears turned the ashen gray on his cheeks to zigzags of black streaks.

Poole and Foucault headed to the back of the truck.

In seconds, Poole was back. He grabbed the driver's jacket and pulled him upright. He dragged him to the cab, opened the door, and shut him inside.

"You're not going to kill me?"

"Not if you do as I say. Drive. You'll be alone in the cab. The rest of us are on the back of the truck and inside the tank. Hiding. You take us through the checkpoints. Remember, if a fight begins, you'll be the first to die."

"Thank you."

"Don't stop until you get to the Kuwaiti border station."

"Not Baghdad?"

"What did I just say?"

"I don't think I have enough petrol."

"Then drive until you run dry."

The driver jammed at the gears until he found the one he needed.

"Now?" he said.

"Wait until I give you the signal."

"What if I have to stop for the police?"

"Tell them lies. Like before. Or just keep on going. Don't worry."

"Don't worry?" His voice a squeak. "They will shoot me."

"They might shoot. They might not. If you disobey, I will shoot you. In the back of the head, with no doubt about it." He gave the man the sign of the finger-pistol that had worked so well with Uday and Qusay.

The Raqi gripped the wheel. "I will drive on."

Poole patted him on the arm. "Don't worry," he said, feeling a chink in his own mean streak. "We don't want to see you dead."

The Raq gave him a look of dismay. Outside his family, he'd probably never heard those words. Coming from an enemy . . .

Poole climbed up onto the back of the truck and rapped on the side of the cab. He gave the driver a smile in the rearview mirror.

The driver eased out the clutch, and the truck lunged forward, one gear clattering on another.

Wrapped in a capsule of heat and leather, Spangler took off his glasses. He wiped them dry and bent the wire frames straight. "How did you beat me back to the Dodge?"

"You're not that fast, General. And hey, my name is Night Runner. You do the math on how fast I can go by day."

"It felt fast. I thought I was melting a path in the snow with my afterburners." He began to giggle.

Night Runner, too.

Spangler sobered up. "What next?"

"You tell me. Why did you come to Montana?"

"To find you."

"But why?"

"To hire you. In the highest interests of national defense."

"Combat?"

"Combat."

Night Runner held up his flapping sleeve, one eyebrow forming a question mark.

"You're the man I want. With or without all your parts."

Night Runner laughed, but bitterly.

"I didn't know you'd lost an arm—"

"Not lost." Night Runner's eyes glazed over. "Taken from me. On a Force Recon mission. In a fight. I got—" He narrowed one eye at Spangler. "A tiger bit it off. And don't tell me you're sorry."

"Holy Mother of God. A tiger?"

They changed seats. Night Runner drove as if he could see through the white. The ride was quiet for a long time, the tires muffled in new-fallen snow.

"To do what?" Night Runner said.

"Lend a hand to a Delta unit inside Iraq."

"Where inside Iraq?"

"They've been out of touch."

"How you going to find them?"

"You tell me."

"You're a regular bull, aren't you, General?"

"Bull?"

"Carry your own china shop around wherever you go."

Spangler kept the silence of awe for a long time. Night Runner rose even higher in his estimation, quoting Churchill at him like that. So . . . *awesome*.

They had cleared the town by a good ways. Night Runner eased the Dodge toward the side of the road. He parked well clear of the road, turned the heater down, and looked Spangler in the eyeglasses.

Spangler could see. Trying to decide. Stay here in Montana and war with the elements? Or go to a real war? To him, one was as dangerous as the other. "Want to know the mission?"

"Doesn't matter. If I go, I go."

Spangler's lips hurt, so wide was his smile.

"What?"

"You're going."

"Why would I? One arm tied behind my back?" He gave a lazy shrug. "So to speak."

"Because being a one-armed Delta man is better than being a one-armed drunk in Heart Butte, Montana."

Night Runner blinked rapidly. "I'm out of shape. I've been . . ."

Moment of silence.

Night Runner swallowed hard. "You're right." He hung his head. "I'm a drunk."

"You don't have to do this, Runner."

"Yes. I do. But . . ."

"What?"

"I've lost my edge. Take me weeks to get up to speed."

"Like riding a bike," Spangler said.

Night Runner's jaw knotted.

"Okay," Spangler said, "that was a stupid thing to say. What do I know about riding *that* bike?"

The wind picked up, battering the side of the Durango.

"Let me at least tell you the mission."

"No."

"What? You won't go?"

"Stop selling. I'm in."

Spangler's face hurt, the size of his grin.

"What's so funny?"

"I can't get used to the feeling of awe I get when I'm around people like you."

Night Runner looked himself over. Greasy and one-armed. "You're an odd man, General."

"*Awed* is the word." He spelled it. "You have no idea how awed."

"Who's in charge?"

"Guy by the name of Ramsey Baker. Former Delta. As far as I know, the only American ever to infiltrate al Qaeda."

"I met him. After the thing in Afghanistan, aboard the carrier. Before they took him off to a hospital ship for a physical."

"What next?"

"Where and when?"

"Savannah, Georgia. Two days."

Night Runner cracked his door.

Spangler shuddered. "One last thing. That guy, Low Speaker—"

"Sneaks Low."

"He woulda killed me back there?"

"Remember that bad guy in *Lonesome Dove*? Blue Duck?"

"Scary guy."

"Sneaks is twice the killer with half the talk. You met him on the prairie a hundred years ago, your last image of him would be his face leaning over yours as he took your hair."

"He has the eyes of a killer."

"Except he might not kill you."

"No?"

"Some things are worse than death."

"Yes." If anybody knew that, it was Spangler.

"Make you wish you were dead."

Spangler gulped.

"Make you kill yourself; and you'd be happy to do it. Do it and die with a smile on your face."

Worse even than the pictures Spangler had imagined on the drive up here.

"Do not ever come here again." Night Runner gazed out into the white nothingness. "I love this land. It never lets you forget that it is all-powerful, like a god unto its own. You don't heed its power, it will kill you. My people come from this. They are of the same stock, and of the same mind. At least until they were civilized by the white men." He hit the *civilized*. "By their religion. Their liquor. Their diseases. Their reservations." He turned to Spangler.

"I'm sorry," Spangler said, the words out there before

he had a chance to think about them. "I'm—" He shut his mouth when the denim sleeve flapped at him.

"Hell," Night Runner said. "Don't be sorry. If we'd had half the chance we'd have done even worse to you."

Spangler gulped. Like those four would have done. Four to one. They had the numbers, whereas their ancestors did not.

"Savannah. Two days." Night Runner pushed the door open.

"You're getting out here? Must be five miles to town."

Night Runner, already out in the wind, just stared at him. A look of *who said I'm going back to town*?

"One thing," Spangler said.

"You got a lot of one things, General."

"Thanks. Thanks for taking on the mission. And thanks for saving my life."

Night Runner waved his flap of denim. "No," he said, "thank you. For saving mine."

Fade to white.

Night Runner was gone.

Spangler locked the Dodge's doors and sat for a full ten minutes immobilized by his emotions.

That kind of a thank-you. From a man like Night Runner. An honor just to know men like him and Ramsey Baker. And to have them know him and not look down on him the way Caranto did, as if he were a snot bubble.

Spangler slid across the seat. It took another five minutes behind the wheel, wiping his eyes dry and waiting for his vision to clear so that he could drive at least no worse than blind through the blizzard.

They rode in a battered taxi, dressed in plain clothes. Karim-Assad had at first supposed they were traveling to the meeting that Saddam had called with the staff and

commanders of the Republican Guard division that had
lost Uday and Qusay. But. A high-level meeting? Dressed
as rug merchants? Saddam in a wrinkled jacket with a
broken button on a breast pocket flap?

Karim-Assad still couldn't grasp it. *Uday and Qusay.
Lost.*

Lost. That was the way Saddam put it. As if some careless adult had taken two toddlers on an outing to a park on
the Tigris and let the children swim alone. As if the toddlers had vanished in the brown swirl.

The driver and another man sat in the front of the taxi.
Karim-Assad recognized them both, both in ordinary
clothes. Personal bodyguards in civilian dress.

At first Saddam seemed chatty and eager, as if dress-
ing down in ordinary clothes and riding in a less than ordinary taxi was a rare adventure. Before long he grew
somber. He folded into himself literally, crossing his legs,
stacking his forearms on his belly, closing his hands into
fists, lowering his head, and pulling a military cap over
his eyes.

Karim-Assad saw no nuance in that. Saddam did not
want to be bothered. It gave him time to think himself.
They were not going to a meeting of military officers.
Such an occasion called for all the trappings of power,
uniforms, medals, pomp. Where, then?

This was no ordinary taxi. The exterior might be battered and dusty, but the inside was spotless. The car felt
heavy. It did not rattle. Karim-Assad turned down the
window a slit.

"Shut it," the driver said, then shut it himself with an
electric control in the front.

"You nearly pinched my fingers." *Have you not heard
that I am Saddam's son? Perhaps only for a day, but at
least for today?*

"Policy."

Karim-Assad stared at the dark, hostile eyes in the rearview mirror. He gave back as dark a look as he could manage. But he had little practice in dark stares.

The driver was not impressed. He stroked the brush of his Saddam mustache. "Policy of the president of Iraq. You want to open a window? You ask him."

A test. Of course.

Karim-Assad had gone from nobody to the son of Saddam. From that moment on, nobody of low station could help but despise him. For part and parcel of living in a low station was to hate those above. Now all those below—and all those in power beside him as well—would hate him. His new peers did not want to share power. Most especially not with a usurper moving up from a low station to the right hand of the giver of all power.

Karim-Assad leaned forward to speak in the man's ear, looking him directly in the mirror-eyes. "I will, indeed, ask him. When I ask him if I might name my replacement in the kitchen as food taster." Karim-Assad put on a wide smile, tipping his head back so it would show in the mirror. "And I will ask you, nicely for now, that if you wish to brief me on any other issues of policy, will you do so in a way that does not risk injury to my person?" He wriggled his fingers beside his face.

The driver gave him an even more hostile glare.

"Or will you not?"

The eyes blinked twice, but the driver kept his silence. A standoff.

Karim-Assad turned to Saddam. "Father, I have a question."

"I-would-rather-brief-you-on-policy," the driver said, running his words together. "In-a-way-that-you-do-not-risk-harm."

Saddam stirred and sat up, a smile playing at his lips.

"What is it, my son?"
"Are we there yet?"

Night Runner tied a bandanna over his ears so they would
not freeze and break off like pork rinds. He put the north
wind at ten o'clock on his right shoulder and struck out.
He put his good hand, the right, his only, Napoleon-style
into his jacket. The one good thing about no hand? No
more worry about frost-bite on the fingers.

He kept cutting into the wind, fighting the tendency to
angle away from a blizzard. In the legendary winter of
1964, entire herds of antelope in eastern Montana turned
their thick, insulated tails to the north wind and walked
blindly for days. They crossed the Missouri River frozen
solid. After the storm, the pronghorns stayed beneath the
sharp edge of the cold front and the minus-thirty temps.
Until the Missouri thawed, trapping them on the south
side of the river. North of the river from Malta to Glas-
gow, hunters had to wait decades for new herds to migrate
from the Dakotas.

Night Runner dropped over the bluffs into Blacktail
Creek's sharp-cut valley. He took his bearings from the
sandstone pillars, ancient sentinels, visible in glimpses between gusts of white. They pointed the way for him. Due
west. Until, finally, in a crook of the frozen Blacktail, hard
against the north bluff, the wind, having done its best to
take him astray and suck him stone-cold, sighed and gave
up trying to kill him. He took off his scarf and stood bare-
headed in the quiet air. Overhead, atop the bluffs, the wind
roared like a rolling thunder. Down here below, he could
have struck a match to light a cigarette. If the shower of
dry snow did not put out the flame. For as soon as the wind
dropped off, so did the snow, piling in long, sweeping
drifts. Just ahead of him beyond one of those drifts at the
base of a cut in the rocks, he saw her front door.

Not your usual Blackfeet lodge. Not the cheap-ass, thrown-up, tribal low-bid duplex. Made of stone, not skins, sandstone chunks picked up at the base of the bluffs, stacked and chinked with mortar from inside. He had mixed the mortar and helped her finish the walls. Inside, the one-room shelter looked like a sandstone cave wind-carved from a single stone. Like those the white men made of mortar on wire in their fake-natural zoo habitats.

Outside, the lodge looked like slabs had fallen from the bluffs and had landed in a rough stack, a pile with each stone on the level. A handful of foot-thick timbers held up the doorposts and supported a ceiling of lodge pole pine stacked to a four-foot peak and covered with blown-on insulating sealant. The place was airtight, except for the door.

Night Runner stepped over the knee-high drift to the doorposts, kept clean by the sweep of wind sliding down a cut in the bluff. He knocked on one doorpost. The door itself was a buffalo robe, hand-tanned, hair side out, Alice's vestigial link to the teepee.

He felt a twinge of alarm as he saw a mark in a skiff of snow near the base of the hide. He was not the first here?

A hand, brown as the buffalo robe and lean as elk jerky, pulled at the hide. Night Runner could see a familiar flash of eyes. He breathed a sigh of relief. Alice's raspy, reedy, ready voice spoke to him. Chiding and greeting him at once.

"What took you so long?" The edges of her English words were sharp. She ran them together in the singsong of their native language, the sentences ending with the up-lilt of a question: *Uttookeeya'sLONG*?

She pulled back the hide to let him in. He slid into the sliver of space, into a stale yellow light of a kerosene lantern, into a cloud of scent rich with wood smoke and rancid with a familiar body odor. She stepped back. Night Runner snugged the robe back against the doorposts and knelt to pull the slack out of it. He held its hem down with granite stones large as bowling balls. The stones taken from teepee rings, circles of rocks on the prairie. Stones that once held down the skirts of teepees.

He stood up. "How long ago was he here?" He wrinkled his nose.

"You smelt him then? Sneaksss?" She turned her head and shot a rope of tobacco spit into a Folger's coffee can by the potbellied stove. "That goddamnt Indin better stop drinking. Or change his name to Stinks High." She hit the ending esses hard, spitting them like watermelon seeds. *Change ees sname to Stinkssigh.*

She wrinkled her own nose. *You don't smell so damnt good your own self.*

Night Runner gave a weak smile. He knew he was one of her favorites, but she availed herself to all the members of the tribe who sought her medicine. An equal opportunity medicine woman.

"If you thought he was sin here, why did you turn your back to fix the stones-ss?"

"I saw a track just outside. Leaving. I guess maybe five minutes ago. At first I was worried."

"About me?"

"You never know."

"You think I just open the door to anybody?"

He glanced at the buffalo hide, billowing inward like a sail. Even with the heavy rocks, anybody could push his way in. Then again, she knew that. For a second there, she looked as if she might actually smile. But she did not. Night Runner smiled for both of them.

"You were expecting me," he said. "Did he tell you we had words?"

"You know betteren to ask."

"Right, the witch doctor–patient confidentiality code of ethics."

"Don't be using them two-dollar wordss on me. I don't

know what they mean, but I know damn well you being a smart-asss."

He was. "What else, Grandmother? What else do you know?"

"You want to be whole again, my son. I know that."

He winced, and his empty sleeve flapped. She reached out and yanked at the sleeve.

"I'm not talking about thiss hand you left in that black forest in the mouth of that lion with the stripes-ss."

Night Runner's head snapped erect. Until today, he had never told anybody on reservation land what had happened to him. He had always dodged the issue, saying the hand was blown off, in a place that he could not talk about. If anybody wanted to think he'd blown off his own damned hand with a grenade, let him.

"You left more than that hand," she said. "You left your spirit. Ever since then your heart has been filled with the darknesss of that forest. You want somebody to blame, somebody to kill, and today you were ready to kill Sneakss. One of your own goddamnt people." She flipped the end of the sleeve toward him and made a swipe at the low ceiling. She turned and uncoiled another rope into the Folger's can. "That's sa bad thing, even if the man deserves skilling."

"And now?"

"You tell me. What do you have in your heart?"

"I want to purify myself of such dark thinking."

"Okay then." She nodded and loosed a hint of a smile, enough to show her brown teeth, half of the uppers missing. "I can help you there."

"Tell me how."

"It's sa long cure. Maybe by spring."

"That bad?"

She did not answer.

Night Runner could not believe his eyes. She was not looking at him, but down at her own trembling fingers. He had never seen that in her before. She had always been strong, powerful, all-knowing, sarcastic, even hostile, but not this. Not afraid.

"Why are you frightened? Did somebody threaten you? Sneaks?"

"Got damn you." Now she stared at him. Drilling him through the eyes with her own. "I don't need you to protect me from the likes sof him. It's syou."

"You're afraid of me?" He threw up his hands, then blushed. He kept forgetting at times like this that he had only the one hand. Until that sleeve flapped at him.

She caught on to him at once. "See that? Your mind is snot right. Your spirit is sall wrong, all out of whack. To purify yourself like thiss against such thingss will take a long time." She spit. "If it can be done at all."

He stood up and walked a small circle, his head bent to keep from bumping into the cave ceiling. "I don't have time, Grandmother. I've been called on to—"

"To be a warrior."

"Yes."

"A warrior for that ugly white man—" She smiled, an inside joke between the two of them about the redundancy.

How did she know?

"The one called Red Eyes swith the starss. He offers syou a war. And you think that will make you whole again."

Night Runner slumped onto a stool. Sneaks. He'd told her about Spangler. The red eyes, the ugly. He'd heard Night Runner call him general, too. But the other things? That he had called him back to fight? Not even Sneaks could have known that. Ah, well, they could have guessed it, though. Why else would a general come all the way out here?

He shrugged. It did not matter if she knew or how she knew. Only that she knew. "You helped me before," he said. "When I needed to find the meaning of courage." Facing a grizzly in the woods alone at night.

"And did that damnt stinking bear give you the courage?"

"No. I found the courage in my heart."

They finished his thought and her words together, aloud, as if reciting a prayer: "Courage is sin a man already."

"If he hass it," she said. "If he don't, then nothing can give it to him."

Useless to argue. "Will you help me?"

"Will you tell Red Eyes sthat you cannot go until spring?"

"No, I have to go now, the war will not wait until spring."

"How long will it wait?"

"Two days."

"You been a drunk for a year, and thiss Red Eyes scan talk you into a war in one day? He should come here. I could learn something about hiss strong medicine."

Night Runner smiled. "Will you help me?"

"Sit down and drink some tea with me." She waved at a stool, her hand still quaking.

"Thank you."

"Don't thank me until you hear my dream."

"Your dream? About me?"

"Yess."

"What happens to me in this dream?"

She turned to him and he could see sudden tears in her eyes. She took a kettle from the woodstove. She did not try to hide her tears.

"This stime," she said, "the bear is snot so forgiving. This time she drags syou into her den and feeds syou to her cubss."

"Well, then." He shook his head. "Maybe I should go. Not even try to purify myself until I come back."

She set the tea before him and returned to her rocker. She drew a wolf skin shawl tight around her shoulders,

the fur yellow with gray turning to black along the spine
and scruff.

"If you go before trying to purify yourself for battle,
you will not come back at all."

"But the bear."

"If you go, you will die in a land where it never rainss,
where grasss does not grow, where riverss do not flow in
their bedss for yearss. Where iss this battle to be?"

He was stunned speechless.

"Iss sit California?" She leaned close to him. "I have
heard bad thingss about thiss California. That it's sa
strange goddamnt place."

She knew California? "Not California."

"Good. That goddamnt place scan be hell on a man."

"What do I do? If I don't purify myself I die in Iraq?"

"Eye-raq?" She nodded. "I heard of that place. Iss sthat
where you're going?"

"Yes."

She pursed her lips and nodded in satisfaction. "At
least it's snot California."

"It's Iraq," he said, biting down on his agitation. "In
this dream? I die in Iraq?"

"Yess. Kilt by another damnt lion with stripes on hiss
face. They have lions sin thiss Eye-raq, do they?"

"I don't know." He shook his head. "But even if I do try
to purify myself, I die here in Montana?"

"I know," she said. "It's a damnt mystery, thiss dream.
But, you know, it'ss only a dream. Sometimess we all get
our dreamss mixed up." She forced a teary smile at him
across her teacup, an antique squat Old Spice shaving
mug, the image of the tri-masted sailing ship thin, like a
faded tattoo.

"So?" He shrugged. *What do I do?*

"You purify yourself before you go," she said. "I been
wrong before. Maybe you could do it in a day. If the med-

icine iss strong enough." She shrugged. "If you believe strong enough."

He could not stifle a smile. "Even if it kills me."

"At least you die at home where you belong."

His stomach fell. Not the medicine he had in mind. If he wanted to die at home, he could go back to town and buy a bottle of Jack.

She read the look on his face. "Come on," she said. "I might be wrong about that dying part, too. Here. Drink your tea, and I will tell you how to conduct your own purification. So you can survive my vision."

"A short purification, right?"

"Short." She shook her head. "Everybody in a goddamnt hurry these dayss. Maybe I should put a drive-up window on thiss lodge. Hand out only the goddamnt instant medicine."

Night Runner bit his mouth shut.

"Short." She spat a brown rope of content into the coffee can. "I'll give you the short cure. But that don't mean itss gonna be the easy cure."

"What doesn't kill you makes you stronger," he said.

"Where did you hear such bullshit ass that?"

He shrugged. "Just a saying."

"A goddamnt stupid-ass saying of the white man." She held up the flap of denim at the end of his arm. "Thiss made you stronger?" *Thiss and the liquor you rode in on?*

He sniffed. *Ouch!*

"Are we there yet?" Saddam said. "What kind of question is that?"

The taxi rolled on heavily, a stiff dark silence radiating from the front seat.

Saddam laughed out loud and patted Karim-Assad on the knee. "Soon enough," he said. He rolled down his own window an inch and stuck his nose into the opening, inhaling deeply. "I love the smell of the restaurant quarter. It's like a perfume to me." He turned his head so the driver could not see him in the mirror. He winked at Karim-Assad. "Open your own window if you wish." He held up a finger and thumb slightly apart. "Just a centimeter or two. Hooligans everywhere. You never know what some rowdy might throw through the window."

Karim-Assad opened his window and put his fingers into the space to hold his nose to the air. He mimicked Saddam's inhaling the fragrance of roasting meat and baking bread. He confirmed that the side glass pane was as thick as the opening he had made for the night air. An armored car. No wonder that it rode so quietly. An armored car disguised as a beat-up taxi.

"Father? I wonder about the meeting you called. With the staff and officers of the Republican Guard division? Are we not going there?"

"A tragedy that. A true tragedy."

"Father?"

"They were struck again. By bombs and bullets from the invading Americans. As they assembled at the meeting place to wait upon my arrival. Can you imagine it? Twice in one day?" He shook his head and made the sound of *tsk-tsk*. "Such a tragedy."

"Father? When did this happen?"

Saddam looked at his watch. "In about ten minutes."

Night Runner found the grizzly den right where Alice Walks With Bears told him to look. It figured. All that time in taverns. First as the fool. The happy drunk, buying for his friends though he had no friends until he began setting up the bar. Then as the madman. Sliding down the declension from wet-lipped folly to stabbing wit to F-tipped sarcasm to one-armed kick-fighting. Until finally, when he had no friends left nor fights nor foes, the last stop. The gulping man. Gulping every breath as if it were his last, gulping every drink as if it were his first. The drowning man. Drowning first his shrinking body, then his festering soul in hard-edged spirits, the cheap stuff, not because he couldn't afford it on his medical pension but because the cheaper, the sharper the bite.

Sharp drink, dull senses. He would not have been too unhappy to find his senses had failed him in full today. Maybe get him lost in the storm. Not find the den.

But no, there it was, just as Alice had painted it in his imagination. The entrance.

She would know where to find any and all bear dens along the Rocky Mountain Front. Why couldn't he choose a mentor who walked with chipmunks?

The blizzard swirling around him as he built a fire inside a sweat lodge. He sat as far away from the super-heated rocks as he could. He brewed and drank the herbal tea she'd given him. In the Folger's can she'd given him. Wondering if she'd ever used it as a spittoon. He found the tea aromatic, sweet, strong. He waited for it to take hold of him. Nothing. He should have brought a flask. A sip of vodka would go good now.

Alice. She'd be pissed that he even thought of drink. She was right to be angry, of course. He had made himself a cripple by thinking it so. By pickling himself in liquor. By letting his muscles atrophy. By letting his warrior's senses erode.

She had told him what he must do. She could not tell him the outcome. Her visions as confused as his consciousness.

Hell, he didn't have to do this. He could drink the tea, have a sweat. Take a nap. Go home. Catch a plane. Who in their right mind would do as this doctor prescribed, the Indian version of Granny Clampett?

Except. Some things—and people—you had to accept

at face value. People like Alice Walks With Bears. He'd had faith in her before. She had worked her magic on him. Besides.

She knew things. Unaccountably. Only three people in the world besides his marine mates knew what happened to his hand.

Spangler. Easy to account for. For he had just told him about the loss of the hand.

Himself. Easiest to account for. For he had lived the loss.

And Alice. Unaccountably. For she had dreamed it. She called it, spot-on. The striped mountain lion in the black forest. The tiger in Vietnam.

For two years, he had doubted himself and his culture and especially those in his culture so close to the original ways. People like Alice.

No more. Alice. She knew things about him.

She sold him because he wanted to believe her. If it was true what she thought in her dream, that he might die today? Just as well. Just as well today as any other day. And if he did not die, he would join Spangler's band of warriors and go fight. Maybe die in battle.

Die as an ancient warrior in a ritual of the bear?

Or die as a modern Delta warrior in *Eye-raq?*

Either way, with dignity. More dignity than to drown in a bottle.

Karim-Assad rode the rest of the way in silent awe of Saddam. Could he, Karim-Assad, ever be so ruthless? He felt so inadequate to the task. Too huge, the distance too far, the climb too steep. He tried out a wish that Uday and Qusay would return unharmed. Did he want to go back to being a simple food tester leading a simple, safe, happy life?

No. He did not want to go back.

There was no going back in any case. Once the evil brothers learned that he had been named third in line, he was a threat to them. They would find a way. Within a week, he would indeed taste poison, in or out of his old job.

The taxi finally stopped. Not in a palace courtyard, though. Rather, in an alley in downtown Baghdad. One of Saddam's bodyguards got out without a word and ran up the stairs to a second-floor apartment. He stood on a rickety balcony and gave a hand signal. The driver waved back and turned to Saddam, who remained inert, leaning against the door of the taxi.

Saddam gave that flip of his hand to Karim-Assad.

"You go," the driver said, a note of glee in his voice.

"To announce me," Saddam said.

"Go," the driver said. "Announce the president of Iraq."

Sneaking out of the palace. Driving through Baghdad in disguise of clothing and taxi. Only to announce the president? There was only one way to find logic in it. He was about to die.

He climbed the steps and stood outside the door. The second bodyguard grasped him by the upper arm. He growled into Karim-Assad's ear, "Keep your mouth shut, little girl." He yanked the door open. "Not a word." He tossed Karim-Assad into the dark room. From outside the doorway, the bodyguard bellowed, "Your president!"

Karim-Assad could see only shapes and shadows in the darkness. He closed his eyes and waited for the bullets to shoot him through and through. He had felt like this before, in his first weeks as food tester, waiting for his throat to clutch, his stomach to cramp after eating samples of Saddam's food.

"Open your eyes."

Karim-Assad did as he was told. To find himself looking across the flame of a single candle into a pair of harsh, glittering eyes. Next to Saddam's, the most frightening eyes he had ever seen. The man behind those eyes would kill him. He would not need to derive any pleasure from it. Given the order, he would just execute it—and his victim. All that was plain in the eyes. This was a soldier practiced in the art.

"Who are you?" the man asked.

Other flames snapped to life around the room, first butane cigarette lighters, then candles. Karim-Assad did not break eye contact with the man in front of him, but he still saw perhaps twenty sets of eyes behind those lights. As the room lightened, he got a fuller picture. Rough men, but not slovenly. Most of them stood against the wall, their arms folded. Some crouched, sitting on their heels. They carried a mix of weapons, mostly new, but a few ancient. Automatic pistols and curved swords, hand grenades for imploding bodies, and hammers for crushing skulls.

"You may call me Karim-Assad. I am Saddam's nephew, although he calls me son. I come to announce him."

The man smiled, not a mocking smile, but one of admiration that Karim-Assad did not quake in the presence of his band of soldiers. Karim-Assad saw it for what it was, a sign of respect. Other men did not understand that once you got over the initial shock of eating every meal with the prospect of poisoning, little else in the world could make you cower.

The man took a step back, easing the threat of his presence.

"Announce him then."

"And so I shall." Karim-Assad narrowed his eyes at the soldier. "First I must know. To whom?"

"Mohammed Bandi-Sadr, captain of your president's Desert Wolves."

Night Runner's sweat lodge was more than eight feet tall on the outside. Because he had no skins to throw over a frame to trap the heat and steam, because he had to use stacks of pine branches to keep in the steam and to keep out the blizzard. Inside though, it was only three feet tall, in one spot. He sat beneath that spot, his head in the little cupola of the rough, fragrant ceiling.

The heat was stifling, of course. To sweat out the toxic elements in him, to numb his senses, to allow the spiritual element in him to break through the noise of his physical self.

Alice had blessed a braid of sweet grass from the Sweet Pine Hills, called the Sweet Grass Hills by white men. He put one end of the grass rope against the hot stones to release its fragrance, a natural sweet incense. He broke off twigs of sage and baked them, too. To fill his lungs with its pungent medicine. At first he made steam by tossing handfuls of snow onto the rocks. But before long the heat from inside the lodge melted ice and snow on the branches, and water droplets kept up a hot cloud inside the lodge. The tea, though. Still no effect on him.

In barely ten minutes, Night Runner wanted to bail out of the lodge. At least he wanted to lie down to escape the heat. He could, too, but what was the point in that? The point was not to stay cool inside the lodge. The point was to bake himself clean and to achieve a higher awareness. Nobody but he would know whether he tried to cheat Alice's prescription. But he would know.

So he sat and baked until he grew dizzy. From the heat, not the tea. He checked his watch, the only thing he wore besides silk briefs. Not exactly original plains warrior fashion, but not proscribed, either.

At thirty minutes he crawled outside and staggered to a spot on the lee side of the lodge, where the snow had drifted two feet deep. He knelt to cup handfuls of snow, one handful at a time trapped against the stump of his left arm, then throwing the powder into the air, showering himself in a frozen mist that melted instantly on his hot body.

In a few minutes he felt clean. Clean of body, keen of mind. For the first time in nearly a year, he felt as if he had a chance to turn his life around. For once he felt as if the rest of his body was not necessarily going to follow that hand down the gullet of the tiger.

He looked around him. There was that bear's den. Go in, she'd told him. Then again. Why? He felt purified already. Reason enough to take another sweat, perhaps to feel even better. Give it a second thought.

Besides, Alice had told him to expect a vision, and none had come. A dizzy spell was hardly the same thing.

He crawled back into the sweat lodge. *More sweat, boss. Go into a bear's den? No way.*

Ramsey Baker picked up on the first ring.

"Ramsey, Roscoe Spangler here." Spangler resisted the urge to say: *Guess where I'm calling from?* "Got a minute?" *An F-16 at thirty thou, man; can you get your head around it?*

"General. Calling to catch up on old times?"

"No. Well, I guess you know better than that."

"I know that every time I hook up with you, somebody kicks my ass."

Spangler cleared his throat. What the hell could he say to that?

"What do you have in mind this time? Hanging? Firing squad? Beheading?"

Spangler made the best chuckle he could, a wet snort. At least try to show he was a good sport. He knew a thing or two about faking the good sport.

"I'd like to come up and visit for a day." *All joking aside.* "Talk to you about a job."

"Don't bother."

Spangler's heart stopped. "Don't bother coming up? Or don't bother talking to you about a job?"

"Neither, General."

"Don't you even want to hear me out?" Spangler heard his own voice squeak. *If begging was what it took to bring back the only good guy ever to get next to bin Laden—*

"Don't need to hear it."

"At least give me a chance to sell you."

"I'm sold."

"Hear me out. I can—*What?*"

"When and where do you want me?"

"Don't you want to know when or where the mission is?"

"I read the papers, General. Watch the CNN."

"Don't you want to know the details?"

"I already have two questions on the table."

"Savannah, Georgia. Tomorrow."

"Address and phone number?"

Spangler told him.

Baker read them back.

"You got it, now—"

"I'm good to go."

"Don't you want to know the deal?"

"Deal?"

"The money? Terms? Timetable?"

"Is it better than the pay for an army captain on medical retirement?"

"Way better. I'm thinking—"

"See you in Savannah."

The line went dead.

The Desert Wolves? Karim-Assad went weak in the knees. These were no tin soldiers of the palace guard.

These were no mere sadists in the secret police who might drag a hapless soul from Saddam's guest bedrooms into the basement of the palace to taunt and torture. The Desert Wolves? Karim-Assad had heard of them, in fact. Not as a living, breathing band of soldiers. But as a legend. The Desert Wolves, half men, half carnivores, mythical creatures conjured up by the Saladins to frighten foreigners, Kurds, and desert outlaws.

"The Desert Wolves?" Karim-Assad said, his voice tiny.

Bani-Sadr tossed his head. In scorn, it seemed to Karim-Assad. "You don't know of the Desert Wolves? A so-called son of Saddam?"

"I know of you only from fairy tales."

"You will soon know of us in great detail, by our deeds. While the rest of the army runs around in circles, running up each others' asses, the Desert Wolves will first find the sons of Saddam." *The true sons,* in the tone of it. "Then we will carry out our vengeance on tonight's invaders. Then we will disappear, and you will not hear of us again until the president needs us to act on his behalf again."

"As I now do."

Every soldier in the room stood to attention, filling Karim-Assad's nostrils with a rush of stale body odor.

Only Karim-Assad moved. He turned to face Saddam, thinking that a second false face had been thrust into the room, one of several doubles that he knew of.

But no, this was Saddam. Karim-Assad recognized him by the broken button on his hunting jacket and the peculiar wrinkles on one breast pocket flap, like pricked dog ears.

Yet it was not the same man. Slumped again. In the presence of such fighters, such legends, how could he do that?

"I regret to relay a radio report, a message I just now received from the new commander of my 100th Republican Guards Division. They have found the car—my sons' armored car. Ambushed, burning, on its side in a wadi. Apparently the men in the front seat, a driver and bodyguard, escaped. Four bodies in the backseat. I assume two of them are my sons."

Karim-Assad's heart leapt like a rabbit, nearly thumping out of his chest.

Saddam's body slumped lower, as if he would topple.

Nobody dared move but Karim-Assad. He stepped to Saddam and took him by the elbow, leading him to the only chair in the room, clearly set up so that he might brief these men on their mission. He hoped the trembling in his arms did not reveal itself through his grip on Saddam. In case it did, he found words to cover the quaking.

"Father, I am shaken. How terrible is your news." *Uday and Qusay dead! Oh joy!* He was now truly a son of Saddam. *The only son!*

Saddam put an elbow on the arm of the chair and cradled his brow in one hand, his eyes downcast.

Karim-Assad took charge, biting down on his smile so it would not show, roughing his voice to sound as if he were grieving instead of celebrating inside. He would not allow his eyelids to blink, letting the eyeballs dry out so they would fill up with tears.

"You may sit down," he told the Desert Wolves. Except for Bani-Sadr, they did as they were told. Nobody in this group saw him as an idiot now, not even the paralyzed bodyguards from the taxi. That settled it for him. He could lead men, direct them with his own hands. If given the chance, he might lead a country.

Bani-Sadr said, "May I speak?"

Karim-Assad looked to Saddam, still downcast. Then he saw Bani-Sadr was asking him. He gave a quick nod before his surprise could show. This desert fighter to rival all the world's sand devils would ask him to speak? The world had tilted on its axis. Toward Karim-Assad.

"May we still have the president's authority to track down the invaders and take our revenge?"

"Yes," Saddam said, his face still shaded by his hand.

"Do you want them dead? Or alive?"

Saddam's hand came away from his face, became a fist, and slammed into the arm of the chair. "Bring me those murderers of my two sons," he said in a low tone. "So I may kill them ten times over."

"Of course." Bani-Sadr took a deep breath. "These are perhaps Delta Force. Or Israeli commandos. If so, they will never surrender. They will fight to the death."

Saddam gave a single tiny nod. "Then give them their death wish. Then bring their heads to me. So I may show all the world the fate of those who invade the sovereign state of Iraq."

Karim-Assad covered his face as if weeping, for he could barely contain his smile.

Inside the sweat lodge, Night Runner felt it coming like the onset of a nap. A picture inside his head coming to life and infusing his body with its own reality. He heard the sounds first. Irregular beating of an imperfect drum. Then he saw himself standing outside his body, watching himself as a spectator. Living in spasms of time.

Now gazing at the rocks. Now standing outside the sweat lodge. He saw himself. In silk shorts, black. Ridiculous.

An elk calf followed the sound of its hoof beats into the clearing. Okay, so that was a vision. Had to be. Elk did not blunder into a man standing in the open. Besides, the elk was struggling too hard for the just six inches of snow it pawed at. *Oh. There.* Behind the calf, Night Runner saw the problem. A wolf yellow as the one whose skin lay over Alice's shoulders, but blended to gray to black along the spine. The wolf clung to a rear quarter of the calf. The calf dragged its killer. Until. The wolf pulled the hindquarters down and held on. The calf beat a tattoo with his front legs, tossing its head as if trying to swim out of a whirlpool. A second wolf. A third joined in the kill. They took hold of the calf's abdomen, near the flank where the skin is thin and soft, staying clear of those front hooves. They tore at the skin, pulling off strips of hide, exposing thin sheets of muscle. The teeth shredded those sheets, exposing the balloon of stomach and coils of gut.

He saw himself shake his head. So realistic. For a vision. Had to be a vision. He was nearly naked and unarmed. Had to be.

In seconds it was over. It happened at the point where the calf must have known it could no longer survive its wounds, even if the wolves gave up and trotted off. The wolves began their feast in earnest. The calf simply lay down to die. The wolves tore deeper into the soft spots, seeking the blood-rich organs. What did they care that their prey had not died? The calf was down and warm and bloody and that was their way.

He heard Alice's voice. In his head. Telling him to act now. His prompter giving him his cue from the wings. Telling him to get into the vision. Giving him his lines. So the Night Runner having the vision gave the lines to the other Night Runner, the one in the vision.

That Night Runner called to the wolves in the language of his people. "Go away, Little Brothers. Go away for a while. Thank you for your kill. I will take what I need and leave you the rest."

He brushed the snow off his pile of clothes at the entrance to the sweat lodge and dug for his hunting knife, a folding piece with a locking blade, the sharpest of blades.

When he turned back to the wolf pack, he saw that they had ignored him. It brought a wry smile to his lips. Another imperfection in Alice's dreams. In her story of the vision, they yielded the elk calf to Night Runner without protest.

Not a glitch that Night Runner could not handle. He leaned over his fire pit where he had heated the large stones for his sweat lodge. In the burned-out space, still warm, he picked up a handful of rocks and cradled them in his left hand against his ribs. This was how he knew the Night Runner of his vision from himself. The Night Runner of his vision had two hands, while he had but the one.

With his first toss, he bounced a golf ball–sized stone off the skull of the largest wolf. The alpha female. She yelped and ran away from the carcass, snapping at one of her sisters as she went by, perhaps blaming the sister for throwing rocks, silly as that was. It was a dream, after all.

Night Runner yelled at the wolves, commanding them to leave in his native tongue. The alpha female turned back and snarled. The others skulked behind the carcass, unwilling to go, using it as a shield. Night Runner arced three more stones their way and got two more hits. The wolves moved back to the edge of the clearing, giving way grudgingly.

Night Runner the dreamer gave control to Night Runner in the dream. That Night Runner stepped up to the carcass. He thanked the calf for giving herself up to his dream. And then, not gently because gentle was not possible, but swiftly, he put his blade to the calf's throat and delivered her from the agony of being eaten alive by wolves.

He looked up and saw that the pack had closed the distance to him by half, not willing to tolerate a thief of their meal. Three more stones and another hit, this time on the alpha male, pushed them away, this time into the margin of the woods.

Night Runner kept his eyes on their eyes, yellow, jealous, and fierce as he knelt and opened the upper belly of the dead animal. He knew the anatomy of a kill. In only a few strokes, he had pulled the calf's liver free of the carcass. He picked up his knife and cut it free in a gush from veins and arteries and ducts.

So much for the easy part. He set the liver and knife aside and washed his steaming hands in the snow, folded his bloody knife, stuck it into the band of his shorts, and stood, shuddering.

Not from the cold, not the cold, although it was below zero. No, because he was afraid of what he had to do. Even in his dream he was afraid.

But do it he must. The Night Runner in the dream had no choice in it. Night Runner gave him no choice. Better the dream Night Runner than himself.

He gave the orders. The other Night Runner took the liver, slippery and hard to handle even with two hands, to the deadfall, the anteroom to the den's door. He knelt and laid it beneath the logs, at the entrance to a tunnel ten feet long. He should give the guy a break. Let him leave his offering and walk away. But no, that was not the dream that Alice had given.

He turned back to face the wolves, to make sure that they had not closed on him instead of the elk carcass. Now that he was bloody. Now that he had knelt down. They might take him for just another prey animal, a crippled, hairless elk calf, slathered with blood. *The better to eat you, my dear.*

But they were gone, every single yellow eye. Not like wolves to give up a fresh kill so easily. Then again, odder things could happen in a dream. And this was certainly a dream. For the Night Runner in it had the two hands, after all.

The taxi ride from the center of Baghdad was somber. Saddam sat wrapped in his grief, the bodyguards in dense silence. Karim-Assad rode ill at ease. On one hand he felt a glow in him, a warmth, an awe of his new station, but he could not give in to it. There was that other, ominous sense.

The quick, dark things in his head. Uday and Qusay. He need not worry about best-case scenarios. If they were dead, he was Saddam's heir. Simple as that. Oh, he would have rivals, other, nearer cousins. Brothers-in-law with more power, those in government. Saddam's half brothers, those he knew about, and those who might surface when he was ready to turn over power. Who knew? More and worse sons of Saddam Hussein might turn up from the slums of Baghdad and Tikrit. He had no practice in holding onto power—for he had never had any. At Saddam's side he might learn how to gain, hold, wield power. He might master the art of keeping others at bay. If he could sit at the hand of Saddam for a time. The living school of the dictator.

But what of the worst-case? What if Uday and Qusay had not died? They were the danger. If the Wolves found them, they would hear that Saddam let Karim-Assad sit at his right hand at the table this very night. The high staff would rush to report it. Either one of the brothers— probably both—would see to it that Karim-Assad went back to work as food tester.

Within a week he would indeed, die of poisoning. Then the entire kitchen staff would die as suspects. The tin soldiers who guarded the kitchen staff for incompetence.

Saddam had blessed such ruthless excess before. Karim-Assad had heard him say it: "Kill ninety-nine innocents if need be, to get at the guilty one. The ninety-nine should have come forward to report that one." And what if none was guilty? "Kill one hundred innocents, and no one man in the next ten thousand will ever risk guilt again."

Uday had already killed one food taster, Kamil Hanna JaJo, another relative. Kamil had made the fatal error of introducing Saddam to a new wife and one who would bear another Hussein half brother, Ali.

"Father." The word was out of Karim-Assad's mouth before he could contain it.

Saddam looked up, his eyes weepy. Karim-Assad was wary. Grief and rage. The two were but a blink apart in Saddam's heart. But he had to be bold, too. He'd cast his die. Now he must wager all before the cube stopped its roll.

"I want to join the Desert Wolves."

Night Runner began a three-legged crawl. His left hand held the hot, slick liver to his chest as he moved into the deadfall. He liked the new idea of a left hand and dug his fingers into the liver.

At the end of the rough wooden tunnel he caught the scent of the bear, rancid, strong, ominous. Very real, for a dream.

This is what had driven the dream wolves away. Of course. They thought him a hairless bear. A bear had taken kills from them before.

At the deep, dark end of the tunnel, a brook lay in ice patches among the rocks. Beyond it was a sluice in the gravel slope, a half-pipe of frozen ground.

Night Runner crawled up the slope. To a slit in the slope. The mouth of the den. Narrow. He felt an oppressive warmth. He could not tell. Was it his own blood boiling? Or the air from inside the cave? Either way, not a good warmth. He looked in. The sluice turned down, into the slit. Into the hillside. Into the blackness. Into the bear's den.

Okay. That was enough. Time to wake up. Let the two-handed Night Runner go the rest of the way on his own. *I'll wait for you in the sweat lodge, marine. Report back*

when you're done. Details, my man, give me details. He'd
need details in case Alice gave him a pop quiz.

The two-handed Night Runner was okay with the mission. He pushed the liver ahead of him into the slit. It fell
away. Night Runner heard it hit bottom with a wet slap.

Okay, good enough. The bear is fed. Why sacrifice the
two-handed man? Why send him in? The bear would be in
and out of sleep all winter. It would awaken, if not today,
then next week. It would find the rich meal at the bottom
of the drop, perhaps not even fully frozen. It might feast
on it, or it might not. Who knew? Certainly not Alice.

Even so. The two-handed version of himself slid into
the slit.

Night Runner decided to follow. Not personally of
course. But in the dream. Roll with it. Give the guy some
moral support.

The two-handed Night Runner could not see, except
with his fingers. Eight fingers, two thumbs.

*Go on, my man. What do you see? Tell me what you see
with those fingers. What do you feel, marine?*

Shoulder blades and potbelly scraping on the ceiling
and floor of the tunnel. The gravel unrolling the waistband
of his silk briefs. Palms scraping on pebbly aggregate.
Fingers probing the silky black for the gel touch of warm
liver.

Finding a soft warmth, recoiling from it.

The warmth of deep fur.

Cold feet. He felt that, too. The tunnel about five feet
long. His feet and ankles still in the air. A chill. Those
wolves. He had left a blood trail. Now his feet stuck out. A
flash on the wolves bringing the calf down. From behind.
Eating it alive.

The urge to draw his feet in. The fear of falling . . .

Into the bear.

Trapped.

Trapped in a dream. Unable to go backward. Unwilling to go forward. Paralyzed in a living coma. The worst of all nightmares.

No. Worse than the worst.

He was no longer giving orders to the two-handed Night Runner. He was the only man in the vision. He was the only man in the cave.

The driver barked when Karim-Assad asked Saddam to join the Desert Wolves. The driver tried to disguise a fit of laughs under a fit of coughs. The other bodyguard hid his face behind both hands. The coughs took hold of him, too.

"The Desert Wolves?" Saddam turned a tiny smile to Karim-Assad. "My son. The training. The trials. And still you might not pass muster."

"I would spend my all in the effort."

"They might well not accept you."

"You could order it."

The fits in the front seat started up again.

Saddam took a case from a cubby behind the driver's seat. By the light of a tiny lamp, he took out his contact lenses and put on a pair of black frames. His eyes floated like huge black marbles in the thick lenses. "Why would I order it? I need you by my side. I need the Desert Wolves to be wild. A novice might slow them down."

"I will train hard."

"I do not doubt your will."

"I want to learn like you."

"There you have it. Stay by my side. Let me teach you my skills."

"I should learn as you did."

Saddam shook his head, confused that he had to argue at all.

"You fought in the streets. You had wounds."

Saddam smiled broadly. Karim-Assad saw that, for now, his two sons were not on his mind.

"That's true." Saddam shook his head. "No, I would worry too much. Perhaps I could give you a tank unit. Promote you to division commander after a decent time. Within a year, if you like."

A snicker from the front.

"Father, I don't want to tell other men where to park their tanks and how to fight them. I want to fight myself." He held up his hands. "I want to kill with these. What better place than among the Desert Wolves?"

"But that might take years." Saddam gave a little smile. "From what I have seen in these last days, I think it might take much less time to learn to command tanks in my regular army." He flapped his hand in that wave that said, *No more.*

Karim-Assad knew. One more step was into a land of peril. He took it.

"How else can I know?" he said, bowing his head in what he thought was respect. "Send me out with them on this mission. Let me learn." He folded his hands and looked up into deadly eyes. "Let me see with my own eyes whether Uday and Qusay are alive." *Let me see them dead.*

Saddam bit his upper lip, the triangles of his eyelids softened. "I am truly touched. To seek my sons? To perhaps go into combat?" Saddam smiled warily, wavered, gave it a second thought, wagged his head. "Too perilous."

"As is fighting in the streets."

Saddam stared at the young man a long time. He was torn. One thing for a sycophant to curry favor. Saddam saw that every day—no, every hour. Nobody ever came to Saddam without wants, if only to live for one more hour.

But this? Asking to go into battle in one of his most fierce units? Begging for the chance to die? Nobody ever asked for such a thing.

So Saddam did not trust it. He was trying to see the angle of self-interest in it.

Karim-Assad nudged him again. "Don't decide now," he said. "Sleep on it. Then send me out to observe on this mission. If I do not shame myself, say yes. I rest my fate with the report of Bani-Sadr."

Saddam set his lips. A twitch of a nod. He might relent.

"If I do not disgrace the Desert Wolves. If I do not eat my vomit. Let me train with them." Yes, there it was, a little nod. "Let me earn my own way. All I ask is that you give me a spot." A full nod. "I will prove myself." Saddam's head bobbing. "Or I will fail."

Karim-Assad saw that he had won before Saddam spoke.

"I will make the call to Bani-Sadr," Saddam said.

"Thank you, Father."

"We are here," the driver said. The taxi pulled into a service gate. Guards stood stiff as the driver pulled level with the post. The driver tossed his head at the backseat. Saddam looked the guard in the eye, his face his pass.

"The garage below ground," Saddam ordered.

He turned to Karim-Assad. "I have a gift for you when you go with the Desert Wolves." He put away his contact lens case. From the same cubby he drew two matched pistols with grips of an exotic purple wood, eagles carved into the wood and enlaid in gold in the slides. He handed one of them to Karim-Assad.

"Take this weapon with you. It is a gift from the German minister of defense to me. Carry it with you on your mission. Use it against our enemies."

"It is loaded." Saddam pulled back the slide with his left hand and let it slam home a round. "A first lesson in using the pistol. Do as I do."

Karim-Assad sent a round home, trying to imitate Saddam's practiced moves, sure and quick.

Saddam reached over. "This is the safety." He flipped the switch on Karim-Assad's weapon. "It is ready to fire."

Saddam pushed the muzzle of Karim-Assad's gun away.

Karim-Assad cringed.

"It is not wise to point a weapon at the president of Iraq, my son. People have been killed for less than that."

Karim-Assad blinked for three counts, the corners of his mouth drawn down. "I am so sorry, Father."

The taxi came to a stop.

"No matter, that is simply lesson two."

"I will not err in that way again."

"Good. Now, here is lesson three. Do as I do."

Saddam raised his pistol. Karim-Assad raised his.

Saddam shot one bodyguard behind his left ear.

Half a second later, Karim-Assad's pistol went off at the right ear of the driver.

Two heads snapped forward. Two clouds of blood burst against the inside of the bulletproof windshield.

Night Runner knew the way out. All he had to do was holler. Wake up. Escape to reality. Try something else. *What? Throw the liver and run? Or just run?*

Run. That made sense. *Get dressed and go home. Forget this. Then call Spangler. Beg off. Forget Iraq.*

What kind of crazy ritual was this anyhow? A crazy woman had told him to go kill himself by bothering a drowsy, never-quite-all-that-asleep bear. What the hell was he thinking? *A crazy woman!*

Ah, well, hell. What was the big deal? It was nothing but a dream anyhow. *Go with it. Play it out.*

Funny. Night Runner caught himself laughing. *Screw it.* He let himself into the den. With one good hand he braked himself. With the other hand, he steered clear of the bear.

He pressed against a side wall of a cave. He was surprised at the warmth of it. His feet still ached from the cold outside. Cold feet, literally, to go with the figurative ones.

He lay still awhile to catch his breath. Let his senses adjust. Very real, this dream. His nose full of the dank, heavy smell of bear breath, bear farts, bear body odor. His eyes began to see things in the dim shaft by the light that found its way down the tunnel. A sparkle of the still-wet liver. A mound of darkness darker than the rest. A very big darkness at that.

Sound. No, sounds. Slow breathing. One, two, three breaths. *Shit!*

Three different breaths. Three darker bulks among the shadows. Three bears.

Damn her! Damn you!

Dammit, Alice! Yes, you told me the bear would have twin cubs. I was thinking the hairless, rat-sized cubs of February. You didn't say hundred-plus-pound yearlings!

To which she would say only: *And did you share a meal with them?*

Shit!

He pulled his knife from the band of his black silk briefs and opened it with his teeth, tasting the blood of liver. He kept from rolling into the griz with his other good hand. That left hand. It was the only thing that kept him in this dream. That hand. He never appreciated it when he had it. Never. He said a prayer, asking for forgiveness that he did not appreciate all his faculties and limbs when he had them. And another prayer to ask forgiveness that he had let liquor diminish the faculties that remained to him.

He stabbed the lump of liver, pulled it toward him, cut a wedge—quickly, for this was the last step of Alice's instructions. Turning the knife so he would not put his eye out, he picked up the wedge in his fingers and put it into his mouth. The liver was warm, rich and energizing. He thought to spit the grit that came with his taste of the elk, but decided to take no chance on waking the bears. He swallowed the chunk of gel without chewing. Grit and all, it went down easy as a shot of vodka.

There, Alice, I shared a bite of liver with the bears. Done.

He folded the knife. He slipped it back into his waistband. He shifted his feet to go. Five feet to crawl. Five feet to consciousness. He stopped. *Hell, this is only a dream.* He should just wake up in the sweat lodge. *Forget this drill.*

Awaken. Go outside. Go home.

He blinked his eyes. Once. Twice. Three times. But each time, he was still in the vision. He could not blink himself out of it.

He put away his knife. He put both hands to his face. He rubbed at his eyes, trying to bring himself out. If he could only escape it with both hands.

Both hands scratched at his face. Both sets of knuckles ground into his eyes. But he did not awaken. When he opened his eyes, he was still in the den. But—

No longer alone.

A shadow. A shadow blocked the light to the den.

Those damned wolves. *Alice!* Did she plant this twist? What did it mean? To be trapped between bears and wolves? Certainly he did not have to worry about wolves coming in here. Not even in a vision would a wolf dare enter the cave of a grizzly bear.

Still. How was he going to get out?

He was tempted to slap his face. Both cheeks with both hands. To bring himself out of this fearful, joyful moment.

The light blinked out. He listened hard: to the sound of gravel falling down the tunnel, to the sound of a body scraping into the space.

Not a wolf after all. *A bear? Another bear?*

Come on, Alice. Play fair.

Nothing made sense. Then again, nothing was supposed to make sense. *Right?* It was a dream. Only a dream. *Remember?*

The appearance of Heavy Runner confirmed it.

Poole walked near the rear of the file of Delta men. They humped it north, away from the road, toward Baghdad. The team stuck to the long shadows cast by the rising sun over the east bank of a wadi.

He felt better after they'd made a mile from the road. That put them out of danger of the Raqis spotting them from any of the convoys grinding back and forth. A perpetual dust cloud, sometimes thin, sometimes thick, hung over the river of talc. The Raqs'd be lucky to see the rig in front of them on that road.

Their only danger for now would come from above. Helicopters plied the skies in every direction, mostly but not always following the roads at low altitude, staying out of the dust cloud.

He gave Solis command of the march. So he could think. He had to noodle the strategic problems. Two in particular. The sons of Satan.

Two Delta men to each. The man in front of Qusay led him by a short tether tied to his flex-cuffed hands, while the man behind kept a loose rein on a tether at his neck. If they needed to put him on the ground, they could throw him like a roped steer.

Uday was a problem of another kind and degree. Because of his gimp leg.

Foucault, ever the MacGyver of the group, had seen the problem coming. When the team un-assed the flatbed, he took two items of OEM along, two five-foot sections of the twenty-foot aluminum ramrod that screwed together to swab the bore of the tank cannon. He detailed two men of about the same height and the same lack of enthusiasm for their jobs. They taped one ramrod section under each armpit of the taller of the Hussein brothers. Then, as they trekked across the desert, each man had the ends of the ramrods on his shoulders. The makeshift litter allowed them to take some of the weight off Uday's bum leg. The litter carriers didn't like it. "Sonofabitch is going to drag his feet, sure as hell," said one.

So Foucault cut a switch from a desert shrub. He gave it to the man on the poles behind Uday. "Like driving a hog at the county fair," he said. Uday got the point as well. The first time he stumbled he earned a sharp twitch on the ear. From then on he carried his weight well enough to avoid the switch.

Poole hated to do it, but he split up the team. He was with half the Delta group, the Uday and Qusay detail. A Hole-in-the-Wall gang. This detail set out for a line of huge rocks in the desert about two hours away. A place to hide.

He left behind a smaller detail. Barret's. To create a fake trail in case the Raqs stopped the semi. They would backtrack to try to find the Delta team. Barret was to ensure they found the fake, if they found a trail at all. Once that was done Barret would catch up.

Taking the truck. That was good. That had put the team thirty miles from the attack site.

The driver might make ten or twenty miles more before getting stopped at a checkpoint. He did the math in a hurry. Fifty miles. Pi r-squared. That made more than 7,500 square miles the Iraqis had to search. A good number. Each night they could expand the radius. Stay hid till D-day. By then the Raqs'd have too much chaos on their hands to keep up a good search.

Solis led the team toward the black basalt boulders, cubes and haystacks scattered on the desert like the liar's dice of giants. The map showed that they were within two miles of an oasis.

They could hide out by day and send a detail for water by night until the real war began.

The bombs and Tomahawks'd shut down Saddam's jammers. Put in a call for helicopters. Get pulled out sooner rather than later. Hole up on a carrier. Debrief the intel types. Get back into the war. Kick some Iraqi ass. A good plan. Except for the one twist. That his odds of pulling it off were about as realistic as winning the lottery.

Heavy Runner. Night Runner's guardian angel on half a dozen Force Recon missions. His ancestor from ancient warrior stock. Heavy Runner, who had tried to make peace with the white man, one of the few Blackfeet chiefs who dared. One who lost his life for the effort. Shot through with a .45-caliber bullet. Killed in winter.

Now here in the bear cave. Here now.

The man who had come to Night Runner to lead him out of the valley of the shadow of death time and again.

He never expected to see Heavy Runner again. Not after he started up with the drink. Not after he felt so sorry for himself.

And now here, Heavy Runner. Heavy Runner had crawled down into this tunnel to appear to him. This was the vision. Heavy Runner's return. It all made sense now. Heavy Runner here to purify him, to lead him away, to— *no*?

Heavy Runner shook his head. He was not here for any of those things?

He looked at the slit in the slope. Still dark. Still the noise of gravel dribbling in.

Night Runner opened his mouth.

Heavy Runner put a finger to Night Runner's lips. So real, the finger smelled of the perfume of smoked meat.

Then the vision went sour.

Heavy Runner. The man who would be his guardian

angel. Heavy Runner did the most wicked thing to his descendent son of a son of a son of warriors.

Heavy Runner leaped upon the largest of the bears, whooping, shaking her awake.

How could this be? Heavy Runner? Siccing the bear on him?

This was the wrong dream, wrong vision. His spiritual kin would not betray him. Would he? Not even in a vision. Would he?

The grizzly came awake with a huff. She rolled in place. She bellowed. Loud enough to hurt his ears. The yearling cubs came awake, keening in surprise.

He opened his mouth to scream. Screaming would bring him awake. Bring him out of this nightmare.

But on the inhale, he smelled it.

The ugly, earthy sweet fragrance of alcohol oxidizing from a man's pores. *Sneaks Low!*

Et tu, Alice?

Letting that bastard into his vision?

The dream jerked into fast motion.

Grunting. A woof. The roar of a griz in the attack. Night Runner felt his body crushed against the gravel wall of the cave. A soft crush, the back of the bear pinning him there. A sudden light. Screaming. Heavy Runner kneeling by the slit. Beckoning.

Come!

Night Runner wanting to call out: *I can't, I'm trapped.*

Heavy Runner hearing his thoughts. Heavy Runner reaching out to slap the bear on the snout.

The bear shifted its weight.

Night Runner sprang into the slit of light and out. His knees hurt, his ribs scraped, his toes and fingers—all ten digits—barely could get a purchase, but he kept scrambling, trying to get back out of the stinking warmth and into the cold. He rolled and came to rest beneath the deadfall. He started scrambling away on all fours. He wanted to call out, to holler. In relief. In joy. In fear—to scare the wolves away. But he could not find his voice.

Like any other man chased by bears in dreams, his limbs were heavy. He could not move except in slow motion. He could not even find breath to shout. He kept trying to shout, kept trying to awaken himself.

But the only sound he heard was a scream.

A scream not his own.

He stopped, turned. The head and shoulders were out of the cave. A bloody face. Sneaks Low. Bitten. Torn. Part of his scalp hanging down the front of his face.

Night Runner turned back. To grasp the man by his jacket. To pull him free of the cave.

Except. Sneaks Low wore a mask of hatred, even in pain. He did not care if he died. Not if he could die with a final act of hatred.

Night Runner did not need anyone, man or spirit, dream or reality, to tell him. If he fell into those grasping hands, Sneaks Low would latch on to him.

The three bears would pull Sneaks into their den. Sneaks would pull Night Runner in as well. Into the den. Into hell.

Inch by inch from below, Sneaks Low pulled away. Into the slit. Night Runner's last glimpse into the dim gave him one last glimmer of hatred in those sickly eyes. A hatred stronger than the fear of death. A hatred more powerful than the pain of death.

Two wide smears of yellow. Then a flash of red, bloody nails pulling pebbles out of the frozen ground. Then. Just the slit.

Night Runner came awake in front of his pile of steaming rocks.

Tired, so tired. He looked outside the sweat lodge. Dark. He'd overdone the steam. He had no energy left. He was too tired now to go on with the rest of it. He could never find an elk in the darkness anyhow. Not that he planned to try.

But he was too tired to go home.

He lay down. To sleep. To finding cool comfort on the floor of his sweat lodge. He hoped not to dream.

Tomorrow. Tomorrow he would go home. Call Spangler. Bag the whole deal. Tomorrow.

Karim-Assad was not so shocked at his first act of murder. He had read the nuance, had seen Saddam telegraph his kill. The look, the subtle change in his voice, the intent in his eyes. When his pistol went up, so did Karim-Assad's. He killed his first man.

Saddam's left hand was on the slide of his pistol at once, keeping the muzzle pointed to the front. Karim-Assad eased his grip loose, so Saddam, ever wary, could take it away.

"I will give it back later. It would not be good for you to be seen in my presence with a loaded pistol after shots were fired," Saddam said. He smiled. Karim-Assad could see the relief. Better for Saddam to have the loaded gun in his own hand.

The back-blast had sprayed Saddam's face.

"You did well," Saddam said.

"Thank you." He wiped his own face. His sleeve came away red-stained.

"Better even than I might have dreamed—or even done myself."

Saddam locked the car doors. "The guards will be here in an instant. Do not try to get out of the car." He laughed. "I do not want you shot by accident. In fact, I do not want you to go out with the Desert Wolves to get shot, either."

Karim-Assad opened his mouth to protest.

Saddam shook his head. "Do not worry. You can go. You have proven yourself. In lesson four."

"Father?"

"Never let an inferior laugh at you. If they live to talk about it, others might laugh as well."

A wary guard knocked on the driver's glass. A squad with automatic rifles backed him up.

Saddam opened the window a crack. "He will not answer," he said. "It is I, Saddam Hussein, president of Iraq."

"Are you—?"

"Quite well, thanks to Karim-Assad here. These two in the front seat tried to kill me. Their treachery is rewarded by instant death. My son here, formerly my nephew, saved my life."

Saddam turned to Karim-Assad and winked.

Outside, the guard, an officer, stood at attention.

Saddam lowered the window another few inches.

"Call off your men and stand them in formation. After we get inside the palace, you may have this car taken away. Leave the bodies inside. Burn the car and the men just as they are."

On the way into the palace, Saddam clasped Karim-Assad to him in a one-armed bear hug.

"Clean up, my son. I will make the calls. You will fly to the combat zone with the Desert Wolves." Saddam shook his head. "One last time."

"Father?"

"You don't have to go. You have proven yourself to me already." He wiped a thumb across Karim-Assad's brow, smearing the clots of gore. "You have been bloodied."

"But I do have to go, Father," Karim-Assad said. "The blood stains prove me to you. But I have to prove myself to me."

Saddam wrapped him in a full bear hug and bussed him on both cheeks. When he released him, Karim-Assad saw a blush of the blood spots. And tears. Streaming down Saddam's cheeks, riding the parentheses marks in rivulets into and out of the mustache. Dripping off his neck. Many times the tears he had shed for his natural sons.

"I could not bear to lose a third son."

"I must do my best to bring back my brothers."

Saddam drew back his head.

Even Karim-Assad was amazed at his own ability to spit out such phrases of incredible goat shit and make them sound credible, sincere, spontaneous.

"Go with God, my son," Saddam said with reverence. He hugged Karim-Assad.

Karim-Assad would not release Saddam until his own eyes had begun to burn and fill up.

"For God and country," he said, holding on for his tears to spill. He came to attention. "And for our great Iraq's incarnation of Saladin." He threw up a crisp salute and snapped it off briskly, the slap of his hand on his thigh a sound to match the pistol shot of his first kill on the road to power. The vehemence of the salute at last sent his tears over the dam of his lower eyelids and coursing down his cheeks. "For you, Father."

He turned away, vowing to work on his weeping, to make it as spontaneous as his goat-shit words.

When he awakened, Night Runner knew that he had slept a long time. The dawn seeped into his sweat lodge through the pinholes between pine branches he used as a door. The rocks of his fire were barely warm.

He needed more sleep, a few hours. He needed conditioning, a few weeks. He needed to get his head right, a few months. Perhaps a lifetime to restore a soul.

Outside, in the light, his heart stopped.

At first the snow looked blotched in black in the early light of day. But no. It was red, the fluff tamped down and stained with blood. He saw wolf tracks. And over them the smaller paw prints of coyotes.

The elk calf in his dream? He saw a trail of blood spots leading to the deadfall. He saw where he had crawled in that vision. He was a good enough tracker to see that a second set of footsteps had followed him in—he remembered now. *The wolves!*

The wolves had not abandoned their kill. Someone had pushed them off it. Sneaks? So that part was reality.

Night Runner felt a twinge of shame. In times past, he would have been too sharp. Nobody could ever slip up on him like that. Least of all a drunk.

He saw signs that covered parts of the boot tracks. A man's handprints, knee prints, bare feet. So he was in the reality, too?

He had been into that deadfall and back? But how? He had only the one hand. He checked the prints in the snow. It was his own sign. It was he who had been there before Sneaks Low. And after him.

He looked down at himself. He saw the blood smears on his chest. He saw the scrapes on his knees, and his ribs, he turned his elbows and saw scratches there, scratches that he had gotten inside the tunnel. He searched the waistband of his briefs and found gravel. He opened his knife and knew before he even saw the specks of blood. He tasted the blade. Liver. Reality enough.

He had purified himself after all?

That was no vision?

Could it be?

He checked the tracks at the edge of the deadfall. Sure enough. A boot print going in. A sole print, as a man knelt down. Scrape marks as a man crawled, dragging the toes of his boots. Two hands had crawled up to that cave behind Night Runner.

And only one set of prints had come out. Definitely reali—

His heart stopped.

Two hands! In the vision, he had two hands. And here were two handprints. A right hand, thumb to the inside. A left hand, thumb to the inside. *No way!*

He dared not look down to the end of his arm. He felt the bloody knife in his right hand. He felt a cold chill in his left hand. He wriggled the fingers. *They worked!* He took a look. To see—

Nothing.

Nothing but a stump. Nothing but reality.

That damned phantom hand. Those damned phantom fingers. The part about his left hand. That was the dream, the vision, the fantasy.

Or was it this?

He closed his eyes. He felt the cold. Very real cold.

He closed the fingers of his left hand. Very real.

He lifted his left hand. Put it to his face. Extended his fingers.

Nothing. He opened his eyes.

Nothing.

He felt flat. Got dressed in clothes so cold and stiff they had to be real. He stamped out the handprints in the snow, the left handprints in particular. He turned to walk out of the woods, not knowing whether he was in a state of fantasy or reality, no longer trusting either.

When Spangler introduced them, Ramsey Baker and Robert Night Runner both looked at him in dismay. Shake hands? Forget it. Each had a hand missing, Night Runner his left, Baker his right. What? Shake stump-to-hand? Or hand-to-stump? Hold hands left-to-right?

Finally Night Runner gave Baker his right hand in a fist, and Baker bumped him with the knuckles of his left.

Both then turned high-beam glares on Spangler.

"I couldn't think of a tactful way to mention it," Spangler said, his face awash in red. "I'm not a good mentioner."

Baker shrugged. "You couldn't say, 'Guy you're going to meet only has one hand'?"

"Sorry."

"You're not a good noticer, either," Baker said.

Spangler squinted his watery eyes. "What, you put on some weight?"

"You don't see?" Baker shook his head. "You're kidding, right?"

"You got a fresh haircut? What?"

Baker wasn't about to say.

"All right, then," Spangler said dubiously. "Can we talk terrorism?" He sat on the bed in the motel room he'd rented in Savannah, a suite with a small conference table. He might not see an awkward situation in advance, but he knew his terrorism. His life vest in the rough seas of ordinary human discourse.

He dropped into the five-paragraph field order. He was deep into it when his cell phone vibrated. He stared at it for a full five seconds before picking it up. He just didn't get that many calls at home. This could only be one person, the one who assigned him the phone.

"Yes?"

Spangler pulled the phone away from his face. A string of curse words leaked into the room. He crammed the phone into his head so Baker and Night Runner could not hear it. From a woman no less. For their parts, Baker and Night Runner did not look away. They kept staring, letting him stew in it. *Didn't even think to say: "The guy's only got one hand"?*

He spoke in grunts and murmurs, the only sounds he could get in edgewise. He grimaced at the pair of one-handed men. Now it occurred to him. Finally. Two guys, only two hands between them. Lady Redcoat still berating him.

An image formed. Lady Redcoat stepping into this very room to meet his crack team of two . . . *amputees?* He had never given it a thought. Until he saw them together. *He was going to get the sons of Satan out of Iraq using two guys with only six limbs between them?*

She must never meet these two.

Even with the phone pressed into his ear snatches of

her words escaped into the open air: *gives a shit . . . get your ass . . . now . . . screwed . . . NOW!*

When it hurt his eardrum too much, he pulled away: *out of touch . . . lost . . . ass with both hands . . . war about to start . . . NOW!*

He cupped the receiver against his skull. Who needed ears? Her instructions penetrated his skull well enough. His ears were—

That was it! Ears!

He cupped his hand over the phone and said to Baker. "Your ears. You got your ears fixed."

Baker laughed and shook his head. "Waste of god-damned money, apparently." A birth defect had left him with tree fungi for ears. After Afghanistan, he spent six months and four surgeries to get ears that looked like ears that were merely odd.

Spangler went back to his phone call. He nodded and nodded. He took quick breath after quick breath. Until he finally caught a bit of dead air—

"Put up a Dirty Bird."

The phone stopped sparking and went silent.

"It's like a Predator," he said. "Launch it with a radio transmitter. Fly it over the team and transmit ground to air from Saudi Arabia on a new frequency set."

More white knuckles.

"Then get a Predator—"

Clearing his throat. Taking charge.

"Try the CIA then."

Blinking. Rapid-fire.

"Line of sight. Burst transmissions."

Quick breaths of impatience.

"Well of course you aren't a techie. Get one of the CIA guys."

Quick, deep breath.

"Shut up and listen so I can tell you."

Big grimace.

"Madelaine?"

Lame smile. He held the phone away from his head. "She said I could call her by her first name but never to use—"

The receiver let out a bark for all in the room to hear: "Ten seconds."

He talked fast. "You only get one shot at this. If you try it twice, the Iraqis will catch on and start shooting artillery or sending in patrols on the flight path. Maybe try a SAM shoot-down."

He held the phone to his ear now. "Even so. Tell them to fly a random pattern. Cover a wide area so the bad guys can't pinpoint the team by charting the flight path. No straight in and out stuff."

Nodding. "Yeah . . . yeah . . . sure . . . fine."

"I've got a flight in an hour."

No shouting now. Nodding to wagging.

"*The* Command Post? Are you sure?"

Mild obscenities leaked from the receiver.

"But Caranto—"

Curse words again.

"Yes, Ma'am." A string of yeses.

Fade to quiet.

Spangler twitched a grim smile at the two former Delta fighters. "A colleague," he said. When they gave him no reaction, he looked at his watch. "Well, we all have planes to catch. Yours is a fast-mover to a Saudi field." He waved a hand at a satchel. "Yours. Orders, authorizations, passports—three apiece—cash, contacts, phones, fake IDs, drop sites for more cash, the works."

"Introductions?" Ramsey said.

"A CIA guy arranged a meeting with a guide, a Kurd name of Omar, which isn't his real name, but that's another story. He's an ally."

"A *reliable* ally?" Baker lifted the stump of his missing

arm. More reliable than his last foray, the one into Afghanistan, in which a reliable ally took off his arm?

Spangler went with the truth. "As reliable as they ever get in that corner of the world, I suppose."

Baker gave a facial shrug.

"Weapons in here. Nobody will open it once you put the Zulu-Black seal on it. Diplomatic immunity. Just don't open it again until you're on the ground in Saudi Arabia and out of their control."

"What about ammo?"

"Hell, they don't care about ammo. Take care," he said. "It's dangerous over there."

Baker and Night Runner both gave him wide smiles.

"What?"

"Not as dangerous as where you're going," Baker said. "You have no idea."

"Don't even ask, General," Night Runner said.

"Ask?"

"I'm not trading spaces with you."

Spangler's laugh had a sardonic edge to it. "I guess I could go AWOL. Hide out with a mutual friend of ours in a safe place."

Night Runner raised one eyebrow.

"Sneaks Low," Spangler said. "Heart Butte, Montana?"

Night Runner's face went askew.

Baker shrugged. "I don't get it. If that's the punch line, what's the joke?"

"Bad joke," Spangler said. "It'd take too long to explain."

"General, you have no idea," Night Runner said.

Spangler fumbled with handshakes with one-handed men. *Damn!* If Lady Redcoat ever saw his A-Team— He didn't even want to think about Caranto seeing these two. Going nuclear did not quite cover what the four-star's re-action'd be.

Three French helicopters settled onto a slab of rock in the
desert. The sunrise was still an hour away. Before the pilot
could take all the weight off the aircraft's wheels, the
Desert Wolves were on the ground and running clear of
the landing area. Not Karim-Assad. He did as Bani-Sadr
told him. Three steps from the helicopter, he went to his
knees and lay flat on the ground. The helicopter took off,
stinging him with pellets of sand and gravel.

Then all went silent, except for wisps of retreating
blade sounds. Pungent exhaust wafted over him. He
opened his eyes and looked across the sleeve of the uniform the Desert Wolves had given him, mottled as the
landscape where he lay.

When he heard the whistle, he got to his knees and
looked around. Nothing. All twenty men had vanished.
The whistle came again. Impatiently this time. He saw the
red dot of a penlight flashing at him from twenty meters
away. He ran toward it, his backpack trying to throw him
off balance.

He arrived at Bani-Sadr's side gasping for breath.

"You lied. To me."

Bani-Sadr laughed. "All out of lungs already? You
should save some of that hot air for the march."

"You said. One of your soldiers. Would stay by my
side."

"Not soldiers, Desert Wolves."

"No matter. Neither was there. By my side. On that
rock."

"Of course not. Too dangerous. Everybody knows the
first man to die in a fight is the one who stays at the landing spot."

Karim-Assad gasped. "Not me."

"Oh, yes." Bani-Sadr put a hand on his shoulder. "Now
including even you."

The hand felt good to Karim-Assad. A reassuring

touch from a true soldier teaching him his first lesson of the desert.

He reached into the pouch on his hip and pulled out a magazine for his Russian rifle, an old SKS.

Bani-Sadr grasped his wrist, this time not to reassure.

"No bullets. Not for you. Not until we get into a fight, and certainly not at night even then."

What he saw in the dim light told Karim-Assad to bite his mouth shut. When he did, Bani-Sadr let go of his wrist.

"Try to keep up," Bani-Sadr said. He looked Karim-Assad up and down. "None of my men will carry you."

Karim-Assad shrugged. Already the straps of his pack dug into his shoulders. His was barely a third the size of the packs that the other men carried, and from the look of it, barely a fraction of the weight.

He looked around casually. "Where are we?"

"About a kilometer from where the attack took place on the Republican Guards."

"A kilometer? Why did we land so far away?"

Bani-Sadr shook his head. "This is a different kind of school, son of Saddam." He let his point sink in. "Here you do not learn by talking. Listen, no talk. Move, no talk. Shoot—when I say to shoot—no talk. Do not talk. If anybody talks, it is I who talks. Then you listen, not talk." Bani-Sadr leaned in close. "Saddam is not here to talk for you or to let you talk. So no talk. Do you understand no talk?"

Karim-Assad opened his mouth.

Bani-Sadr stuck a finger under his nose.

Karim-Assad closed his eyes and nodded. When he opened his eyes, he saw Bani-Sadr had crept away five meters without making so much as a crunch of sand.

"Sit here," he said in a low tone. "Watch." A raised eyebrow.

Karim-Assad folded on the spot, sitting in place. *No talk.*

He saw only shadows of the Desert Wolves working the area nearby as if looking for lost coins. In time they moved out in all directions, until he could see them no more.

Other men watched over the search parties from hiding spots. They chose their spots well, blending into the shadows of the rocks and clumps of desert foliage. In time, Karim-Assad could pick them out.

Bani-Sadr. He was firm but did not insult him. He did not play the petty games of the tin soldiers at table in Saddam's palaces. He never made a move or spoke a word without a purpose to it. So much to learn from Bani-Sadr. If only he weren't so tired.

Last night Bani-Sadr's men had given him gear and a weapon, a rusted Russian rifle, the SKS, which he had to learn to shoot and to clean spotless and oil-less before he could sleep. So. Only an hour's nap on the flight from the airport on the outskirts of Baghdad. Now the letdown after a night of shooting at targets. This made Karim-Assad more respectful of military men, and weary.

He thought he heard a distant whistle but decided it was a bird and did not even open his eyes. The next whistle he heard, in the same pitch, was in his ear.

Bandi-Sadr gave him a leer when he startled awake.

"Eyes open at all times, except for a blink now and then," Bani-Sadr said. "A short blink."

Karim-Assad opened his mouth, then slapped his own finger over his lips before Bani-Sadr could.

Bani-Sadr nodded gravely. "Perhaps you are wiser than you look, after all." He flashed his gray teeth in the imitation of a smile. "Come. Look. Listen. Learn."

The flight was short and swift for Ramsey Baker. He slept in a reclining seat aboard the air force VIP craft. Also short and swift was the drive from the desert airfield to the Iraqi border in an air-conditioned Mercedes SUV.

Quite the contrast from his last trip to the region—first strapped to a gurney in the back of a cargo plane, then tied to the back of a groin-splitting mountain pony with quad jackhammers for legs.

They met their contact, a CIA man, and their guide in the glow of head-on headlights at the Iraqi-Saudi border two hours before dawn.

Baker knew the CIA man, Brian Carnes. He had guided him into Afghanistan his last time out. Carnes had known him before his arm was cut off. He did not make a point of either looking at it or not looking at it. Carnes simply embraced him then held him by both shoulders at arm's length.

"You got your ears fixed," he said. "They look good."

"Thanks."

The CIA man was all of six-two, two hundred. The wide receiver type of athlete.

But he looked puny next to the Kurd guide, a good six inches taller and half again as wide as the CIA man. The defensive end type, big, fast, and mean. There was no way to know how much he weighed for the bulk of wool wraps.

Baker had heard of rug merchants. This guy was a cutlery merchant. A pair of flat throwing knives strapped to the outside of each calf. Two curved swords at his waist, hand-guards forward. A jewel-handled dagger stuck in his belt. A chopping blade on a leather loop around his neck, again without a sheath. And in his right hand, not one but two spears, their steel blades a full eighteen inches long, one with double straight-edges, the other a wavy, gleaming blade that looked like a flicker of silver flame.

The guy a conversation-stopper and knew it. Letting the newcomers—inferiors to him—stare at him while he looked over their heads with black, deep set eyes, two piss-holes in the sand.

"Nice knives," Baker said with a straight face.

The Kurd lowered his eyes to glare at Baker. *The viewing is now over.* "Fair words butter no parsnips."

Baker put his hand up to pinch a smile out of his face. He'd met an Afghan warlord before who talked in Middle-East bumper stickers, too.

Carnes spoke up. "He wants to get going before sunup. You got something for him?"

The exchange of bona fides went off without a hitch. A satchel half full of cash to the Kurd, who handed off to an aide without looking inside. The aide did look. He nodded at the Kurd and drove the cash away on a motorcycle with an engine like that of a leaf blower.

Ramsey handed the CIA man a clear plastic bag with a like amount of cash. Carnes held it up to the Kurd. He looked away in disdain, as if money meant nothing to him. Carnes slung the bag over his shoulder. He was to keep it until the Kurd guided Baker and Night Runner to a spot in the desert, the last known GPS coordinates of the Delta team.

Baker produced a map to the spot.

The Kurd studied the lay of the land, turning his back on the Americans to orient the map to the ground, not visible in the dark except for the distant horizon. After a few seconds he turned back to them and handed the map over.

"I know this place," he said in English.

"Before we go, I'm Ramsey Baker." He stuck out his hand. "Pleased to meet you, Omar."

Carnes winced. The right side of the Kurd's face lifted into a sneer.

"Who is this Omar?" He looked down at Baker's hand as if the American was trying to pass off a dog turd.

"That's a code name," Carnes said in a hurry. "We don't use your real name when we talk about you."

Baker tried to be quick on the uptake. "Right. Your real name is a secret."

Carnes shook his head. *You couldn't let me handle it?*

"What secret?" The Kurd pounded the sand with the hafts of his two spears. "My name no secret. Everybody know Adnil Mustafa Qasim Zimnako Jalal Massoud Saladin ji Kirkuk. Iraqi bastards know my name. They fear to say it but they know it."

"They call him The Angry Kurd," Carnes said.

The Kurd snorted for emphasis.

"No shit," Baker said. "What do we call him for short? Adnil? Or just Mad?"

"Go with Adil?" Night Runner said.

"Not *Adil*. My name *Adnil* Mustafa Qasim Zimnako Jalal Massoud Saladin ji Kirkuk."

"No way," Baker insisted.

The Kurd loomed in fury.

"*Ramsey-ee-e*," Carnes stepped between them and whispered. "Trying to cause an international incident?"

"We can't call the guy that," Baker said. "We get into a scrape, we'll get overrun by the time we say his name on the radio."

"What is scrape?" the Kurd wanted to know.

"Omar," Carnes said, tamping down the air in front of his chest with both hands, trying to lower the Kurd's emotions. "It's just your code name. For secrecy, my men will call you Omar."

"Omar." The Kurd gave it a long taste before nodding. "For short, Omar is okay. My own men will not call me Omar. They will call me my name in full." By his tone they did not have an option.

Baker's hand was out, offering to shake again.

"He wants to be your friend," Carnes said.

Omar closed his left fist on one of his scimitars. "The Kurds have no friends except the mountains."

Baker withdrew his only good hand. "And the horse he rode in on."

"No horse." Omar pointed his spears at a white Toyota pickup with a topper on it. "We go." He put his spears in a tool rack on the topper alongside a pair of shovels. He growled, and eight rough men, of the desert, well-armed with rifles and pistols, lowered their heads and climbed into the back.

"You and Runner in the front with big guy."

"Thanks loads. I guess we'll get along in English and what he knows of the Arabic dialects," Baker said.

"Stick to English," Carnes said. "He hates all Arabs, not just the Iraqis. It wouldn't do to reveal your heritage flat-out."

"Figures. Another little detail that Spangler neglected to mention."

"I'm sorry—"

Baker waved off the apology. *Forget it.* "What matters is, can we trust him?"

Carnes shrugged. "As much as you can trust any man in this part of the world, I suppose."

"Huge comfort, Brian, just huge. You and Spangler selling me the same load of crap."

"They don't trust, okay? After Desert Storm they learned not to rely on the staying power of Americans. They treat their friends—"

Baker held up the hand. "I know the proverb, Brian. They treat their friends like they'll be enemies tomorrow. What I want to know is, will they treat their enemies like friends tomorrow?"

Omar started the pickup.

Carnes shook his head. "This is one Kurd who hates the Iraqis more than any other—on that you can rely. There is no circumstance I can imagine in which he would be friends with an Iraqi, let alone Saddam."

Omar honked the horn.

"All he's gonna do is take us a few miles into the desert, right?" Baker said.

"That's it." Carnes put up the palms of both hands. "Take you in, drop you off, turn over the truck." He hefted the garbage sack off his shoulder. "A hundred grand. He turns that truck over to you, you give him a signed hall pass. I give him the bag. End of story. Piece of—"

"Don't say cake."

"Pie."

"Bastard." Baker shook Carnes's hand.

"Guy makes me queasy."

"That's a good thing. Help you keep your edge."

Baker turned to Night Runner at his shoulder. "Anything to add?"

"I call shotgun," Night Runner said.

"Jeez. Don't make me sit by him, Runner." Baker held up his left hand. "I only got the one. If he hits a pothole and some of that cutlery flies up—" He shut up when Night Runner held up his own stump.

Bani-Sadr stood in a clutch of his men.

Karim-Assad marveled. He could see the design in the way the Desert Wolves formed. They stood and knelt and sat in a loose circle, one that let them shift and fight back in any direction, should they come under attack. Never did these men take things for granted. There was no chance an enemy would be at this spot, so close to the place where the tank division was attacked. And yet.

Yet they stayed ready for just such an attack. Come to think of it, even last night as he took target practice in a courtyard just outside the palace walls, he saw it. These men never did drop their guard. Only one man at a time helped to train him. The others stood apart, out of the light, at the ready. Unlike the tin soldiers, they never stood around in a group to smoke cigarettes and tell stories about women and the pranks they'd pulled in the barracks. These men were always ready to fight.

Bani-Sadr nodded to him. Karim-Assad shrugged. What had he done wrong now?

Then he saw it. A spot in the perimeter left open. He gave a look to Bani-Sadr. *For me?* Another nod.

He filled the space and sat sideways like the other men. He did as they did, keeping an ear to the speaker, rather than turning to watch him. His eyes he used to scan the desert, shimmering in heat already at barely eight o'clock in the morning. His heart shimmered, too, with pride.

They had left a space for him in their circle.

"Who has a report?" Bani-Sadr.

"I, Nabil." Karim-Assad had not heard the voice before, soft, like a woman's. He was tempted to look so he could match the voice to the face, but he dared not.

"Half a kilometer's distance from here. A helicopter landing site. Two helicopters. Blackhawks, by the shape and size of the triangle formed with the landing wheels. Twelve men. Americans, by the patterns on their boot soles."

"I found their trail," said a second, much rougher voice. "Up there to the north, just short of the crest of the ridge where they looked down on the division headquarters. They held meetings. I put two men to work reading other clues. By the time we get to the camp, they will have more to reveal."

"A good report, Salim," Bani-Sadr said. "Any other reports?"

Silence.

"Let us go see what the others have to tell us."

Spangler and Lady Redcoat and Caranto sat in a cafeteria in the Pentagon. Glum. Pensive. Together but aloof. Better here than the ops center, where they had no function in the continuing loss of contact with the Delta team. They weren't exactly big buddies now—Caranto still could not mask his hatred of Spangler and barely tried—but all their tensions went flat after the failure to contact the Delta team. Nothing was more important than Delta to Spangler. Nothing was more important than Delta's captives to Caranto and Lady Redcoat. The vacuum left them in an awkward state: nothing to fight about. So they accepted an inadvertent, undeclared truce, with none of the three quite able to grasp how to act toward the other two. An aimless, latent, sterile hostility hung in the air, waiting for one or another of them to pick at a scab that would trigger a two-on-two feeding frenzy among three stunned, starving sharks. The only questions? Which were the feeders? And which was the feed-ee?

One of the scouts met Bani-Sadr at the crest of the hill. Karim-Assad stood by so he could hear the report.

The scout told Bani-Sadr, "Two groups. One group bypassed the outpost, while another split itself again to attack."

The scout spoke and pointed like a guide at a historical museum to show how the battle unfolded. Somehow these men could read the ground, smell the battle, taste the air. For them to touch the footprint impressions was to see through a window into the past.

"One thing I do not understand," the scout said, still pointing. "Almost all of the division's return fire struck in three spots. Here, here, and up there."

Karim-Assad watched in his peripheral vision. Below him, the Desert Wolves had fanned out and worked their way downhill in ones and twos, eyes glued to the ground.

The headquarters area was a shambles. Bullet-riddled tents had burned. Equipment lay strewn, both damaged and abandoned whole. Garbage everywhere.

"Blood trails?" Bani-Sadr asked.

"Plenty from the Iraqi positions. Most of them shot from behind."

Bani-Sadr cocked his head. "By their own men?"

"I doubt it. Almost every spot has brain matter. That many head shots? Not likely from the headquarters soldiers, even if they tried."

"No enemy positions with blood?"

"None. Not a single drop of bloodshed in those spots. You can see, the foliage torn to pieces by tank and machine-gun fire. Mortars, shrapnel. All from our own guns."

Bani-Sadr smiled. "These were men with huge balls. To get between the security force and the headquarters, then kill them from behind."

Karim-Assad had never thought to respect an enemy. *Another lesson learned.*

"No rifle brass?" Bani-Sadr wanted to know. "No footprints?"

"Only fragments of footsteps in the kill zones. One man."

Karim-Assad saw the scout remove his hat and scratch at his head.

"The same man," the scout said. "He was in all three positions. He did something there in each place to draw the fire of anybody down below who could see to shoot."

"And yet he left no brass?" Bani-Sadr said.

"No. Not here."

Karim-Assad saw out of the corner of his eye that Bani-Sadr was not all that puzzled. He shrugged it off. "The Americans. They do have their toys and their tricks. This man created some kind of illusion or diversion. Later we will talk to one who survived the battle. He will tell us why so much firepower was directed at only those spots." He laughed out loud. "As the enemy went down the slope to bring hell on earth."

"We did find brass from two rifle shots," the scout said. "One there, and another there."

"And?"

"To kill the sentries. One was head-shot. The officer of the guard in the neck."

Bani-Sadr had seen enough. "Let us go get the report from below." He turned to Karim-Assad. "Just the preliminaries," he said. "A little bit of history so we can identify our enemy. Once we know him, we will pick up the pace of our schooling. We will teach you how to find these men—no matter how good they are as soldiers, men who are not as familiar with the desert life as we."

Karim-Assad shook his head in awe. *How could any man know as much about the desert as these men?*

"You will learn as much as a city mouse can." He clasped an arm around Karim-Assad. "I have watched you. You learn fast."

Karim-Assad opened his mouth, caught himself, and put a finger to his lips.

"Very fast." Bani-Sadr pointed the way downhill. "Watch your step. There are many unexploded rounds in the Iraqi arsenal. If you kick one by accident—"

The scouts gave their reports as before, only faster. Everybody picked up the pace of speech, gesture.

Karim-Assad learned that the boot prints of the dead American—about all that remained intact were his boots—matched those of the attacker who had visited all three sites up above to play his trick on the soldiers of the 100th Division. Soldiers tramping about had obliterated most of the footprints in this area. Several Iraqis died at the site, blown up when the American booby trap when off. They had surrounded the body, shooting at him at close range.

"Idiots." Bani-Sadr shook his head. "Killing a dead man. Only to kill themselves."

Farther down the gully and across the road the Desert Wolves had a bit more trouble reading signs. Firefighters, rescue crews, gawkers—there were few clues to the Americans left.

The Desert Wolves sent scouts in wide circles around the burned-out hulk of the SUV. Karim-Assad felt his pulse race. Uday and Qusay had ridden in that car. They could not have lived through that crash. Could they?

Bani-Sadr answered his digital phone and went out of Karim-Assad's hearing to talk.

When he came back to the circle, the scouts shook their heads. They'd found no signs of a trail leading away from the site of the attack on the SUV.

"A helicopter?" Bani-Sadr asked.

"Not possible," Nabil said. "None could land so close to the division after an attack."

Bani-Sadr smiled. "Exactly. The Americans hijacked a truck. A huge truck carrying a damaged tank away from the camp. They traveled inside the tank and even in the cab with the driver."

Karim-Assad's jaw dropped. His look said what his mouth dared not: *You can tell all this by reading tracks?*

"A truck driver was killed within the hour at a road-block. Before he died he claimed to have taken the Americans away from here. We have a report of a full-scale fight. Fourteen killed, twice as many wounded." Bani-Sadr gave the weakest of smiles. "No enemy casualties." He shook his head. "No Americans involved, in fact."

Karim-Assad opened his mouth and, remembering, slammed it shut. *Our soldiers killing each other?*

"Call for our helicopters," Bani-Sadr said, holding up three fingers. "One to follow the track between here and the roadblock, looking for signs where the Americans jumped off the truck." He closed one finger into this fist. "A second team to scout the watering spots." He folded a second finger.

Karim-Assad shrugged. *The third?*

"We've been ordered to make a personal report." Bani-Sadr pointed a forefinger at the sky, inclined his head toward Karim-Assad, then brought down the finger to aim it

at the former food taster. "You and I. To our president."
He sighed.

And no wonder. An audience with Saddam? During
times of stress? Such a trip might well be his last. Karim-
Assad thought he saw the first chink in the confidence of
the mighty chief of the Desert Wolves—there was a tiny
rattle in that deep sigh. To think of it, he didn't feel so
well himself. All those times of eating all that rich food
and curry. Seldom did he feel so close to vomiting as he
did now.

Dawn of the second day in Iraq. The team lay among the
warming black rocks on a stretch of land in an ancient
seabed where lava flows once seeped through cracks in the
earth's crust. For as far as Poole could see, camel humps
of lava as big as the projects, house-sized lumps of basalt.
Pool-table sized sandstone chunks lay about where they'd
fallen when the basalt broke through. On his map he saw
the sterile birds-eye view that did not even hint at the hell-
hole reality of the spot. To the northeast was the oasis
where Solis went, ten miles away. To the north, about fifty
miles away, was Buhayrat ar Razazah, a thirty-five-mile-
long lake near Karbala. Beyond that lay Baghdad.

Solis had led the team on a heading to the oasis while
the sun was still low. In case an air scout spotted their
tracks. On the theory that the spotter would draw a line to
the oasis and look for them there.

Instead Poole and the Delta captives cut hard left, into
the lava bed to hide a mile offset from Solis's line. A good
piece of misdirection. Solis kept two men to make a track
to the oasis. Poole left a man to brush away the signs
they'd left after making the left turn.

By daylight, each of the details Poole had split off had
to hide out. He'd have to gather his chicks in the dark tonight. No radios, no unity, no peace of mind. This war was

getting to be a bitch and it wasn't even scheduled to begin until day after tomorrow.

He'd sent Barret and two other Delta men off to create a second false trail from the spot where'd they'd bailed off the flatbed. Barret went due south, toward Saudi Arabia. A second piece of misdirection. If the Iraqis found that set of tracks, they might think Delta had left the country.

Funny thing. He even hated being out of radio contact with Mr. Pain-in-the-Butt-Staff-Guy. He'd welcome a call now, a lifeline back to the world. But no. Every time he turned his radio on, he heard the music of jamming. At just a hundred meters between radios, it overpowered the team's radios, even with direct line of sight. So he couldn't talk to Solis at the oasis or Barret, who was even farther away—hell, he couldn't even talk to his track-hider, who was stuck in a cluster of rocks less than a klick away. He was a commander out of touch with his men. Nothing ground an officer's gut more. If a light squad of Iraqis were to stumble onto any one of the group . . . well, he'd have to give it a Scarlett O'Hara pass and think about it tomorrow.

Last night was so frigid. He couldn't wait for the sun. Now that he'd gotten his wish, Poole couldn't wait for the dark. He kept shifting to stay in the shade.

Poole had put his part of the team to bed. They needed rest. He could not sleep himself. So he stayed awake, keeping eye-to-eye with Saddam's sons.

But not before detailing two men to give them drinking water. He watched the two suck down the water greedily as Artemis and Foucault handled them with more respect.

Uday spoke up to Foucault, who turned to Poole.

"Man's gotta piss again."

Poole shrugged. Sometimes a leader had to delegate. This was one of those times, telling his top NCO in body language: *Deal with it.*

Foucault wasn't going down so easily. "All right if I take off the flex cuffs?"

Poole shrugged and made his best call of the war so far. To keep his fat mouth shut. *Or you could unzip, hold it, and shake it for him. Your call, 'cuz I ain't buying into this one.*

Night Runner felt ill at ease. It wasn't the speed so much, or the roughness of the journey.

It was rough, though. The Toyota bounced across the desert track for thirty minutes or so, then fed into a wider track. Somebody had maintained this road in the distant past, scraping a shallow roadway the width of a bulldozer blade. Omar drove the bladed road as if it were an eight-lane autobahn.

Carnes was so sure the fix was in with the Iraqis. That Omar was free to travel the country as safely—and as fast—as Saddam himself.

Night Runner wasn't so sure. All bets were off now that Delta had Saddam's sons. He didn't trust any of these people. Hell, he didn't even trust his own body. The purification itself had taken a lot out of him. Then the travel. The lack of sleep.

But the worst? The idea that any Iraqi private who wasn't in on Omar's fix could pull them over on a whim at the point of an AK.

At sunup Omar stopped the Toyota in the center of the road. He bailed out of the pickup and urinated into the dust.

The men in the back of the truck piled out, too. Night Runner followed suit, afraid a full bladder couldn't take the pounding.

Omar stretched, spat, and said his first words to the Americans since leaving Carnes behind.

"You ride in back now." He flapped a hand at them. "Batman show you." He spoke to one of his Kurds.

The man tugged at their empty sleeves and led them to the tailgate.

"Did he just say *Batman*?" Night Runner said.

The Kurd smiled, showing off brown teeth and tapping himself on the chest. "Batman." He pronounced it *Botmahn*.

"It's a Kurd name," Baker said. "Spelled just like the guy from Gotham City, though."

"Too bad we didn't use it as a code name instead of *Omar*. It's got more pizzazz."

They piled into the rear of the Toyota, and six men climbed in behind them, packing them toward the front.

Making Night Runner feel all the more vulnerable. For now he could not see, could not brace himself against the road, and if they came under attack, he could not fight.

Soon enough, he didn't care about any of that. All he cared about was getting one fresh breath. The Toyota first raised a dust cloud, then sucked it into the topper through its wake, sifting that talc onto the men. Like the Kurds, all the Americans could do was close their eyes and clap wet cloths to their faces to filter the air. Every man had to keep moving his cloth as the spaces between the weave filled up with silt.

Even so Night Runner fell asleep. Until he felt the truck coast to a stop.

Every man among the Kurds produced a paint brush and went to work cleaning the action of his weapon.

The Kurd at the rear of the topper finished brushing his weapon first, an Uzi submachine gun, a short and wicked weapon capable of firing a stream of bullets on automatic. The Kurd knelt on one knee and practiced sweeping the gun back and forth across the tailgate. If the wrong guy opened that topper—

The rest of the Kurds knelt along the sides of the topper. Night Runner saw for the first time that he was not so helpless after all. Four of the Kurds each put one hand on a quick release clip that held the topper to the back of the pickup. With their feet under them, they could release the clips, stand up, and throw off the topper. Every gun could then join the fight.

A harsh voice called out. In Arabic. Ramsey Baker spoke in his ear.

"It's an Iraqi military cop. He wants to know what Omar is doing on this—"

Omar spoke up brusquely.

"Whoa! Guys got balls. Give him that."

"What?" Night Runner said.

"Omar says he's Mukhabarat," Baker whispered, translating the exchange. "On a high-level secret-police mission—Jesus, he speaks the language better than most Iraqis—hell better than I do."

IRAQI COP: *Everybody in the country is on a high-level mission.*

"He's being sarcastic."

OMAR: *No more important than my mission.*

IRAQI COP: *You're trying to get the reward, too?*

OMAR: *Reward?*

IRAQI COP: *For finding the sons of Saddam. You haven't heard? Ten million dinars.*

OMAR: *I have heard, but not about the reward. My reward will be in finding them and returning them to Saddam.*

IRAQI COP: *If you don't care then give me the twenty million.*

OMAR: *You said ten.*

IRAQI COP: *Ten for each. Can you imagine? Those two lost in the desert?*

OMAR: *Imagine, yes. Lost? No, I have never been lost.*

IRAQI COP: *Your papers and credentials. Just a formality.*

OMAR: *Our lives are filled with formalities.*

A sympathetic snort. Night Runner could hear a rustling of papers.

IRAQI COP: *Now a quick look at your cargo.*

OMAR: *I have no cargo. I delivered rations and water to a border post.*

IRAQI COP: *That's a secret mission?*

OMAR: *It was on the way.*

IRAQI COP: *Even so. I have my orders. To look in every vehicle where a man might hide.*

OMAR: *Even one coming back into the country?*

The Iraqi laughed.

IRAQI COP: *You might be bringing Uday and Qusay to their father. And I might insist on a share of that reward you do not care about.*

A door of the Toyota snapped open.

OMAR: *I do have something for you, a taste of my cargo. Call your friend over. I have a taste for him as well.*

IRAQI COP: *I thought your truck was empty.*

OMAR: *It is empty for anybody but you and your friend here.*

Every man in the back of the Toyota tensed for action, including Night Runner and Baker. One of the Kurds shushed at Baker to stop his whispering.

Night Runner heard the crunch of gravel on the left side of the Toyota. The Iraqi called out. A second Iraqi voice called back.

Then nothing.

A sharp intake of breath. A second gasp. Night Runner heard two bodies hit the ground.

Then came a series of knocks on the topper: two raps, then one, then two more. The Kurds relaxed.

Omar began talking rapid-fire in his own tongue, and the Kurds went into action, spilling out on the road.

Out on the ground, they took only a moment to stretch. Then they pulled a spear from each of the two bodies lying on the ground. Two Kurds took down a shovel each from the tool rack and began digging a hasty grave for the dead cops. Two men took positions where they could out-post up and down the road. The rest of them looked over the Volvo van that belonged to the Iraqis.

"I will take their truck," Omar said to Baker. "Instead of walking out of the country after I leave you."

Night Runner spoke in a low voice into Baker's ear, "Does he know you speak the Iraqi language?"

Baker shook his head.

"Ask him what the cop wanted. In English. See if he lies."

Baker asked without hesitation.

Omar blinked twice before saying, "He was looking for two lost men in the desert."

Baker did not miss a beat, wagging a thumb between Night Runner and himself. "Us? Do you think he meant us? That Saddam knows we are in Iraq?"

"No. He was looking for the sons of Saddam. Uday and Qusay."

"Uday and Qusay."

"Yes. He spoke of a large reward." Omar narrowed his eyes at Baker. "Is this why I guide you into Iraq? So you can recover the sons of Saddam before he does?"

"No." Baker's turn to blink. He was every bit as quick in his lie. "I have no use for those two. If I found them, I would end the matter with two well-placed bullets."

"Indeed." Omar pooched his lips. "Perhaps you seek the world's most potent weapons then, the so-called weapons of mass destruction."

"No." Baker was quick again. "If that were the case, I could not say. But it is not the case at all. My mission has to do with the Iraqi air defenses"—he flapped his empty sleeve at Omar—"and that is all I can say about it."

"I understand." Omar smiled. "You part with your head but not with your secret. That is okay on me. As long as I get paid my bags of money." He swept his arm at the Volvo, taller and longer than the Toyota. "Now I have an even better truck." He pointed at the Toyota. "You drive. Stay close to me. Do not stop for a checkpoint unless I do."

They were on their way in minutes, gobbling up the dusty miles. All the Kurds having piled into their new ride, leaving Baker and Night Runner alone in the Toyota.

Night Runner helped with the shifting, as Baker drove—two one-armed men using their good arms in the cause of driving one truck.

"At least he didn't lie," Baker said.

"No, at least he didn't lie."

"Then what? Something's eating at you."

"I don't trust him."

"Why not? He passed your test."

Night Runner held his silence, trying to answer Baker's question for himself.

Afternoon limped into evening. Poole wasn't thinking tactics or strategy. *Just trying to find some damned shade.* Trying to snatch a nap, working his way around a boulder with the shade. Shade hot as hell.

Nothing in his head but heat. Even his thoughts hot and oppressive. How many more days of this crap? A week? At least. No telling how long for the ground forces to pass by.

When the hell—?

Gunshots. Small arms. Then explosions. *Boomers? From the oasis?*

Solis? Solis and the two Delta men?

In a fight?

Shit!

Solis tried. He tried to hide. Tried to spend the day out of sight. Tried to wait for the night so they could backtrack to Poole and the boys. Tried to wipe out every sign that they'd been at the oasis. Tried to hide in the hills well away from the damp sand seep, a grassy, tree-lined pool. Tried to stay out of fight, out of mind. Honest to God tried.

The Iraqis swooped in by air. Not on their tracks. More like a random air search. Check off all the water holes. One turn around the seep. Then off into the wild blue—

A sudden bank. The chopper swapped ends. And came back to land near the well.

Four Iraqis hit the ground. Well-armed, fit, swarthy, serious fighters. Dressed in billowing pants, loose shirts, draped in light cloaks. High-tech boots on the bottom, head wraps on the top. The color of the desert. If Solis looked over his binos, the men blended into the sand.

Three other desert men stayed on board.

As the three on the ground went prone, alert, clear of the blade disk, the blades turning at flat pitch.

As one guy took a slow turn around the well. He put down each foot with care. He kept his eyes on the sand. Until.

He stood up and pointed at the false trail Solis's detail had laid down and then brushed out so it wouldn't look too-o-o obvious.

"They gonna take the bait?" Ballard.

The tracker knelt on one knee.

"No. He ain't buying." Miller.

"On my word," Solis said. "Take out the chopper first. On my word. Top, you and I drill the pilots. Miller, you pin down the four on the ground."

The Iraqi turned, still on one knee. He took a long look over each shoulder.

Solis saw him shudder. A sixth sense. As if he could feel Miller's .17-cal on his back.

"Now!"

Miller fired on the word.

The Iraqi leapt to his feet. Bent back. Waved. First to his men to flatten. Then to the chopper to take off. Fell over.

Solis pasted white asterisks across the windshield of the chopper.

The craft grew light on its wheels.

Ballard fired on the windshield, cracking and crazing it like a sudden frost. A web of white fell away.

Still. The chopper wobbled into the air.

Both of them raked the cabin on auto fire.

Still. The nose lifted.

Two bodies tumbled out of the cabin. Two rag dolls flopped onto the sand.

Still. The chopper blades found clean air and began a climb-out.

Ballard cursed and fired. Solis cursed and fired some more. "Miller. Help out here. It can't get off," he hollered. "We can't. Let them. Get. Away." The rattle of his M-4 between words.

Miller was on the scout. He'd shot the man in the ass as he leaped up. The Iraqi tried to hobble-crawl to the safety of the stone wall at the well. Miller killed him with a shot to the ear.

Then he shifted fire. Not that a puny .17-cal was going to do much good. He shot for the only vulnerable spot.

He put a pair of slugs into the tail rotor disk. Maybe hit a blade. Chance of one in thirty.

Still. The chopper gained fifty feet.

"Can't. Get. Off." Solis said.

Miller sent another needle-nose slug into the transparent disc. The tail rotor disintegrated.

The chopper spun, dropped, rolled, and hit. Main rotor blades first in the water of the seep beside the well. It rolled and lay on its back, belly-up.

Solis had a new prayer. "Sink. Sink, you bastard."

But the seep was too shallow, and this prayer's answer was *no*.

Three Iraqis left.

Three Iraqis turned on the Delta team. And attacked

across the open. Into the face of three guns. And kept coming. Even after being shot through.

Two of them, shot more than four times each would. Not. Stop. They closed to twenty yards before Solis and Miller took them both out with a pair of boomers.

Solis reloaded and lay still. Aiming. In case the bastards came back to life like they did in films. This wasn't the Iraqis he'd seen on tape from Desert Storm. Hands up. Big grins. No, these guys were crazy. They did not panic, did not run, did not even try to hide or fight from cover. These guys attacked. Like Delta.

Movement! In the water!

One of the Iraqi devils had survived the crash.

He swam away from the ship, but not away from them. He waded ashore. He came at them.

"Kill him?" Miller asked.

Solis was in awe.

At the man. As he staggered through the sand, bypassing a dead Iraqi's rifle. He ran like a drunk, but he ran. At the Delta ambush.

He had no weapon.

"He's not going to—" Ballard.

But he was, and he did.

"Out of his mind." Miller.

He stopped to pick up rocks.

"Kill him." Solis.

"Think they got off a radio call?" Ballard.

The Iraqi slung his rocks at them. One hit Ballard on the shoulder.

"That's what I'm afraid of," Solis.

And kept coming.

"Snot what I'm afraid of." Miller. He drew a bead on the Iraqi's head. And put him down with a single through the eye. "I'm afraid there's more where this guy came from."

Baker drove. Night Runner kept track of their progress on the map.

They came out of a long, shallow, grinding climb to the crest of a ridge, and the Volvo came to an abrupt stop.

"Now what?" Baker said.

"Below this ridge," Night Runner said tapping a forefinger on the map. "There's a cross-road not far from where the Delta team hit the Iraqis." He opened his door to step out as Omar strode back to the Toyota.

"Is not safe to go on," Omar said. "We hide out until night. Then—"

Omar turned about and cupped his hands behind his ears. He shook his head. "Turn off your motor so I can hear."

Baker shut down the Toyota and stepped out of the cab.

"What is it?" he asked.

"Silence," Omar said.

Baker turned to Night Runner across the hood of the Toyota. He pointed to his own ears and mouthed: *I can't hear a thing*.

"A firefight," Omar said. "We get off the road now."

Night Runner turned his binoculars toward the horizon and kept staring until the Volvo left the road ahead of them.

Baker kept the Toyota in the tire tracks of the Volvo, following it across the desert. Before long they descended into a shallow gully. The Volvo kept to the shady side of the gully until they were out of sight. Unless a helicopter flew overhead, nobody was going to spot them.

"I got the new ears," Baker said to Night Runner, "but I can't hear a damn bit better than I ever could."

"The guy has ears like a mule deer. I heard an explosion, but not the firefight." Night Runner shook his head in disgust. "Ten, maybe fifteen miles from here."

"What's wrong?"

"I used to be able to hear that well."

"What'd you see?"

"I saw a helicopter go down. I couldn't tell if it was a crash or not. But it went down fast. No smoke, no fire."

Baker waved at the windshield. "Here comes Omar. What do you think about him taking us the rest of the way at night?"

"Not much."

"Then what?"

"Send him back."

"Back?"

"Back to Saudi Arabia. Back to the CIA man. We'll go it alone."

Baker did not argue. Omar balked.

"You can't get past the roadblocks," he said. "Not safe for you. They will soon look for those dead Iraqi cops."

Night Runner stepped in. "That's why you should go."

"What?"

"You have the Volvo. You make it a risk for us. Go back and leave us alone."

"You cannot do it without me."

"Yes." Night Runner narrowed his eyes. "Without you."

The Kurd snorted. "In a flat country this hillock thinks he is a mountain."

Baker shrugged. "What the hell does that mean?"

Night Runner didn't care what it meant. "No." He flapped a hand Saudi Arabia's way. "Go. Collect your pay." Night Runner walked away.

Omar tried to sway Baker. But he took a note card from his pocket, wrote a pre-agreed note in Arabic: *Two goats delivered on time.* He signed it and handed it to Omar.

"Give that to Carnes. He'll pay you what's due."

Omar shook his head. "The devil takes a hand in what is done in haste."

Baker shook his head again. No dice. He turned away and caught up with Night Runner. "What was that all about?"

"Sorry, I know you're in command here."

"Forget that. What's the deal?"

"I don't trust a guy that tries to be so helpful."

Night Runner sat at the very crest of the hill looking back down the road toward Saudi Arabia. When the Volvo passed by, Omar did not deign to look at them.

"Come to think of it, I don't trust him, either," Baker said. "Guy that talks in bumper stickers? He's just spouting bullshit he can't think up on his own."

Minutes before sunset, a voice in his ear jolted Poole awake. He poked a finger into his head to reset his earbug. When did he fall asleep? How long had it been? His only clue was the long rays of the sun. Must have been a couple hours since the firefight at the oasis? Wait a minute. *There was a firefight, right?*

He asked Foucault. A nod of the long, solemn face told him so.

Damn! Out of touch with Solis. Out of touch with the world.

"Did you just hear a voice in your ear-bug—?"

"Prosper Zero-Six, this is Three-Three, over." The staff officer, real as life. The words pouring through the static and warble. Somehow the desk jockeys had figured out how to break the wall of jam. *Hot damn!* Poole took back all the bad words he'd said about staff weenies in the last two days.

He croaked into the radio, cleared his throat, and croaked again. "Zero-Six, over."

"Stand by for burst download. Intel you have to have. Ten-second window max." Even as he said it, the voice began to fade.

Poole gulped a swig of warm water. He tried his voice again and found that it worked: "Roger."

"Can you bring up your TPDA?"

Poole rogered and opened up his shirt-pocket computer the size of a pack of cards, mostly screen.

The screen came to life. Three-Three had already sent his download. Poole touched the blinking icon with the tip of a rifle cartridge, the best stylus a field soldier could use, always sharp, always at hand, never as messy as the tip of a ballpoint pen.

A tactical map blinked into view. Too large a scale to get oriented. Poole zoomed out with half a dozen quick touches of the stylus. A linear deployment of Iraqi symbols.

"What have we got here?"

Three-Three tried to tell him, but the warp and woof of the interference turned his voice into a kind of jazz fusion.

He saw a second download filling up a run scale on-screen. Until—

A streak of fire. A white flashbulb in the sky. A blast. Then. Nothing.

Nothing but static. The jamming again.

Spangler whispered a curse. Lady Redcoat said hers aloud.

"SAM?" Spangler said.

"Affirm, Sir, definitely a SAM shootdown," said the major, name of Shaw, call sign Three-Three.

"We lost the Predator?"

"Yes, Ma'am."

All three sets of eyes glued to Shaw's computer screen with the feed from an airborne radar from an AWACS craft flying deep inside Saudi Arabia.

"Think they got the download?" Spangler asked.

"Very likely, Sir. Most of it."

"What next?"

"At least we have a spot on them, Ma'am."

"Five spots," Spangler corrected. "Five areas of PER-

LOBE returns." Five personal beacon locations. A single at the attack site, possibly—no, probably—a casualty, a kid named Michelotti. Three from one spot, four each from two other sites, with one offset by only six hundred meters.

"Which one is Poole?" Spangler wanted to know.

Shaw pointed to a spot on the screen.

"What the hell is he doing down there?" Spangler wanted to know. "Why did he separate his team?"

Shaw shrugged.

"What the hell is he doing with the Hussein brothers?" Lady Redcoat wanted to know. "Why isn't he trying to get them out of country?"

"What the hell are you doing in here?" Caranto wanted to know as he burst into the special command post set up to direct this operation.

"Who wants to know?" Lady Redcoat.

"This is a restricted area, Ma'am."

"He's with me."

Caranto looked as if he would like to get it on with her, but he didn't have the rocks that she had. She looked at Caranto with the deadly intent of somebody pulling off one sandal to deal with an ant on the kitchen counter. Caranto turned his lasers of hate on Spangler.

Truce over.

Spangler put on a blank stare and shrugged a look of helplessness toward Caranto. Thumbing back a pair of hammers in his mind. Dealing with Caranto in this state was going to take both barrels. *Can you kill, Roscoe? Can you kill?* The question was rhetorical, of course. He already knew that he could not go through with a literal homicide—he'd learned that of himself with Bowers in the hospital. *Praying the rosary?*

But professional homicide? Ruin a career of the likes of Caranto? Now there was a hit he could make in a New York minute. With relish.

Adnil Mustafa Qasim Zimnako Jalal Massoud Saladin ji Kirkuk kept his eye on the pair in his left mirror.

When the Americans were just two more stones on the rear horizon, he spoke to the man next to him in the Volvo. "Ezmir, how fast are we going?"

Ezmir pointed to the speedometer. "You can see for yourself." But after a backhand to the face, he was only too happy to recite the instrument reading. "Sixty-five. Sixty-five kilometers per hour."

"When I stop, slide over here, count to ten, and drive on. As quickly as you can, get to sixty-five. Drive out of sight. No faster, no slower. Stop just short of the border checkpoint and wait for me to call."

"All night?"

"For the rest of your life, if need be." He checked the mirror when the Volvo dropped into a swale in the road. The van was out of sight of the Americans. He stopped the Volvo and collected the rest of his men. The last two tumbled out of the van as Ezmir sped off, getting up speed.

After thirty minutes, Night Runner decided he could wait no more to see if Omar would double back. He used the time to brief Baker on a plan.

"I'm not trying to take command here," Night Runner said. "Just an idea."

Baker flapped a sleeve at him. "Forget the military protocol. You're the scout. And I'll tell you when I have an opinion worth listening to."

Night Runner started off at a brisk walk down the road toward the last known Delta sighting. Baker drove the Toyota at the greatest distance he could and yet keep Night Runner in sight. If Night Runner spotted danger, he was to signal Baker, then hide to the side of the road. If Baker saw danger in his rearview mirrors, he would honk his horn and flash his lights as a signal to Night Runner to hide.

Night Runner would hide and Baker would bluff. Baker had the fake credentials and language skills to talk his way out of a situation. Nobody would suspect him of being a deserter, since he had only the one arm. And the Toyota held no contraband, only two cases of bottled water. Night Runner carried all the weapons—both their pistols, his own M-4 carbine, his sword, and the set of NVGs. Baker was just a fella, a tired, disabled vet on the way to visit kin in Karbala.

Night Runner, though, could not pass scrutiny. He looked Indian. He spoke only English and French.

He traveled that way until dusk, down the ridge and out onto the flat-scape of the desert. It was a good plan. Night Runner was glad to have had a good idea. He could not remember the last one. This one, though—its only drawback that he was getting tired—reminded him of his previous great idea. To come here. He should have stayed out of it. Until he had the legs for war.

The helicopter barely touched down at Baghdad's international airport before an ambulance streaked across the tarmac toward it. Karim-Assad saw two bodyguards pile out of the rear doors and duck beneath the transparent spinning rotor disk to meet Karim-Assad and Bani-Sadr. Two of Saddam's most trusted. Two cousins of his and Karim-Assad's.

Karim-Assad tried to hang back. He was in no hurry to get into the back of that vehicle. He was not so shaken that he did not notice Bani-Sadr subtly trying to hang back as well. Neither one of them, not even the brave chief of Desert Wolves wanted to be first into a sealed box. Karim-Assad braced himself as if to taste three tablespoons of butter before a meal. It gave him the courage to walk a step ahead of Bani-Sadr.

To Karim-Assad's relief the bodyguards did not disarm him. They did not pinch his arm just above the elbow. Karim-Assad had felt that particular pain many a time inside the palaces.

No, the bodyguards ushered them inside, then joined them. The pair sat near the doors, silent, solemn, not giving a hint at what might come next. The ambulance backed, turned, and careened across the tarmac.

The inside of the box was not even a pretense of a medical vehicle. Padded benches with armrests, a drop-down conference table, a refrigerator, and a bank of radios, and other electronic gear. One of Saddam's, comfortable as a limousine and safe from air strikes. And armored, too. Instead of rear-door glass, steel plates.

The ambulance came to a sudden stop. Karim-Assad and Bani-Sadr braced. The bodyguards put their hands to their weapons. They sat in silence until a knock on the rear doors. An exchange of sign and countersign through a squawk box in one of the doors.

Karim-Assad recognized the voice outside.

The doors flew open, and there stood Saddam, the huge indoor emptiness of an airplane hangar behind him. His arms wide in welcome.

The tension gushed from the box.

Because Saddam wore a smile broad and genuine. It left Karim-Assad delirious. Even the grave Bani-Sadr grinned. So did the solemn bodyguards. Not the usual stupid grins that because the president of Iraq smiled so did everybody else in the room. This was an occasion for joy. He was not in a mood for blood. He had good news. He—Karim-Assad's stomach sank. It was going to be terrible good news.

"They're alive!" Saddam brayed. "Uday and Qusay."

The bodyguards broke into applause. Karim-Assad and Bani-Sadr joined in.

"It's true. I have autopsy results," Saddam yelped. "Russian doctors and French forensic experts confirm it." His spit flew. "Thank Allah, they did not die among the four in the vehicle!"

So much for the intuition that he had not walked into a disaster. This was worse than eating a tub of butter.

He swallowed his vomit. "God is great!" he whooped. *Even if I am not feeling so great myself.*

⁂

Poole spent the last hour of faint light bent over his PDA, trying to make sense of the burst downloads. It was a map with live animations of Iraqi troop dispositions since the attack on the Republican Guards—what was it, a month ago? It *felt* like a month ago.

As he watched, the lines, arrows, and unit ID boxes flowed across the LED map. They looked like symbols for a cold front sweeping across the country on the Weather Channel.

The first animation gave him hope. The head of the snake-line, an Iraqi column, drove back toward Poole's original attack site and encircled it. *Okay,* he decided, *the division was going to secure the site.* Why, he could not guess. Maybe it was just something to do to look like you were doing something in the general chaos.

Or maybe to secure the site for the Iraqi equivalent of CSI. That made sense.

A second download was a snaking line with an arrow for its pointed head. It uncoiled as a tank column that drove through the attack site heading straight north, on a line more or less toward Baghdad. Okay, Saddam had re-called the division to the capital. Maybe to reinforce his defenses there. Maybe as a personal bodyguard of tanks.

In any case, that division didn't matter anymore. Certainly not to him and his men with the boots on the ground. The line to Baghdad would miss him and the Delta team by fifteen miles. He could even hear the distant roar. When he looked up he could see a curtain of dust rising to redden the setting sun.

The team was going to get a free pass, after all. The column would take hours to clear. Delta could hide out. Find water. Wait for the U.S. attack. Hunker down and stay out of the fight. Maybe even use the fog of combat to sneak out of the country and into Saudi Arabia.

Home free now. No sweat. All he had to do was recover Solis and Barret. Wait for the war. Deliver the goods. Go home. Bask in the glory. Life was good.

Right?

Karim-Assad and Bani-Sadr were back in the air just thirty minutes after their brief meeting with Saddam.

Bani-Sadr wore a headset and rode in a jump seat behind the two pilots. He studied a map spread out across his legs, pointing out the windshield and poking his finger at the map.

Bani-Sadr had little to say since the meeting with Saddam.

Karim-Assad understood why. It was one thing for the president of Iraq to order the Desert Wolves to find his sons' assassins. They could kill any number of people on the ground, not even Americans, and say they had done their best. Soon he would have plenty of American bodies to take to the president. Bani-Sadr could claim that any of them were the killers of Uday and Qusay.

But this mission? Bring back Uday and Qusay? Alive? There was no way to fake it. He had to deliver—

All at once Bani-Sadr grabbed the ear cups of his headset. He stared at his feet and spoke back. Two more exchanges. Then he reached forward and tapped both pilots by the shoulders. He pointed out the windshield to a low ridge beside the road.

The pilot turned sharply and set up for a landing.

Karim-Assad saw a second Desert Wolves helicopter on the ground, rotors turning.

After they landed, Bani-Sadr sent both helicopters away to loiter in the air beyond the horizon.

Karim-Assad kept up with Bani-Sadr on the jog from the landing area. He no longer felt tired. So much learning in so short a time invigorated him.

He hunkered down near Bani-Sadr, keeping his back to him. Like the others, he stayed on the alert for an enemy, although he had yet to see one.

For the tenth time today, Karim-Assad took out his shaving brush and began to whisk away the grit on the moving parts of his rifle.

"Nabil?"

"Yes?"

Bani-Sadr nudged Karim-Assad. "He found signs leading away from the road."

Karim-Assad raised his chin and dipped it again toward Nabil, a sign of his respect, and then went back to brushing his rifle.

Bani-Sadr asked for a full report.

"To the north of the road, a trail of up to a dozen men perhaps."

"The sons of Saddam among them?" Bani-Sadr wanted to know.

"Difficult to tell," Nabil said. "They brushed over their tracks. I think I saw a long drag mark in the sand. Perhaps a lame man—I cannot say for certain."

Karim-Assad stopped brushing. His heart stopped as well. *Uday?*

"What else?"

"A fake trail to the south," Nabil said. "Three men made the tracks to a helicopter takeoff area. Once walking forward, once walking backward. They left the impressions of helicopter wheels on the ground. Then they walked backward to this spot where we sit." He shrugged. "They crossed the road and joined the others in that direction." He pointed. "Toward Baghdad, not away."

"To make us believe they have left the country," Bani-Sadr said. "Tell this young man how you know the wheel impressions are fake."

"The wheel impressions are very good," Nabil said. "But they are too far apart for a Blackhawk, by a full ten centimeters. The tail mark is too close to the front wheels by almost half a meter, and the angle is skewed. The wind itself could not distort those distances."

Karim-Assad shook his head in wonder.

"Besides," Nabil said, "it is absurd that they would use two helicopters to bring in the attackers and only one to take them out—even with the loss of one man. A poor fake." Nabil turned his head to spit.

"He is disgusted," Bani-Sadr said.

Karim-Assad cocked his head.

Nabil's soft voice turned harsh. "Because they treat us like inferiors."

Bani-Sadr moved the tactical meeting across the road to the well-camouflaged trail leading north. Karim-Assad bent close to the spot where Nabil pointed. If it was a trail, he did not see it. Until he dropped to his knees, where he could see the brush marks as of a rough broom.

Nabil smiled and shook his head. "If you look too closely, you'll see the grains of sand but not the desert. Step back. Take in the landscape to the horizon. From that point of view, you can see it like a tarmac highway."

Karim-Assad looked, then shook his head. He could not see the track of the Americans.

Nabil shrugged. No matter to him. "We have them," he said to Bani-Sadr. "We own them like goats."

Bani-Sadr's own smile was lame in reply. He told them

of his new orders. All at once, Nabil—for that matter, all of the Desert Wolves—seemed not quite as eager for combat with the Americans. The handicap of trying to kill without killing Uday and Qusay was too great to enjoy a meeting with the enemy on better than even terms.

Bani-Sadr told his radio man to call the loitering helicopters back. "Also our third craft," he said. "The one patrolling the watering holes."

The Desert Wolves waited on board, the helicopters running, for a full ten minutes. Still that third craft did not join them. Bani-Sadr made several calls into his radio set, and as he waited five minutes more, his complexion grew darker, his eyes more flinty than ever.

Finally Bani-Sadr had had enough. He tapped on the pilot's shoulder and pointed at a spot on the map. The spot on the map before Bani-Sadr's nail was a splash of green with a blue dot in the center.

The pilot took off and flew out of his own cloud of dust. Up on one knee, Karim-Assad looked out the windshield. A stand of low trees in the distance, green, just as on the map, only brighter green, caught in the last, low rays of sunshine before dusk. The blue dot he could guess at.

An oasis.

Night Runner kept going into the darkness, marching down the center of a shallow wadi at a pace not fast, but steady. Baker wore the NVGs. He let the Toyota close up with Night Runner as the night came on. Finally Night Runner was walking beside Baker's open window.

"Need a lift?"

Night Runner stopped in his tracks.

Baker saw massive basalt shapes all around.

"Cut the engine."

Night Runner stepped away from the ticking sound of the hot engine, turning a complete circle.

"What?" Baker whispered.

"We're here."

"Where?"

"We're at the spot where Poole was supposed to be," Night Runner said. He shrugged. "I mean at the last place the GPS beacons had him."

"How do you know?"

Night Runner shook his head. "I may have lost my edge, but I can still read a map."

"What do we do now?"

"You freeze!"

Night Runner and Baker cursed as one. "Americans," they said in unison. "We're Americans."

"Lay down on your belly and spread out like a puddle of vomit," yelled a voice from the darkness. "Now! Before we blow your American asses away."

Two hours after sunset. Time to move again. Barret and his team had made it back by double-timing since dusk. Poole had briefed. The team, such as it was, stood around in an uneasy tension, shifting combat packs and web gear to ride in the grooves of their shoulders and dents in their backs on the coming trek. The bodyguards had Uday and Qusay on their feet—no whining from Uday for a change. He lifted his arms to accept the poles that would take the weight off his bum knee.

All Poole had to say was, *Move out.* The point man was ready to go. Scouts were already out to the flanks.

Poole hated making a second move without Solis. But he didn't dare to spend too much time in one spot, or even two. Solis would have to catch up.

All eyes were on him. He raised his hand to give the signal. He opened his mouth to say the words.

"Uh-oh." The sound came from Foucault's instead of his own mouth. "Houston, we have a problem."

"What up?"

Foucault handed over a set of high-powered NVGs. Poole took in the picture in one sweeping glance. The Iraqi column. No longer was it a snake. Every vehicle had stopped in line. Every one had changed direction at once. Coming right at the Delta team on a line.

A search party. An entire division sweeping toward them. One long line, one vehicle deep, a line that stretched fifteen miles.

The search party was going to sweep over this position. At the rate the Iraqis were moving, he might have an hour to clear the area. Maybe he could get wide enough to clear the end of the sweep before the Iraqis came by. An hour to travel seven miles? In the dark? For a Delta Force team, no prob. But with two prisoners? One a crip?

No way.

A voice yelped inside Poole: *Do something, even if it's wrong.*

Give it the old college try. He opened his mouth again to give the order to move out on the double-time. "Shit."

He didn't need to explain it to any of his team—they had the eyes to see for themselves. The Iraqis were coming with full white lights on, headlights and tanks searchlights winking at them with every turn of the steering wheel, every dip in the desert.

"What next?"

"Oh, there's more." Foucault.

"I don't want to hear it."

Foucault gave it to him anyhow. "They're also traveling on full IR."

"Any ideas?"

Nobody had one.

He could think of one, but didn't have the balls to say it. *Fight it out.*

Right. Against an armored division. Maybe the Iraqis would be stupid. Circle the wagons and open fire into the center. Kill themselves, letting the Americans walk away with their prisoners. *Yeah.* Or maybe the Iraqis would just laugh themselves to death.

The Desert Wolves found the helicopter lying on its back, belly-up like a dead fish.

Karim-Assad could not believe that the craft could be one of theirs. These men not invincible? The helicopters banked sharply and flew a wide loop around the oasis. Karim-Assad saw the dead men in the gloom of dusk. He recognized the uniforms as they flew over. It was, indeed, part of Bani-Sadr's team.

The brace of helicopters, landing together like geese, touched down nearly a kilometer from the oasis, in an area so flat it could not hide an enemy.

Karim-Assad watched as the Desert Wolves rushed the oasis in a three-prong formation of alternating moves and stops. Bani-Sadr did not know he existed now.

That was fine with him. In their vengeful moods, he was happy to stay out of sight, out of their school of the desert.

The Desert Wolves rushed past the oasis, past the dead bodies and onto the high ground beyond. Karim-Assad caught up with them there.

Nabil and three others set off toward the west, jogging, pointing at the ground, following a trail.

Bani-Sadr ordered his team to gather up the dead. "Take them to our base camp," he said. "Notify the families."

"You go back with them," Bani-Sadr said.

"As you wish." This was no time to argue, and he knew it.

Bani-Sadr shook his head. "Only three."

Karim-Assad held his silence, confused.

"Only three Americans, and they were able to do all

this." He shook his head. "They suffered no casualties. The Desert Wolves are not used to fighting such men as this, men who can win a fight even with fewer numbers."

"Trickery? Luck?"

Bani-Sadr put a hand on his shoulder and directed Karim-Assad back down the slope. "Never assume luck with your enemy," he said. "These are good fighters. Just as the Desert Wolves are the best fighters in our country."

Bani-Sadr stopped him short of the helicopter.

"Please do not tell our president that I said anything to disparage our military forces."

"But you haven't."

"So now I will. The Russian agents who advise our president tell us that the Americans will likely start the war tomorrow. Their air force will battle our air force." He snickered. "That will be a short fight. Their armies will battle our armies. That will be a longer fight because there are so many more of our tanks to destroy than our jet fighters." He squeezed Karim-Assad's shoulder. "Here is the part that I want you to keep to yourself. The Americans will win the war."

"I fear it, too."

"Tell our president this: No matter what happens in this war, the Desert Wolves will track down the Americans who took his sons. The best Iraqi fighters will kill every one of America's best. We will have that victory at least."

"I want to fight with you," Karim-Assad said, unable to keep from blurting the words.

"It's too much of a risk."

"I'm not afraid to die."

"Nor am I afraid for you to die. The risk is not to you. The risk is to us if we take you along."

Karim-Assad winced.

A pat on the shoulder. "We have to move across the desert at night. You're in no condition."

"Perhaps then after you deal with them. Even if we lose the war. If I have to die, I would rather do it with real men than with those tin soldiers who strut around the palaces."

Bani-Sadr took his hand from Karim-Assad's shoulder and cupped it to the young man's cheek.

"I did not mean that which I said just now. I do not wish for you to die at all." Gently he turned Karim-Assad's head and pushed him toward the waiting helicopter. "Later. If there is a later, you can rejoin us and continue to learn. I would be proud to have you in my command."

Poole heard a crackle in his headset. Three-Three breaking through the jamming? No.

"Six, this is Green Six." Solis.

"What's your twenty?" Poole's voice flat, pulse spiking, mind dropping the clutch and going through the gears. He called out, both into his radio mike and to the Delta team. "Heads up. Solis and his crew are hard by." They had to be close. Or else the radio wouldn't work.

He heard the word passed out by word of mouth, then come back.

"Clear, Cap." Foucault. "Word's out."

"You're clear in," Poole said.

"Coming from the east with one helluva surprise."

"You got a helicopter gonna beam us up?"

"Not quite. But I do have a Toyota pickup, and that's not even the good part."

A Toyota? If Solis jacked a truck and the Raqs sent up an alarm— He saw the surprise. "Night Runner?"

The Blackfeet brave who'd been with Poole in Afghanistan smiled.

Poole was seeing a ghost. Had to be. He walked up to him, touched the face, worked his fingers all over it, taking off the NVGs and tactical soft cap to feel his hair. He ran his hands down the apparition's arms. Finding no left hand, he rolled back the sleeve to the stump. He touched the hard smooth scar. "Night Runner."

"Affirm."

"Where's the rest of you?"

Night Runner held up the stump. "Vietnam."

"How?"

Night Runner shrugged like a guy tired of talking about the same old. "We can catch up later." He tossed a nod over Poole's shoulder, toward the sight and sound of the approaching armored division. "Deal with that first?"

"Sons of bitches fragged a dozen air strikes to me, then took them back, the first time I wanted to use them."

"A dozen?" Night Runner gave him a weak smile. "I don't know, Captain. Two dozen, three dozen? Ten dozen might not even be enough."

It broke the tension built up inside Poole. He laughed. Hard. Shook his head. What the hell. "Got any ideas?"

"We can put some guys in the Toyota with your payload. Make a run for it."

"Toyota." Poole looked to Solis, smiling all the way back to his ears. "You weren't BS'ing."

"Nope."

"Where is it?"

Solis jerked a thumb over his shoulder. "A klick yonder, sitting in defilade in a wadi with another former Delta guy. We sneaked up on these two on our way back. Good thing they was talking American or we might notta bothered sneaking."

Poole gave Night Runner a look. *Sneaked up on you?* But kept his trap shut about it when the Indian ducked his head, embarrassed. "Two former Delta guys? And a truck?"

"Spangler worked it out," Night Runner said.

"Ah-h-h." Poole got it. "Figures." He shook off all the

extraneous racing thoughts. "Okay, what?" he said to Night Runner without consulting Solis or his own NCOs. "Take the whole crew back to the truck?"

Night Runner looked around him, counting noses first, then taking in the basalt formations. "Not the whole team. We might squeeze everybody in the truck, but it'd bog down in the sand." He looked around. "Understand you have some prisoners besides?"

Poole twitched his head. "They're off a ways."

"No place to hide in the wadi," Night Runner said. "Better cover here."

"Here."

Night Runner shrugged. *Better'n nothing.*

The drone of the armor column was its own urgency. Poole detailed four men to take the Hussein brothers back to the Toyota. Baker went with them.

After they left, Poole looked relieved. Hell, he felt relieved. Now that he was shed of those two. Whatever else might have been here, he might be able to say—just might—that this singular Delta team, under his feeble command, at least performed its mission.

The rest of them? Well. They were trapped.

"Fight it out?" Poole said.

Night Runner snickered along with the other Delta men within hearing. Fight it out with a tank division. Right.

"Got any other ideas?"

"One," Night Runner said. "Won't be easy."

"Easy? I been thinking of setting a suicide ambush for a tank division. What do I know about easy? Give me the hardest idea you got."

"The idea is easy. The hard part is the execution."

The tanks grew louder. White lights now cast faint shadows. Soon the Raqi IR would pick up the heat returns from their bodies and paint them as hotspots against the cold desert.

Night Runner waited for the word. Poole saw an uncertainty there.

Was there a trembling in his fingers? Night Runner nervous? Did he smell fear in him? *Night Runner afraid?* He didn't want to think about it.

"What's the play?" he said. "Youda man with a plan? I want to hear it."

"Circle up the troops. So I can brief them all at once. There's no time to repeat it, no chance to debate it. You're going to have to trust me."

Poole gave him a wide smile. "That's the easy part."

They stood with a basalt boulder shielding them from the Raqis. Night Runner talked fast and loud over the encroaching sounds: tracks grinding, metal squealing, engines laboring. The shadows cast by the lights grew sharper edges.

Night Runner finished to silence. He mopped his face with his empty sleeve. *Night Runner sweating?*

"Questions."

"There were none."

"Let's get to it," Poole said, his passion for the plan not all that real. But what the hell. Fake or real, it didn't matter anyhow. Bad as Night Runner's plan sounded, he didn't have a better one. "We don't have a lot of time."

Baker vowed he'd never go into combat again. Not after tonight. *Uday and Qusay!* First the trip into Afghanistan, coming face-to-face with Osama bin Laden.

Now this! The sons of Saddam. The NVGs that he borrowed from one of the Delta men pinched his head, but he could not stop to adjust them. Not now. He had to clear of the line of tanks moving at him. Screw the torpedoes, balls to the wall.

Nothing seemed real, not even the desert unreeling before him at warp speed, green and in one-dimension like an arcade game on expert level.

But this was no game. He was taking Uday and Qusay out of Iraq. *Uday and Qusay, for God's sake!* Kidnapping the sons of Saddam.

He couldn't go back to any war after this. Not after this. Any other war would be too boring.

Night Runner sent half the team—Solis's men—to a basalt boulder the size of a school bus. He watched them climb it, heard the grunts and groans loud and clear, the Delta men's way of letting him know. *This is bullshit.*

The second rock was broader and wider, more like a one-room cinderblock house with a flat roof with no doors or windows. There he put Poole's squad. These men groaned even louder. Because the top of this boulder was lower than the first.

Once the two Delta teams were in place, Night Runner began to work around the base of the rocks. He brushed out every trace of footsteps that he could find. He knew he could not find them all, so he focused on each rock, working with the branch of the weed with very fine tendrils. The base of each of these rocks would get the passing glances, the second looks from troops on the ground. Here the wind had done its best work, sweeping up the sand, creating hollows on one side of the rock and piles on the other. Here lay piles of rubble that fell away from the mother stones. If the Iraqis did find an enemy here he'd find him at the base of these boulders. Overhead shelter from artillery in the overhangs. Natural fighting positions behind the rubble. Even the most tired Iraqis would not be so depleted as to ignore these spots. Night Runner smiled.

Because this gave the Delta men their edge.

The Iraqi eyes would focus downward, to the danger

zones. Not up to the level higher even than the IR tank searchlights.

If every man on the Delta team kept his head down, the Iraqi thermal optics would not pick up any returns. Because the tops of the boulders were higher.

Finally, Night Runner could do no more. The irregular line of tanks and trucks had moved to within a hundred meters. He had to hide.

He climbed up to the top. Keeping flat, he slithered across the stone, raspy as fine sandpaper. He took off his night vision goggles and hid them beneath the flat of his left sleeve so the glass could not pick up a stray light beam, reflect it, and betray the team. Before his eyes could adjust he knew he was lying beside Poole. His nose told him that. To his right, and not far away he smelled Foucault. He never told the white men that he could tell them apart by their body odors, that he could remember them for all his life by their scent. He lifted his nose into the breeze, testing. No Michelotti. He wanted to ask where the kid was, yet didn't want to hear the answer.

"Runner?" Poole.

"You've got good night vision, Captain."

"No, no offense."

"What?"

"You been drinking?"

A non-Indian could smell him? "Not for three, maybe four days."

"The hand?"

"Something like that." *More like the head, or the heart. Maybe even the spirit.* Whatever, it was not only his hand that was lost to him for the past year.

A white man could smell him? Make that a black man. Nothing could humiliate him more. If he ever got back to the world, he would never drink again. Never.

The roar of Iraqi tanks made Night Runner hug the top of the stone. He figured about half the team bought into his plan. The half that knew him from the mission into Afghanistan. The new guys didn't know him. They could not believe what he was asking them to do, let alone trust him. But they had to. There were no choices left. Embrace the impossible. The improbable. The incomprehensible. The insanity of hiding in plain sight.

He did not have time to sell it. To tell them he often hid in the open where creatures had many times the powers of hearing, sight, smell, and touch as the Iraqi soldiers now combing the desert within spitting distance.

The hard part was to believe it could be done. Then to lie still. To close your eyes. So no light could reflect to one of the Iraqis.

It did not depend on camo. It depended on the viewer's frame of mind. He'd watched Indian women in Montana seeking edible plants and herbs on the prairie, so intent on identifying a plant they would pluck one from beneath a sleeping prairie rattler lying in plain sight.

The Iraqi soldiers were tired. The attack on their own. Constant tension. Lack of sleep. Searching the desert by day and night in vehicles the temperature of toaster ovens for hours on end. They were looking for American soldiers ten feet tall, draped with weapons, perhaps hundreds of them, weapons the size of Minuteman missiles.

But all they'd seen, for days and endless nights on end, were rocks and rubble and bushes and foxes and rabbits and snakes and spiders and each other.

He'd told the Delta men: *If you don't give them anything unusual to see, they won't see you. If you hide in a place they don't expect, they won't even look. They will look at bushes, to see behind bushes. They will look at holes, to find the glint of eyeballs looking out. They will send the infantry into caves and under cliffs and overhangs. They will lift up every stone that looks suspicious. But they will not see nine men lying in plain sight because they can't even imagine such a thing possible.*

So simple to say. *Lie down in plain sight. Close your eyes. Lie still. Don't breath. Don't peek. Let the Iraqis go on by. Hope. Have faith. Pray. Make peace.*

The unsaid part, they already knew: *If I'm wrong, get ready to die.*

The boulder shook as the tanks came near. The roar of diesel engines filled his ears, his head, his chest. He could not tell his own trembling from that of the earth. Was this fear? Or just a withdrawal from alcohol? How dare he risk the lives of good men while he was on the very verge of the DTs?

His last thought before the first Iraqi tank came abreast of the boulder was a reassuring one. He did not want to die. He wanted to walk the path of a warrior. To kill the enemy, not himself. A good thought for a warrior. Now. If only he didn't stink.

He opened one eye and peeked beneath his left elbow.

To find himself face-to-face with an Iraqi tank commander not two feet away.

The pressure was on Ramsey Baker. He knew he was not a great choice for driver. He was a natural righty, and his left hand was his only hand. Which made it tough to shift, even with an automatic tranny. But the Delta men refused to drive. *Not to make a big deal about it, crip, but we gotta fight.*

They were probably right about that. Still. Only a year out of the business and already over the hill. Not to mention one-handed.

"What are you slowing down for?" the Delta NCO in the front with Ramsey Baker wanted to know. Winston.

"A road up ahead. It gets a lot of traffic."

"More than a whole Republican Guard division out there bearing down on our asses?"

Baker kept his cool. He kept the Toyota idling forward,

but slowly. The last thing he wanted to do was charge across that road in front of an Iraqi combat vehicle. One thing to bluff your way out of a stop in broad daylight. Quite another to try it with a white truck. Driving at night. Cross-country. With four soldiers armed to the teeth. And, oh yeah, Uday and Qusay.

He was right to be wary. All the commotion came from the right side, the lights and noise. Let Winston obsess over that. Baker kept checking left. Until he saw it, the glitter of the light bar of an Iraqi police vehicle coming from that way—toward the tank division, barreling down the road. Lights on bright, the top of the car sparkling red and white.

Baker let it pass. Then he gassed the Toyota. He plunged into the rooster tail of dust behind the police car and turned right. Driving half-blind, staying in the flicker of the lights.

All he had to make was a quarter mile. If he could beat the tank division to the intersection, it was a sharp left to the road to Saudi Arabia. He stayed in the dust cloud and, when he could no longer see the headlights and flashers of the police car, hinged up his NVGs and turned on his own headlights—it was far too conspicuous to be running this road without lights. From a half mile distance, a set of oncoming headlights winked in and out of the dust at him. His heart clutched a stroke, then picked up a faster pace.

"Jesus, man," Winston said. "You got some cajones."

It didn't call for a reply. Baker jammed down on the gas and plowed ahead. He had to beat that Iraqi vehicle to the turn.

He felt the seat pressed back and realized that Winston was pressing his own feet on the floorboard. As if he could make the truck go faster.

Go he did. Faster and blinder, until Baker couldn't see anything past his brown-fogged headlights, maybe ten meters to the front. He glanced out his door glass and found that at least he could see the edge of the road.

"Tell me if I'm about to run up that guy's ass," he said to Winston.

Winston grunted through one very tight throat.

Baker saw the rock cairn.

He slowed. Made the left. Drove out of the cloud. The police car went on. The oncoming lights slid past, first in the right-side mirror, then the left.

Winston gasped in relief.

But Baker knew. They were not out of danger until . . .

Halfway up the ridge, the road curved. Only when the bend hid the Toyota from the tank division below and behind them did Baker let out a gush of air.

"Nice call," Winston said.

"Thanks." Baker could not have been more proud. A compliment like that. From a Delta fighter. Better than his Medal of Honor.

Out of the danger zone. Nothing but a straight shot to Saudi Arabia on a road less traveled. Baker turned off the headlights and dropped his NVGs down over his eyes again.

"Man," Winston said. "Am I ever proud to be with you."

Baker thought his heart might burst out of his chest.

A tank commander. Right in front of his face. Night Runner knew it was a tank commander because he could see the open clamshell hatch on the cupola behind the man's shoulder. The tank stopped with the Iraqi right in his face.

Move on!

But no, the vehicle stood in place, the engine chugging at idle. The tank commander hauled himself out of the cupola, planted his butt on the turret and slid down to the rear deck. He stamped his feet on the grills over the engine. And stepped up to the basalt, eye-level with Night Runner.

Night Runner cursed himself. He had not dreamed this. A firefight, maybe. If one of the men—one of the other men—was spotted. But not *this*. The Iraqi was going to see him. He could not even shift his body, could not risk the tiniest of movements to bring his right hand beneath his belly and close his fist on the reassuring grip of his short, curved sword.

A glow of white light lit up the Iraqi. Night Runner lay in the shadow of those very lights. But at this distance—

A hand came up to the edge of the basalt boulder, the tank commander's left hand.

The Iraqi leaned in toward Night Runner. Yes, he was reaching for him. But why? Why not sound the alarm?

Night Runner tensed, ready to uncoil at the man.

Now barely a foot from his face. The hand closed on the edge of the basalt.

The man didn't see him yet? The man didn't smell that alcohol stink?

Night Runner had to move. A hasty plan of action. Pull his sword. Hit the Iraqi. Leap to the ground. Dash to the rear. Try to draw the Iraqis toward him. Away from the Delta team. Away—

What the hell was he thinking?

That was so crazy anyhow. Why not go all the way?

Why not run to the front of the tank? Climb up the front slope of the T-72? Take the driver's head off with his keen blade? Pull out the corpse? Crawl into the hatch?

Drive on. Maybe later park the tank and—

A cry from below. In Arabic.

The tank commander laughed and pulled away from the brink. Night Runner could smell the man's stale breath.

A slight snicker from beside him. Poole.

Night Runner's body ached from the tension in his muscles. His head hurt from trying to keep focus, as . . .

The tank commander's head bounced up and down, in and out of sight, in and out, as he stood on the tank's rear deck.

Night Runner got it at last. The Iraqi was packing himself into his pants. He'd stopped to pee. A soldier had walked by. The tank commander had pissed over the side onto one of his own.

He found himself smiling like a mad man, cold from the sweat that drenched him. The Iraqi clambered up into his cupola, feet-first, and tugged his commo helmet down over his ears. The tank lurched away, leaving the team in a sudden darkness and growing silence.

From below came the plodding, grinding footsteps of boots in the sand. Tired men on foot. Tired and grumbling. He did not know the language, but he knew the sentiment: *Bad enough that the assholes in the tank corps gave you grief day in and day out. But pissing on you? That's over the line.*

Night Runner shook his head clear. He'd almost done it. Almost jumped off the boulder onto the Iraqi. He'd nearly given away the Delta team. Talk about pissing on your own troops.

"Shit!" Winston said it at the instant Baker thought it.

A pair of headlights, maybe two miles ahead between the Toyota and Saudi Arabia. Winking at them just moments after they topped the ridge.

"Any ideas?" Winston said.

Baker took it as high praise that a Delta man would look to him for an idea. "It just so happens that I do."

He knew this ground. He kept driving in the dark until he saw this afternoon's tire tracks. Omar had led him into that gully out of sight next to the road before Night Runner banished him.

Baker turned off, following the tracks to the very spot. "We'll wait him out."

He stopped the truck with the hand brake to avoid flashing the taillights. Then he turned off the engine.

Winston and the Delta men took up positions at the four corners of the truck to guard their precious cargo. Baker sat in the truck.

Nothing left to do now but wait.

Night Runner wasn't in the groove exactly, but he did feel cleansed. He had sweated mightily on top of that monument of basalt, close enough to literally spit into the eye of the Iraqi tank commander. It was a near-death experience worthy of life. He rewarded himself with fully half a canteen of water to restore what he had lost in sweat.

Poole assembled the men at the base of one boulder. There was some chatter, some shaking of heads, a bit of the giddy laughter that they had defied all the odds against them. Foucault translated the hot exchange between the tank commander and one wet-down soldier. The guffaws trailed off to an uneasy silence. These men were pros. They knew they weren't out of the desert yet.

Night Runner waited with the others for Poole to give them a plan.

But Poole gave the nod to Night Runner. "You da man," he said. "Take us home. After what we just got away with, you could tell me to sprout wings, and I'd be checking my flaps for feathers."

Night Runner surprised himself. He began talking at once. As if he had hatched a plan already.

"We let the Iraqis go on their way," he said. "Give them an hour. Then take a southwest heading toward Saudi Arabia. Hole up by day, travel by night. We should be out in three days."

Poole simply said, "You and Barret on point." He shrugged. "If that's okay with you."

"Better than okay." Behind his night vision goggles Night Runner closed his eyes. He had worth again. He had worth as a man, a warrior, as a leader with credentials of skill rather than rank. All he had to do was help lead the team to safety. Get out of Iraq. Go home. Start a regimen to restore the exterior. Once he had his body and his senses back. Then maybe he could tackle the other, the soul of a warrior.

He wanted to be whole again—as much as he could. He could live as a warrior—even a one-handed warrior if need be.

This. This companionship, this combat. It was his nature, his destiny, his very being. For the first time in a year this let him feel truly alive. For the first time in his life he understood why. This. Against all the civil incivility he'd learned in the Ivy League, this was his mission. This war.

Adnil Mustafa Qasim Zimnako Jalal Massoud Saladin ji Kirkuk just smiled and smiled. The stories he would tell in his home town of Kirkuk. A man standing in the middle of the road, arms outstretched. A flashlight in each hand. From four kilometers away, it looked like the headlights of a truck two kilometers distant. If the man bowed at the waist and twisted left and right, he became a moving truck.

That's all it took to drive the Toyota into hiding. That's all it took to deliver the sons of Saddam into his hands.

The man the Americans called Omar gave his men the signal. They began creeping up on the Toyota. Even before the one-armed driver had shut down the motor, they were within striking range.

While they waited for the last of the hour to pass, Night Runner and Poole caught up on old news. Poole let Night Runner be as vague as he needed to be about the year-plus between Afghanistan and yesterday.

Then Poole asked, "What about this guy, Omar?"

Night Runner gave it a moment's thought. "Think of him as the Kurdish version of Spangler."

"Meaning?"

"Smart—"

"You mean clever."

"Focused—"

"Obsessed."

"Ruthless—"

"Ruthless."

Night Runner screwed up his face.

"And you don't trust him besides?"

Night Runner shook his head. "Spangler I trust because I have a general idea of his motives. This guy? Anybody's guess."

"A Kurd? And he's not on our side?"

Night Runner shrugged. "He was when I left him. Or at least he acted like it. But he's only on one side. His own."

Night Runner fell in step beside Barret. Together they stepped off into the night ahead of the Delta team. *Walking point on a combat mission!*

This was where he belonged. He felt hotter; he felt colder. He felt meaner; he felt bolder.

Think hot, act cold, think mean, act bold. The chain of thought gave him a rush. All at once he was alive and sure and strong and decidedly undead. Because he *felt*.

He felt the will to fight, to win, to live on in the service of men like these. *IF.*

If only his body did not let him down.

On the outside he shivered from the cold. Inside he shivered from a fear. Not fear of combat. That fear was normal; that fear was good—it made a man assess risk before taking chances. But this. This was fear of failure, fear that he would not measure up. Fear that he was so far out of physical condition and mental acuity that he might put these Delta men at risk.

On the outside he stunk. From the sick smell of alcohol working its way out of his body, clinging to his clothes, reeking. His body was wet from the stinking sweat, the fear. And so he shivered and stunk.

On the outside he stumbled. Used to be his feet had an ability to find obstacles in his path, feel them, gauge them, sidestep them. Used to be his feet had eyes. Now he clumped along like a white man.

No, that was an insult to Barret. Next to him Barret glided across the desert in ballet slippers. Next to Barret Night Runner was a Blackfeet Frankenstein in concrete shoes.

Instead of hearing the night, a white noise roared like surf in his ears. His blood pressure. Again the lack of conditioning. Out of shape. A stranger to stress. Again, the drinking.

His night vision had lost its clarity, because in the last year he had no reason to see at night. Once he had been able to see at night almost as well as the white man using night vision goggles. Better in one respect, in that his field of vision was not limited to the narrow tunnel of the NVGs.

He felt a hand on his shoulder. Barret. Did he sense his frenzy? A gentle grip to buoy him? Or just a check on the noise of his concrete feet?

Next time he would be in shape. Next time he would be a better soldier, a better warrior. Next time Spangler asked him to—

Barret's iron grip dragged him to his knees.

As a harsh voice called out. From straight ahead, not twenty meters away. An Iraqi voice.

Night Runner felt a wash of shame. A mistake of the recruit fresh off the streets. Inside his head instead of keeping vigil on the danger zone of Iraq.

Barret spoke up to answer the voice.

Night Runner did not speak Arabic, but he could read Barret. It was a tired, impatient answer. He murmured to Night Runner, "He wants to know who goes here."

Barret's tone said: *Who the hell wants to know?*

The exchange went on in the guttural squish of Arabic. Night Runner filled in the words.

IRAQI: *What are you doing running around in the night?*
The tension gone from his voice now.
BARRET: *Good question. I'd rather be home in bed—your home, with your wife.*

A laughter of several men. An infantry patrol. Stragglers. Maybe the man who got peed on.

IRAQI: *Come up and join us for a smoke.*
BARRET, SPEAKING LOUDER: *No can do. We have to catch up.*
IRAQI: *What's the hurry that you can't stop for a cigarette?*

Barret whispered to Night Runner, "He wants us to show ourselves before we pass by. No can do, Abu."

Barret called out again: *No can do, Abu.* He was shouting, his radio mike open. To warn Poole and the team.

Night Runner forced himself out of his head. He had to act. He pried Barret's fingers loose and began to crawl. Forward. Action. Action against the enemy. Get into it. That was the way to recover from his blunder. He tired before he made ten meters. He had to stop, catch his breath. So his panting did not give him away.

The Iraqi voice grew impatient, angry, demanding. He was telling Barret to show himself. And Barret's tone was, by turns, dumb, harried, indignant. *Keep him on the line, Bo.*

As long as the Iraqi kept talking, the Delta team was in no danger of getting shot at. Barret might pull it off, might talk his way past. Go around.

Night Runner bit his lip. This was his fault. *Stragglers? You never thought of stragglers?* Why not wait *two* hours before striking out? Was he so dull?

He shook his head, to clear it. His night vision goggles slid off-center. He fixed them. *There!* A man. Finally. The Iraqi yapping at Bo. Four more Iraqis came into focus. Right there all along, but he hadn't seen them. A year ago, when he was sharper, he would already be standing behind them by now, his short sword drawn.

A year from now.

What did that matter in the here and now? Nothing. What mattered was how Delta was going to get out of this pickle. Fight? Or flee?

Night Runner figured flee. No need to fight with this squad, smoking, joking, squatting, sitting on their helmets, rifles not at the ready.

He could see the insignia of rank, the two pips of a lieutenant on the Iraqi doing all the talking. Calling out between drags on his cigarette. No big deal. Not as if men didn't get lost in the desert now and then. Goes with the territory.

Bo should just shut up. Go quiet and slip away. Night Runner could act as a rear guard. These guys didn't look up to a chase in the dark. They were at ease.

True, they did have night vision devices, the monoculars the Russians had stopped using before they had stopped being the Soviet Union. The L-T and two others wore theirs on lanyards around their necks. They didn't care about Bo's voice enough to try to spot him.

Night Runner decided to slip back to Bo and lead the team wide. He no sooner shifted his weight when a direct current of alarm shot through him.

A second man, an NCO stood up and spoke into the officer's ear. The Iraqi officer pulled the lanyard off his head and handed over his monocular. The NCO scanned over Night Runner's head toward Bo's voice.

Just as Bo called out again. Night Runner clamped his jaws tight. For Bo. *Shut up, Bo. Back off*.

The NCO handed back the monocular, shook his head, screwed up his face. He had not spotted Bo. But he was leery. He unslung his rifle, an AK-50, the carbine version of the AK-47, short barrel, a telescoping metal stock.

In slow motion, the NCO dropped to one knee. He worked the bolt to the rear, then eased it forward. He slid a round home. He bumped the bolt with the heel of his hand, seating the round in the chamber.

Night Runner put his hand to radio mike. *A warning round? To show a soldier this was no joke? The NCO would pull a stunt like that?*

It was a stunt. Surely. If he was truly alarmed, he'd have made his men take cover. Still. The danger of a Red-on-Red firefight was all too real. Popping off a round at night? With an enemy threat? Pure nuts.

By now, these men knew that the sons of Saddam were missing. By now, nobody in Iraq would joke around.

The lieutenant, also in slow motion, also dropped to one knee. The rest of the Iraqis took heed. They sat erect, grasped their weapons, put on their helmets. No more smoking, no more joking.

The banter with Bo went silent. Maybe Bo had left an insult hanging in the air. Maybe a twang in his accent. A wrong answer.

The NCO pressed a release button and extended the metal stock of his carbine.

The lieutenant pulled a piece of paper from his breast pocket. Night Runner knew. The games were over.

He aimed his pistol. The Glock's silencer made the gun muzzle-heavy. He felt another twinge of shame. His hand trembled as he laid the EOTECH reticle on the Iraqi NCO's face, the red center dot the size of a period. He had lost his edge. But did his nerve have to fail him, too?

He laid the silencer across a round, smooth stone the size of a bowling ball.

The officer read from his paper. He called out a word. A preset verbal signal, the sign in a two-part password. No way could Barret know the countersign reply.

Hoping he was still in radio range, Night Runner spoke into his boom mike. "Bo, get down. Get down and—"

The round, smooth stone, the size of a combat helmet lurched at the sound of his voice.

Another voice spoke. An Iraqi voice. Right in front of him. In Arabic, no doubt as to the words: *What the hell?*

The NCO with the carbine heard the ruckus. He shifted his aim, lowering the barrel of the AK-50 toward the sound. Giving Night Runner a point of view like no other. Point blank. An open eye, its pupil encircled by an iron peep sight. A closed fist around the forestock of the weapon. One squinted eye to the side, three fingers below the weapon, the trigger finger hidden behind the hand on the forestock and by the trigger guard. A folded bayonet. A sling swivel.

A front post sight, long and pointed. Below that and at the center of it all he could see an immense dot: the ultimate exclamation point. The bore of a rifle in the shape of a perfectly black, perfectly circular circle.

Ramsey Baker checked his watch. Half an hour. Time enough for the lights to have cleared. Yet they had not passed by. *What up?*

The Delta men still stood their posts at the four corners of the truck. Two at each fender. All looking outward. All on the alert.

Winston not so much. He stood next to Baker. He kept his back to the truck, looking out, but he didn't mind passing the time with idle chatter. Didn't mind telling Baker he was from Nevada. That the desert was a piece of cake to him. That he loved the desert.

"Even the snakes. Ever see a sidewinder? Coiled up? Like any other rattler to most people. Y'know, except for the sharp hoods over the eyes. But moving? A regular optical illusion. No mistaking that move."

Baker let it go with no more than a grunt or two. Until.

The sound of gunfire. In the distance. A weapon on auto, a burst of ten. An odd shot grouping, lacking in fire discipline.

"An AK," Baker and Winston said as one.

"I gotta go check out the road," Winston said.

"I don't know," Baker said. "We should saddle up and go."

"There's a fight." More gunfire, a real firefight now. Winston clenched his jaw. "Somebody on our tail?"

Baker reached across his body with his left hand and put the truck into gear. "I'm not arguing here. I'm just saying—those lights. We should wait till they pass—"

Winston gave him a hard look. "They should have been by already."

"Right," Baker said. "Let's go. We gotta get our cargo out of the country."

He checked all three mirrors. His heart leapt. He counted four men. Five with Winston. One too many.

"We've got company."

He snatched at the 9-mm pistol in his belt. He pulled back the hammer with a flick of his thumb and put the muzzle under one thigh.

He glanced at Winston. He had not moved. His face was the expression of a gas pain.

"What?"

Winston's face softened, almost a dreamy look in his eyes.

Ramsey barked at him. "Get to the rear. Get—"

Then he saw it, the tip of a spear. Dark and wet, breaking through the front of Winston's jacket from low and below the center of his chest.

The passenger door flew open. The man who stood there was not Delta Force. *One of Omar's!* Baker opened his mouth to call out a warning. He could not speak for the pain in his neck.

He had felt pain before, beatings at the hand of an ally, his arm cut off as he watched. But nothing had felt so damned, well . . . *fatal* as this. A spike through the left side of his neck and out the right, rasping through his windpipe for ever and ever. As if. A spear. Had run. Him through.

In the left mirror he saw Omar's face, straining at the effort of leveraging against his pierced neck. In his left ear, Omar strained the words: "Parting is such sweet sorrow, especially when you must part with your head."

Baker slammed the gas pedal to the floor. The Toyota lurched forward. But. All four tires dug into the sand. The Toyota buried itself up to the hubs in seconds. He hadn't intended to do that. A reflex to the pain. He realized he'd clenched his pistol grip, too. He smelled the cordite. He'd fired off a round. Funny, he didn't even hear it go off. He could barely feel the pain of shooting himself in the leg.

He only felt the pain in his neck. Dragged from the vehicle by the pain, even as his blood ran down his throat and into his lungs. He coughed. He thought of seawater inhaled on a hot day.

Over. It was over for him.

He could have stayed home.

But no. He had to come here to die. In disgrace. A Stone Age weapon through the neck. Omar using the shaft to fork him out of the truck as if he were gigging a frog.

Failure. So. This is how failure feels. His job was to take Uday and Qusay out of Iraq. *Failure.*

The spear came clean from his throat, and he fell to the ground.

Beneath the pickup, he could see a thin slit to the other side. A dead man. One of Omar's. At least he'd hit the guy there with the bullet that passed through his leg. Not a complete failure.

In the distance, he heard the sounds of the firefight die off.

At least there the men had put up a fight. Unlike here. One damned shot the only resistance.

So he did the last thing he could think of to do. His left hand beneath the Toyota still held the 9-mill. He might swing it clear. He might get off a shot at Omar.

No. He saw the smile on Omar's face. He saw a blur against the night sky. He felt another hot poker. In his chest. The spear going through him, pinning him to the ground. He could not pull the pistol free of the truck.

He had come back from the dead once. In Afghanistan. *Not this time.* Survival was not an option.

He did the only thing he could. He started firing. Maybe the Delta team would hear the shots.

With luck he might pierce the Toyota bed and kill Uday or Qusay.

No, he smelled gasoline. *Hell.* All he did was shoot out the gas tank. *Ah, well, shit!*

He couldn't see. But he could hear. *Omar. Cursing.* It gave him cause to smile. At least he had pissed off the sonofabitch. Left him without a ride.

A happy thought, considering. Considering that he was feeling a blade sawing back and forth across his throat. Considering that Omar was cutting off his head. *No way out of it this time. Not this time. Not—*

Night Runner's world came undone in muzzle flashes.

The Iraqi NCO's rifle chattered on auto, a long burst. Loud. Harsh.

Night Runner snapped off three quick shots. He could do that with the EOTECH sight. It let him shoot with both eyes open. Let him pick up a target in an instant.

The first round, at the NCO, struck the helmet that rose up in front of the Glock. The guy just trying to get out of the line of fire. Too late. Night Runner shot off his helmet. Then the NCO shot off the man's face, splattering Night Runner with a warm spray and solid chunks.

Night Runner's second shot went wild. The NCO dove to the desert floor. He kept firing. Night Runner's third shot missed, too, low and off-line. At least it stung the Iraqi NCO in the face with sand. Giving Night Runner time for a fourth shot.

The other Iraqis ran for cover.

The L-T went for a radio. Night Runner's fourth shot blew the handset out of the L-T's fist. In front of the man's lips. The slug went on into the L-T's mouth. The officer slumped forward into a sand nap. He opened his mouth in a wide, hurtful yawn. He closed his fists on the dirt and closed his teeth, lips bared, on the desert dust, his drool his blood.

The NCO had shot his AK dry. Men shouted, curses probably.

Night Runner heard bolts. Bolts yanked to the rear.

Bolts let go. Bolts slamming home. He also heard a screeching. In his own throat as he took aim and fired again and again, waiting for the slugs to hit him.

Three, maybe four weapons went off at once. Not aimed fire, but a high volume, the Iraqis spraying and praying. And somewhere in the back of his hearing, he heard the spitting sounds of silenced weapons. From the side of the Iraqi hasty battle position.

One by one, the Iraqis went still. They dropped their weapons. They buried their faces in the sand.

As the Delta team swept over them from the flank, firing at close range.

Night Runner lay still himself. He wished he could burrow into the sand.

Now was the worst time in combat. Every wounded man was at his most lethal. Each had a loaded weapon at his side, maybe even an armed grenade. One sound, one word, one footstep. Any of these things would bring on another attack from a crazed dying man, another volley of fire, explosions. The works.

The Delta men would shoot at any twitch now, so Night Runner did not twitch.

Not that it mattered to him. He had never felt more shame than now. And a new kind of fear. That the Delta men would know his fear, the badge of the coward.

For he had pissed his pants. How? The fight played back at him in hot flashes. The Iraqi NCO. Shooting up an entire clip at him on auto. Point blank. Throwing up geysers. Shooting twigs off low desert bushes. Showering him with sand and toothpicks. The rest of the Iraqis aiming at where the NCO was shooting.

All that focus on killing him. They missed; he pissed?

Surely not. It must be a wound. He patted himself down and smelled the wetness. No. The smell disappointed him. It was not blood.

He lay in place, in disgrace, watching the Delta Force

pros sweep across the battle zone, prying weapons from lifeless fingers. The Delta men checked for radios, armed grenades, each man, living or dead was patted down for anything of intel value.

Poole leaned over the NCO. He spoke to him in Arabic. The NCO was calm, perhaps even bemused. Or maybe just delirious. He turned his head and spat in answer to one of Poole's questions. Poole spoke to one of his own, Artemis, who produced flex cuffs to put on the NCO.

When Artemis lifted up the NCO's wrist, the arm came free of the Iraqi's body. The NCO gave a weak, wry smile, before fainting. Artemis turned the Iraqi over. The massive loss of blood from his chest, shoulder, and back meant the NCO would not awaken.

Night Runner wished he could trade places.

Poole went to a second wounded Iraqi, now the sole survivor. Gut-shot, he would live awhile. Poole took a cigarette from the man's pocket and lit it for him. The Iraqi smoked. His eyes rolled up at the taste, as if it were dope. The Iraqi began talking in a low voice.

Artemis stepped up with the flex cuffs. "What's he saying, Cap?"

"He wants to know if I'm going to off him."

Artemis tweaked his face. *And?*

Poole shook his head.

Artemis grimaced: *Want me to do it?*

"He's a soldier, not a terrorist," Poole said quietly. "Besides, he's going to die before we finish burying the rest."

"We're going to bury the bastards?"

Poole gave him a sharp look. "To hide the bodies."

"Right, right." Artemis slapped himself on the side of the head. "Iffen we don't they're going to know it's us."

Poole walked away from the killing zone.

Artemis used the unused flex cuffs on this man, putting his hands in front so he could smoke, fixing his elbows together in back with a strap so he could not do any more than lift the smoke to his lips and rest his hands in his lap. Foucault walked onto the scene of death—eight Iraqis by Night Runner's count. Foucault, the interrogator, spoke softly.

As Night Runner lay in shame. How to get out of this disgrace? Walk away? Come back tomorrow? Tell them he got lost? No, Poole would never buy—

Poole called out. "Barret? Bo?" A second time. No answer. A third time.

Night Runner's heart began to pound the sand beneath his chest.

He knew Bo. This wasn't his style.

"Runner?"

"Here," he said. He stood up and turned away to hide the muddy spot. But now he worried about an even worse disaster.

He followed his own drag marks in the sand, back to where he'd left Bo. *No!* He saw the inert figure.

Barret. On his back, one knee bent under him.

Night Runner bent over his favorite Delta man, Travis "Bo" Barret. He took his knee and lifted it, freeing the ankle, pulling the leg straight.

"Bo?"

But Barret was dead.

"Bo?" Poole. "Dead? Ah, man, no. Not Bo."

Night Runner sobbed. Bo dead, shot through the forehead, killed in an instant, his head turned and twisted at an acute angle, dropping where he'd knelt, the perpetual Bo Barret smirk still pasted across his face. His death mask still no different from his broadest sappy grin.

"Can't be," Poole whispered. "He's like . . . a super-hero." Poole turned the super-soldier's head straight. "How could these piss-poor excuses for real soldiers kill Bo? How could anybody? How? Can't be."

But it could. Night Runner had seen it time and again. A random act. As combat often is. And senseless, as it usually is. An accident . . . well, almost an accident. A scared Iraqi hit the dirt. Tried to flatten himself into the dark desert floor, one hand tearing at the crust of earth, fingers raking like dog claws after a squat, scooping out a pathetic hollow for his body, the other hand holding down the trigger of his rifle, firing on auto, tearing up the dirt ten yards away, peppering the empty blue midnight above, hoping, praying that a shield of slugs could protect him if only he would get lucky.

As one Iraqi did. One wild shot killed Bo.

"Just like Michelotti," Poole said. "Damn, man. What's up with this freaking mission?"

Night Runner knelt, wet and muddy. As pathetic as any of the terrified Iraqis.

This was his fault. Because of his blunders. Because he wasn't fast enough, wasn't alert enough, wasn't careful enough in his aim.

He had as much as killed Bo. Might as well have put his pistol to Barret's head and put that dark, wet circle above his right eyebrow on purpose.

It did not take long for the word to pass among the Delta men.

Bo dead.

Artemis went nuts. He wanted to go down the line and kill the wounded Iraqi. Then double tap the dead. "Step off, Captain Poole," he pleaded. "Just go off a ways and take a leak or something. Guy tries to escape, I'll shoot 'em in the face—no, the back of the head."

"You step off," said Poole, no anger, no emotion whatever in his voice. "We're not going to murder this guy."

"He's a terrorist."

Poole shook his head. "He's a soldier." Artemis went silent. "Just like you—just like Bo."

Artemis just stared. To him calling an Iraqi in Saddam's army a soldier instead of a terrorist was a distinction without a difference. He blinked a few times as

Poole's reasoning leaked past his fury and into his head. Artemis dropped his head as a new insight took root. "You mean like I used to be," he said. "I ain't a soldier no more."

Night Runner's very thought. More than that, he doubted he could ever call himself a warrior again.

Adnil Mustafa Qasim Zimnako Jalal Massoud Saladin ji Kirkuk saw that his men were working in vain to throw dirt on the gasoline fire of the Toyota. The truck was lost. A piece of bad luck, that.

The rest of his luck all good. Very good. He had overcome the Americans. Five of them at the cost of only one man lost.

He now owned the sons of Saddam. Well worth the cost. To keep them, he would have to clear the area fast. The Iraqis would send troops, perhaps a helicopter to investigate the source of the fire. Just one thing first.

He had the blindfolds removed from the two prisoners. He told them his name and asked if they knew him. Except for a twitch in Qusay's eyes, he gave no sign. But Uday could not stop his own eyes from going wide in alarm. One thing to be a captive of Americans. Quite another to be in the hands of a Kurd, one of the peoples that Saddam persecuted so vigorously, a survivor of a nerve gas attack.

The Kurd pulled the tape from Uday's mouth.

"As you might expect," the Kurd said to him in their language, "this fire will draw the interest of your army. So it is imperative that I remove you from here quickly. If they should find us, they will try to kill us."

Uday licked his lips.

"That would be too bad for you, because, before I die, you die." He produced a satellite telephone. "Now. Listen to reason. I have a phone call to make." He shrugged.

"Unfortunately, I do not know the number." He pasted on a wide grin and beamed it at Uday. "Fortunately, you know the number." He held the phone in his right hand and poised a fingertip to touch the numbers. "Your father. Give me the number, or I will hurt you."

Qusay grunted behind his gag. Uday began blinking rapidly, the wrinkles on his bald pate bunching like the zigzag pattern of a tire tread.

The Kurd took the chopping blade from the lanyard around his neck. "I have heard it said that it is easier to make a camel jump a ditch than to make a fool listen to reason." He laid the edge of the blade flat on Uday's thigh. "I tell you one more time to listen. Listen a hundred times; ponder a thousand times; then speak once but tell me the first time what I want to know. Before you decide to answer, you should know that I intend to trade you to your father alive and in one piece." He fanned the chopping blade over Uday's belly. "But if you do not give me the number right away, I will begin cutting pieces from your body—important pieces—until you tell me the number."

Uday tried to talk, choked, cleared his throat, and said, "I do not know the number."

"Take off his trousers," the Kurd said, and three other Kurds not involved in trying to put out the fire fell on Uday, leaving him naked from the waist down in seconds.

"Hold him down." One Kurd threw Uday and held him down by the neck. The other two pulled his legs apart and leaned on them. Uday screamed, hollering about the pain of the steel pin in his leg.

"Sit him up," Adnil Mustafa Qasim Zimnako Jalal Massoud Saladin ji Kirkuk said. "So he can see. I repeat, we have no time for delay. If we had time, I would go easy on you, starting with fingers, one at a time." He knelt between the lanky legs of the six-five Uday and grasped his penis. "Have you heard our Kurdish proverb? It is better to be a man for one day than a woman for ten." He pulled the penis taut. "You have had your day as a man. If your next words are not numbers, you will be half a man. If the next words after that are not numbers, you will be a woman."

He put the blade to Uday's foreskin. Just the touch of the keen edge opened a slit in the pocket of velvet skin, the start of a radical circumcision.

Uday began screaming. Numbers poured from his shrieking throat.

Poole had never seen a Delta Force unit so shaken. They had lost men before, good men, even excellent men. Mitch was a top hand. But Bo. The invincible Bo? *Dead?* No way. Except . . .

Night Runner. He did this.

He shoulda known. The Indian was thin, dull, agitated— one-armed, for shit's sake. Fear in the eyes, rot in the soul.

And half-armed. *A soldier?* A soldier was not complete without all his sticks. Both hands. Both legs.

And the stink. The stink of booze.

A straight line to this. The man had pissed himself, for chrissake, pissed himself in a firefight.

A guy could puke before a football game. Hell, he'd done it. Out of pure anxiety. But piss himself?

The other men saw it. They knew. Night Runner, the so-called natural genius original last-of-the-fucking-Mohicans. Pissing his pants.

Bury the Raqis, sure. But Bo? Dig a hole for Bo Barret? Leave their best soldier, their strongest spirit, their combat leader to rot in the desert? All because of a stinking drunk? A stinking Indian? A civilian, for chrissake?

Came down to one thing. How could Poole let this happen?

Good question. The guys in Delta had a right to ask it. Let Bo go off on point with a fricking one-handed civilian?

Pathetic. That's what they were thinking. He knew it.

Pathetic is right. Poole watched Night Runner try to pitch in digging, but he was the one-armed paper hanger, no good for papering, no good for digging holes. The Delta men did not have shovels or entrenching tools, and neither did any of the dead Iraqis. Some of Poole's men used bayonets to break up the earth, and others used Raqi helmets to scoop away the loosened dirt. The job took two hands.

For awhile, Night Runner knelt, leaning on his left elbow, scooping dirt with his hand. Trying to hide his wet pants is what he was doing.

Poole couldn't take it, couldn't stand to watch. He had to get Night Runner away from his men. Goddam him, he had to get the stinking sonofabitch out of his sight, out of his nose. Spare himself and the others the disgust.

He touched Night Runner on the shoulder.

"Take a turn around the position," Poole said. "A security check."

Night Runner gave a nod, but didn't raise his head to look into Poole's eyes. He turned to go, his tail between his wet legs like any other whipped, piddling, dribbling puppy.

"Before you go out there, check in with security." Poole shook his head. "I can't afford to lose another man."

No conviction in it. Just saying it was insult enough. Used to be, he could trust Night Runner to sneak away in plain sight. Not now. Couldn't trust him to do anything right now. *Oh by the way,* in the tone of it, *be sure to tell them that I told you to check in so none of them shoots you on purpose.*

What now? What the hell else could go wrong?

He pushed the negative vibes out of his head. *Think positive, baby. Can't afford to get superstitious. Forget the vibe. Cancel the Karma.*

Dammit. Nothing was going to go wrong. Right?

"Let's gitter done and get out."

"Captain?"

Night Runner? What was he doing back? *Somebody didn't shoot your ass yet?*

Then Poole saw. To the east, searchlights swiveling on tank turrets. Headlights sweeping the horizon. The Raqs were turning? Why?

Night Runner nudged him. *With his goddamned stump?* Poole turned to follow the point of Night Runner's M-4 muzzle. To see a glow on the horizon not three miles away.

A fire. An angry orange inferno. *A fuel fire?* A vehicle burning like a beacon. At a spot where Baker and four more good men would have had to pass. With Uday and Qusay. And he'd wanted to know: *What else?*

"Is Bo covered?" he said.

A murmur in the affirmative.

"Forget the rest. The Raqs know we're here." He shook his head. "We gotta get to that fire before they do."

Mohammed Bandi-Sadr, captain of the Iraqi Desert Wolves, was so sure he'd waylay the Americans. After he saw the tanks sweeping his way, he set a series of two- and three-man ambushes along the track. Let the tanks push the Americans back toward him. Spring the ambushes. Get his revenge.

He might recover the sons of Saddam. Perhaps not. At any event, he would repay the Americans for what they did to his Desert Wolves at the oasis.

But then the tanks turned. Just wheeled about in the night and began pushing back over the ground they had just traveled. Leaving him to hang out in the dark. After half an hour with no sign of the Americans, he did the only thing he could.

He recalled his helicopters so he could renew his search from the air.

A deadline for war with America was to come at midnight. Likely a long and ugly bombing campaign. The skies swarming with fighters and bombers and those damned cruise missiles. If he didn't settle this tonight, those helicopters would be of no value to him tomorrow. He and the Desert Wolves could survive to old age living in the desert, but might never see another sunset if they had to rely on trucks and helicopters.

Poole sent two of his best scouts ahead to recon as they drew near the fire. It was a vehicle fire, and one of the scouts soon came back to say it was the white Toyota.

Behind them, the Raqs came on. The tank lights stabbed into the sky and blinked out in turn as the vehicles rocked and rolled across the desert landscape. A cheap laser light show and a head game all at once. Horizon to horizon, the lights swept up and down, side to side. An invisible array of IR beams peering into the night as well—these he could not see, except in his imagination, the worst place possible. He confirmed that Artemis in the rear was watching their six. Artemis confirmed that the sweep was now on course toward the fire. Poole decided not to turn around anymore. Sure, it was a form of denial. Sure, the enemy was going to be back there whether he looked or not. He didn't have to look at them, though, did he?

Of all the rotten luck. They had evaded the Raqs not an hour ago. Now, by some shit piece of luck, they had to do it all over again. Or fight it out.

The point men double-timed toward the burning beacon in the night that was drawing the Iraqis. *Insane.* Delta should be running away from this fire, not at it.

Uday and Qusay would not be at the Toyota. Not un-

less they were dead. He could only hope his own four men
were alive. A small hope it was.

As he drew near the fire, Poole saw one of his scouts
give him a thumbs-down.

Not good. Not good at all.

The scouts swept around the sides of the blaze. By
hand signals Poole directed his men to find cover. He went
into the circle of light. To see the disaster eyeball-to-
eyeball. He imagined the worst possible.

He was wrong. What he found was worse than the
worst possible. His four men dead, overkilled at that.

Every face smashed to pulp. Their bodies hacked up.
Four good men killed, four heads removed. Only one dead
Kurd, shot down at the passenger door of the Toyota.

And Ramsey Baker.

Ramsey Baker. Poole did not know him. But there was
a one-armed corpse—another of Spangler's damned one-
armed guys—lying near the open driver's door. The body
was afire. The truck's tires had burnt off already and the
chassis had settled into the sand. Baker's head was no doubt
crushed under the Toyota, burned beyond recognition—

No! Poole saw the face now. On Ramsey Baker's head.
Balanced on a shovel handle, the spade end driven into the
desert floor. The face slack and bloody, the expression
very sad, the downturned mouth asking: *How could you
let this happen to me, boys?*

The shovel handle was slimed with blood, baked and
blistered on the side toward the burning truck, glistening
like dew on the far side. Poole wished he had not looked
now. He'd never get that look of sadness out of his own
head. Baker. He'd trusted Night Runner. So had Poole.
They both had been wrong to do so.

The back of the Toyota was open. The burning topper
was nothing but a sagging skeleton. No bodies. No Uday.
No Qusay. End of mission. A fiasco, flat-out, no putting a
shine on it now.

All because of one sorry gin-soaked bastard.
Night Runner.
Where the hell was that sonofabitch anyways?

Karim-Assad was in the taxi with Saddam when the phone rang in the briefcase between them. Saddam stared at the briefcase. The phone rang on.

"Father?"

Saddam shook his head. "Only two people alive know the number to that phone," he said.

Karim-Assad gulped hard. "My brothers."

"Uday and Qusay." Yet he dared not open the briefcase.

"Father, shall I?" When Saddam nodded, Karim-Assad took out the phone. He did not know the proper button to answer it, but Saddam poked at the receiver to make it stop ringing.

"Yes, who is it?" Karim-Assad grimaced. After a long moment he covered the mouthpiece and spoke a name into the backseat of the taxi. "I'm not sure I have all of it," he said.

"The Kurd?" Saddam whispered.

"Yes, The Kurd." Karim-Assad felt a faint glimmer of hope. He knew *The Kurd* by reputation, the hatred, the promises of revenge, spoken and unspoken. *The Mad Kurd.* "He says he has—"

"My sons!" Saddam took the phone. As Karim-Assad's head swam. He caught only snatches of Saddam's conversation.

"Trickery . . . What proof of life can you give . . . ?" Saddam held the phone away from his ear, and Karim-Assad heard a tiny scream. It was a sincere scream, a scream of words. Saddam grimaced. "And Qusay?" Another scream, not quite as desperate, but altogether as genuine. "Alive . . . ? How much . . . ? And what else . . . ? How can I be sure?"

Saddam's hopeful words, a distant gruff voice, the tiny screams. All sounds of Karim-Assad's world coming undone.

He could not even rely on the hatred of the Kurds for the Husseins? Was there nothing left to trust in the world?

Where was he? More to the point, *what* was he? *A coward? A traitor? A deserter?*

Night Runner asked all these questions of himself. The very questions he had seen in the faces of the Delta men. Questions he could not answer for them. Questions he could not answer for himself.

As he ran away. He was running away. Into the chill night, leaving the Toyota fire behind, the darkness hiding him from all but himself, Night Runner running away. He'd dreamed of bears and lions. But run away? Never this. Never in any dream did he run from his own men.

He ran for a long time. And would have gone longer if he were in better shape. All he could see in the distance to his right were the lights of the Iraqis. If he looked to his rear he would see that faint orange glow of the Toyota. In his mind's eye was Baker's face. On a pike. So he did not look back.

Ramsey Baker. A man he barely knew, but well enough to admire. A hero. A hero whose name the country would never know.

All at once a figure stood before him, blocking his path.

Night Runner gasped. He had done it again. Blundering along like a white man, all in his skull. Leaving no senses on duty to warn him of danger.

Until it was too late. Nothing left to do but attack. He fumbled with his M-4, strapped to his right side with its bungee sling. He pulled at it but lost the grip. He was done. He lunged into the attack.

Karim-Assad went with Saddam to a lavish hospital room in a residential neighborhood of Baghdad. A hospital with no patients. Nobody in the hospital but top military staff arriving in paper medical gowns and government cabinet officers arriving in ambulances. The men tore off their gowns at the door. The hospital was full of conference rooms and communications centers instead of patient wards and operating theaters.

"I must ask you to undertake a mission requiring the utmost trust," Saddam said. He took Karim-Assad by the arm and moved him out of hearing of the bodyguards just inside the door. "This is a mission you will relish."

"Back to the desert?" What could he relish more than that?

"Yes."

"With the Desert Wolves?" Yes, that. But . . .

Saddam shook his head. "This is a mission for family alone. Our family."

Karim-Assad was barely able to keep his jaw from dropping open as Saddam told him of the Kurdish ransom demands.

"A helicopter is being made ready even now," Saddam said. "Five million dollars American. And the contents of this briefcase—" He held out a satchel to Karim-Assad. "Papers. Certain promises by me to allow an independent Kurdish state in return for their support in case of war with the Great Satan America."

Karim-Assad took the satchel and an envelope. *A Kurdish state?* He could hardly believe it spoken from those thick lips. The very people Saddam had tried to exterminate? Independent? *A Kurdistan?* Carved out of Iraq?

Saddam said, "In that envelope is the combination to open the briefcase. Make sure to give it to the Kurd as well." He handed a phone to Karim-Assad. "Take this. It will ring for you after you are in the air. The Kurd will give directions for you to relay to the pilot—do you remember which button to push to answer it?" Karim-Assad nodded. "He will give you directions; and you will relay them to the pilots." Saddam gave a crooked smile. "He does not trust, this Kurd. He thinks I will send troops or bombs if I know where he is." Saddam shook his head. "Bombs that might harm my sons?" Three rapid beats of Karim-Assad's heart. "Those Kurds."

Karim-Assad forced a hopeful smile onto his face and lifted the satchel. "And these things will bring back my brothers?"

"By the grace of God."

Or the grace of Satan. "And you trust this Kurd?"

Tears welled up in Saddam's eyes. "What else can I do? He has my very blood in his hands."

Karim-Assad felt as if he might cry himself. Although for not the same reason. It made for a long, awkward moment. Until Saddam hugged him and kissed him on both cheeks, then held him at arm's length.

"You must go now, my son. The helicopter awaits you, and my staff and cabinet await me." He threw up his hands. "A kidnapping to resolve tonight; a war perhaps tomorrow."

Karim-Assad gave him a weak smile. *A tyrant's work is never done.*

He left Saddam to compose himself, dabbing at his eyes with a kerchief, blowing his nose. In the hallway outside the bedroom, Karim-Assad set the briefcase on the floor to adjust the German automatic pistol at the back waistband of his trousers. As he bent down to pick up the satchel, he heard Saddam speaking. Not in the soft voice he had used with Karim-Assad, but in the rough voice he used as president of Iraq.

"Bani-Sadr," Saddam said in his telephone voice, and

Karim-Assad's heart leapt. His heroic mentor. "Well, get him."

Karim-Assad heard Saddam's footsteps. He dashed to the turn in the hall before Saddam could catch him eavesdropping.

Bani-Sadr. Saddam was talking to the captain of the Desert Wolves. It could only mean one thing. He was sending the Desert Wolves to punish The Kurd after he, Karim-Assad, ransomed the sons of Saddam.

Heavens! The very heavens were conspiring against him.

Poole's thoughts raced. Okay, Night Runner was gone. AWOL? Artemis called it AWOL, but that was so much nonsense. The guy not even a soldier. A contractor working for Spangler could come and go as he pleased. Whatever. He was glad to be shed of him. Now he wouldn't have to look at the man. Wouldn't have to smell him.

Whatever. He had to get the guy out of his head.

The grinding, roaring, light-waving Raqi tank division was racing to the orange beacon lighting the way to the Delta team.

Face it. This mission is lost. No Uday, no Qusay. No hope of finding Omar's trail in the dark. No Bo, no tracker. Worst of all, *no time.*

On the bright side, they had no prisoners to lag, no Uday to lug. They could run free. They might even get away without a fight. The Irāqis were reacting to the blaze. They wouldn't dream that the Americans were here. Only an idiot would stand around a fire waiting for a tank division to come looking for him. Poole shook his head—only an idiot like him.

Poole hollered for a huddle. No time for the five paragraph field order. Just the big picture.

"Were going to un-ass the area," he said. "At the double-

time. Security on the fly." They didn't have time to leave a
rear guard, no luxury of moving by leaps and bounds.

"Fight like hell if we have to, run like hell if we
don't." He took a deep breath. What the hell was he missing? "Any questions?"

"Where we going, Cap?"

"Details, details," he said. It brought a laugh. Men in
danger, men in combat, hell, men at the point of death and
still able to laugh in its face. "Back to where it all began."
He said it as quickly as the idea flew into his head.
"Where we bit the Raqs on the ass that first night."

A few grunts of assent.

"Last place they'll look for our asses," he said. He tried
to sound more confident than he felt. "Tomorrow night we
E and E to Saudi Arabia."

He heard grunts in the right tone. They liked it.

He took out his pocket compass. He turned the compass, rotated the bezel line until it aligned with the needle
over north, then pointed with his arm. "Three-zero-zero
magnetic," he said. "Move out."

*Got no time for meditation, cogitation, conversation, or
navigation. Get with the exfiltration. Make with the evacu-
ation. Un-ass the area.*

Night Runner uncoiled and threw himself at the figure in
his path. He drew the curved sword and swung it in one
motion. All for nothing. He hit nothing but the ground.
Hard. The sweep of the blade across his body was strong,
but he met no resistance and he could barely stop the arc
of the blow from hitting his own knee on the follow-
through. His M-4 clattered among the rocks and hung up.
He pulled at the bungee cord that served as a sling. The
carbine came free and hit him in the face.

Tears in his eyes, Night Runner bounced into a low
crouch, trying to find a target for the M-4. To be sure, he

was no more agile than a three-legged cat, but he felt a new energy. He felt the will to live.

He whirled in place, looking for his enemy. He found him. The figure stood astride the tracks that Night Runner had made. But. The figure was not his enemy.

Night Runner dropped to his knees in relief. He hung his head.

Only an illusion. Heavy Runner. The Blackfeet chief slain in 1870 when he walked out from his winter camp to meet an attack of cavalry. Heavy Runner. Who had waved a piece of paper, a white man's recognition of his peaceful nature and intentions. Heavy Runner. Who was greeted by a .45-caliber rifle slug to the chest. Heavy Runner. Who had come to Night Runner in the past at times of his own weakness and indecision. A hallucination at worst, a vision at best.

Night Runner seethed. Heavy Runner. What kind of spiritual patron was he anyhow? Why did he not save his left hand? Why not save him from despair? From alcohol? From disgrace tonight? Why now? After it was all done? After he was all done? After he had peed—

He took a blow to the head. Hard. He went down.

Was that bright light inside his head? Or was it all around him? And another thing—why was he lying on his side?

For that matter why was a grizzly bear standing over him? Swiping at him? Trying to cuff him again? Was this the bear from the cave?

A helluva vision, if it was. A vision that could knock you over. One that could draw blood from the right side of your head and make it run down, tickling, over your face, into your eyes, shutting out the night.

Poole and every member of the Delta Force team heard it at one time. *Incoming.*

A shriek in the night air. That's all it took for the team to sprawl flat. A flash of light against closed eyelids. More shrieks, more explosions. Then the rumble of distant cannons. *Artillery.*

Hearing the shrieks. That was a good thing. The sounds of rounds passing by. The explosions and flashes beyond. The Raqs shooting long.

Moments later a second barrage. This time the flashes and explosions first, then the shrieks. The Raqs shooting short.

"Up and at 'em," he hollered. The Delta men needed no urging. Shooting long, then short, was not good news. The Raqs were bracketing. Firing long, then adjusting. Firing short. Next the Raqi gunners would split the difference, try to catch something in the bracket. Fire for effect with an all-out barrage.

They ran like hell. Toward the spot where the first rounds hit.

Poole already felt lucky. It was when you didn't hear any sound, when only the lights flashed, that you were in a bad way. That you were as good as dead.

Strange. The night air felt good, chilly and clean as a drink of water. He felt alive. He was alive. The Iraqi shrapnel had not sliced them to pieces. They could run. They could run fast. New mission—run for your life.

Run wild. *Oh, yeah, baby.* Running for your life was a thrilling thing, a real gasser, if you got away with it. What was it that Spangler was always crowing about? The thing about the thrill of getting shot at and missed?

Night Runner felt the earth move beneath him. It lifted. It bucked. It shifted and buzzed, rocked and rolled, swayed and sank. And lifted again. He heard the buzz and singing of metal whizzing through the air. And explosions. The crack of lightning nearby, the boom of thunder in the distance. Air bursts near and cannon from afar. He knew the shrill sound high above, shells whistling through the air.

He opened his eyes, but could not see. *Blind!*

No, not blind, just blinded for a moment. He rubbed his eyes, clearing them of grit and the dark film of his own blood.

An artillery attack. He put his hand to the side of his head and felt the wound. The wound cut him, slicing his finger with a sharp edge. He closed his fingers on it, the blade of some rough knife, and pulled. It came free of the wound. Shrapnel. A curved piece of shrapnel.

Just an artillery strike. No heavy Runner. No grizzly bear. Just a dream. It was only a dream.

He reached for the sword that he had dropped. Still on his knees he looked around for his carbine. He found it outside the rocks where—

He'd fallen into a foot-high fortress of stones.

He put away his sword in his belt sheath and stood up.

He got it at last. Heavy Runner—or the bear, something in that vision—had knocked him down among these rocks. Had saved him from getting cut to pieces. He checked out his carbine. The glass in its EOTECH sight was shattered, no more transparent than a snowball. The magazine was dented above the clip. He could not pull the clip free. He tried the bolt. Jammed shut. No good. He threw the gun away.

He found the NVGs. Dented. Useless. He tossed them aside.

He took a long pull on his canteen. The first few gulps of warm water put that vodka tingle into the back of his throat. He had to let down the canteen and inhale deeply to see if alcohol fumes would take his breath away. *Water.* It was a relief to taste plain water.

Maybe it was the blow to the head. Or just the water. The vision. Something. He did feel better than he had a right to feel. Something had been lifted from his chest. That feeling of gloom, of despair. Gone.

For some reason, he could see. Even without the NVGs. Sure, the moon was full, but . . .

He had his night vision. No more need to rely on the white man's toys. This was a gift. Heavy Runner had found him here, had come, had given this to him. It filled him with hope.

He knew what he must do. He began walking. In an arc, sweeping across armored vehicle tracks and wheel ruts. Looking for a track to follow.

He could not run away. Not anymore. If he ran into the Delta men before finding Omar, he would go to them and apologize. He would help them recover Uday and Qusay, if they let him. If they told him to leave, he would do that, too. Anything but run away from his fellow warriors. If he could, he might, just might, redeem himself in the eyes of the Delta Force troopers.

If he ran into Omar and the Kurds first, he would take on an even harder task. To redeem himself in his own eyes.

The Delta team settled into an easy pace that ate up the miles.

For Poole, the hot flash of the thrill had passed. Spangler was right. Nothing felt so ass-kicking good as to be shot at and missed. *Funny.* As if Spangler would know about taking fire.

Whatever. Nobody was shooting at them now. Now he knew that nobody had spotted them. The Raqs just firing a random pattern of artillery fire to cover the area around the vehicle fire. Stabbing a finger at the map and spanking the ground with airbursts. Shucking and jiving. Trying to get lucky.

Behind him, the artillery kept up its screeching,

rolling thunder. The Raqi tanks pressed forward. And now probing ahead of the line with machine-gun fire. When you can't get results, recon by fire; make a lot of noise and light instead.

Bullets snapped overhead. He could hear the twang of ricochets.

"Hold up," he called out. He kept his voice low, and heard the order passed ahead of him. The Delta men didn't need to be told twice. No more Delta deaths from wild bullets. Bo and Mitch were two too many.

"I got no idea what's going on," Poole said.

"It's a whole division on line," Foucault said. "Reconning by fire."

"I can see that," Poole said. "What I don't get is why. That kind of shooting? Guy'd get the idea they don't care about offing Uday and Qusay anymore."

Night Runner felt strong enough to jog awhile. Too soon he had to walk. Thinking his lungs must have shrunk to the size and color of walnuts in the last year.

He pushed himself outside his head as he let his body recover. A strange feeling, confidence. The air felt good, clean, chill, pure; it filled him up. He could hear for a change. Over and above even the sounds of the artillery and the grinding, squealing, roaring approach of the Iraqi division. A bird in flight, its wings whistling. *Not a night bird.* Then. The rustling of small, quick feet across the crust of the desert. *A rodent. A large one.* Given time, he would learn this desert, know how to identify each animal by its sound, its pace.

Except he had no time. Just tonight. And only while he remained in the zone of this ultra-sensory perception.

He cut the track in ten minutes. Eight men, one walking apart—Omar. He walked softer than the others of his party, setting his foot down sole first, rather than crashing through the crust of the desert heel-first. He pushed off, not with his toes, not by throwing up a tiny rooster-tail of sand, but by lifting the foot all at once with his thigh muscles. Not a good technique for Olympic sprinting, but a soundless way to cover ground at night. He walked apart from the others because the others made noise. An enemy shooting at noise alone would not hit him except by accident.

The others walked in a group. One set of drag marks among them. *Uday.* One set of prints irregular. A stumbling man, his hands tied, his toes dragging. A tired man. *Qusay.*

One set of tracks on either side of each son. One man walking behind, now and then turning in his footsteps, throwing up a tiny berm of sand on the outside of his right foot and another on the inside of his left. A trail man looking over his right shoulder as he walked.

Night Runner saw all this in a glance. No need to study it. The Kurds were in a rush. Running from the Iraqi artillery—an equal opportunity killer? Or were they hurrying to a specific spot? It did not matter. Not now. Now that he was onto them.

A gentle breeze blew from the southwest. Night Runner kept to the downwind side of the track as far away as he could—so the trail scout would not see him on it or near it. He traveled as quickly as he could without making noise.

He didn't worry about an ambush. Not while the Iraqis kept pushing the Kurds. He still had a chance.

His pants had dried out. The mud had flaked off. All he had left to remind him was a burning sensation on his thighs. He could get over that. If he could catch up. If nothing happened to change Omar's pace.

As soon as he thought it, he saw them.

The Kurds. And the sons of Saddam. Ahead. On a hillock.

Night Runner found a spot to watch the two brothers through the sight of his pistol, laying the center dot on each of them in turn, rehearsing. *First shot to Qusay's head.* Shift aim. *Two shots to Uday's chest.* Then, if he had time, shift again to take out the two guards. Then run like hell, using the little fold in the earth behind him as cover. It would give him thirty meters of clear sailing, if he ran bent over. If he got to the flank of the Kurds he might—

Hell, he wasn't going to get away with it. All he'd accomplish for sure was the killing of Qusay. Uday would throw his body down and try to burrow into the sand like the snake he was. The guards would open up and dive for cover. He might get Qusay anyhow, Qusay for sure, the worst of the pair. But it wasn't enough. Even if he killed them both. He wanted Omar. He had a debt to pay, Ramsey Baker's life.

Omar. He was talking on a small radio, no, a digital phone.

Uday and Qusay sat side by side, their eyeballs on high beam, white and bright in the ambient light they reflected to Night Runner's NVGs. Qusay showed more stress at being in the hands of the Kurds than when the Delta men had him. For the little time that Night Runner had observed him in the hands of Delta Force, he had a smirk set onto his face. A kind of look that said: *Just wait until Daddy catches up with you guys.* Now he and his brother could not get the looks of fear off their faces.

Omar knelt between Uday and Qusay and held out a pistol and the phone. He said something to them, then fired the pistol between their heads. The two boys began shrieking into the phone as one.

Omar smiled and stood up, talking into the phone, walking away from the pair. Night Runner saw what was going on, a proof of life situation, something to inspire Saddam to ransom his sons.

Which meant Night Runner needed a Plan B. And he had to work quickly.

He dropped back into the fold of the desert so none of the Kurds could see him take off his pants. They chafed his thighs, but more than that he wanted to cut down the sound of fabric rasping against fabric. That and the smell of urine that might give him away. Next he took off his jacket and shirt and stacked them in a pile with the pants. From the pack he took a pair of boomers and a roll of duct tape.

That done, he strapped on his pistol belt and holster, cinching it tight on his right hip. No sense in going *too* native. If the enemy started shooting, a few pistol shots would be the kind of reply to keep heads down. He pulled out his short, curved sword, which had served him in so many scrapes before, starting in this very country so many years ago when he took it off a desert fighter.

A few turns of tape and he felt ready to go collect some scalps.

The pilots flew due north, a heading given them by Saddam. When the phone vibrated in Karim-Assad's trouser pocket, he jumped as if it were a snake. So keyed were his nerves, so lost was he in thought about the imminent disastrous return of Uday and Qusay.

He spoke into the phone, "Yes."

The Kurd identified himself with that name a kilometer long. He spoke Arabic as well as Saddam. If it truly was the Kurd.

"If you are really who you say you are, let me speak to my brothers," he said. "I mean, Uday and Qusay, of course . . ."

Screaming followed a gunshot in the phone. Two voices. He recognized both. For a moment he thought about aggravating the Kurd further. Maybe if he were vexed enough, he would kill them outright. But no, that was merely a fantasy.

And anyhow the Kurd was already giving him instructions, asking him if he understood.

"Yes. You want me to have the pilots fly a course of two-seven-zero—"

The Kurd disconnected, so Karim-Assad called out the heading to the pilots. "I will get course corrections if you need them. Watch for a red light on the ground," he said. "Land to that light and wait."

That was all? Not likely. The Kurd would not arrive at a landing zone with the sons of Saddam to pick up his ransom. *Who but an idiot would? What sane man would not expect Saddam to try a trick? Who would leave open the chance to lose all if a squad of secret police landed?*

So. The Kurd would have tricks of his own. Karim-Assad's heart lifted. Perhaps he would try to steal the ransom and keep Uday and Qusay besides. Perhaps even kill them, deliver their heads only. Karim-Assad doubted he could be so lucky.

He leaned back against the stack of ghastly green. American dollars, a pallet full of paper bricks shrink-wrapped in plastic. He did not care about money. He cared about good luck. If he were to have it this night, he would have to manufacture his own.

"Got a gunshot, boss." Foucault. The Delta team had slowed to a walk since outrunning the artillery strike.

Poole, gasping for breath, did not need the report. There was nothing wrong with his hearing, just his lungs.

"Heard. It," Poole said. "Single shot. Maybe. A pistol. Anybody. With better flaps. Than mine hear. Anything else?"

Artemis spoke up. "A scream." He shrugged. "Could have been my ears. Playing tricks on me. You know? But I thought I heard. Big scream." Then, when nobody else spoke up. "Or maybe. Nothing."

"Me too," Poole said, his lungs near fully recovered.

"What?" Foucault said. "An Iraqi? Maybe lost? Calling for help?"

"I don't know," Artemis said. "Sounded like somebody in pain."

"Or scared to death." Poole stood up. "Anybody see anything?"

He said this to the two men who had turned their backs to him to scan the horizon with night vision binoculars.

"Nothing," they both said at once.

"Go check?" Poole hesitated to suggest it. "Maybe it's one of the Hussein boys?"

"More likely a Raqi Beetle Bailey," Artemis said. "Some lost guy. What do we care?"

"Good point." Poole sure as hell didn't care. He saw no need to go out and look for a man to kill. The way his luck was running? Stumble over some poor snake-bit Private Ali Doe? The guy firing off his weapon in panic, killing four or five Delta guys? *Screw that.*

There was one thing, this forlorn hope. Maybe it was Night Runner. They should try to find him. Apologize. Man had an off-night. Could happen to any man.

But stumble off into the night? Maybe run into a screaming Raq? That was just plain asking for it.

Night Runner kept thinking too much about the stalk of the three Kurds. It felt like a mechanical drill, crouch low, lift left foot high, extend left foot, touch down left toe-first, test weight, lower heel, transfer weight evenly, lift right foot high . . .

He used to flow across the landscape. Now it was as if he had to list every move before making it. Where was his head? More to the point, why was he spending all his time inside his head?

He kept moving, but did, indeed, take the first step out-

side his skull in years. To focus on the Kurds. All three of
them without night vision goggles. Not a bad situation.
Without NVGs, they felt inferior, so they clung to each
other.

They stood shoulder to shoulder. Like him, they had
heard Omar shouting in the center of their small perimeter.
Unlike him they could not see Omar growing impatient
with Uday and Qusay. Whatever it was Omar wanted them
to say, the gunshot made them begin to babble like a brook.

After their initial shock, the trio of Kurds jostled each
other and laughed. Making fun of the Husseins. Or mocking each other for being on edge. Either way, comforting
each other with low chatter.

Not knowing that Night Runner had slipped behind
them into their circle, that he'd fallen into his flow, that he
was low and close, creeping ever closer, stalking like one
of the great cats.

Night Runner even felt like one of the great cats he had
seen. Once he had set up a still camera in the woods below
the Continental Divide in Montana. It was a motion-
activated camera to snap pictures of wildlife passing by at
night. Deer, elk, a grizzly sow with two cubs. Routine
wildlife pictures, but nothing he could not see for himself.
Except for one striking photo. A mule deer, a doe, standing tense, eyes wide, reflecting the flash. Long ears
cocked forward. Her legs were bent slightly, her muscles
coiled for her best, most fantastic leap to get away from
some threat she felt. If only she knew which direction to
bound.

Behind her, a mountain lion, barely a foot away, his
nose practically touching the black-tipped rope of the
deer's tail. Crouched, but only slightly, perhaps not even
hungry, possibly just practicing his art of the sneak.

Night Runner was enthralled by the photo. Its tension.
The contrast of the deer's anxiety to the lack of tension in
the lion.

Night Runner could see the reason for that. The full belly of the lion. It did not want to kill. It could, but there was no need.

Unlike him.

He had the need, the will, the means. Best of all he had the hunger. This was no prank. In combat, you did not toy with a victim, did not take chances, did not talk, did not make the clever Arnold Schwarzenegger remarks. You closed with the enemy. You killed him. You made damned sure. Because if a dying man has a mere three seconds of life left in him, he'd find a way to pull a trigger. This was the thing that the people who never faced the ultimate life-and-death situation never understood. They would judge you in the aftermath of battle. They would count bodies. They would find all your mistakes and point out ways that a lesser application of force would have sufficed. *No need to double tap. Try to take prisoners. Offer a way out to the enemy short of fighting.* All things right out of Hollywood. People in the press especially, all of them having learned their conduct of war from the movies. He'd like to have one of them embedded with him right now, in the attack against three men. Try to take them alive. *Right.*

Above all, he had the anger. Rather, the anger had him. The loss of the hand. The loss of a friend. The loss of a soul. Such losses as these must be answered. There was a cost to such wrongs. Somebody had to pay them at a dear price.

In his right hand, he held his boot dagger, short, stout, double-bladed. He led with his left. He stepped right, braced, threw his weight left, swinging across his body.

The man at the right of the Three Stooges cluster died with no sound but the snick of Night Runner's sword passing through his neck. It was the small, quick crack of split kindling. A tiny blast of air escaped through his open windpipe, a long puff, like a pipe smoker's. His head hit the ground with more noise than his dying.

The second man was not so easy. He gargled, choking on a torrent of blood let loose in his throat. Night Runner's blade stuck in the neck. His stroke not strong enough to take two necks.

Because he wasn't strong enough. He had known it, even as he was taping his short sword to the stump of his left forearm.

Even so this second man was dead, too. He said not a word about his fate. He simply gave up living and went down. As he fell, he pulled Night Runner's arm down with him, slumping into the man at the far left of the group.

This third Kurd didn't like getting bumped. He bitched in the tone of: *Hey, watch what you're doing, asshole!*

His last words. As Night Runner thrust upward with his right fist, the blade catching the last Kurd standing, entering his skull beneath his right ear. Night Runner drove hard, hooking with his fist, landing the blow all the way up to his thumb. Even without the blade, he would have knocked him down, maybe out. With the blade . . .

Forget them, all three. Night Runner put them out of his head. He looked around, quickly, to see whether anybody had spotted him.

He cranked on his left elbow, working at it until his sword blade came free of the neck bone. The exertion had him panting for breath. If he died tonight, it was going to be for lack of conditioning.

He crept away, looking for the hiding place that he had already chosen. It was a spot in plain view. From there he could wait to pick off his next target. After they found the bloody mess he'd just left.

Only one regret. That he did not have time to take scalps. That he did not give Omar a sight to dread.

He heard footsteps. *One man.* Coming to check the outpost. About to fall prey to the worst of all a soldier's enemies. Fear rising to the sudden pitch of panic.

Nobody had spotted him as he knelt in the sand, easing into a natural divot barely ankle-deep.

He scooped the edges of the divot against his knees and boots. He folded his body tightly, and with one hand poured fistfuls of dirt over his body and head, breaking up the outline of a human body. He shut his eyes and imagined himself just one more slight bump in the desert floor. With that, he became the desert floor.

Until a voice called out. Then he opened one eye only. To watch. •

As the Kurds called out again, concerned, moving toward the three-man outpost. Closer but slower now that nobody had answered him. Seeing the three men from a distance, thinking—hoping—that they'd fallen down on the job to nap. Calling with a quaver in his voice. Yelping at the sight of three mutilated corpses, bled out, lying in sopping sand.

The Kurd dropped to one knee. He fired his weapon on automatic, one long burst into the night. Outside the perimeter. Calling over his shoulder to his fellow Kurds. Shooting blindly, not to hit an enemy as much as to reassure himself that he was still alive.

The Delta team hit the ground at the sound of gunfire.

Ambush!

That was the word in every mind. But by the time they had made their landings, Poole knew better. The gunfire was not directed at them. Not loud enough. And no slugs flying by before the sound reached them.

"What the hell?" Solis. *Ambush?*

"The same idiot that was calling out?" Foucault.

Poole shut his eyes, the better to think. "No," he said, "that was a pistol before." *This was a rifle. On auto. But at what?*

"The Iraqis ambushing one of their own patrols?"
Armies were always shooting up their own.

A few grunts: *Maybe, probably, who knows?*

Poole's mind on the main issue: *What are you going to do now, soldier?* No matter what the men were guessing, what they did depended on his decisions. The men laying back first-guessing. Later, if his decision was wrong, they'd begin the second-guessing.

Poole shook his head. There was no school solution to this one.

He decided to make his own educated guess. *Some petrified Raqi out there, that was all. Scared to death. Shooting at shadows.*

But not at Delta men. Not now and not later. Because he wasn't taking his troops over there. He was taking his troops out of this hot zone. Find a hideout. E and E as soon as they could. *You betcha. Hide out before sunup. Find water. Get some shade. Get some rest.*

Tomorrow night. Escape and evade. Get the hell out of Dodge.

Night Runner could barely contain a smile. *A break.* Finally, he had caught a lousy break. Things were going his way.

They came on, rushing to the scared sentry-checker, Omar and one other man, Omar hanging back. They dropped to their knees. They scanned the landscape, again outside the perimeter. The moon was so bright, his vision so well restored, he dared to think that he was back to his old form.

He came up into a crouch behind them, his arm drawn back. He flung a grenade. Outside the perimeter, exactly where they were looking.

Before the grenade went off, he turned his back to it, so the flash would not wash out his night vision.

After the blast, he moved like a lizard, keeping his belly to the earth.

Taping the short sword to the stump of his arm. What an idea that had been. It helped him creep and crawl. Toward the very center of the Kurds' perimeter.

The grenade flattened the Kurds for a full ten seconds. They tried to see what was going on, but they were tactically blind from the flash-bang. They did the only thing left to a blind man in combat. They shot up the desert blindly.

Night Runner was the cat again, now at the backs of the mule deer. All of them looking the wrong direction, poised to leap away from him but not knowing where to land. Omar and the others shooting wild. Literally blinding themselves with muzzle flashes, deafening themselves by pounding blasts into their own ears.

He had maybe a minute. *A world of time.*

He'd need no more than a few seconds.

Poole hit the ground again and heard his team sprawl behind him. This time he was back up on his feet at once. That flash. That crack. Louder and sharper than any other ordnance he knew.

"That's a boomer," he said. "One of ours." No grenade like it in the world. "Night Runner?"

"Cap," said Solis. "Think. Not the Indian. The Kurds. Remember? They probably took boomers off of our guys after—" Solis slammed his mouth shut as he realized what he had just said.

"Exactly," said Poole. "Either Night Runner is in a tussle, or Omar is over there with a couple of bad boys that belong to us."

"Yeah," said Foucault. "Hell, yeah. If it is Omar, who the hell else is he fighting?"

Poole didn't care who Omar was fighting. He had only

the two thoughts. *The Hussein brothers? He was actually getting a chance to recover the Hussein brothers?* He didn't wait around for anybody to argue. He took off, striding toward the sounds of gunfire, now heavy. No more than two hundred meters away.

Behind him he heard the Delta team hustling to catch up. *Now this. Was more like it.*

Night Runner used the edge of his curved blade with more finesse this time. He swung it as hard, but kept his elbow bent. This time he did not rely on brute force to chop. This time he whipped the forearm like a soccer player's lower leg. He let the keen blade slide, not chop. Into the tendons at the back of the neck behind the skull and into the brainstem. Like cutting tomatoes in the info-mercials—*Let the blade do the work, people. See how easy? Perfect slices every time.* The Kurd's head fell forward, his chin on his chest as if nodding off. Dead or dying. No factor.

The second Kurd was the first to fight back. At least try. He saw or sensed the death at his left. He swung his AK-47. Away from Uday and Qusay. Toward Night Runner.

He never made it. His left hand still on the forestock, still holding the rifle, flinched. Expecting the recoil. There was none.

The Kurd and Night Runner both glanced down at the same time. Night Runner could see why. The Kurd was still wondering. *Why?* Why did the rifle not fire? He was pulling the trigger as hard as he could, wasn't he? His fist was still clamped onto the pistol grip, wasn't it? Nothing. Until the Kurd released his grip of his left hand. Until his severed right arm fell off, the rifle still in its grip. He opened his mouth to scream.

He never made a sound. Night Runner plunged his right hand into the Kurd's solar plexus. Burying the dag-

ger. Driving hard, stealing first his breath. Then, flexing
his wrist as a pivot point, he swept the blade in an arc inside the chest cavity, stealing the Kurd's life.

Night Runner gave a quick glance toward Omar and
the last of his force. Still shooting. Into the empty night.
He still had time. To get to the brothers.

Uday. The warm spray of the dying Kurd had painted
his face like a Jackson Pollack painting. He began to chatter inanities. Qusay tried to roll away. He got to his knees.
He bent his forehead down to lever his body up. He got to
his feet to run. Pathetic. For all he could do was hop with
his ankles tied. The side of his face was puffy from the
beating the Kurds had given him. Night Runner shook his
head. Poor bastards. One side, then the other, seemed bent
on killing the Husseins. Now a one-armed naked savage
was up to the same thing.

Night Runner stepped up to Uday and slapped the flat
blade of the dagger, still wet, across his mouth. The blow
was gentle. Uday saw it could as easily have been fatal.
He shut up. Night Runner cut the cords around his ankles
and shoved him into the darkness. He did the same for
Qusay, leaving the wrists tied on both men. He watched
them go. Into the desert, stumbling, each in his turn
falling. Each got to his feet and ran. In no time they were
separated. Uday called to his brother. Qusay kept going.
Away. Away from the Kurd, the worst of all enemies. Not
so eager as his brother to reunite.

Night Runner didn't care, either. He could round them
up later. Their absence now was the essence of his plan.

He found a new divot and stepped into it.

The night went quiet. Omar called out. Now a question,
now a command. To the two men on guard over Uday and
Qusay. They did not answer. Could not.

Night Runner lay on his side. He pulled sand around
his legs. He poured dirt over his back and head a fistful at

a time, blending with the desert in his divot like the ant lion. He closed his eyes, becoming the desert. Waiting for the pismires to pass by.

Poole knelt, waiting for his men to catch up.

Foucault went to his knees at one shoulder, Solis at the other. Both wanting to know: "What?"

"Crazy."

"What?"

"Not what. Who? Look like a drunk. Guy fell down. Just fell down."

"Who?"

Poole gave Solis a smirk: *That's what I asked.* "Tall guy. Tall guy with a limp." As if he didn't dare say the name.

"Uday," Foucault said. He had his night binos jammed into his face.

"Not the time to screw with me," Poole said. "Not the time."

"No. I'm not kidding—*Jesus!*"

"What?"

"And the other one, too."

Poole saw a second head, caked with sand from his fall. True, he had Qusay's hair. He had the Hussein eyebrows. He had the 'stache. He looked like the favorite son of Saddam. But—

"Holy shit!" Artemis. "I got Uday. Want me to take him?"

"Yes—*No!*" Poole couldn't believe it. "Wait!" It had to be some kind of trap. Had to be. Omar. The bastard just laying for them. Just waiting for them to step out. Something. *This isn't right.* Still. *If it wasn't a trap, then what?* "Take him."

"Got him."

"No, no."

"Cap." Foucault and Solis as one.

"You're thinking blanks, Cap. You gotta make up your mind." Solis.

"Right." Blanks. "I mean *alive*," Poole hollered. "I want them both alive."

Foucault cleared his throat.

Think!

Could it be? Could it be too good to be true? He could recover all that he had lost?

Foucault said, "Give us a plan, Cap. So we can take them."

Right. An order. "Alberto, take your detail. Bring them back alive. Alive." He cleared his throat. "Foucault?"

"Yes, sir."

"You, me, and the rest on fire support." It wasn't much. But it was a plan.

Poole dropped the reins. He had to. No more for him to do. From here on out, it was up to his men. They had their jobs.

Now get out of the way. Let them do what they knew how to do.

His job was to jump ahead to new issues. *What are you going to do next, Captain?* Think. Get those two thugs back. Get them out of Iraq.

Oh, yeah. One more thing. Connect with Night Runner.

Who else? It had to be him who hit the Kurds. Had to be him who'd set these two free. Had to be Night Runner.

Night Runner kept his eyes closed. His ears told him the story well enough. No more shooting—easy enough to discern. Omar called out again, twice. First another order. Then a question.

And again. The third time a plea. *Don't let this be what I think it is.*

The last three Kurds argued. What were their choices?

Open fire? Omar would never allow that. Run away? No way. Give up Uday and Qusay? The keys to Saddam? No way, no how. He would try to get them back.

Silence. Then whispering.

Night Runner held back a smile. Omar did not whisper well. His voice was a low drone. He took charge. Using threats, gruff and growling. Then whines of assent. Two tentative sets of footsteps came his way. Two scared men huffing at the brink of panic. Behind them a third set of steps even more tentative. Omar. So he could see what was going on with as little risk as possible.

Night Runner felt a sense of deep calm. He had his gift back, the power of his senses, the ability to see the situation with his ears.

One gasp, then another. As the Kurds saw their own dead soldiers. And no Hussein brothers.

They called out to Omar. Omar growled back.

Night Runner opened one eye. He saw the pair of Kurds. Heads down, pointing at the ground. Walking on the tracks of Uday and Qusay.

From Omar, deep breaths now. Alone. Not daring to come near, not willing to stay back. At the edge of panic now. Afraid at ordering the others away, afraid of being alone. Coming on.

Closer.

One. Two. Three steps closer.

Come on! Four more steps. Four steps to write the end of Omar.

One step. Two. Three.

A shot in the dark. A cry in the night. A boomer. A firefight? It could only be . . .

Poole and the Delta team!

Night Runner smiled.

Until he heard feet on the run. *Omar's.*

Poole couldn't believe his luck. Good luck for a change. Those days of lying in the white heat, waiting for sundown. Those nights of lying in the black cold, waiting for a break to go his way. Getting no breaks.

Then, in just a few seconds, everything broke for him.

He watched Solis grab Qusay by the hair and propel him toward the Delta position. One of his men took the Qusay handoff, grabbing him by the elbow and jogging him back to the Foucault line. Qusay smiling, as happy as if he had good sense. Poole could see his teeth gleaming beneath his Sadman 'stache. There was no good place for him to be in this desert, but there were worse places. With the Kurds, for one.

Solis's men ran back to the line in two rough clutches, and Poole studied them until he saw what he wanted to see. Almost a head taller, Uday hustled back toward the line, his feet barely touching the sand, striding ten feet at a time as they held his weight off the ground. No smile on his face. Poole could see he was not faking the pain in his leg.

The Delta men threw Uday to the ground and hit the deck beside him.

"Nice work," Poole said.

"I think I'm going to have to quit"—Solis said, gasping for breath—"quit the Force. One mission—and I've already got—enough war stories—for a lifetime."

Too many. Still, Poole needed an ending to this one before he could call it a story. He looked for it at the edge of darkness in his NVGs. And there it came, stumbling across the desert. Two of Omar's Kurds, trying to run at night in NVGs. A tough deal if you didn't have the practice. Hard to get up to speed when your feet looked far enough away to be somebody else's.

Not that it mattered to the two Kurds anymore.

Poole didn't need to say a word about when or how. Foucault knew his job. And one of his sharpshooters knew his. The crack of a .17-caliber rifle. One shot, and the first Kurd pitched forward onto his face into a one-point landing, headfirst. He plowed a face-furrow a foot long, his heels came up to kick himself in the butt, and then went straight, his toes digging in like a tailhook on a carrier landing. The dust drifted away. The Kurd lay still.

The second Kurd made the same landing. Something was wrong, though, because the rifle shot did not come until after the man had laid out for a belly flop and crashed out of sight in a fold of the desert floor. A Kurdish curse word told him what had happened. The Kurd had tripped and fallen on his own initiative. The NVGs had saved his life.

The Kurd opened fire. Wild fire not aimed at them but to the oblique. Poole's men looked down the sights of their rifles, waiting for their enemy to show his head. He did not. He just kept firing wildly from where he lay, out of sight.

"Boomer?" The call from one of Foucault's men.

"Boomer out," Foucault said.

Poole buried his face like everybody else. To protect his night vision. To plug his ears. Even as his tactical mind skipped ahead to the next issue. He had the Hussein brothers. Fine and dandy. That meant a half a dozen people still out there, including Omar.

Attack? No. Too Hollywood. Get out of town with two wild and crazy guys. *Leave a mobile rear guard. Let Omar try to catch up. Just let him try.*

The boomer went off in the 2.7 seconds it took his mind to paint the plan on the mission board inside his head.

Night Runner lay still and low. Until he was sure the firefight was over.

Then, when the firing stopped he shot to his feet. A

tower of dust settled. He ran, leaving a cloud of dust in his wake.

After Omar. Toward the man he had to kill. For Baker and for himself.

A strobe light behind him. A slap on the back. *A boomer.*

It threw him to the ground.

It saved his life.

Before he hit the sand, he saw.

Omar.

Facing him.

One of his primitive, deadly spears in one hand level, a spare in the other. Arm cocked. A grim, wide smile. A face sure of victory.

The fist came forward. Then the shove in the back. Then the spear sailing over his shoulder.

No. Not over his shoulder. Into his back.

The ground coming up to meet his face.

The pain in his back fierce. The pain of knowing he'd just lost his life to Omar was even worse.

After the slap of air from the boomer, Poole called out two simple commands, one to Foucault one to Solis. With no more than that, they were on the way. He found himself jogging beside Solis.

Omar? He could forget Omar, unless the stupid bastard made the mistake of trying to follow. Then deal with him. That wasn't going to happen. The Husseins could not have escaped from the Kurds on their own. It had been Night Runner. *Had to be.* He had not gone AWOL after all.

No. He left to take care of Omar. There was the revenge thing, the shame thing, the Indian thing, that need to make things right with the world.

Hell, Night Runner didn't need Delta.

Leave Night Runner to take care of his own business. He'll be fine.

Night Runner felt the shock like a jolt of lightning.

Shock. That Omar was going to kill him.

Shock at the searing hot wounds, one in the meaty back of his shoulder, another in his buttocks.

Shock that he was so careless.

Shock. That he had taken on most of the Kurds and beat them. Only to impale himself on Omar's spear point. Odd. He saw it go by his face. It was the spear with the wavy head.

Shock. That he had sent Uday and Qusay to Poole and his Delta team. He had saved their lives, only to lose his.

Shock. That the impact of the boomer had saved his life for a few moments more.

Shock. At the sight of Omar, the smile.

Shock. Literally, at hitting the ground, at gulping for air and drawing dust. Coughing.

Shock. That he could think like this when his life was at stake.

Night Runner drove his right fist into the desert floor, and kicked with his right foot. He rolled his body left.

Shock that his body would not bend, that it was kept straight by the shaft and blade of that spear stitched into his body in two places along his back. The shaft still sticking out of his shoulder alongside his right ear. The blade still in his right buttock.

Shock. That he heard the sound of a metal blade sheathing itself in the sand. A sound that he felt as much as he heard.

Shock. That it might have sheathed itself in his back.

Shock. That on his back he was helpless. In near panic, he struck upward with his left hand-arm-sword.

He felt it strike and chop through three sticks, *snick-snack-snick.*

He tried to roll to his belly. But he could not find leverage. He lay like a turtle on his back. He swung in an arc over his head. Waiting for the parry and thrust.

The blow never came.

Just the return of the shock. At a howl that rose up in the night. It sent a chill rippling along his skin. To the soles of his feet back up to prickle his scalp.

He had heard the sound before. In the early morning hours. In Montana. A lion calling out to the mountains, a warning, a threat, a promise to every creature in hearing. A sound to curdle the blood.

Then he saw Omar. Not in the attack. Just standing. His face raised to the sky. His mouth wide open in his scream of the wild cat.

He saw that he had cut more than Omar's spear in his up-thrust. He had cut off the Kurd's right fist above the wrist.

It was a shock. That he could see Omar at all such detail, bathed in white light, now his equal in hands.

Shock. That he could feel the buzz of teeth-rattling, lip-tickling, skin-tingling, mind-numbing vibration more than hear it, the very air agitated, the very desert excited, as wisps of dust began rising from the sand like steam leaking from vents in the cracked and seamy earth around Yellowstone Park.

Shock. At what it meant.

"Chopper!" Poole yelled.

What the hell. If he had to yell over the roar, he didn't need to tell the Delta men. They had the ears to hear.

In the only move left to him, Night Runner swung low
with his left arm, using his own curved blade like a
scythe. He swept it along the ground at ankle-height. His
blade hit metal.

He saw it in the glow of the white light. The clatter of
his blade against the half-buried point of Omar's spear.
Striking sparks steel-to-steel. Knocking the spear off kil-
ter, breaking the grip of the armless fist, sending Omar's
severed hand flying.

Now he was done. The spear in his back. No time to
get another swing before Omar—

Omar?

Omar was gone?

Or was he? Night Runner looked left-right-left-above.
*Nothing. Nothing but a tail boom of a chopper passing
over on final.*

Nothing of Omar but that hand lying in the sand, palm
up, opening and closing in quick jerks, an addict's fist trying to pump up a vein, something right out of a B movie.
Except this was no movie.

A blast of rotor wash pelted Night Runner with flying
sand and gravel.

Adnil Mustafa Qasim Zimnako Jalal Massoud Saladin ji
Kirkuk, ran toward the helicopter. His open wrist leaked
blood no matter how much pressure he applied with the
thumb of his good hand.

Nobody on the helicopter saw him coming from the
left rear. He saw only the two pilots and one other man. A
surprise. He thought Saddam would send a platoon of secret police. But he had not.

In the cargo area, bracing himself against a block of
cash the size of a carton of UN rations, one man. Perhaps
the little weasel he had spoken to on the phone.

He ducked down next to the vibrating craft and dialed the telephone number. He waited, heard the ring in his headset, saw the weasel startle as if hit with an electrical shock, and began speaking as soon as he heard the weasel's voice.

"Throw out the satchel and tell the pilots to take off on a heading of due north."

"No—"

"Do as I say, weasel." But no, the weasel wagged his head, plugging his off-ear, shouting into the phone.

"No," he yelled, "not until I have the sons of Saddam aboard."

The weasel tried to peer into the darkness, and although he was looking directly at him, did not see. He was a young one, a little bastard. If he did not throw out that satchel . . . . *Damn him!*

"They are at a second spot. Throw out the satchel here. Then take off due north. You will see a second red light less than a kilometer away. Land there, pick up Uday and Qusay, and drop off the millions of dollars. Then it is over You will have room to take them home."

Karim-Assad was confused at the instructions. Of course he did not dare to trust the Kurd. But then again, did he dare to mistrust?

All he could say for certain was that he did not care about the satchel. Uday and Qusay were not here—only that much seemed certain—if they were here, he would show them and demand that the cash be pushed off the aircraft. If he did as he was told, if he threw out the satchel and took the cash to the next landing spot, perhaps there he would find Uday and Qusay.

They were all he cared about now.

He heaved the satchel out the left side of the open

cargo compartment and hollered for the pilots to take off.

Adnil Mustafa Qasim Zimnako Jalal Massoud Saladin ji Kirkuk cared about nothing but that satchel. Not the sons of Saddam. Not the cash. Right now, not even his hand. If he had to drop the phone and pull his pistol. If he had to risk bleeding to death—

The satchel flew his way.

Now. How to carry it and keep from bleeding to death until the Volvo came for him.

He saw the aircraft begin to lift on its wheels. He felt the breeze off its rotors as they screwed into the air.

He closed his eyes and waited for the sandblasting to begin and end.

He saw a brightness of day behind his eyelids.

He felt himself thrown into the air.

Poole ducked at the sounds and sights. Two more choppers. Two more sets of lights. Over the roar of turbines and buzz of blades came the *scratch-pop-sizzle-POW!* of rocket fire.

"Bite it!" He hit the ground feeling just plain stupid. Telling Delta men not to stand up in the face of a rocket attack? What the hell had come over him?

Rocket fire? How did the damned Iraqis even know where they were?

The helicopter bucked and spun until it threw Karim-Assad out the left door. He landed on his face, but not so hard he could not get to his knees and crawl. He did not get far. A weight landed on him and pinned him to the desert floor. He heard guns. A battle was going on? What was going on out here?

Then again, he did not care.

For he could not breathe. He would surely die. The treachery. That damned Kurd. He had shot down the helicopter. One of those shoulder-fired missiles very likely.

Now he understood. The Kurd would get his country and his cash.

For one moment, Night Runner felt he should just lie still.

He heard the firefight nearby. Let the Delta men take care of this business. Then call for help.

But. A warrior could not quit. Not while he had strength and blood and breath in him. A Blackfeet warrior could never give up. *A warrior! He dared not shame himself in Heavy Runner's eyes.* A vision in his head gave him all he needed.

He pushed off with his left heel and threw his left arm across his chest. It was enough to roll him onto his face.

His right hand felt numb—from the spear wound. But it was his only hand. It had to work for him, no excuses.

He closed his eyes against the pain. He willed away the cramps of his torn shoulder muscles around the shaft of that lance. He gave the commands for his hand to reach. First up. Then to touch his ear.

He told the fingers to walk up behind his ear. Into his hair. To find the wooden shaft. He ordered the fingers to close.

He could not tell by the fingers that they gripped the lance. A sudden new sharp pain in the wound told him that.

He directed his muscles to raise the arm above his head.

He felt the second pain. Of the buttocks wound. He clamped his teeth down on a cry. He pulled as hard as he

could. When the pain let up, he knew that the point of the
lance had pulled free of his glute.

He tried bending his knees and found that he could.
No longer was he held straight by the lance stitching up
his back.

He got to his feet. He bent over at the waist and felt the
blade bounce on his hip. The shaft tore at the wound, but
he could bear it now. This was no worse than the pain of
the sun dance. He had done that. He could do this.

He gave the order for the hand to reach behind him,
gingerly, so as not to cut off his fingers. He ordered the
hand to grasp the wooden shaft above the spear head. To
inch the shaft downward. And again. And again.

A new pain stabbed him in the back each time he
jerked at the shaft.

Until finally it finished its travel through the tunnel of
his flesh and fell free.

Night Runner took a deep breath. Relief. He acted as
his name told him he must. He began running into the
darkness, toward a small fire. To a crashed helicopter now
beginning to burn.

For all the good it would do him to catch up to Omar.
His right arm, his only good arm, was now useless, flapping at his side. His right leg barely worked. He didn't
bother to stop to try to find his pistol. To pick it up and
aim and fire was too much.

He felt light-headed. From the loss of blood, he
guessed. It made him flighty. He even laughed at his
ridiculous state, his only hand practically worthless.

He might have to get a new Blackfeet name. No-Arm.

Adnil Mustafa Qasim Zimnako Jalal Massoud Saladin ji
Kirkuk knew what it was even before he could shake off
its effects, clear his head, and get to his feet. *A rocket at-*

tack! Not the first that Saddam's helicopters had directed at him, the treacherous bastard.

The rockets had shot long. If not the shrapnel of the warheads, then the concussion or flash or all these things had made the pilots try to evade at an altitude too close to the ground. The blades had struck sand. The helicopter crashed. He saw that the weasel was thrown clear. He was nearly buried beneath a mountain of bundled cash. He was scrabbling at the desert, trying to get free.

The weasel might be useful. He pulled his pistol and arranged his hand so he could use the grip of the weapon to cut off the circulation to his wound. Then he ran to the Iraqi, now getting onto his feet, and shouted into his face. "Come here, Weasel, before I kill you."

The Iraqi stood up stiff. "My name is Karim-Assad."

Plenty of guts, this kid. "Fair enough. Come here, Karim-Assad. Carry that satchel for me."

The Iraqi youth picked up the satchel.

He pointed with the pistol. "That way. Run." He glanced over his shoulder, toward the noise of a battle. "And quickly before your people come—if they come, I will shoot you."

The Iraqi did not make a move. "I will carry your independent Kurdish state, but only if you lead me to Uday and Qusay."

"What?" The defiance of the Iraqi made him check his good hand to see that he indeed was clenching the threat of the pistol and pointing it at the youth. He was. Yet the youth showed no fear. "What did you say?"

"Uday and Qusay. I will carry your independent state only if they are at the end of my journey."

"What are you talking about? Independent state?"

"Kurdistan. It's in here. In the satchel. The papers."

"Papers? There'd better not be papers, ass. There'd

better be VX agent and anthrax vials enough to wipe out a city ten times the size of Baghdad."

The young Iraqi's eyes went wide. "Nerve gas? Anthrax? What treachery is this?"

"Treachery? No treachery. It is my bargain for the lives of Saddam's sons."

"Uday and Qusay?"

"Of course Uday and Qusay. Who else?" The Kurd laughed. "You?"

The Iraqi weasel shook his head. "Of course not. Where are they?"

It cost him nothing to lie. "Uday and Qusay are that way." He pointed with both arms and the pistol, his hand still clamped onto the veins above his seeping wrist. "Hurry. I have a truck waiting, a Volvo, with the pair of them safely in the back." He lifted up his bloody hand and empty wrist. "Back there are Americans. They have shot down your helicopter. They are coming for us, for Uday and Qusay. We must run. If you are not a flower, then at least don't be a thorn. Now run, Karim-Assad, run."

Poole couldn't get his head around it. Okay, the Raqs were coming in hot in two more helicopters—he got that. Firing with everything they had, kitchen sinks and toilet bowls included—he could see that. *But firing at their own lead helicopter?*

Each of the attack helos had a rocket pod fixed on one side of the craft and a machine gun on the other side. White lights blazing. Rockets shearing the night. Machine guns peppering the sky with lazy silly-strings of tracers. And from the sides of the helicopters small-arms fire from inside shooting out.

The Raqs were landing troops, ready to make a ground attack. Fine. But on top of Delta? *Nuh-uh.* They were going after their own lead chopper. They didn't even know Delta was here. No other way to explain it.

He saw it for what it was. A break he wanted—hell, needed. The Raqs had not spotted the Delta team. They would touch down. Kick the troops out. Sit in the LZ at flat pitch for maybe ten seconds, tops, to let the dust dissipate before they took off again.

Bottom line, the Raqs were going to put troops on the ground, and he had to stop them.

The tactics did not matter. Only the physics. Any helo was a duck on landing. A goose on the ground. An albatross at takeoff.

"Take them," he yelled into the racket. Only the man beside him, Foucault, could hear. He and his NCO led by example. They riddled the nose of the first helicopter.

That's all it took. The Delta men opened up as if Poole had a nerve circuit directly from his trigger finger to theirs.

Night Runner saw the pair run away from the downed helicopter. He set a course to intercept.

He hoped he had the right angle to cut them off. He'd never been this lame in the attack, so he couldn't gauge the distance so well. There was the cold wet on his back below the hot spot. His right foot sloshed in his boot from the flow down the back of his leg. His hamstring felt numb. It was all he could do to drag the leg, throwing it ahead of him, pushing off, riding his weight over it like a vaulting pole.

Matter of time before the leg gave out. Or before he bled to death. He felt it in his chest. A light and airy sense of being out of gas. Running on fumes.

As he ran across the desert with the satchel, Karim-Assad felt the blow of a sudden insight. The sand dragged at his feet. The insight dragged down his heart. *Saddam. He did this. Not the Americans.*

Saddam was ruthless enough. Saddam was treacherous enough. The Kurd had not shot down the helicopter. Neither had the Americans. An Iraqi helicopter had done it. Trying to kill the Kurd, even at the risk of killing Karim-Assad. For the love of Allah. *At the risk of killing his own sons?*

Well. Uday, Karim-Assad could understand. *But Qusay?* Saddam positively doted on Qusay. Qusay on a track to be the next president.

It all fit. The sounds of battle. The Desert Wolves. That phone call from the hospital from Saddam to Bani-Sadr. He had launched them in a mission to follow the ransom helicopter. To attack and kill the Kurds and everybody else. Including his sons. All three, if need be.

Saddam didn't care about five million dollars. He didn't care about his sons or his nephew. He only cared about killing the Kurds, no matter what the cost. Kill them all. So they could not extort him. Kill them all. So he would not lose face in the Arab world. This was Saddam. A man who had no weak points. Not even family. The Kurd was beaten and didn't even know it. There was no Kurdish state to be. Ever. And there were no weapons of mass destruction in that briefcase. If anything at all was in there it was a bomb. Waiting for the Kurd to set it off by opening it. Saddam would pay any price to keep himself in power. Even this.

It was a lesson not lost on Karim-Assad. *Pure, evil treachery had no limit, no boundary, no extreme.*

Karim-Assad had learned the lesson. For all the good it did him. Because now he had no place to go.

Saddam would kill him if he went back.

He would not—*could* not—ever go back.

The Kurd would kill him if he stayed.
It left him with only one aim in life—no, two.
Aim One: Uday. Aim Two: Qusay.

Poole kept up his part of the firefight. Even as he tried to
put his mind on the next step. He needed an escape plan.
A strategy to get him to his hideout. All this racket. The
Republican Guard division would turn again. It would
come after them on the ground, if this airborne batch of
troops pinned them down.

Forget tomorrow. Delta had to make its break.

If they didn't bring down those choppers and kill every
Raq within the next ten minutes, there was no tomorrow.

Adnil Mustafa Qasim Zimnako Jalal Massoud Saladin ji
Kirkuk felt his heart pound against his chest. Not just
from the trial of running. Not even from the shock of his
wound. No. Because there was the Volvo. His man Ezmir
at the wheel. He had his escape assured now.

He did not need the Iraqi weasel. He was near to success. A satchel with his weapons. Weapons, which he
would indeed use to wreak mass destruction on the bastard Saddam. Weapons as leverage to negotiate with the
lame Americans. He would get his own state of Kurdistan.
And his presidency. Not from a batch of worthless papers
and empty promises from Saddam. But from the power in
that satchel the weasel carried—

The Iraqi balked not two meters from the door of the
Volvo.

"Karim-Assad, put the satchel in the truck."

"First I want to see them."

"See who—?"

"The sons of Saddam, of course."

"Why, of course."

"Where are they?"

"In the rear of the truck, of course."

"I don't believe you."

"See for yourself, Karim-Assad. Put the satchel down and see."

"I will hold the satchel until I see."

Adnil Mustafa Qasim Zimnako Jalal Massoud Saladin ji Kirkuk checked his good hand again to reassure himself that he still had the threat of the pistol in his hand. He did indeed. Though for some reason the Iraqi seemed not to think it a threat. He called out to the man behind the wheel, "Start the motor, Ezmir." He nodded to the youth. "See for yourself then."

Karim-Assad stepped toward the back of the truck.

Adnil Mustafa Qasim Zimnako Jalal Massoud Saladin ji Kirkuk raised his pistol and aimed it at the back of the young man's head.

Karim-Assad opened the door to the van. "Empty. You liar!"

The Kurd was angry, too. That Ezmir did not start the truck.

"Ezmir," he hollered. Then, to the Iraqi: "Enough of your Arab rudeness."

Karim-Assad turned. "What did you—?" He gave a little cry as the full moon showed him the glint of steel from the pistol. He began to pray aloud.

"Forget your prayers," the Kurd said. "A camel is not an animal, and an Arab is not a human being. There is no heaven for you."

Karim-Assad closed his eyes to take a bullet, fumbling for the key to the satchel. If Saddam was as cruel as he thought, the explosives would detonate the moment he opened it.

The sons of Saddam were likely already dead. Nothing to do now but—

He flinched at the sound. Not a gun shot, but the rough noise of a hatchet chopping the head off a goat. Then came a cry of pain from the Kurd.

Karim-Assad opened his eyes. He had not yet engaged the satchel lock with the key. But now there was no need to blow himself up.

The Kurd still pointed his arms at him, but no more did he hold the pistol. For he had no hands, just two spurting forearms.

And beside him a ghost. A half-naked man with a sword in his left hand—no, no left hand. Somehow an epidemic had struck off the hands of men. This one had just a sword taped to one arm.

Poole and Delta did all too good a job.

The first volley of fire from Foucault and Poole would have been enough. They riddled the chopper's windshield, killing both pilots.

One of the Raqs fell over the cyclic control stick. The craft tucked its nose. A main rotor blade screwed into the sand.

The rotor broke up, the chopper broke apart, and the mission for both Raqs and Delta went to hell.

Omar shrieked. A pained call for help, an agonized order for action.

"Ezmir will not come," Night Runner said. "Ezmir is dead."

Omar blinked in Morse code. Then he put on a smile. Night Runner saw it coming, the art of the con. He grinned back.

"Why do you smile?" Omar said. He pointed at the crash site with his stumps. "There's cash on that aircraft," he said. "Five millions American. It's for me." He cocked his head. "I can share it." He nodded to Night Runner. *With you.*

Night Runner gave a bare tweak of one side of his mouth. "Fair words butter no parsnips."

Omar laughed bitterly at having his proverb thrown back at him. "All right then. Take it all. I'll be happy with just my life." Omar threw up his bloody stumps, spattering Night Runner's face. "I'm sorry. Take the cash. All of it. It's yours. Just stop the bleeding before I die."

Night Runner blinked once.

So Omar tried again. "Saddam sent me weapons." He tossed a sprinkle of blood at the case. "In that satchel. Nerve gas. And anthrax. We could use it to end this war. Send the Iraqis into panic."

Night Runner blinked twice.

Omar went to the next con with barely a hitch in his delivery. He dropped to his knees. "Don't kill me. I am a lion of my people. I am an ally of America."

Lion? He calls himself a lion?

"I give you my neck," Omar said. He bent and put his face to the sand. "I beg for your mercy."

This is it. Alice had seen this very lion kill Night Runner? At least she thought she had.

Not now. There was no way for the lion to harm him. The lion had no hands, no claws, no way to wield a weapon.

This was it. Night Runner's moment of truth. One warrior, flesh and blood, against another warrior, flesh and blood. No tiger, no lion. Just a handless man. Reality versus vision. Extra emphasis on the blood.

Night Runner's moment of redemption. If Alice's vision came true, he was to die a warrior, faithful to the warrior's duty. Die fighting. If he lived, he would redeem himself as a warrior and live to fight again. But could he do it? Could any man defeat a vision, a gift from a spirit greater than any man? It was in his own hand now.

Nothing else mattered. Nothing else existed. Not the satchel, not the Iraqi youth, not the war, not even the firefight raging behind him.

Just this pathetic, defeated lion, now tame and toothless. He was useless as a warrior. A man who could do him no harm. If he left Omar here, he would bleed out. As good as dead.

The fight was over. If he killed Omar now, it was murder.

Omar raised his head, smiling, his face as irregular as a topo map of the mountains. He knew he'd won his life.

Night Runner read the look. *Americans did not murder. Americans were merciful. Americans fought by rules.*

"When the cat wants to eat her kittens, she says they look like mice," Omar said. "But not you. You have no more appetite. You have seen the truth with your mind," Omar said through a pained smile. "And you have heard me with your heart." He held out his spurting forearms. "I pardon you the injury—everything is pardoned the brave. When I am king, you shall have an entire country at your command. You will have more wealth than even the five millions. Here, stop my bleeding."

The wrecked chopper bounded and rolled at Poole and Foucault.

The Delta team broke left and right, diving away from its path.

Raqi bodies flew from the craft like fleas off a dog.

Poole kept up the fire, as if his bullets could hold back the bulk of the craft rolling toward him.

When that did not work, he dove left.

"I am not an American," Night Runner told the Kurd. "I am a Blackfeet warrior."

"I don't understand this."

Night Runner's answer was on his face.

Omar read the look at once. "No. You have to let me live. It is . . . it is . . . it is the rules."

"No rules."

"You cannot kill me. I give up. I am sorry. God bless the USA. I love America." At last Omar had given up the con. "I surrender to you under the rules of war. Spare *me-e-e,*" he squealed.

Night Runner spoke under his breath.

"What? What did you say? What did—?"

Night Runner put an end to it with a short, swift slash of his sword. The blade tip passed first through Omar's right ear, then his left, below the startled eyes. The top of his skull stayed in place a second before sliding off. His headpiece fell off. Like Uday, the lion of the Kurds was bald. The full moon glistening off his severed pate.

"I said, 'You've been watching too many movies.'"

His sword did not whistle as movie swords whistled. It made only the sound of a meat cleaver splitting a chicken. Omar dropped to his knees. He still smiled his pained smile, a bit more painful now.

The Iraqi youth gasped. Not at the sight of the Kurd who fell face-first at his feet. But at the touch of the sword blade to his own neck.

Night Runner prodded him. Karim-Assad stumbled to the driver's side of the Volvo. He was to drive? He shrugged. "I don't know how to drive."

The American did not care. He made Karim-Assad drag the dead man from the seat of the van and get inside. He put the satchel on the seat between them. He put both hands on the wheel and gave a pitiful grimace.

Night Runner understood. That made two of them who could not drive. What, with the sword still taped to his left arm? He was a danger to them both. The Volvo had an automatic transmission. They could work it out.

He started the Volvo with his not-so-good good hand and made signs for the Iraqi to step on the brake. Then he bumped the shift lever into *Drive* and touched the gas pedal with the tip of his sword.

The Iraqi got the idea.

Night Runner pointed to the fight. The Iraqi steered them that way, jerking and bouncing the Volvo over the desert floor.

As they neared the fight, Night Runner could see that the battle was over. *Good.* He doubted he could add any value to it.

So much for one night already.

He let a smile crease his face. He had taken the head of his lion. He had bested Alice's vision.

In a single stroke, the lion was off his back. He had his redemption from drink. He had come back from the loss of face. He had restored faith in himself.

Only one thing left to do. Recover his reputation with the Delta team.

A chunk of tail boom rolled up Poole's back. He lay pinned as the second chopper danced in the air. It wavered, leaned, jerked, then fell to the sand.

Funny. He felt no pain. Not even claustrophobia. Too much going on? Flames. Bodies flying. Noise. Screams. Shots.

Now that. Was a crash.

Even so, four Raqi soldiers came out alive. They ran at him, their clothes in flames.

Now he felt. *Panic.* That he could not get his hands free to fight.

To his right, his Delta men opened up with small arms. The Iraqis shot back. He heard steps. He shut his eyes and waited for a killing shot.

"How's it going, boss?" Foucault.

"Oh, it's you. Thank Christ. I can't move."

Foucault tossed a boomer in a high arc.

"Boomer out!" he hollered.

The Raqs fired on his call. The tail boom rattled with hits.

Until the blast ended the fight.

"Delta here," Artemis called out.

"Delta here." Ballard.

"Delta." Solis.

"Uday and Qusay?" Poole wanted to know.

"Here, boss," Foucault said. "I got them both right here."

Poole's spirits rose. His heart lifted when he heard three more men call out: *Delta. Delta here. Delta.* His men. And then . . .

"Night Runner here."

Night Runner? "Jeez, Night Runner." He turned his head and felt the pressure on his chest. "Foucault, bring him in." His tactical mind went back to work. "Have Ballard take three men and sweep the area." He could hear a roar of tank engines. "Then we gotta book." He dropped his head in the sand beneath the tail boom.

"Gotta get the hell outta here," he said. *War over.*

He knew he wasn't going with them.

Night Runner came into the light in a crouch. He dragged one leg behind. He looked like a scab oozing out of the dark.

At the point of his sword was a young Arab with a satchel.

Ballard took the Iraqi and pushed him into the huddle next to Uday and Qusay. They looked startled at the sight of him.

Foucault clawed at the desert floor beneath Poole, like a dog digging.

"I got claustrophobia, Runner," Poole said. "You think of a thing worse than this?"

Night Runner looked at Foucault. They both saw it. Something worse. A fuel fire creeping at him, inch by inch.

Foucault flinched from the heat. He ducked his head, kept digging.

Solis came into the glow of light and tried to lift the tail boom. To no avail. "The transmission is still hooked on," he said. "Too heavy."

"Fire." Poole yelled. "I feel it. Get out. Before the Raqs come."

"I can't leave you, Cap," Solis said.

"Get. Out. Do I have to say it?"

"Can't leave you, Cap. Even if you give me the old direct order."

"You have to. It's Uday and Qusay. They're the mission now. You have to get them out."

"We're all going or we're all staying."

"Negative. That's an order."

Now it was Solis's turn to laugh. "Look who's giving orders." It was not a joke, and his was a pale laugh.

"I think my back is broken. I can't feel anything." Poole's anguish was intense, but not from pain. "You have to go. And you have to—"

"Not the double tap thing."

"Yes."

"Negative."

"You bastard, Solis. You been balking at me like a mule this whole mission."

"I know. I'm sorry, Cap."

"Forget sorry. You have to do this, you have to, you have to."

Solis gulped.

"You can't leave me here alive."

"I can't kill you, Cap, I can't."

"Go." A new voice.

"Night Runner." Poole and Solis said it at the same time.

"You scared the shit out of me," Solis said. "Man, you look like shit."

"Make him go," Poole said.

Night Runner looked at Solis. "I brought a truck, a Volvo. Go get it. We'll use it to push this thing off him."

"He wanted me to—"

"I know what he wanted. Go. Get the truck." Night Runner pointed the way to the Volvo. "Now."

When he was gone, Poole said, "I'd rather you shot me. I'm done anyhow. Man, they hurt me in eleven places. I got no future in Delta now." He half laughed, half cried out in pain. "I'm already paralyzed. Hell, the ride alone is going to kill me." Pleading.

"No."

"Some friend you are."

"They do wonders at Walter Reed," Night Runner said. "You should see the prosthetic hand they gave me."

Poole didn't even try to hear him. "You can do this," he said. "You have to do it fast, like ripping off a Band-Aid." The Volvo came rumbling out of the dark. "Do it now before—"

A pistol shot cut off his words. A second shot. Then a third shot sparked in the night.

Karim-Assad will keep it fresh in his mind for all the time he has left in his pathetic life.

Uday and Qusay try to talk to him. Whispering like school kids.

"How did you get here?" Uday.

"Did Father send men to rescue us?" Qusay.

"Yes." Karim-Assad. Both his eyes are open. Staring ahead but taking it all in. The fire. The terror. The rage. The debate. The action. He'd done this every night as the food taster. Standing by at meals. Gauging men by the tiny things. A twitch, a nuance, a blink. Signs to their emotions. Clues to their actions.

As he waits for his own time to come once more. The trick is to know it for what it is, when it comes. The key is to act on it.

He sees it coming. All eyes go to the Volvo driving out of the dark.

He slips a hand into the band of his trousers. He pulls the pistol.

Qusay sees. He smiles. He thinks it is his moment to get free.

Uday sees. He blinks. He does not know what to think. Until.

Karim-Assad points it into his face. Until he pulls the trigger.

Qusay knows now. He tries to roll away. Karim-Assad shoots him twice in the body.

He keeps pulling the trigger. Even as the American with the sword taped to his arm tackles him. Two more shots. Until the gun pressed between their two bodies will fire no more.

Until the man with the sword for an arm goes limp.

The first bombings in Iraq began just minutes before daylight, when two F-117 stealth fighters armed with two two-thousand-pound bunker buster bombs apiece, unloaded on a reported bunker complex on a farm not far from Baghdad. The strikes came not long after the final forty-eight-hour ultimatum from President George W. Bush to Saddam Hussein and his two sons to leave Iraq.

In fact, the military and CIA had developed the target eight hours before the ultimatum ran out. But the president would not authorize the hit. "No," he said. "I gave Saddam forty-eight hours, and I'm a man of my word."

For days nobody knew to a certainty whether the strikes had hit Saddam. But in one isolated command post everybody knew the CENTCOM strike did not hit Uday and Qusay. Because they knew his sons were not with him.

At least they thought they knew, after nearly three days out of contact with the Delta team that reported capturing the pair.

The first wave of strikes after the attempt on Saddam
went to demolish the command and signal structure of the
Iraqis, especially the transmitters that were jamming
satellites and other communications. The effect of this
wave was immediate and obvious.

The ops center, now run by a four-star named Caranto,
had managed to get some spare strike missions fragged to
him for the Delta team, but he had no targets. Until the
jamming stopped. Then, in an instant, he had contact with
the Delta team, an officer named Solis.

Caranto didn't care that he wasn't talking to Captain
Poole, the original officer in command. He wanted to
know, "Do you still have the sons of Saddam in your custody?"

The answer was halting, unsteady, uncertain.

"Confirm your last," Caranto said. "You do have Uday
and Qusay in your possession."

Caranto had the radio on speaker, and the answer
from the field raised a chorus of cheers inside the command post.

Poole, riding in the back of the Volvo truck, lying beside
the unconscious Night Runner heard one side of the exchange.

"Affirmative," said Solis. "We have the sons of Saddam."

Poole found a smile tingling the inside of his chest,
even if he didn't feel it on his face. All that had gone on
from the time they'd captured the two, lost them, recap-
tured them, and lost them again. Yet, strictly speaking, Solis had not told a lie.

"Tell him," Poole whispered. "Tell him the truth."

"Roger, Cap," Solis said. Then, cringing, he spoke into
his radio mike: "Be advised that Uday and Qusay are
KIA. We have them with us, but they're both dead."

Lady Redcoat sank into a chair looking small and forlorn.

Caranto wouldn't accept it. He went into a tirade at the officer on the other end of the radio, denying the death, demanding an explanation, threatening a group court-martial.

"Roger that," said the officer named Solis.

Spangler heard the man laugh before he cut off his transmit button. It brought a smile to his own face. What did Caranto know about these Delta men? *Threatening to court-martial one of them? After what they'd just been through?*

"Roger on the court-martial," Solis said as he came back on the radio, the tone in his voice a dare: *Just try it, you rear-echelon MF.* "That ain't gonna bring these two bastards back to life. We need medics and an evac chopper soonest. For a couple people who are alive."

Before the stunned Caranto could cut loose on Solis again, Spangler spoke up from the periphery of the ops center. "I have an idea."

Caranto went at Spangler instead of Solis. "I got an idea, too. I got an idea this is your fault."

Too funny. Spangler laughed—just like Solis and damned proud of it. "How is it my fault that Frick and Frack are dead?"

"You're going down for this, squid-face."

"We're all going down for it." Lady Redcoat.

Before the stunned Caranto could cut loose on somebody—*anybody*—again, Spangler said, "Wanna hear my idea?"

"No." Caranto.

"Yes." Lady Redcoat.

"I can."

"Do what?"

"I can bring them back to life."

Lady Redcoat perked up. "You can?"

"In a manner of speaking."

"What the hell are you talking about?" Caranto wanted to know.

Spangler pointed at the situation maps that flickered to life on the screens in the ops center, a cluster of PER-LOBE beacons on the road to Saudi Arabia. "I suggest you frag those strikes at the tank column following our boys toward Saudi Arabia. And at the checkpoint manned by the Iraqis." Spangler winced. "And I suggest you find a way to meet those Delta boys with a helicopter and some refrigerated coffins. We don't want Uday and Qusay to decompose before we get some mileage out of them."

Four months later, Uday and Qusay were found dead after an afternoon battle inside Iraq, long after the conventional fighting had ended.

Dozens of attempts to negotiate with Saddam for their release had failed. Saddam never made a serious attempt to respond to the taped pleas of his nephew, Karim-Assad Ibrahim al-Hasan al-Tikriti. Whether Saddam thought it a trick or whether he was not persuasively approached, he never negotiated.

The first photos of the bodies showed them with full beards and long hair as well as fresh wounds and bruises. Spangler was the evil genius who arranged for the wound makeup, wigs, and fake beards to account for the time that the pair were on the run while they were dead. The blood was freshly transfused, the bodies thawed and warmed in advance of the first shots. The body of Karim-Assad Ibrahim al-Hasan al-Tikriti was never put on display. Although he reputedly died in the same battle, clean-shaven, alongside his cousins, his body was never kept in evidence and assumed, somehow lost.

Spangler. He lost his guardian angel in the red coat, his Madelaine. All might have been forgiven her, if the sons of Saddam had come out of Iraq alive. But no. She was summoned to the White House one last time. Then she vanished into obscurity.

Leaving Spangler under another wing. That of the four-star, Caranto. Who got his court-martial going, after all.

Before preferring charges, he faced Spangler down.

"You're bluffing," Spangler hooted, bluffing himself. "That business with Bowers—"

"Forget Bowers. This is about misappropriation of U.S. funds. To the tune of three-quarters of a million dollars."

"Are you kidding? I only spent a quarter-mill, tops."

Caranto grinned wide.

Spangler's knees buckled, as he sank into a chair that wasn't there. He'd just confessed. He knew Lady Redcoat would never be tied to the funds she gave him. He alone had signed for the cash and government credit card. She was too smart; he was too dumb.

And now, in the most painful moment of his life, aside from the paralysis in his tailbone when he hit the floor with his ass, he'd let that idiot, Caranto, outfox him.

Forget the court-martial. He didn't deserve one. *Outfoxed by Caranto.* He didn't deserve to live. But he didn't deserve the dignity of his coming prosecution, either. The shame of getting beat by that buffoon was enough of a conviction for any man.

Karim-Assad Ibrahim al-Hasan al-Tikriti. That night the war began in earnest against Iraq, he rode in the Volvo van sitting up next to Poole. Poole, whose legs had recovered their feeling after being pinned beneath the helicopter. Poole, who realized that Night Runner had saved his life. Not just by thinking to use the van to push the tail boom off his back. Night Runner who would not let anybody shoot Poole, saved Poole's life. His career, too, for that matter. By the time the bouncing Volvo reached Saudi Arabia, he had the feeling back in his legs in full. By the time he met the evac chopper, he could walk to it under his own power. He made a full recovery. The army asked him to return to command in Delta.

But no. Not after . . .

Not after that night. When he tried to order himself shot.

It was nice to be alive, of course. He had talked to Night Runner's inert body for a full ten minutes once they crossed into Saudi Arabia and he could be alone with his savior. At the end of his disordered diatribe, he tried to sum up simply. "The short answer is thanks," he said to Night Runner. Night Runner did not react. But the sentiment brought tears to his own eyes.

Christ, the man had saved his life.

But, under the circumstances, he would not go back to Delta. What if it had been another man? What if he had killed a fellow Delta soldier with the same conviction? What if he had been as wrong?

Poole took the offer of a medical discharge. Oh, he passed a medical with high marks. But as he could tell anybody who could ask but never did, not all disabilities are in the body.

Night Runner took two bullets to the chest from a young Raq who claimed to be the son of Saddam.

Before they crossed into Saudi Arabia, Poole, speaking

in Arabic, asked the kid his name, out of curiosity, thinking, if he did go on and kill the little bastard in an escape attempt, he'd know his name at least.

"Karim-Assad," the young man said, stripes of blood streaking down his cheeks like tiger stripes. "I am a cousin to those two bastards there."

"Karim-Assad," said Poole pensively. "Karim the Lion."

Nobody in the Volvo saw the eyes of Night Runner flash open, flicker, and go shut.